# HIGH CITADEL

DESMOND BAGLEY was born in 1923 in England's Lake District and emigrated to Africa after the war. He held a number of jobs in Nairobi, Rhodesia and South Africa, and then became a journalist there. In 1962 he began to write a novel, *The Golden Keel*; after its successful publication in 1963 he and his wife returned to England, and he has been a full-time novelist ever since. He now lives in Guernsey.

Desmond Bagley has now written twelve highly-praised novels, each more successful than the last: all have been bestsellers in England and America, and they have now been translated into nineteen foreign languages. William Collins published his most recent book, *Flyaway*, in 1978.

DESMOND BAGLEY

# High Citadel

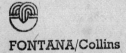

FONTANA/Collins

First published in 1965 by William Collins Sons & Co Ltd
First issued in Fontana Books 1967
Twenty-third Impression June 1980

© Desmond Bagley 1965

Made and printed in Great Britain by
William Collins Sons & Co Ltd, Glasgow

TO JOHN DONALDSON
AND BOB KNITTEL

# Chapter I

The bell shrilled insistently.

O'Hara frowned in his sleep and burrowed deeper into the pillow. He dragged up the thin sheet which covered him, but that left his feet uncovered and there was a sleepy protest from his companion. Without opening his eyes he put his hand out to the bedside table, seized the alarm clock, and hurled it violently across the room. Then he snuggled into the pillow again.

The bell still rang.

At last he opened his eyes, coming to the realisation that it was the telephone ringing. He propped himself up on one elbow and stared hatefully into the darkness. Ever since he had been in the hotel he had been asking Ramón to transfer the telephone to the bedside, and every time he had been assured that it would be done to-morrow. It had been nearly a year.

He got out of bed and padded across the room to the dressing-table without bothering to switch on the light. As he picked up the telephone he tweaked aside the window curtain and glanced outside. It was still dark and the moon was setting—he estimated it was about two hours to dawn.

He grunted into the mouthpiece: "O'Hara."

"Goddammit, what's the matter with you?" said Filson. "I've been trying to get you for a quarter of an hour."

"I was asleep," said O'Hara. "I usually sleep at night —I believe most people do, with the exception of Yankee flight managers."

"Very funny," said Filson tiredly. "Well, drag your ass down here—there's a flight scheduled for dawn."

"What the hell—I just got back six hours ago. I'm tired."

"You think I'm not?" said Filson. "This is important —a Samair 727 touched down in an emergency landing and the flight inspector grounded it. The passengers are mad as hornets, so the skipper and the hostess have sorted out priorities and we've got to take passengers to the coast. You know what a connection with Samair means to us; it could be that if we treat 'em nice they'll use us as a regular feeder."

"In a pig's eye," said O'Hara. "They'll use you in an

5

emergency but they'll never put you on their time-tables. All you'll get are thanks."

"It's worth trying," insisted Filson. "So get the hell down here."

O'Hara debated whether to inform Filson that he had already exceeded his month's flying hours and that it was only two-thirds through the month. He sighed, and said, "All right, I'm coming." It would cut no ice with Filson to plead regulations; as far as that hard-hearted character was concerned, the I.A.T.A. regulations were meant to be bent, if not broken. If he conformed to every international regulation, his two-cent firm would be permanently in the red.

Besides, O'Hara thought, this was the end of the line for him. If he lost this job survival would be difficult. There were too many broken-down pilots in South America hunting too few jobs and Filson's string-and-sealing-wax outfit was about as low as you could get. Hell, he thought disgustedly, I'm on a bloody escalator going the wrong way—it takes all the running I can do to stay in the same place.

He put down the hand-set abruptly and looked again into the night, scanning the sky. It looked all right here, but what about the mountains? Always he thought about the mountains, those cruel mountains with their jagged white swords stretched skywards to impale him. Filson had better have a good met. report.

He walked to the door and stepped into the corridor, unlit as usual. They turned off all lights in the public rooms at eleven p.m.—it was that kind of hotel. For the millionth time he wondered what he was doing in this godforsaken country, in this tired town, in this sleazy hotel. Unconcernedly naked, he walked down towards the bathroom. In his philosophy if a woman had seen a naked man before then it didn't matter —if she hadn't, it was time she did. Anyway, it was dark.

He showered quickly, washing away the night sweat, and returned to his room and switched on the bedside lamp wondering if it would work. It was always a fifty per cent chance that it wouldn't—the town's electricity supply was very erratic. The filament glowed faintly and in the dim light he dressed—long woollen underwear, jeans, a thick shirt and a leather jacket. By the time he had finished he was sweating again in the warm tropical night. But it would be cold over the mountains.

From the dressing-table he took a metal flask and shook it tentatively. It was only half full and he frowned. He could

6

wake Ramón and get a refill but that was not politic; for one thing Ramón did not like being wakened at night, and for another he would ask cutting questions about when his bill was going to be paid. Perhaps he could get something at the airport.

O'Hara was just leaving when he paused at the door and turned back to look at the sprawling figure in the bed. The sheet had slipped revealing dark breasts tipped a darker colour. He looked at her critically. Her olive skin had an underlying coppery sheen and he thought there was a sizeable admixture of Indian in this one. With a rueful grimace he took a thin wallet from the inside pocket of his leathery jacket, extracted two notes and tossed them on the bedside table. Then he went out, closing the door quietly behind him.

## I I

When he pulled his battered car into the parking bay he looked with interest at the unaccustomed bright lights of the airport. The field was low-grade, classed as an emergency strip by the big operators, although to Filson it was a main base. A Samair Boeing 727 lay sleekly in front of the control tower and O'Hara looked at it enviously for a while, then switched his attention to the hangar beyond.

A Dakota was being loaded and, even at that distance, the lights were bright enough for O'Hara to see the emblem on the tail—two intertwined " A's," painted artistically to look like mountain peaks. He smiled gently to himself. It was appropriate that he should fly a plane decorated with the Double-A; alcoholics of the world unite—it was a pity Filson didn't see the joke. But Filson was very proud of his Andes Airlift and never joked about it. A humourless man, altogether.

He got out of the car and walked around to the main building to find it was full of people, tired people rudely awakened and set down in the middle of nowhere in the middle of the night. He pushed his way through the crowd towards Filson's office. An American voice with a Western twang complained loudly and bitterly, " This is a damned disgrace—I'm going to speak to Mr. Coulson about it when I get back to Rio."

O'Hara grinned as he pushed open the door of the office. Filson was sitting at his desk in his shirt-sleeves, his face shiny with sweat. He always sweated, particularly in an emergency and since his life was in a continual state of crisis it was a wonder he didn't melt away altogether. He looked up.

"So you got here at last."

"I'm always pleased at the welcome I get," observed O'Hara.

Filson ignored that. "All right; this is the dope," he said. "I've contracted with Samair to take ten of their passengers to Santillana—they're the ones who have to make connections with a ship. You'll take number one—she's being serviced now." His voice was briskly businesslike and O'Hara could tell by the way he sonorously rolled out the words "contracted with Samair" that he saw himself as a big-time air operator doing business with his peers instead of what he really was —an ageing ex-pilot making a precarious living off two twenty-five-year-old rattling ex-army surplus planes.

O'Hara merely said, "Who's coming with me?"

"Grivas."

"That cocky little bastard."

"He volunteered—which is more than you did," snapped Filson.

"Oh?"

"He was here when the 727 touched down," said Filson. He smiled thinly at O'Hara. "It was his idea to put it to Samair that we take some of their more urgent passengers, so he phoned me right away. That's the kind of quick thinking we need in this organisation."

"I don't like him in a plane," said O'Hara.

"So you're a better pilot," said Filson reluctantly. "That's why you're skipper and he's going as co-pilot." He looked at the ceiling reflectively. "When this deal with Samair comes off maybe I'll promote Grivas to the office. He's too good to be a pilot."

Filson had delusions of grandeur. O'Hara said deliberately, "If you think that South American Air is going to give you a feeder contract, you're crazy. You'll get paid for taking their passengers and you'll get their thanks—for what they're worth—and they'll kiss you off fast."

Filson pointed a pen at O'Hara. "You're paid to jockey a plane—leave the heavy thinking to me."

O'Hara gave up. "What happened to the 727?"

"Something wrong with the fuel feed—they're looking at it now." Filson picked up a sheaf of papers. "There's a crate of machinery to go for servicing. Here's the manifest."

"Christ!" said O'Hara. "This is an unscheduled flight. Do you have to do this?"

"Unscheduled or not, you're going with a full load. Damned if I send a half empty plane when I can send a full one."

O'Hara was mournful. "It's just that I thought I'd have an easy trip for a change. You know you always overload and it's a hell of a job going through the passes. The old bitch wallows like a hippo."

"You're going at the best time," said Filson. "It'll be worse later in the day when the sun has warmed things up. Now get the hell out of here and stop bothering me."

O'Hara left the office. The main hall was emptying, a stream of disgruntled Samair passengers leaving for the antiquated airport bus. A few people still stood about—those would be the passengers for Santillana. O'Hara ignored them; passengers or freight, it was all one to him. He took them over the Andes and dumped them on the other side and there was no point in getting involved with them. A bus driver doesn't mix with his passengers, he thought; and that's all I am—a bloody vertical bus driver.

He glanced at the manifest. Filson had done it again—there were *two* crates and and he was aghast at their weight. One of these days, he thought savagely, I'll get an I.A.T.A. inspector up here at the right time and Filson will go for a loop. He crushed the manifest in his fist and went to inspect the Dakota.

Grivas was by the plane, lounging gracefully against the undercarriage. He straightened when he saw O'Hara and flicked his cigarette across the tarmac but did not step forward to meet him. O'Hara crossed over and said, "Is the cargo aboard?"

Grivas smiled. "Yes."

"Did you check it? Is it secure?"

"Of course, Señor O'Hara. I saw to it myself."

O'Hara grunted. He did not like Grivas, neither as a man nor as a pilot. He distrusted his smoothness, the slick patina of pseudo good breeding that covered him like a sheen from his patent leather hair and trim toothbrush moustache to his highly polished shoes. Grivas was a slim wiry man, not very tall, who always wore a smile. O'Hara distrusted the smile most of all.

"What's the weather?" he asked.

9

Grivas looked at the sky. "It seems all right."

O'Hara let acid creep into his voice. "A met. report would be a good thing, don't you think?"

Grivas grinned. "I'll get it," he said.

O'Hara watched him go, then turned to the Dakota and walked round to the cargo doors. The Dakota had been one of the most successful planes ever designed, the work-horse of the Allied forces during the war. Over ten thousand of them had fought a good war, flying countless millions of ton-miles of precious freight about the world. It was a good plane in its time, but that was long ago.

This Dakota was twenty-five years old, battered by too many air hours with too little servicing. O'Hara knew the exact amount of play in the rudder cables; he knew how to nurse the worn-out engines so as to get the best out of them —and a poor best it was; he knew the delicate technique of landing so as not to put too much strain on the weakened undercarriage. And he knew that one day the whole sorry fabric would play a murderous trick on him high over the white spears of the Andes.

He climbed into the plane and looked about the cavernous interior. There were ten seats up front, not the luxurious reclining couches of Samair but uncomfortable hard leather chairs each fitted with the safety-belt that even Filson could not skip, although he had grumbled at the added cost. The rest of the fuselage was devoted to cargo space and was at present occupied by two large crates.

O'Hara went round them testing the anchoring straps with his hand. He had a horror that one day the cargo would slide forward if he made a bad landing or hit very bad turbulence. That would be the end of any passengers who had the ill-luck to be flying Andes Airlift. He cursed as he found a loose strap. Grivas and his slip-shod ways would be the end of him one day.

Having seen the cargo was secured he went forward into the cockpit and did a routine check of the instruments. A mechanic was working on the port engine so O'Hara leaned out of the side window and asked in Spanish if it was all right. The mechanic spat, then drew his finger across his throat and made a bloodcurdling sound. "*De un momento a otro.*"

He finished the instrument check and went into the hangar to find Fernandez, the chief mechanic, who usually had a bottle or two stored away, strictly against Filson's orders.

O'Hara liked Fernandez and he knew that Fernandez liked him; they got on well together and O'Hara made a point of keeping it that way—to be at loggerheads with the chief mechanic would be a passport to eternity in this job.

He chatted for a while with Fernandez, then filled his flask and took a hasty gulp from the bottle before he passed it back. Dawn was breaking as he strode back to the Dakota, and Grivas was in the cockpit fussing with the disposal of his brief-case. It's a funny thing, thought O'Hara, that the brief-case is just as much a part of an airline pilot as it is of any city gent. His own was under his seat; all it contained was a packet of sandwiches which he had picked up at an all-night café.

"Got the met. report?" he asked Grivas.

Grivas passed over the sheet of paper and O'Hara said, "You can taxi her down to the apron."

He studied the report. It wasn't too bad—it wasn't bad at all. No storms, no anomalies, no trouble—just good weather over the mountains. But O'Hara had known the meteorologists to be wrong before and there was no release of the tension within him. It was that tension, never relaxed in the air, that had kept him alive when a lot of better men had died.

As the Dakota came to a halt on the apron outside the main building, he saw Filson leading the small group of passengers. "See they have their seat-belts properly fastened," he said to Grivas.

"I'm not a hostess," said Grivas sulkily.

"When you're sitting on this side of the cockpit you can give orders," said O'Hara coldly. "Right now you take them. And I'd like you to do a better job of securing the passengers than you did of the cargo."

The smile left Grivas's face, but he turned and went into the main cabin. Presently Filson came forward and thrust a form at O'Hara. "Sign this."

It was the I.A.T.A. certificate of weights and fuel. O'Hara saw that Filson had cheated on the weights as usual, but made no comment and scribbled his signature. Filson said, "As soon as you land give me a ring. There might be return cargo."

O'Hara nodded and Filson withdrew. There was the double slam as the door closed and O'Hara said, "Take her to the end of the strip." He switched on the radio, warming it up.

11

Grivas was still sulky and would not talk. He made no answer as he revved the engines and the Dakota waddled away from the main building into the darkness, ungainly and heavy on the ground. At the end of the runway O'Hara thought for a moment. Filson had not given him a flight number. To hell with it, he thought; control ought to know what's going on. He clicked on the microphone and said, "A.A. special flight, destination Santillana—A.A. to San Croce control—ready to take off."

A voice crackled tinnily in his ear. "San Croce control to Andes Airlift special. Permission given—time 2.33 G.M.T."

"Roger and out." He put his hand to the throttles and waggled the stick. There was a stickiness about it. Without looking at Grivas he said, "Take your hands off the controls." Then he pushed on the throttle levers and the engines roared. Four minutes later the Dakota was airborne after an excessively long run.

He stayed at the controls for an hour, personally supervising the long climb to the roof of the world. He liked to find out if the old bitch was going to spring a new surprise. Cautiously he carried out gentle, almost imperceptible evolutions, his senses attuned to the feel of the plane. Occasionally he glanced at Grivas who was sitting frozen-faced in the other seat, staring blankly through the windscreen.

At last he was satisfied and engaged the automatic pilot but spent another quarter-hour keeping a wary eye on it. It had behaved badly on the last flight but Fernandez had assured him that it was now all right. He trusted Fernandez, but not that much—it was always better to do the final check personally.

Then he relaxed and looked ahead. It was much lighter in the high air and, although the dawn was behind, the sky ahead was curiously light. O'Hara knew why; it was the snow blink as the first light of the sun caught the high white peaks of the Andes. The mountains themselves were as yet invisible, lost in the early haze rising from the jungle below.

He began to think about his passengers and he wondered if they knew what they had got themselves into. This was no pressurised jet aircraft and they were going to fly pretty high—it would be cold and the air would be thin and he hoped none of the passengers had heart trouble. Presumably Filson had warned them, although he wouldn't put it past that bastard to keep his mouth shut. He was even too stingy

12

to provide decent oxygen masks—there were only mouth tubes to the oxygen bottles to port and starboard.

He scratched his cheek thoughtfully. These weren't the ordinary passengers he was used to carrying—the American mining engineers flying to San Croce and the poorer type of local businessman proud to be flying even by Andes Airlift. These were the Samair type of passengers—wealthy and not over fond of hardship. They were in a hurry, too, or they would have had more sense than to fly Andes Airlift. Perhaps he had better break his rule and go back to talk to them. When they found they weren't going to fly over the Andes but *through* them they might get scared. It would be better to warn them first.

He pushed his uniform cap to the back of his head and said, "Take over, Grivas. I'm going to talk to the passengers."

Grivas lifted his eyebrows—so surprised that he forgot to be sulky. He shrugged. "Why? What is so important about the passengers? Is this Samair?" He laughed noiselessly. "But, yes, of course—you have seen the girl; you want to see her again, eh?"

"What girl?"

"Just a girl, a woman; very beautiful. I think I will get to know her and take her out when we arrive in—er—Santillana," said Grivas thoughtfully. He looked at O'Hara out of the corner of his eye.

O'Hara grunted and took the passenger manifest from his breast pocket. As he suspected, the majority were American. He went through the list rapidly. Mr. and Mrs. Coughlin of Challis, Idaho—tourists; Dr. James Armstrong, London, England—no profession stated; Raymond Forester of New York—businessman; Señor and Señorita Montes—Argentinian and no profession stated; Miss Jennifer Ponsky of South Bridge, Connecticut—tourist; Dr. Willis of California; Miguel Rohde—no stated nationality, profession—importer; Joseph Peabody of Chicago, Illinois—businessman.

He flicked his finger on the manifest and grinned at Grivas. "Jennifer's a nice name—but Ponsky? I can't see you going around with anyone called Ponsky."

Grivas looked startled, then laughed convulsively. "Ah, my friend, you can have the fair Ponsky—I'll stick to my girl."

O'Hara looked at the list again. "Then it must be Señorita Montes—unless it's Mrs. Coughlin."

Grivas chuckled, his good spirits recovered. "You find out for yourself."

"I'll do that," said O'Hara. "Take over."

He went back into the main cabin and was confronted by ten uplifted heads. He smiled genially, modelling himself on the Samair pilots to whom public relations was as important as flying ability. Lifting his voice above the roar of the engines, he said, "I suppose I ought to tell you that we'll be reaching the mountains in about an hour. It will get cold, so I suggest you wear your overcoats. Mr. Filson will have told you that this aircraft isn't pressurised, but we don't fly at any great height for more than an hour, so you'll be quite all right."

A burly man with a whisky complexion interjected, "No one told me that."

O'Hara cursed Filson under his breath and broadened his smile. "Well, not to worry, Mr.—er . . ."

"Peabody—Joe Peabody."

"Mr. Peabody. It will be quite all right. There is an oxygen mouthpiece next to every seat which I advise you to use if you feel breathing difficult. Now, it gets a bit wearying shouting like this above the engine noise, so I'll come round and talk to you individually." He smiled at Peabody, who glowered back at him.

He bent to the first pair of seats on the port side. "Could I have your names, please?"

The first man said, "I'm Forester." The other contributed, "Willis."

"Glad to have you aboard, Dr. Willis, Mr. Forester."

Forester said, "I didn't bargain for this, you know. I didn't think kites like this were still flying."

O'Hara smiled deprecatingly. "Well, this is an emergency flight and it was laid on in the devil of a hurry. I'm sure it was an oversight that Mr. Filson forgot to tell you that this isn't a pressurised plane." Privately he was not sure of anything of the kind.

Willis said with a smile, "I came here to study high altitude conditions. I'm certainly starting with a bang. How high do we fly, Captain?"

"Not more than seventeen thousand feet," said O'Hara. "We fly through the passes—we don't go over the top. You'll find the oxygen mouthpieces easy to use—all you do is suck." He smiled and turned away and found himself held.

14

Peabody was clutching his sleeve, leaning forward over the seat behind. "Hey, Skipper. . . ."

"I'll be with you in a moment, Mr. Peabody," said O'Hara, and held Peabody with his eye. Peabody blinked rapidly, released his grip and subsided into his seat, and O'Hara turned to starboard.

The man was elderly, with an aquiline nose and a short grey beard. With him was a young girl of startling beauty, judging by what O'Hara could see of her face, which was not much because she was huddled deep into a fur coat. He said, "Señor Montes?"

The man inclined his head. "Don't worry, Captain, we know what to expect." He waved a gloved hand. "You see we are well prepared. I know the Andes, señor, and I know these aircraft. I know the Andes well; I have been over them on foot and by mule—in my youth I climbed some of the high peaks—didn't I, Benedetta?"

"*Si, tío*," she said in a colourless voice. "But that was long ago. I don't know if your heart . . ."

He patted her on the leg. "I will be all right if I relax; is that not so, Captain?"

"Do you understand the use of this oxygen tube?" asked O'Hara.

Montes nodded confidently, and O'Hara said, "Your uncle will be quite all right, Señorita Montes." He waited for her to reply but she made no answer, so he passed on to the seats behind.

These couldn't be the Coughlins; they were too ill-assorted a pair to be American tourists, although the woman was undoubtedly American. O'Hara said inquiringly, "Miss Ponsky?"

She lifted a sharp nose and said, "I declare this is all wrong, Captain. You must turn back at once."

The fixed smile on O'Hara's face nearly slipped. "I fly this route regularly, Miss Ponsky," he said. "There is nothing to fear."

But there was naked fear on her face—air fear. Sealed in the air-conditioned quietness of a modern jet-liner she could subdue it, but the primitiveness of the Dakota brought it to the surface. There was no clever décor to deceive her into thinking that she was in a drawing-room, just the stark functionalism of unpainted aluminium, battered and scratched, and with the plumbing showing like a dissected body.

O'Hara said quietly, "What is your profession, Miss Ponsky?"

"I'm a school teacher back in South Bridge," she said. "I've been teaching there for thirty years."

He judged she was naturally garrulous and perhaps this could be a way of conquering her fear. He glanced at the man, who said, "Miguel Rohde."

He was a racial anomaly—a Spanish-German name and Spanish-German features—straw-coloured hair and beady black eyes. There had been German immigration into South America for many years and this was one of the results.

O'Hara said, "Do you know the Andes, Señor Rohde?"

"Very well," he replied in a grating voice. He nodded ahead. "I lived up there for many years—now I am going back."

O'Hara switched back to Miss Ponsky. "Do you teach geography, Miss Ponsky?"

She nodded. "Yes, I do. That's one of the reasons I came to South America on my vacation. It makes such a difference if you can describe things first-hand."

"Then here you have a marvellous opportunity," said O'Hara with enthusiasm. "You'll see the Andes as you never would if you'd flown Samair. And I'm sure that Señor Rohde will point out the interesting sights."

Rohde nodded understandingly. "*Si*, very interesting; I know it well, the mountain country."

O'Hara smiled reassuringly at Miss Ponsky, who offered him a glimmering, tremulous smile in return. He caught a twinkle in Rohde's black eyes as he turned to the port side again.

The man sitting next to Peabody was undoubtedly British, so O'Hara said, "Glad to have you with us, Dr. Armstrong —Mr. Peabody."

Armstrong said, "Nice to hear an English accent, Captain, after all this Spa——"

Peabody broke in. "I'm damned if I'm glad to be here, skipper. What in hell kind of an airline is this, for godsake?"

"One run by an American, Mr. Peabody," said O'Hara calmly. "As you were saying, Dr. Armstrong?"

"Never expected to see an English captain out here," said Armstrong.

"Well, I'm Irish, and we tend to get about," said O'Hara.

"I'd put on some warm clothing if I were you. You, too, Mr. Peabody."

Peabody laughed and suddenly burst into song. "'I've got my love to keep me warm'." He produced a hip flask and waved it. "This is as good as a top-coat."

For a moment O'Hara saw himself in Peabody and was shocked and afraid. "As you wish," he said bleakly, and passed on to the last pair of seats opposite the luggage racks.

The Coughlins were an elderly couple, very Darby and Joanish. He must have been pushing seventy and she was not far behind, but there was a suggestion of youth about their eyes, good-humoured and with a zest for life. O'Hara said, "Are you all right, Mrs. Coughlin?"

"Fine," she said. "Aren't we, Harry?"

"Sure," said Coughlin, and looked up at O'Hara. "Will we be flying through the Puerto de las Aguilas?"

"That's right," said O'Hara. "Do you know these parts?"

Coughlin laughed. "Last time I was round here was in 1912. I've just come down here to show my wife where I spent my misspent youth." He turned to her. "That means Eagle Pass, you know; it took me two weeks to get across back in 1910, and here we are doing it in an hour or two. Isn't it wonderful?"

"It sure is," Mrs. Coughlin replied comfortably.

There was nothing wrong with the Coughlins, decided O'Hara, so after a few more words he went back to the cockpit. Grivas still had the plane on automatic pilot and was sitting relaxed, gazing forward at the mountains. O'Hara sat down and looked intently at the oncoming mountain wall. He checked the course and said, "Keep taking a bearing on Chimitaxl and let me know when it's two hundred and ten degrees true bearing. You know the drill."

He stared down at the ground looking for landmarks and nodded with satisfaction as he saw the sinuous, twisting course of the Rio Sangre and the railway bridge that crossed it. Flying this route by day and for so long he knew the ground by heart and knew immediately whether he was on time. He judged that the north-west wind predicted by the meteorologists was a little stronger than they had prophesied and altered course accordingly, then he jacked in the auto pilot again and relaxed. All would be quiet until Grivas came up with the required bearing on Chimitaxl. He sat in repose and watched the ground slide away behind—the dun and olive foothills, craggy bare rock, and then the shining snow-covered peaks. Presently he munched on the sandwiches he took from his brief-case. He thought of washing them down with a drink from his flask but then he thought of Peabody's whisky-sodden face. Something inside him seemed to burst and he found that he didn't need a drink after all.

Grivas suddenly put down the bearing compass. "Thirty seconds," he said.

O'Hara looked at the wilderness of high peaks before him, a familiar wilderness. Some of these mountains were his friends, like Chimitaxl; they pointed out his route. Others were his deadly enemies—devils and demons lurked among them compounded of down draughts, driving snow and mists. But he was not afraid because it was all familiar and he knew and understood the dangers and how to escape them.

Grivas said, "Now," and O'Hara swung the control column gently, experience telling him the correct turn. His feet automatically moved in conjunction with his hands and the Dakota swept to port in a wide, easy curve, heading for a gap in the towering wall ahead.

Grivas said softly, "Señor O'Hara."

"Don't bother me now."

"But I must," said Grivas, and there was a tiny metallic click.

O'Hara glanced at him out of the corner of his eye and stiffened as he saw that Grivas was pointing a gun at him—a compact automatic pistol.

He jerked his head, his eyes widening in disbelief. "Have you gone crazy?"

Grivas's smile widened. "Does it matter?" he said indifferently. "We do not go through the Puerto de las Aguilas this trip, Señor O'Hara, that is all that matters." His voice hardened. "Now steer course one-eight-four on a true bearing."

O'Hara took a deep breath and held his course. "You must have gone out of your mind," he said. "Put down that gun, Grivas, and maybe we'll forget this. I suppose I have been bearing down on you a bit too much, but that's no reason to pull a gun. Put it away and we'll straighten things out when we get to Santillana."

Grivas's teeth flashed. "You're a stupid man, O'Hara; do you think I do this for personal reasons? But since you mention it, you said not long ago that sitting in the captain's seat gave you authority." He lifted the gun slightly. "You

18

were wrong—this gives authority; all the authority there is. Now change course or I'll blow your head off. I can fly this aircraft too, remember."

"They'd hear you inside," said O'Hara.

"I've locked the door, and what could they do? They wouldn't take the controls from the only pilot. But that would be of no consequence to you, O'Hara—you'd be dead."

O'Hara saw his finger tighten on the trigger and bit his lip before swinging the control column. The Dakota turned to fly south, parallel to the main backbone of the Andes. Grivas was right, damn him; there was no point in getting himself killed. But what the hell was he up to?

He settled on the bearing given by Grivas and reached forward to the auto pilot control. Grivas jerked the gun. "No, Señor O'Hara; you fly this aircraft—it will give you something to do."

O'Hara drew back his hand slowly and grasped the wheel. He looked out to starboard past Grivas at the high peaks drifting by. "Where are we going?" he asked grimly.

"That is of no consequence," said Grivas. "But it is not very far. We land at an air-strip in five minutes."

O'Hara thought about that. There was no air-strip that he knew of on this course. There were no air-strips at all this high in the mountains except for the military strips, and those were on the Pacific side of the Andes chain. He would have to wait and see.

His eyes flickered to the microphone set on its hook close to his left hand. He looked at Grivas and saw he was not wearing his earphones. If the microphone was switched on then any loud conversation would go on the air and Grivas would be unaware of it. It was definitely worth trying.

He said to Grivas. "There are no air-strips on this course." His left hand strayed from the wheel.

"You don't know everything, O'Hara."

His fingers touched the microphone and he leaned over to obstruct Grivas's vision as much as possible, pretending to study the instruments. His fingers found the switch and he snapped it over and then he leaned back and relaxed. In a loud voice he said, "You'll never get away with this, Grivas; you can't steal a whole aeroplane so easily. When this Dakota is overdue at Santillana they'll lay on a search—you know that as well as I do."

Grivas laughed. "Oh, you're clever, O'Hara—but I was

cleverer. The radio is not working, you know. I took out the tubes when you were talking to the passengers."

O'Hara felt a sudden emptiness in the pit of his stomach. He looked at the jumble of peaks ahead and felt frightened. This was country he did not know and there would be dangers he could not recognise. He felt frightened for himself and for his passengers.


III


It was cold in the passenger cabin, and the air was thin. Señor Montes had blue lips and his face had turned grey. He sucked on the oxygen tube and his niece fumbled in her bag and produced a small bottle of pills. He smiled painfully and put a pill in his mouth, letting it dissolve on his tongue. Slowly some colour came back into his face; not a lot, but he looked better than he had before taking the pill.

In the seat behind, Miss Ponsky's teeth were chattering, not with cold but with conversation. Already Miguel Rohde had learned much of her life history, in which he had not the slightest interest although he did not show it. He let her talk, prompting her occasionally, and all the time he regarded the back of Montes's head with lively black eyes. At a question from Miss Ponsky he looked out of the window and suddenly frowned.

The Coughlins were also looking out of the window. Mr. Coughlin said, "I'd have sworn we were going to head that way—through that pass. But we suddenly changed course south."

"It all looks the same to me," said Mrs. Coughlin. "Just a lot of mountains and snow."

Coughlin said, "From what I remember, El Puerto de las Aguilas is back there."

"Oh, Harry, I'm sure you don't really remember. It's nearly fifty years since you were here—and you never saw it from an airplane."

"Maybe," he said, unconvinced. "But it sure is funny."

"Now, Harry, the pilot knows what he's doing. He looked a nice efficient young man to me."

Coughlin continued to look from the window. He said nothing more.

James Armstrong of London, England, was becoming very bored with Joe Peabody of Chicago, Illinois. The man was a positive menace. Already he had sunk half the contents of his flask, which seemed an extraordinarily large one, and he was getting combatively drunk. "Whadya think of the nerve of that goddam fly-boy, chokin' me off like that?" he demanded. "Actin' high an' mighty jus' like the goddam limey he is."

Armstrong smiled gently. "I'm a—er—goddam limey too, you know," he pointed out.

"Well, jeez, presen' comp'ny excepted," said Peabody. "That's always the rule, ain't it? I ain't got anything against you limeys really, excep' you keep draggin' us into your wars."

"I take it you read the *Chicago Tribune*," said Armstrong solemnly.

Forester and Willis did not talk much—they had nothing in common. Willis had produced a large book as soon as they exhausted their small talk and to Forester it looked heavy in all senses of the word, being mainly mathematical.

Forester had nothing to do. In front of him was an aluminium bulkhead on which an axe and a first-aid box were mounted. There was no profit in looking at that and consequently his eyes frequently strayed across the aisle to Señor Montes. His lips tightened as he noted the bad colour of Montes's face and he looked at the first aid-box reflectively.


I V


"There it is," said Grivas. "You land there."

O'Hara straightened up and looked over the nose of the Dakota. Dead ahead amid a jumble of rocks and snow was a short air-strip, a mere track cut on a ledge of a mountain. He had time for the merest glimpse before it was gone behind them.

Grivas waved the gun. "Circle it," he said.

O'Hara eased the plane into an orbit round the strip and looked down at it. There were buildings down there, rough cabins in a scattered group, and there was a road leading down the mountain, twisting and turning like a snake. Someone had thoughtfully cleared the air-strip of snow, but there was no sign of life.

He judged his distance from the ground and glanced at the altimeter. "You're crazy, Grivas," he said. "We can't land on that strip."

"You can, O'Hara," said Grivas.

21

"I'm damned if I'm going to. This plane's overloaded and that strip's at an altitude of seventeen thousand feet. It would need to be three times as long for this crate to land safely. The air's too thin to hold us up at a slow landing speed—we'll hit the ground at a hell of a lick and we won't be able to pull up. We'll shoot off the other end of the strip and crash on the side of the mountain."

"You can do it."

"To hell with you," said O'Hara.

Grivas lifted his gun. "All right, I'll do it," he said. "But I'll have to kill you first."

O'Hara looked at the black hole staring at him like an evil eye. He could see the rifling inside the muzzle and it looked as big as a howitzer. In spite of the cold, he was sweating and could feel rivulets of perspiration running down his back. He turned away from Grivas and studied the strip again. "Why are you doing this?" he asked.

"You would not know if I told you," said Grivas. "You would not understand—you are English."

O'Hara sighed. It was going to be very dicey; *he* might be able to get the Dakota down in approximately one piece, but Grivas wouldn't have a chance—he'd pile it up for sure. He said, "All right—warn the passengers; get them to the rear of the cabin."

"Never mind the passengers," said Grivas flatly. "You do not think that I am going to leave this cockpit?"

O'Hara said, "All right, you're calling the shots, but I warn you—don't touch the controls by as much as a finger. You're not a pilot's backside—and you know it. There can be only one man flying a plane."

"Get on with it," said Grivas shortly.

"I'll take my own time," said O'Hara. "I want a good look before I do a damn thing."

He orbited the air-strip four more times, watching it as it spun crazily beneath the Dakota. The passengers should know there was something wrong by this time, he thought. No ordinary airliner stood on its wingtip and twitched about like this. Maybe they'd get alarmed and someone would try to do something about it—that might give him a chance to get at Grivas. But what the passengers could do was problematical.

The strip was all too short; it was also very narrow and made for a much smaller aircraft. He would have to land on the extreme edge, his wingtip brushing a rock wall. Then there was the question of wind direction. He looked down at the cabins, hoping to detect a wisp of smoke from the chimneys, but there was nothing.

"I'm going to go in closer—over the strip," he said. "But I'm not landing this time."

He pulled out of orbit and circled widely to come in for a landing approach. He lined up the nose of the Dakota on the strip like a gunsight and the plane came in, fast and level. To starboard there was a blur of rock and snow and O'Hara held his breath. If the wingtip touched the rock wall that would be the end. Ahead, the strip wound underneath, as though it was being swallowed by the Dakota. There was nothing as the strip ended—just a deep valley and the blue sky. He hauled on the stick and the plane shot skyward.

The passengers will know damn well there's something wrong now, he thought. To Grivas he said, "We're not going to get this aircraft down in one piece."

"Just get me down safely," said Grivas. "I'm the only one who matters."

O'Hara grinned tightly. "You don't matter a damn to me."

"Then think of your own neck," said Grivas. "That will take care of mine, too."

But O'Hara was thinking of ten lives in the passenger cabin. He circled widely again to make another approach and debated with himself the best way of doing this. He could come in with the undercarriage up or down. A belly-landing would be rough at that speed, but the plane would slow down faster because of the increased friction. The question was: could he hold her straight? On the other hand if he came in with the undercarriage down he would lose airspeed before he hit the deck—that was an advantage too.

He smiled grimly and decided to do both. For the first time he blessed Filson and his lousy aeroplanes. He knew to a hair how much stress the undercarriage would take; hitherto his problem had been that of putting the Dakota down gently. This time he would come in with undercarriage down, losing speed, and slam her down hard—hard enough to break off the weakened struts like matchsticks. That would give him his belly-landing, too.

He sighted the nose of the Dakota on the strip again. "Well, here goes nothing," he said. "Flaps down; under-carriage down."

As the plane lost airspeed the controls felt mushy under his hands. He set his teeth and concentrated as never before.

23

As the plane tipped wing down and started to orbit the air-strip Armstrong was thrown violently against Peabody. Peabody was in the act of taking another mouthful of whisky and the neck of the flask suddenly jammed against his teeth. He spluttered and yelled incoherently and thrust hard against Armstrong.

Rohde was thrown out of his seat and found himself sitting in the aisle, together with Coughlin and Montes. He struggled to his feet, shaking his head violently, then he bent to help Montes, speaking quick Spanish. Mrs. Coughlin helped her husband back to his seat.

Willis had been making a note in the margin of his book and the point of his pencil snapped as Forester lurched against him. Forester made no attempt to regain his position but looked incredulously out of the window, ignoring Willis's feeble protests at being squashed. Forester was a big man.

The whole cabin was a babel of sound in English and Spanish, dominated by the sharp and scratchy voice of Miss Ponsky as she querulously complained. "I knew it," she screamed. "I knew it was all wrong." She began to laugh hysterically and Rohde turned from Montes and slapped her with a heavy hand. She looked at him in surprise and suddenly burst into tears.

Peabody shouted, "What in goddam hell is that limey doing now?" He stared out of the window at the air-strip. "The bastard's going to land."

Rohde spoke rapidly to Montes, who seemed so shaken he was apathetic. There was a quick exchange in Spanish between Rohde and the girl, and he pointed to the door leading to the cockpit. She nodded violently and he stood up.

Mrs. Coughlin was leaning forward in her seat, comforting Miss Ponsky. "Nothing's going to happen," she kept saying. "Nothing bad is going to happen."

The aircraft straightened as O'Hara came in for his first approach run. Rohde leaned over Armstrong and looked through the window, but turned as Miss Ponsky screamed in fright, looking at the blur of rock streaming past the starboard window and seeing the wingtip brushing it so closely. Then Rohde lost his balance again as O'Hara pulled the Dakota into a climb.

It was Forester who made the first constructive move. He was nearest the door leading to the cockpit and he grabbed the door handle, turned and pushed. Nothing happened. He put his shoulder to the door but was thrown away as the plane turned rapidly. O'Hara was going into his final landing approach.

Forester grabbed the axe from its clips on the bulkhead and raised it to strike, but his arm was caught by Rohde. "This is quicker," said Rohde, and lifted a heavy pistol in his other hand. He stepped in front of Forester and fired three quick shots at the lock of the door.

## VI

O'Hara heard the shots a fraction of a second before the Dakota touched down. He not only heard them but saw the altimeter and the turn-and-climb indicator shiver into fragments as the bullets smashed into the instrument panel. But he had no time to see what was happening behind him because just then the heavily overloaded Dakota settled soggily at the extreme end of the strip, moving at high speed.

There was a sickening crunch and the whole air frame shuddered as the undercarriage collapsed and the plane sank on to its belly and slid with a tearing, rending sound towards the far end of the strip. O'Hara fought frantically with the controls as they kicked against his hands and feet and tried to keep the aircraft sliding in a straight line.

Out of the corner of his eye he saw Grivas turn to the door, his pistol raised. O'Hara took a chance, lifted one hand from the stick and struck out blindly at Grivas. He just had time for one blow and luckily it connected somewhere; he felt the edge of his hand strike home and then he was too busy to see if he had incapacitated Grivas.

The Dakota was still moving too fast. Already it was more than half-way down the strip and O'Hara could see the emptiness ahead where the strip stopped at the lip of the valley. In desperation he swung the rudder hard over and the Dakota swerved with a loud grating sound.

He braced himself for the crash.

The starboard wingtip hit the rock wall and the Dakota spun sharply to the right. O'Hara kept the rudder forced right over and saw the rock wall coming right at him. The nose of the plane hit rock and crumpled and the safety glass in the windscreens shivered into opacity. Then something hit him on the head and he lost consciousness.

He came round because someone was slapping his face. His head rocked from side to side and he wanted them to stop because it was so good to be asleep. The slapping went on and on and he moaned and tried to tell them to stop. But the slapping did not stop so he opened his eyes.

It was Forester who was administering the punishment, and, as O'Hara opened his eyes, he turned to Rohde who was standing behind him and said, "Keep your gun on him."

Rohde smiled. His gun was in his hand but hanging slackly and pointing to the floor. He made no attempt to bring it up. Forester said, "What the hell did you think you were doing?"

O'Hara painfully lifted his arm to his head. He had a bump on his skull the size of an egg. He said weakly, "Where's Grivas?"

"Who is Grivas?"

"My co-pilot."

"He's here—he's in a bad way."

"I hope the bastard dies," said O'Hara bitterly. "He pulled a gun on me."

"You were at the controls," said Forester, giving him a hard look. "You put this plane down here—and I want to know why."

"It was Grivas—he forced me to do it."

"The *señor capitan* is right," said Rohde. "This man Grivas was going to shoot me and the *señor capitan* hit him." He bowed stiffly. " *Muchos gracias.*"

Forester swung round and looked at Rohde, then beyond him to Grivas. "Is he conscious?"

O'Hara looked across the cockpit. The side of the fuselage was caved in and a blunt spike of rock had hit Grivas in the chest, smashing his rib cage. It looked as though he wasn't going to make it, after all. But he was conscious, all right; his eyes were open and he looked at them with hatred.

O'Hara could hear a woman screaming endlessly in the

passenger cabin and someone else was moaning mono-
tonously. "For Christ's sake, what's happened back there?"

No one answered because Grivas began to speak. He
mumbled in a low whisper and blood frothed round his mouth.
"They'll get you," he said. "They'll be here any minute
now." His lips parted in a ghastly smile. "I'll be all right;
they'll take me to hospital. But you—you'll . . ." He broke
off in a fit of coughing and then continued: ". . . they'll
kill the lot of you." He lifted up his arm, the fingers curling
into a fist. "*Vivaca*. . . ."

The arm dropped flaccidly and the look of hate in his eyes
deepened into surprise—surprise that he was dead.

Rohde grabbed him by the wrist and held it for a moment.
"He's gone," he said.

"He was a lunatic," said O'Hara. "Stark, staring mad."

The woman was still screaming and Forester said, "For
God's sake, let's get everybody out of here."

Just then the Dakota lurched sickeningly and the whole
cockpit rose in the air. There was a ripping sound as the
spike of rock that had killed Grivas tore at the aluminium
sheathing of the fuselage. O'Hara had a sudden and horrible
intuition of what was happening. "Nobody move," he shouted.
"Everyone keep still."

He turned to Forester. "Bash in those windows."

Forester looked in surprise at the axe he was still holding
as though he had forgotten it, then he raised it and struck
at the opaque windscreen. The plastic filling in the glass
sandwich could not withstand his assault and he made a hole
big enough for a man to climb through.

O'Hara said, "I'll go through—I think I know what I'll
find. Don't either of you go back there—not yet. And
call through and tell anyone who can move to come up front."

He squeezed through the narrow gap and was astonished
to find that the nose of the Dakota was missing. He twisted
and crawled out on to the top of the fuselage and looked aft.
The tail and one wing were hanging in space over the valley
where the runway ended. The whole aircraft was delicately
balanced and even as he looked the tail tipped a little and
there was a ripping sound from the cockpit.

He twisted on to his stomach and wriggled so that he could
look into the cockpit, his head upside-down. "We're in a jam,"
he said to Forester. "We're hanging over a two-hundred
foot drop, and the only thing that's keeping the whole

27

bloody aeroplane from tipping over is that bit of rock there."
He indicated the rock projection driven into the side of the
cockpit.

He said, " If anyone goes back there the extra weight
might send us over because we're balanced just like a see-saw."

Forester turned his head and bawled, " Anyone who can
move, come up here."

There was a movement and Willis staggered through the
door, his head bloody. Forester shouted, " Anyone else?"

Señora Montes called urgently, " Please help my uncle—
oh, please."

Rohde drew Willis out of the way and stepped through the
door. Forester said sharply, " Don't go in too far."

Rohde did not even look at him, but bent to pick up Montes
who was lying by the door. He half carried, half dragged him
into the cockpit and Señorita Montes followed.

Forester looked up at O'Hara. " It's getting crowded in
here; I think we'd better start getting people outside."

" We'll get them on top first," said O'Hara. " The more
weight we have at this end, the better. Let the girl come
first."

She shook her head. " My uncle first."

" For God's sake, he's unconscious," said Forester. " You
go out—I'll look after him."

She shook her head stubbornly and O'Hara broke in
impatiently, " All right, Willis, come on up here; let's not
waste time." His head ached and he was panting in the thin
air; he was not inclined to waste time over silly girls.

He helped Willis through the smashed windscreen and
saw him settle on top of the fuselage. When he looked into
the cockpit again it was evident that the girl had changed
her mind. Rohde was talking quietly but emphatically to her
and she crossed over and O'Hara helped her out.

Armstrong came next, having made his own way to the
cockpit. He said, " It's a bloody shambles back there. I
think the old man in the back seat is dead and his wife is
pretty badly hurt. I don't think it's safe to move her."

" What about Peabody?"

" The luggage was thrown forward on to both of us. He's
half buried under it. I tried to get him free but I couldn't."

O'Hara passed this on to Forester. Rohde was kneeling
by Montes, trying to bring him round. Forester hesitated,
then said, " Now we've got some weight at this end it might
be safe for me to go back."

O'Hara said, "Tread lightly."

Forester gave a mirthless grin and went back through the door. He looked at Miss Ponsky. She was sitting rigid, her arms clutched tightly about her, her eyes staring unblinkingly at nothing. He ignored her and began to heave suitcases from the top of Peabody, being careful to stow them in the front seats. Peabody stirred and Forester shook him into consciousness and as soon as he seemed to be able to understand, said, "Go into the cockpit—the cockpit, you understand."

Peabody nodded blearily and Forester stepped a little farther aft. "Christ Almighty!" he whispered, shocked at what he saw.

Coughlin was a bloody pulp. The cargo had shifted in the smash and had come forward, crushing the two back seats. Mrs. Coughlin was still alive but both her legs had been cut off just below the knee. It was only because she had been leaning forward to comfort Miss Ponsky that she hadn't been killed like her husband.

Forester felt something touch his back and turned. It was Peabody moving aft. "I said the cockpit, you damned fool," shouted Forester.

"I wanna get outa here," mumbled Peabody. "I wanna get out. The door's back there."

Forester wasted no time in argument. Abruptly he jabbed at Peabody's stomach and then brought his clenched fists down at the nape of his neck as he bent over gasping, knocking him cold. He dragged him forward to the door and said to Rohde, "Take care of this fool. If he causes trouble, knock him on the head."

He went back and took Miss Ponsky by the arm. "Come," he said gently.

She rose and followed him like a somnambulist and he led her right into the cockpit and delivered her to O'Hara. Montes was now conscious and would be ready to move soon.

As soon as O'Hara reappeared Forester said, "I don't think the old lady back there will make it."

"Get her out," said O'Hara tightly. "For God's sake, get her out."

So Forester went back. He didn't know whether Mrs. Coughlin was alive or dead; her body was still warm, however, so he picked her up in his arms. Blood was still spurting from her shattered shins, and when he stepped into the cockpit

29

Rohde drew in his breath with a hiss. "On the seat," he said. "She needs tourniquets now—immediately."

He took off his jacket and then his shirt and began to rip the shirt into strips, saying to Forester curtly, "Get the old man out."

Forester and O'Hara helped Montes through the windscreen and then Forester turned and regarded Rohde, noting the goose-pimples on his back. "Clothing," he said to O'Hara. "We'll need warm clothing. It'll be bad up here by nightfall."

"Hell!" said O'Hara. "That's adding to the risk. I don't——"

"He is right," said Rohde without turning his head. "If we do not have clothing we will all be dead by morning."

"All right," said O'Hara. "Are you willing to take the risk?"

"I'll chance it," said Forester.

"I'll get these people on the ground first," said O'Hara. "But while you're at it get the maps. There are some air charts of the area in that pocket next to my seat."

Rohde grunted. "I'll get those."

O'Hara got the people from the top of the fuselage to the ground and Forester began to bring suitcases into the cockpit. Unceremoniously he heaved Peabody through the windscreen and equally carelessly O'Hara dropped him to the ground, where he lay sprawling. Then Rohde handed through the unconscious Mrs. Coughlin and O'Hara was surprised at her lightness. Rohde climbed out and, taking her in his arms, jumped to the ground, cushioning the shock for her.

Forester began to hand out suitcases and O'Hara tossed them indiscriminately. Some burst open, but most survived the fall intact.

The Dakota lurched.

"Forester," yelled O'Hara. "Come out."

"There's still some more."

"Get out, you idiot," O'Hara bawled. "She's going."

He grabbed Forester's arms and hauled him out bodily and let him go thumping to the ground. Then he jumped himself and, as he did so, the nose rose straight into the air and the plane slid over the edge of the cliff with a grinding noise and in a cloud of dust. It crashed down two hundred feet and there was a long dying rumble and then silence.

O'Hara looked at the silent people about him, then turned his eyes to the harsh and savage mountains which surrounded them. He shivered with cold as he felt the keen wind which blew from the snowfields, and then shivered for a different reason as he locked eyes with Forester. They both knew that the odds against survival were heavy and that it was probable that the escape from the Dakota was merely the prelude to a more protracted death.

## VIII

"Now, let's hear all this from the beginning," said Forester.

They had moved into the nearest of the cabins. It proved bare but weatherproof, and there was a fire-place in which Armstrong had made a fire, using wood which Willis had brought from another cabin. Montes was lying in a corner being looked after by his niece, and Peabody was nursing a hangover and looking daggers at Forester.

Miss Ponsky had recovered remarkably from the rigidity of fright. When she had been dropped to the ground she had collapsed, digging her fingers into the frozen gravel in an ecstasy of relief. O'Hara judged she would never have the guts to enter an aeroplane ever again in her life. But now she was showing remarkable aptitude for sick nursing, helping Rohde to care for Mrs. Coughlin.

Now there was a character, thought O'Hara; Rohde was a man of unsuspected depths. Although he was not a medical man, he had a good working knowledge of practical medicine which was now invaluable. O'Hara had immediately turned to Willis for help with Mrs. Coughlin, but Willis had said, "Sorry, I'm a physicist—not a physician."

"Dr. Armstrong?" O'Hara had appealed.

Regretfully Armstrong had also shaken his head. "I'm a historian."

So Rohde had taken over—the non-doctor with the medical background—and the man with the gun.

O'Hara turned his attention to Forester. "All right," he said. "This is the way it was."

He told everything that had happened, right back from the take-off in San Croce, dredging from his memory everything Grivas had said. "I think he went off his head," he concluded.

Forester frowned. "No, it was planned," he contradicted. "And lunacy isn't planned. Grivas knew this air-strip and he knew the course to take. You say he was at San Croce airfield when the Samair plane was grounded?"

"That's right—I thought it was a bit odd at the time. I mean, it was out of character for Grivas to be haunting the field in the middle of the night—he wasn't that keen on his job."

"It sounds as though he *knew* the Samair Boeing was going to have engine trouble," commented Willis.

Forester looked up quickly and Willis said, "It's the only logical answer—he didn't just steal a plane, he stole the contents; and the contents of the plane were people from the Boeing. O'Hara says those big crates contain ordinary mining machinery and I doubt if Grivas would want that."

"That implies sabotage of the Boeing," said Forester. "If Grivas was expecting the Boeing to land at San Croce, it also implies a sizeable organisation behind him."

"We know that already," said O'Hara. "Grivas was expecting a reception committee here. He said 'They'll be here any minute.' But where are *they*?"

"And *who* are they?" asked Forester.

O'Hara thought of something else Grivas had said: ". . . they'll kill the lot of you." He kept quiet about that and asked instead, "Remember the last thing he said—'*Vivaca*'? It doesn't make sense to me. It sounds vaguely Spanish, but it's no word I know."

"My Spanish is good," said Forester deliberately. "There's no such word." He slapped the side of his leg irritably. "I'd give a lot to know what's been going on and who's responsible for all this."

A weak voice came from across the room. "I fear, gentlemen, that in a way I am responsible."

Everyone in the room, with the exception of Mrs. Coughlin, turned to look at Señor Montes.

## Chapter II

Montes looked ill. He was worse than he had been in the air. His chest heaved violently as he sucked in the thin air and he had a ghastly pallor. As he opened his mouth to speak again the girl said, "Hush, *tío*, be quiet. I will tell them."

She turned and looked across the cabins at O'Hara and

Forester. "My uncle's name is not Montes," she said levelly. "It is Aguillar." She said it as though it was an explanation, entire and complete in itself.

There was a moment of blank silence, then O'Hara snapped his fingers and said softly, "By God, the old eagle himself." He stared at the sick man.

"Yes, Señor O'Hara," whispered Aguillar. "But a crippled eagle, I am afraid."

"Say, what the hell is this?" grumbled Peabody. "What's so special about him?"

Willis gave Peabody a look of dislike and got to his feet. "I wouldn't have put it that way myself," he said. "But I could bear to know more."

O'Hara said, "Señor Aguillar was possibly the best president this country ever had until the army took over five years ago. He got out of the country just one jump ahead of a firing squad."

"General Lopez always was a hasty man," agreed Aguillar with a weak smile.

"You mean the government arranged all this—this jam we're in now—just to get you?" Willis's voice was shrill with incredulity.

Aguillar shook his head and started to speak, but the girl said, "No, you must be quiet." She looked at O'Hara appealingly. "Do not question him now, señor. Can't you see he is ill?"

"Can you speak for your uncle?" asked Forester gently.

She looked at the old man and he nodded. "What is it you want to know?" she asked.

"What is your uncle doing back in Cordillera?"

"We have come to bring back good government to our country," she said. "We have come to throw out Lopez."

O'Hara gave a short laugh. "To throw out Lopez," he said flatly. "Just like that. An old man and a girl are going to throw out a man with an army at his back." He shook his head disbelievingly.

The girl flared up. "What do you know about it; you are a foreigner—you know nothing. Lopez is finished—everyone in Cordillera knows it, even Lopez himself. He has been too greedy, too corrupt, and the country is sick of him."

Forester rubbed his chin reflectively. "She could be right," he said. "It would take just a puff of wind to blow Lopez over right now. He's run this country right into the ground in the last five years—just about milked it dry and salted

33

enough money away in Swiss banks to last a couple of life-times. I don't think he'd risk losing out now if it came to a showdown—if someone pushed hard enough he'd fold up and get out. I think he'd take wealth and comfort instead of power and the chance of being shot by some gun-happy student with a grievance."

"Lopez has bankrupted Cordillera," the girl said. She held up her head proudly. "But when my uncle appears in Santillana the people will rise, and that will be the end of Lopez."

"It could work," agreed Forester. "Your uncle was well liked. I suppose you've prepared the ground in advance."

She nodded. "The Democratic Committee of Action has made all the arrangements. All that remains is for my uncle to appear in Santillana."

"He may not get there," said O'Hara. "Someone is trying to stop him, and if it isn't Lopez, then who the hell is it?"

"The *comunistas*," the girl spat out with loathing in her voice. "They cannot afford to let my uncle get into power again. They want Cordillera for their own."

Forester said, "It figures. Lopez is a dead duck, come what may; so it's Aguillar versus the communists with Cordillera as the stake."

"They are not quite ready," the girl said. "They do not have enough support among the people. During the last two years they have been infiltrating the government very cleverly and if they had their way the people would wake up one morning to find Lopez gone, leaving a communist govern-ment to take his place."

"Swapping one dictatorship for another," said Forester. "Very clever."

"But they are not yet ready to get rid of Lopez," she said. "My uncle would spoil their plans—he would get rid of Lopez and the government, too. He would hold elections for the first time in nine years. So the communists are trying to stop him."

"And you think Grivas was a communist?" queried O'Hara.

Forester snapped his fingers. "Of course he was. That explains his last words. He was a communist, all right—Latin-American blend; when he said '*vivaca*' he was trying to say '*Viva* Castro.'" His voice hardened. "And we can expect his buddies along any minute."

"We must leave here quickly," said the girl. "They must not find my uncle."

O'Hara suddenly swung round and regarded Rohde, who had remained conspicuously silent. He said, "What do you import, Señor Rohde?"

"It is all right, Señor O'Hara," said Aguillar weakly. "Miguel is my secretary."

Forester looked at Rohde. "More like your bodyguard."

Aguillar flapped his hand limply as though the distinction was of no consequence, and Forester said, "What put you on to him, O'Hara?"

"I don't like men who carry guns," said O'Hara shortly. "Especially men who could be communist." He looked around the cabin. "All right, are there any more jokers in the pack? What about you, Forester? You seem to know a hell of a lot about local politics for an American businessman."

"Don't be a damn fool," said Forester. "If I didn't take an interest in local politics my corporation would fire me. Having the right kind of government is important to us, and we sure as hell don't want a commie set-up in Cordillera."

He took out his wallet and extracted a business card which he handed to O'Hara. It informed him that Raymond Forester was the South American sales manager for the Fairfield Machine Tool Corporation.

O'Hara gave it back to him. "Was Grivas the only communist aboard?" he said. "That's what I'm getting at. When we were coming in to land, did any of the passengers take any special precautions for their safety?"

Forester thought about it, then shook his head. "Everyone seemed to be taken by surprise—I don't think any of us knew just what was happening." He looked at O'Hara with respect. "In the circumstances that was a good question to ask."

"Well, I'm not a communist," said Miss Ponsky sharply. "The very idea!"

O'Hara smiled. "My apologies, Miss Ponsky," he said politely.

Rohde had been tending to Mrs. Coughlin; now he stood up. "This lady is dying," he said. "She has lost much blood and she is in shock. And she has the *soroche*—the mountain-sickness. If she does not get oxygen she will surely die." His black eyes switched to Aguillar, who seemed to have fallen asleep. "The Señor also must have oxygen—he's in grave danger." He looked at them. "We must go down the mountain. To stay at this height is very dangerous."

O'Hara was conscious of a vicious headache and the fact that his heart was thumping rapidly. He had been long enough in the country to have heard of *soroche* and its effects. The lower air pressure on the mountain heights meant less oxygen, the respiratory rate went up and so did the heart-beat rate, pumping the blood faster. It killed a weak constitution.

He said slowly, "There were oxygen cylinders in the plane —maybe they're not busted."

"Good," said Rohde. "We will look, you and I. It would be better not to move this lady if possible. But if we do not find the oxygen, then we must go down the mountain."

Forester said, "We must keep a fire going—the rest of us will look for wood." He paused. "Bring some petrol from the plane—we may need it."

"All right," said O'Hara.

"Come on," said Forester to Peabody. "Let's move."

Peabody lay where he was, gasping. "I'm beat," he said. "And my head's killing me."

"It's just a hangover," said Forester callously. "Get on your feet, man."

Rohde put his hand on Forester's arm. "*Soroche*," he said warningly. "He will not be able to do much. Come, Señor."

O'Hara followed Rohde from the cabin and shivered in the biting air. He looked around. The air-strip was built on the only piece of level ground in the vicinity; all else was steeply shelving mountainside, and all around were the pinnacles of the high Andes, clear-cut in the cold and crystal air. They soared skyward, blindingly white against the blue where the snows lay on their flanks, and where the slope was too steep for the snow to stay was the dark grey of the rock.

It was cold, desolate and utterly lifeless. There was no restful green of vegetation, or the flick of a bird's wing—just black, white and the blue of the sky, a hard, dark metallic blue as alien as the landscape.

O'Hara pulled his jacket closer about him and looked at the other huts. "What is this place?"

"It is a mine," said Rohde. "Copper and zinc—the tunnels are over there." He pointed to a cliff face at the end of the air-strip and O'Hara saw the dark mouths of several tunnels driven into the cliff face. Rohde shook his head. "But it is too high to work—they should never have tried. No man can work well at this height; not even our mountain *indios*."

"You know this place then?"

36

"I know these mountains well," said Rohde. "I was born not far from here."

They trudged along the air-strip and before they had gone a hundred yards O'Hara felt exhausted. His head ached and he felt nauseated. He sucked the thin air into his lungs and his chest heaved.

Rohde stopped and said, "You must not force your breathing."

"What else can I do?" asked O'Hara, panting. "I've got to get enough air."

"Breathe naturally, without effort," said Rohde. "You will get enough air. But if you force your breathing you will wash all the carbon dioxide from your lungs, and that will upset the acid base of your blood and you will get muscle cramps. And that is very bad."

O'Hara moderated his breathing and said, "You seem to know a lot about it."

"I studied medicine once," said Rohde briefly.

They reached the far end of the strip and looked over the edge of the cliff. The Dakota was pretty well smashed up; the port wing had broken off, as had the entire tail section. Rohde studied the terrain. "We need not climb down the cliff; it will be easier to go round."

It took them a long time to get to the plane and when they got there they found only one oxygen cylinder intact. It was difficult to get it free and out of the aircraft, but they managed it after chopping away a part of the fuselage with the axe that O'Hara found on the floor of the cockpit.

The gauge showed that the cylinder was only a third full and O'Hara cursed Filson and his cheese-paring, but Rohde seemed satisfied. "It will be enough," he said. "We can stay in the hut to-night."

"What happens if these communists turn up?" asked O'Hara.

Rohde seemed unperturbed. "Then we will defend ourselves," he said equably. "One thing at a time, Señor O'Hara."

"Grivas seemed to think they were already here," said O'Hara. "I wonder what held them up?"

Rohde shrugged. "Does it matter?"

They could not manhandle the oxygen cylinder back to the huts without help, so Rohde went back, taking with him some mouthpieces and a bottle of petrol tapped from a wing tank. O'Hara searched the fuselage, looking for anything that might be of value, particularly food. That, he thought, might turn out to be a major problem. All he found was half a slab of milk chocolate in Grivas's seat pocket.

Rohde came back with Forester, Willis and Armstrong and they took it in turns carrying the oxygen cylinder, two by two. It was very hard work and they could only manage to move it twenty yards at a time. O'Hara estimated that back in San Croce he could have picked it up and carried it a mile, but the altitude seemed to have sucked all the strength from their muscles and they could work only a few minutes at a time before they collapsed in exhaustion.

When they got it to the hut they found that Miss Ponsky was feeding the fire with wood from a door of one of the other huts that Willis and Armstrong had torn down and smashed up laboriously with rocks. Willis was particularly glad to see the axe. " It'll be easier now," he said.

Rohde administered oxygen to Mrs. Coughlin and Aguillar. She remained unconscious, but it made a startling difference to the old man. As the colour came back to his cheeks his niece smiled for the first time since the crash.

O'Hara sat before the fire, feeling the warmth soak into him, and produced his air charts. He spread the relevant chart on the floor and pin-pointed a position with a pencilled cross. " That's where we were when we changed course," he said. " We flew on a true course of one-eighty-four for a shade over five minutes." He drew a line on the chart. " We were flying at a little over two hundred knots—say, two hundred and forty miles an hour. That's about twenty miles —so that puts us about—*here*." He made another cross. Forester looked over his shoulder. " The air-strip isn't marked on the map," he said.

" Rohde said it was abandoned," said O'Hara.

Rohde came over and looked at the map and nodded. " You are right," he said. " That is where we are. The road down the mountain leads to the refinery. That also is abandoned, but I think some *indios* live there still."

" How far is that?" asked Forester.

" About forty kilometres," said Rohde.

" Twenty-five miles," translated Forester. " That's a hell of a long way in these conditions."

" It will not be very bad," said Rohde. He put his finger on the map. " When we get to this valley where the river runs we will be nearly five thousand feet lower and we will breathe more easily. That is about sixteen kilometres by the road."

"We'll start early to-morrow," said O'Hara.

Rohde agreed. "If we had no oxygen I would have said go now. But it would be better to stay in the shelter of this hut to-night."

"What about Mrs. Coughlin?" said O'Hara quietly. "Can we move her?"

"We will have to move her," said Rohde positively. "She cannot live at this altitude."

"We'll rig together some kind of stretcher," said Forester. "We can make a sling out of clothing and poles—or maybe use a door."

O'Hara looked across to where Mrs. Coughlin was breathing stertorously, closely watched by Miss Ponsky. His voice was harsh. "I'd rather that bastard Grivas was still alive if that would give her back her legs," he said.


II

Mrs. Coughlin died during the night without regaining consciousness. They found her in the morning cold and stiff. Miss Ponsky was in tears. "I should have stayed awake," she sniffled. "I *couldn't* sleep most of the night, and then I had to drop off."

Rohde shook his head gravely. "She would have died," he said. "We could not do anything for her—none of us."

Forester, O'Hara and Peabody scratched out a shallow grave. Peabody seemed better and O'Hara thought that maybe Forester had been right when he said that Peabody was only suffering from a hangover. However, he had to be prodded into helping to dig the grave.

It seemed that everyone had had a bad night, no one sleeping very well. Rohde said that it was another symptom of *soroche* and the sooner they got to a lower altitude the better. O'Hara still had a splitting headache and heartily concurred.

The oxygen cylinder was empty.

O'Hara tapped the gauge with his finger but the needle stubbornly remained at zero. He opened the cock and bent his head to listen but there was no sound from the valve. He had heard the gentle hiss of oxygen several times during the night and had assumed that Rohde had been tending to Mrs. Coughlin or Aguillar.

He beckoned to Rohde. "Did you use all the oxygen last night?"

Rohde looked incredulously at the gauge. "I was saving some for to-day," he said. "Señor Aguillar needs it."

O'Hara bit his lip and looked across to where Peabody sat. "I thought he looked pretty chipper this morning."

Rohde growled something under his breath and took a step forward, but O'Hara caught his arm. "It can't be proved," he said. "I could be wrong. And anyway, we don't want any rows right here. Let's get down this mountain." He kicked the cylinder and it clanged emptily. "At least we won't have to carry this."

He remembered the chocolate and brought it out. There were eight small squares to be divided between ten of them, so he, Rohde and Forester did without and Aguillar had two pieces. O'Hara thought that he must have had three because the girl did not appear to eat her ration.

Armstrong and Willis appeared to work well as a team. Using the axe, they had ripped some timber from one of the huts and made a rough stretcher by pushing lengths of wood through the sleeves of two overcoats. That was for Aguillar, who could not walk.

They put on all the clothes they could and left the rest in suitcases. Forester gave O'Hara a bulky overcoat. "Don't mess it about if you can help it," he said. "That's vicuna—it cost a lot of dough." He grinned. "The boss's wife asked me to get it this trip; it's the old man's birthday soon."

Peabody grumbled when he had to leave his luggage and grumbled more when O'Hara assigned him to a stretcher-carrying stint. O'Hara resisted taking a poke at him; for one thing he did not want open trouble, and for another he did not know whether he had the strength to do any damage. At the moment it was all he could do to put one foot in front of the other.

So they left the huts and went down the road, turning their backs on the high peaks. The road was merely a rough track cut out of the mountainside. It wound down in a series of hairpin bends and Willis pointed out where blasting had been done on the corners. It was just wide enough to take a single vehicle but, from time to time, they came across a wide part where two trucks could pass.

O'Hara asked Rohde, "Did they intend to truck all the ore from the mine?"

"They would have built a telfer," said Rohde. "An endless rope with buckets. But they were still proving the mine. Petrol engines do not work well up here—they need superchargers." He stopped suddenly and stared at the ground.

In a patch of snow was the track of a tyre.

"Someone's been up here lately," observed O'Hara. "Supercharged or not. But I knew that."

"How?" Rohde demanded.

"The air-strip had been cleared of snow."

Rohde patted his breast and moved away without saying anything. O'Hara remembered the pistol and wondered what would happen if they came up against opposition.

Although the path was downhill and the going comparatively good, it was only possible to carry the stretcher a hundred yards at a time. Forester organised relays, and as one set of carriers collapsed exhaustedly another took over. Aguilar was in a comatose condition and the girl walked next to the stretcher, anxiously watching him. After a mile they stopped for a rest and O'Hara said to Rohde, "I've got a flask of spirits. I've been saving it for when things really get tough. Do you think it would help the old man?"

"Let me have it," said Rohde.

O'Hara took the flask from his hip and gave it to Rohde, who took off the cap and sniffed the contents. "*Aguardiente*," he said. "Not the best drink but it will do." He looked at O'Hara curiously. "Do you drink this?"

"I'm a poor man," said O'Hara defensively.

Rohde smiled. "When I was a student I also was poor. I also drank *aguardiente*. But I do not recommend too much." He looked across at Aguilar. "I think we save this for later." He recapped the flask and handed it back to O'Hara. As O'Hara was replacing it in his pocket he saw Peabody staring at him. He smiled back pleasantly.

After a rest of half an hour they started off again. O'Hara in the lead, looked back and thought they looked like a bunch of war refugees. Willis and Armstrong were stumbling along with the stretcher, the girl keeping pace alongside; Miss Ponsky was sticking close to Rohde, chatting as though on a Sunday afternoon walk, despite her shortness of breath, and Forester was in the rear with Peabody shambling beside him.

After the third stop O'Hara found that things were going better. His step felt lighter and his breathing eased, although the headache stayed with him. The stretcher-bearers found that they could carry for longer periods, and Aguillar had come round and was taking notice.

O'Hara mentioned this to Rohde, who pointed at the steep slopes about them. "We are losing a lot of height," he said. "It will get better now."

After the fourth halt O'Hara and Forester were carrying the stretcher. Aguillar apologised in a weak voice for the inconvenience he was causing, but O'Hara forbore to answer —he needed all his breath for the job. Things weren't that much better.

Forester suddenly stopped and O'Hara thankfully laid down the stretcher. His legs felt rubbery and the breath rasped in his throat. He grinned at Forester, who was beating his hands against his chest. "Never mind," he said. "It should be warmer down in the valley."

Forester blew on his fingers. "I hope so." He looked up at O'Hara. "You're a pretty good pilot," he said. "I've done some flying in my time, but I don't think I could do what you did yesterday."

"You might if you had a pistol at your head," said O'Hara with a grimace. "Anyway, I couldn't leave it to Grivas— he'd have killed the lot of us, starting with me first."

He looked past Forester and saw Rohde coming back up the road at a stumbling run, his gun in his hand. "Something's happening."

He went forward to meet Rohde, who gasped, his chest heaving, "There are huts here—I had forgotten them."

O'Hara looked at the gun. "Do you need that?"

Rohde gave a stark smile. "It is possible, señor." He waved casually down the road with the pistol. "I think we should be careful. I think we should look first before doing anything. You, me, and Señor Forester."

"I think so too," said Forester. "Grivas said his pals would be around and this seems a likely place to meet them."

"All right," said O'Hara, and looked about. There was no cover on the road but there was a jumble of rocks a little way back. "I think everyone else had better stick behind that lot," he said. "If anything does break, there's no point in being caught in the open."

They went back to shelter behind the rocks and O'Hara

told everyone what was happening. He ended by saying, "If there's shooting you don't do a damned thing—you freeze and stay put. Now I know we're not an army but we're likely to come under fire all the same—so I'm naming Doctor Willis as second-in-command. If anything happens to us you take your orders from him." Willis nodded.

Aguillar's niece was talking to Rohde, and as O'Hara went to join Forester she touched him on the arm. "Señor."

He looked down at her. "Yes, señorita."

"Please be careful, you and Señor Forester. I would not want anything to happen to you because of us."

"I'll be careful," said O'Hara. "Tell me, is your name the same as your uncle's?"

"I am Benedetta Aguillar," she said.

He nodded. "I'm Tim O'Hara. I'll be careful."

He joined the other two and they walked down the road to the bend. Rohde said, "These huts were where the miners lived. This is just about as high as a man can live permanently—a man who is acclimatised such as our mountain *indios*. I think we should leave the road here and approach from the side. If Grivas did have friends, here is where we will find them."

They took to the mountainside and came upon the camp from the top. A level place had been roughly bulldozed out of the side of the mountain and there were about a dozen timber-built huts, very much like the huts by the air-strip.

"This is no good," said Forester. "We'll have to go over this miniature cliff before we can get at them."

"There's no smoke," O'Hara pointed out.

"Maybe that means something—maybe it doesn't," said Forester. "I think that Rohde and I will go round and come up from the bottom. If anything happens, maybe you can cause a diversion from up here."

"What do I do?" asked O'Hara. "Throw stones?"

Forester shook with silent laughter. He pointed down the slope to beyond the camp. "We'll come out about there. You can see us from here but we'll be out of sight of anyone in the camp. If all's clear you can give us the signal to come up." He looked at Rohde, who nodded.

Forester and Rohde left quietly and O'Hara lay on his belly, looking down at the camp. He did not think there was anyone there. It was less than five miles up to the air-strip by the road and there was nothing to stop anybody going up there. If Grivas's confederates were anywhere, it was not

43

likely that they would be at this camp—but it was as well to make sure. He scanned the huts but saw no sign of movement.

Presently he saw Forester wave from the side of the rock he had indicated and he waved back. Rohde went up first, in a wide arc to come upon the camp at an angle. Then Forester moved forward in the peculiar scuttling, zigzagging run of the experienced soldier who expects to be shot at. O'Hara wondered about Forester; the man had said he could fly an aeroplane and now he was behaving like a trained infantryman. He had an eye for ground, too, and was obviously accustomed to command.

Forester disappeared behind one of the huts and then Rohde came into sight at the far end of the camp, moving warily with his gun in his hand. He too disappeared, and O'Hara felt tension. He waited for what seemed a very long time, then Forester walked out from behind the nearest hut, moving quite unconcernedly. "You can come down," he called. "There's no one here."

O'Hara let out his breath with a rush and stood up. "I'll go back and get the rest of the people down here," he shouted, and Forester waved in assent.

O'Hara went back up the road, collected the party and took them down to the camp. Forester and Rohde were waiting in the main "street" and Forester called out, "We've struck it lucky; there's a lot of food here."

Suddenly O'Hara realised that he hadn't eaten for a day and a half. He did not feel particularly hungry, but he knew that if he did not eat he could not last out much longer—and neither could any of the others. To have food would make a lot of difference on the next leg of the journey.

Forester said, "Most of the huts are empty, but three of them are fitted out as living quarters complete with kerosene heaters."

O'Hara looked down at the ground which was criss-crossed with tyre tracks. "There's something funny going on," he said. "Rohde told me that the mine has been abandoned for a long time, yet there's all these signs of life and no one around. What the hell's going on?"

Forester shrugged. "Maybe the commie organisation is slipping," he said. "The Latins have never been noted for good planning. Maybe someone's put a spoke in their wheel."

"Maybe," said O'Hara. "We might as well take advantage of it. What do you think we should do now—how long should we stay here?"

Forester looked at the group entering one of the huts, then up at the sky. "We're pretty beat," he said. "Maybe we ought to stay here until to-morrow. It'll take us a while to get fed and it'll be late before we can move out. We ought to stay here to-night and keep warm."

"We'll consult Rohde," said O'Hara. "He's the expert on mountains and altitude."

The huts were well fitted. There were paraffin stoves, bunks, plenty of blankets and a large assortment of canned foods. On the table in one of the huts there were the remnants of a meal, the plates dirty and unwashed and frozen dregs of coffee in the bottoms of tin mugs. O'Hara felt the thickness of the ice and it cracked beneath the pressure of his finger.

"They haven't been gone long," he said. "If the hut was unheated this stuff would have frozen to the bottom." He passed the mug to Rohde. "What do you think?"

Rohde looked at the ice closely. "If they turned off the heaters when they left, the hut would stay warm for a while," he said. He tested the ice and thought deeply. "I would say two days," he said finally.

"Say yesterday morning," suggested O'Hara. "That would be about the time we took off from San Croce."

Forester groaned in exasperation. "It doesn't make sense. Why did they go to all this trouble, make all these preparations, and then clear out? One thing's sure: Grivas expected a reception committee—and where the hell is it?"

O'Hara said to Rohde, "We are thinking of staying here to-night. What do you think?"

"It is better here than at the mine," said Rohde. "We have lost a lot of height. I would say that we are at an altitude of about four thousand metres here—or maybe a little more. That will not harm us for one night; it will be better to stay here in shelter than to stay in the open to-night, even if it is lower down the mountain." He contracted his brows. "But I suggest we keep a watch."

Forester nodded. "We'll take it in turns."

Miss Ponsky and Benedetta were busy on the pressure stoves making hot soup. Armstrong had already got the heater going and Willis was sorting out cans of food. He called O'Hara over. "I thought we'd better take something with us when we leave," he said. "It might come in useful."

"A good idea," said O'Hara.

Willis grinned. "That's all very well, but I can't read Spanish. I have to go by the pictures on the labels. Someone

45

had better check on these when I've got them sorted out."

Forester and Rohde went on down the road to pick a good spot for a sentry, and when Forester came back he said, "Rohde's taking the first watch. We've got a good place where we can see bits of road a good two miles away. And if they come up at night they're sure to have their lights on."

He looked at his watch. "We've got six able-bodied men, so if we leave here early to-morrow, that means two-hour watches. That's not too bad—it gives us all enough sleep."

After they had eaten Benedetta took some food down to Rohde and O'Hara found himself next to Armstrong. "You said you were a historian. I suppose you're over here to check up on the Incas," he said.

"Oh, no," said Armstrong. "They're not my line of country at all. My line is medieval history."

"Oh," said O'Hara blankly.

"I don't know anything about the Incas and I don't particularly want to," said Armstrong frankly. He smiled gently. "For the past ten years I've never had a real holiday. I'd go on holiday like a normal man—perhaps to France or Italy—and then I'd see something interesting. I'd do a bit of investigating—and before I'd know it I'd be hard at work."

He produced a pipe and peered dubiously into his tobacco pouch. "This year I decided to come to South America for a holiday. All there is here is pre-European and modern history—no medieval history at all. Clever of me, wasn't it?"

O'Hara smiled, suspecting that Armstrong was indulging in a bit of gentle leg-pulling. "And what's your line, Doctor Willis?" he asked.

"I'm a physicist," said Willis. "I'm interested in cosmic rays at high altitudes. I'm not getting very far with it, though."

They were certainly a mixed lot, thought O'Hara, looking across at Miss Ponsky as she talked animatedly to Aguillar. Now there was a sight—a New England spinster schoolmarm lecturing a statesman. She would certainly have plenty to tell her pupils when she arrived back at the little schoolhouse.

"What was this place, anyway?" asked Willis.

"Living quarters for the mine up on top," said O'Hara. "That's what Rohde tells me."

Willis nodded. "They had their workshops down here, too," he said. "All the machinery has gone, of course, but

46

there are still a few bits and pieces left." He shivered. "I can't say I'd like to work in a place like this."

O'Hara looked about the hut. "Neither would I." He caught sight of an electric conduit tube running down a wall. "Where did their electricity supply come from, I wonder?"

"They had their own plant; there's the remains of it out back. The generator has gone—they must have salvaged it when the mine closed down. They scavenged most everything, I guess; there's precious little left."

Armstrong drew the last of the smoke from his failing pipe with a disconsolate gurgle. "Well, that's the last of the tobacco until we get back to civilisation," he said as he knocked out the dottle. "Tell me, Captain; what are you doing in this part of the world?"

"Oh, I fly aeroplanes from anywhere to anywhere," said O'Hara. Not any more I don't, he thought. As far as Filson was concerned, he was finished. Filson would never forgive a pilot who wrote off one of his aircraft, no matter what the reason. I've lost my job, he thought. It was a lousy job but it had kept him going, and now he'd lost it.

The girl came back and he crossed over to her. "Anything doing down the road?" he asked.

She shook her head. "Nothing. Miguel says everything is quiet."

"He's quite a character," said O'Hara. "He certainly knows a lot about these mountains—and he knows a bit about medicine too."

"He was born near here," Benedetta said. "And he was a medical student until——" She stopped.

"Until what?" prompted O'Hara.

"Until the revolution." She looked at her hands. "All his family were killed—that is why he hates Lopez. That is why he works with my uncle—he knows that my uncle will ruin Lopez."

"I thought he had a chip on his shoulder," said O'Hara.

She sighed. "It is a great pity about Miguel; he was going to do so much. He was very interested in the *soroche*, you know; he intended to study it as soon as he had taken his degree. But when the revolution came he had to leave the country and he had no money so he could not continue his studies. He worked in the Argentine for a while, and then he met my uncle. He saved my uncle's life."

"Oh?" O'Hara raised his eyebrows.

"In the beginning Lopez knew that he was not safe while my uncle was alive. He knew that my uncle would organise an opposition—underground, you know. So wherever my uncle went he was in danger from the murderers hired by Lopez—even in the Argentine. There were several attempts to kill him, and it was one of these times that Miguel saved his life."

O'Hara said, "Your uncle must have felt like another Trotsky. Joe Stalin had him bumped off in Mexico."

"That is right," she said with a grimace of distaste. "But they were communists, both of them. Anyway, Miguel stayed with us after that. He said that all he wanted was food to eat and a bed to sleep in, and he would help my uncle come back to Cordillera. And here we are."

Yes, thought O'Hara; marooned up a bloody mountain with God knows what waiting at the bottom.

Presently, Armstrong went out to relieve Rohde. Miss Ponsky came across to talk to O'Hara. "I'm sorry I behaved so stupidly in the airplane," she said crossly. "I don't know what came over me."

O'Hara thought there was no need to apologise for being half frightened to death; he had been bloody scared himself. But he couldn't say that—he couldn't even mention the word *fear* to her. That would be unforgivable; no one likes to be reminded of a lapse of that nature—not even a maiden lady getting on in years. He smiled and said diplomatically, "Not everyone would have come through an experience like that as well as you have, Miss Ponsky."

She was mollified and he knew that she had been in fear of a rebuff. She was the kind of person who would bite on a sore tooth, not letting it alone. She smiled and said, "Well now, Captain O'Hara—what do you think of all this talk about communists?"

"I think they're capable of anything," said O'Hara grimly.

"I'm going to put in a report to the State Department when I get back," she said. "You ought to hear what Señor Aguillar has been telling me about General Lopez. I think the State Department should help Señor Aguillar against General Lopez *and* the communists."

"I'm inclined to agree with you," said O'Hara. "But perhaps your State Department doesn't believe in interfering in Cordilleran affairs."

"Stuff and nonsense," said Miss Ponsky with acerbity.

"We're supposed to be fighting the communists, aren't we? Besides, Señor Aguillar assures me that he'll hold elections as soon as General Lopez is kicked out. He's a *real* democrat just like you and me."

O'Hara wondered what would happen if another South American state did go communist. Cuban agents were filtering all through Latin America like woodworms in a piece of furniture. He tried to think of the strategic importance of Cordillera—it was on the Pacific coast and it straddled the Andes, a gun pointing to the heart of the continent. He thought the Americans would be very upset if Cordillera went communist.

Rohde came back and talked for a few minutes with Aguillar, then he crossed to O'Hara and said in a low voice, "Señor Aguillar would like to speak to you." He gestured to Forester and the three of them went to where Aguillar was resting in a bunk.

He had brightened considerably and was looking quite spry. His eyes were lively and no longer filmed with weariness, and there was a strength and authority in his voice that O'Hara had not heard before. He realised that this was a strong man; maybe not too strong in the body because he was becoming old and his body was wearing out, but he had a strong mind. O'Hara suspected that if the old man had not had a strong will, the body would have crumpled under the strain it had undergone.

Aguillar said, "First I must thank you gentlemen for all you have done, and I am truly sorry that I have brought this calamity upon you." He shook his head sadly. "It is the innocent bystander who always suffers in the clash of our Latin politics. I am sorry that this should have happened and that you should see my country in this sad light."

"What else could we do?" asked Forester. "We're all in the same boat."

"I'm glad you see it that way," said Aguillar. "Because of what may come next. What happens if we meet up with the communists who should be here and are not?"

"Before we come to that there's something I'd like to query," said O'Hara. Aguillar raised his eyebrows and motioned him to continue, so O'Hara said deliberately, "How do we know they are communists? Señorita Aguillar tells me that Lopez has tried to liquidate you several times. How do you know he hasn't got wind of your return and is having another crack at you?"

Aguillar shook his head. "Lopez has—in your English idiom—shot his bolt. I *know*. Do not forget that I am a practical politician and give me credit for knowing my own work. Lopez forgot about me several years ago and is only interested in how he can safely relinquish the reins of power and retire. As for the communists—for years I have watched them work in my country, undermining the government and wooing the people. They have not got far with the people, or they would have disposed of Lopez by now. I am their only danger and I am sure that our situation is their work."

Forester said casually, "Grivas was trying to make a clenched fist salute when he died."

"All right," said O'Hara. "But why all this rigmarole of Grivas in the first place? Why not just put a time bomb in the Dakota—that would have done the job very easily."

Aguillar smiled. "Señor O'Hara, in my life as a politician I have had four bombs thrown at me and every one was defective. Our politics out here are emotional and emotion does not make for careful workmanship, even of bombs. And I am sure that even communism cannot make any difference to the native characteristics of my people. They wanted to make very sure of me and so they chose the unfortunate Grivas as their instrument. Would you have called Grivas an emotional man?"

"I should think he was," said O'Hara, thinking of Grivas's exultation even in death. "And he was pretty slipshod too."

Aguillar spread his hands, certain he had made his point. But he drove it home. "Grivas would be happy to be given such work; it would appeal to his sense of drama—and my people have a great sense of drama. As for being—er—slipshod, Grivas bungled the first part of the operation by stupidly killing himself, and the others have bungled the rest of it by not being here to meet us."

O'Hara rubbed his chin. As Aguillar drew the picture it made a weird kind of sense.

Aguillar said, "Now, my friends, we come to the next point. Supposing, on the way down this mountain, we meet these men—these communists? What happens then?" He regarded O'Hara and Forester with bright eyes. "It is not your fight—you are not Cordillerans—and I am interested to know what you would do. Would you give this dago politician into the hands of his enemies or . . ."

"Would we fight?" finished Forester.

"It's my fight," said O'Hara bluntly. "I'm not a Cordilleran, but Grivas pulled a gun on me and made me crash my plane. I didn't like that, and I didn't like the sight of the Coughlins. Anyway, I don't like the sight of communists, and I think that, all in all, this is my fight."

"I concur," said Forester.

Aguillar raised his hand. "But it is not as easy as that, is it? There are others to take into account. Would it be fair on Miss—er—Ponsky, for instance? Now what I propose is this. Miguel, my niece and I will withdraw into another cabin while you talk it over—and I will abide by your joint decision."

Forester looked speculatively at Peabody, who was just leaving the hut. He glanced at O'Hara, then said, "I think we should leave the question of fighting until there's something to fight. It's possible that we might just walk out of here."

Aguillar had seen Forester's look at Peabody. He smiled sardonically. "I see that you are a politician yourself, Señor Forester." He made a gesture of resignation. "Very well, we will leave the problem for the moment—but I think we will have to return to it."

"It's a pity we had to come down the mountain," said Forester. "There's sure to be an air search, and it might have been better to stay by the Dakota."

"We could not have lived up there," said Rohde.

"I know, but it's a pity all the same."

"I don't think it makes much difference," said O'Hara. "The wreck will be difficult to spot from the air—it's right at the foot of a cliff." He hesitated. "And I don't know about an air search—not yet, anyway."

Forester jerked his head. "What the hell do you mean by that?"

"Andes Airlift isn't noted for its efficiency and Filson, my boss, isn't good at paperwork. This flight didn't even have a number—I remember wondering about it just before we took off. It's on the cards that San Croce control haven't bothered to notify Santillana to expect us." As he saw Forester's expression he added, "The whole set-up is shoe-string and sealing-wax—it's only a small field."

"But surely your boss will get worried when he doesn't hear from you?"

"He'll worry," agreed O'Hara. "He told me to phone him from Santillana—but he won't worry too much at first. There have been times when I haven't phoned through on his say-so and had a rocket for losing cargo. But I don't

51

think he'll worry about losing the plane for a couple of days at least."

Forester blew out his cheeks. "Wow—what a Rube Goldberg organisation. Now I really feel lost."

Rohde said, "We must depend on our own efforts. I think we can be sure of that."

"We flew off course too," said O'Hara. "They'll start the search north of here—when they start."

Rohde looked at Aguillar whose eyes were closed. "There is nothing we can do now," he said. "But we must sleep. It will be a hard day to-morrow."


### III


Again, O'Hara did not sleep very well, but at least he was resting on a mattress instead of a hard floor with a full belly. Peabody was on watch and O'Hara was due to relieve him at two o'clock; he was glad when the time came.

He donned his leather jacket and took the vicuna coat that Forester had given him. He suspected that he would be glad of it during the next two hours. Forester was awake and waved lazily as he went out, although he did not speak.

The night air was thin and cold and O'Hara shivered as he set off down the road. As Rohde had said, the conditions for survival were better here than up by the air-strip, but it was still pretty dicey. He was aware that his heart was thumping and that his respiration rate was up. It would be much better when they got down to the *quebrada*, as Rohde called the lateral valley to which they were heading.

He reached the corner where he had to leave the road and headed towards the looming outcrop of rock which Rohde had picked as a vantage point. Peabody should have been perched on top of the rock and should have heard him coming, but there was no sign of his presence.

O'Hara called softly, "Peabody!"

There was silence.

Cautiously he circled the outcrop to get it silhouetted against the night sky. There was a lump on top of the rock which he could not quite make out. He began to climb the rock and as he reached the top he heard a muffled snore. He shook Peabody and his foot clinked on a bottle—Peabody was drunk.

"You bloody fool," he said and started to slap Peabody's

face, but without appreciable result. Peabody muttered in his drunken stupor but did not recover consciousness. "I ought to let you die of exposure," whispered O'Hara viciously, but he knew he could not do that. He also knew that he could not hope to carry Peabody back to the camp by himself. He would have to get help.

He stared down the mountainside but all was quiet, so he climbed down the rock and headed back up the road. Forester was still awake and looked up inquiringly as O'Hara entered the hut. "What's the matter?" he asked, suddenly alert.

"Peabody's passed out," said O'Hara. "I'll need help to bring him up."

"Damn this altitude," said Forester, putting on his shoes.

"It wasn't the altitude," O'Hara said coldly. "The bastard's dead drunk."

Forester muffled an imprecation. "Where did he get the stuff?"

"I suppose he found it in one of the huts," said O'Hara. "I've still got my flask—I was saving it for Aguillar."

"All right," said Forester. "Let's lug the damn fool up here."

It wasn't an easy thing to do. Peabody was a big, flabby man and his body lolled unco-operatively, but they managed it at last and dumped him unceremoniously in a bunk. Forester gasped and said, "This idiot will be the death of us all if we don't watch him." He paused. "I'll come down with you—it might be better to have two pairs of eyes down there right now."

They went back and climbed up on to the rock, lying side by side and scanning the dark mountainside. For fifteen minutes they were silent, but saw and heard nothing. "I think it's okay," said Forester at last. He shifted his position to ease his bones. "What do you think of the old man?"

"He seems all right to me," said O'Hara.

"He's a good joe—a good liberal politician. If he lasts long enough he might end up by being a good liberal statesman —but liberals don't last long in this part of the world, and I think he's a shade too soft." Forester chuckled. "Even when it's a matter of life and death—*his* life and death, not to mention his niece's—he still sticks to democratic procedure. He wants us to vote on whether we shall hand him over to the commies. Imagine that!"

"I wouldn't hand anyone over to the communists," said O'Hara. He glanced sideways at the dark bulk of Forester.

"You said you could fly a plane—I suppose you do it as a matter of business; company plane and all that."

"Hell, no," said Forester. "My outfit's not big enough or advanced enough for that. I was in the Air Force—I flew in Korea."

"So did I," said O'Hara. "I was in the R.A.F."

"Well, what do you know." Forester was delighted. "Where were you based?"

O'Hara told him and he said, "Then you were flying Sabres like I was. We went on joint operations—hell, we must have flown together."

"Probably."

They lay in companionable silence for a while, then Forester said, "Did you knock down any of those Migs? I got four, then they pulled me out. I was mad about that —I wanted to be a war hero; an ace, you know."

"You've got to get five in the American Air Force, haven't you?"

"That's right," said Forester. "Did you get any?"

"A couple," said O'Hara. He had shot down eight Migs but it was a part of his life he preferred to forget, so he didn't elaborate. Forester sensed his reserve and was quiet. After a few minutes he said, "I think I'll go back and get some sleep—if I can. We'll be on our way early."

When he had gone O'Hara stared into the darkness and thought about Korea. That had been the turning point of his life: before Korea he had been on his way up; after Korea there was just the endless slide, down to Filson and now beyond. He wondered where he would end up.

Thinking of Korea brought back Margaret and the letter. He had read the letter while on ready call on a frozen airfield. The Americans had a name for that kind of letter—they called them "Dear Johns." She was quite matter-of-fact about it and said that they were adult and must be sensible about this thing—all the usual rationalisations which covered plain infidelity. Looking back on it afterwards O'Hara could see a little humour in it—not much, but some. He was one of the inglorious ten per cent of any army fighting away from home, and he had lost his wife to a civilian. But it wasn't funny at all reading that letter on the cold airfield in Korea.

Five minutes later there was a scramble and he was in the air and thirty minutes later he was fighting. He went into battle with cold ferocity and a total lack of judgment. In three minutes he shot down two Migs, surprising them by sheer recklessness. Then a Chinese pilot with a cooler mind shot *him* down and he spent the rest of the war in a prison cage.

He did not like to think of that period and what had happened to him. He had come out of it with honour, but the psychiatrists had a field day with him when he got back to England. They did what they could but they could not break down the shell he had built about himself—and neither, by that time, could he break out.

And so it went—invalided out of the Air Force with a pension which he promptly commuted; the good jobs—at first—and then the poorer jobs, until he got down to Filson. And always the drink—more and more booze which had less and less effect as he tried to fill and smother the aching emptiness inside him.

He moved restlessly on the rock and heard the bottle clink. He put out his hand, picked it up and held it to the sky. It was a quarter full. He smiled. He could not get drunk on that but it would be very welcome. Yet as the fiery fluid spread and warmed his gut he felt guilty.


IV


Peabody was blearily belligerent when he woke up and found O'Hara looking at him. At first he looked defensive, then his instinct for attack took over. "I'm not gonna take anything from you," he said shakily. "Not from any goddam limey."

O'Hara just looked at him. He had no wish to tax Peabody with anything. Weren't they members of the same club? he thought sardonically. Fellow drunks. Why, we even drink from the same bottle. He felt miserable.

Rohde took a step forward and Peabody screamed, "And I'm not gonna take anything from a dago either."

"Then perhaps you'll take it from me," snapped Forester. He took one stride and slapped Peabody hard on the side of the face. Peabody sagged back on the bed and looked into Forester's cold eyes with an expression of fear and bewilderment on his face. His hand came up to touch the red blotch on his cheek. He was just going to speak when Forester pushed a finger at him. "Shut up! One cheep out of you and I'll mash you into a pulp. Now get your big fat butt off that bed and get to work—and if you step out of line again I swear to God I'll kill you."

The ferocity in Forester's voice had a chilling effect on Peabody. All the belligerence drained out of him. "I didn't mean to——" he began.

"Shut up!" said Forester and turned his back on him. "Let's get this show on the road," he announced generally.

They took food and a pressure stove and fuel, carrying it in awkwardly contrived packs cobbled from their overcoats. O'Hara did not think that Forester's boss would thank him for the vicuna coat, already showing signs of hard use.

Aguillar said he could walk, provided he was not asked to go too fast, so Forester took the stretcher poles and lashed them together in what he called a *travois*. "The Plains Indians used this for transport," he said. "They got along without wheels—so can we." He grinned. "They pulled with horses and we have only manpower, but it's downhill all the way."

The *travois* held a lot, much more than a man could carry, and Forester and O'Hara took first turn at pulling the triangular contraption, the apex bumping and bouncing on the stony ground. The others fell into line behind them and once more they wound their way down the mountain.

O'Hara looked at his watch—it was six a.m. He began to calculate—they had not come very far the previous day, not more than four or five miles, but they had been rested, warmed and fed, and that was all to the good. He doubted if they could make more than ten miles a day, so that meant another two days to the refinery, but they had enough food for at least four days, so they would be all right even if Aguillar slowed them down. Things seemed immeasurably brighter.

The terrain around them began to change. There were tufts of grass scattered sparsely and an occasional wild flower, and as they went on these signs of life became more frequent. They were able to move faster, too, and O'Hara said to Rohde, "The low altitude seems to be doing us good."

"That—and acclimatisation," said Rohde. He smiled grimly. "If it does not kill you, you can get used to it—eventually."

They came to one of the inevitable curves in the road and Rohde stopped and pointed to a silvery thread. "That is the *quebrada*—where the river is. We cross the river and turn north. The refinery is about twenty-four kilometres from the bridge."

"What's the height above sea-level?" asked O'Hara. He was beginning to take a great interest in the air he breathed —more interest than he had ever taken in his life.

56

"About three thousand five hundred metres," said Rohde.

Twelve thousand feet, O'Hara thought. That's much better.

They made good time and decided they would be able to have their midday rest and some hot food on the other side of the bridge. "A little over five miles in half a day," said Forester, chewing on a piece of jerked beef. "That won't be bad going. But I hope to God that Rohde is right when he says that the refinery is still inhabited."

"We will be all right," said Rohde. "There is a village ten miles the other side of the refinery. Some of us can go on and bring back help if necessary."

They pushed on and found that suddenly they were in the valley. There was no more snow and the ground was rocky, with more clumps of tough grass. The road ceased to twist and they went past many small ponds. It was appreciably warmer too, and O'Hara found that he could stride out without losing his breath.

We've got it made, he thought exultantly.

Soon they heard the roar of the river which carried the melt-water from the snow fields behind them and suddenly they were all gay. Miss Ponsky chattered unceasingly, exclaiming once in her high-pitched voice as she saw a bird, the first living, moving thing they had seen in two days. O'Hara heard Aguillar's deep chuckle and even Peabody cheered up, recovering from Forester's tongue-lashing.

O'Hara found himself next to Benedetta. She smiled at him and said, "Who has the pressure stove? We are going to need it soon."

He pointed back to where Willis and Armstrong were pulling the *travois*. "I packed it in there," he said.

They were very near the river now and he estimated that the road would have one last turn before they came to the bridge. "Come on," he said. "Let's see what's round the corner."

They stepped out and round the curve and O'Hara suddenly stopped. There were men and vehicles on the other side of the swollen river and the bridge was down.

A faint babble of voices arose above the river's roar as they were seen and some of the men on the other side started to run. O'Hara saw a man reach into the back of a truck and lift out a rifle and there was a popping noise as others opened up with pistols.

He lurched violently into Benedetta, sending her flying

57

just as the rifle cracked, and she stumbled into cover, dropping some cans in the middle of the road. As O'Hara fell after her one of the cans suddenly leaped into the air as a bullet hit it, and leaked a tomato bloodiness.

## Chapter III

O'Hara, Forester and Rohde looked down on the bridge from the cover of a group of large boulders near the edge of the river gorge. Below, the river rumbled, a green torrent of ice-water smoothly slipping past the walls it had cut over the æons. The gorge was about fifty yards wide.

O'Hara was still shaking from the shock of being unexpectedly fired upon. He had thrown himself into the side of the road, winding himself by falling on to a can in the pocket of his overcoat. When he recovered his breath he had looked with stupefaction at the punctured can in the middle of the road, bleeding a red tomato and meat gravy. That could have been me, he thought—or Benedetta.

It was then that he started to shake.

They had crept back round the corner, keeping in cover, while rifle bullets flicked chips of granite from the road surface. Rohde was waiting for them, his gun drawn and his face anxious. He looked at Benedetta's face and his lips drew back over his teeth in a snarl as he took a step forward.

"Hold it," said Forester quietly from behind him. "Let's not be too hasty." He put his hand on O'Hara's arm. "What's happening back there?"

O'Hara took a grip on himself. "I didn't have time to see much. I think the bridge is down; there are some trucks on the other side and there seemed to be a hell of a lot of men."

Forester scanned the ground with a practised eye. "There's plenty of cover by the river—we should be able to get a good view from among those rocks without being spotted. Let's go."

So here they were, looking at the ant-like activity on the other side of the river. There seemed to be about twenty men; some were busy unloading thick planks from a truck, others were cutting rope into lengths. Three men had apparently been detailed off as sentries; they were standing with rifles in their hands, scanning the bank of the gorge. As they watched, one of the men must have thought he saw something move, because he raised his rifle and fired a shot.

Forester said, "Nervous, aren't they? They're firing at shadows."

O'Hara studied the gorge. The river was deep and ran fast—it was obviously impossible to swim. One would be swept away helplessly in the grip of that rush of water and be frozen to death in ten minutes. Apart from that, there were the problems of climbing down the edge of the gorge to the water's edge and getting up the other side, not to mention the likelihood of being shot.

He crossed the river off his mental list of possibilities and turned his attention to the bridge. It was a primitive suspension contraption with two rope catenaries strung from massive stone buttresses on each side of the gorge. From the catenaries other ropes, graded in length, supported the main roadway of the bridge which was made of planks. But there was a gap in the middle where a lot of planks were missing and the ropes dangled in the breeze.

Forester said softly, "That's why they didn't meet us at the air-strip. See the truck in the river—downstream, slapped up against the side of the gorge?"

O'Hara looked and saw the truck in the water, almost totally submerged, with a standing wave of water swirling over the top of the cab. He looked back at the bridge. "It seems as though it was crossing from this side when it went over."

"That figures," said Forester. "I reckon they'd have a couple of men to make the preliminary arrangements— stocking up the camp and so on—in readiness for the main party. When the main party was due they came down to the bridge to cross—God knows for what reason. But they didn't make it—and they buggered the bridge, with the main party still on the other side."

"They're repairing it now," said O'Hara. "Look."

Two men crawled on to the swaying bridge pushing a plank before them. They lashed it into place with the aid of a barrage of shouted advice from terra-firma and then retreated. O'Hara looked at his watch; it had taken them half an hour.

"How many planks to go?" he asked.

Rohde grunted. "About thirty."

"That gives us fifteen hours before they're across," said O'Hara.

"More than that," said Forester. "They're not likely to do that trapeze act in the dark."

Rohde took out his pistol and carefully sighted on the bridge, using his forearm as a rest. Forester said, "That's no damned use—you won't hit anything at fifty yards with a pistol."

"I can try," said Rohde.

Forester sighed. "All right," he conceded. "But just one shot to see how it goes. How many slugs have you got?"

"I had two magazines with seven bullets in each," said Rohde. "I have fired three shots."

"You pop off another and that leaves ten. That's not too many."

Rohde tightened his lips stubbornly and kept the pistol where it was. Forester winked at O'Hara and said, "If you don't mind I'm going to retire now. As soon as you start shooting they're going to shoot right back."

He withdrew slowly, then turned and lay on his back and looked at the sky, gesturing for O'Hara to join him. "It looks as though the time is ripe to hold our council of war," he said. "Surrender or fight. But there may be a way out of it—have you got that air chart of yours?"

O'Hara produced it. "We can't cross the river—not here, at least," he said.

Forester spread out the chart and studied it. He put his finger down. "Here's the river—and this is where we are. This bridge isn't shown. What's this shading by the river?"

"That's the gorge."

Forester whistled. "Hell, it starts pretty high in the mountains, so we can't get around it upstream. What about the other way?"

O'Hara measured off the distance roughly. "The gorge stretches for about eighty miles down stream, but there's a bridge marked here—fifty miles away, as near as dammit."

"That's a hell of a long way," commented Forester. "I doubt if the old man could make it—not over mountain country."

O'Hara said, "And if that crowd over there have any sense they'll have another truckload of men waiting for us if we do try it. They have the advantage of being able to travel fast on the lower roads."

"The bastards have got us boxed in," said Forester. "So it's surrender or fight."

"I surrender to no communists," said O'Hara.

There was a flat report as Rohde fired his pistol and, almost immediately, an answering fusillade of rifle shots, the sound redoubled by echoes from the high ground behind. A bullet ricocheted from close by and whined over O'Hara's head.

Rohde came slithering down. "I missed," he said.

Forester refrained from saying, "I told you so," but his expression showed it. Rohde grinned. "But it stopped them working on the bridge—they went back fast and the plank dropped in the river."

"That's something," said O'Hara. "Maybe we can hold them off that way."

"For how long?" asked Forester. "We can't hold them off for ever—not with ten slugs. We'd better hold our council of war. You stay here, Miguel; but choose a different observation point—they might have spotted this one."

O'Hara and Forester went back to the group on the road. As they approached O'Hara said in a low voice, "We'd better do something to ginger this lot up; they look too bloody nervous."

There was a feeling of tension in the air. Peabody was muttering in a low voice to Miss Ponsky, who for once was silent herself. Willis was sitting on a rock, nervously tapping his foot on the ground, and Aguillar was speaking rapidly to Benedetta some little way removed from the group. The only one at ease seemed to be Armstrong, who was placidly sucking on an empty pipe, idly engaged in drawing patterns on the ground with a stick.

O'Hara crossed to Aguillar. "We're going to decide what to do," he said. "As you suggested."

Aguillar nodded gravely. "I said that it must happen."

O'Hara said, "You're going to be all right." He looked at Benedetta; her face was pale and her eyes were dark smudges in her head. He said, "I don't know how long this is going to take, but why don't you begin preparing a meal for us. We'll all feel better when we've eaten."

"Yes, child," said Aguillar. "I will help you. I am a good cook, Señor O'Hara."

O'Hara smiled at Benedetta. "I'll leave you to it, then."

He walked over to where Forester was giving a pep talk. "And that's the position," he was saying. "We're boxed in and there doesn't seem to be any way out of it—but there is

61

always a way out of anything, using brains and determination. Anyway, it's a case of surrender or fight. I'm going to fight—and so is Tim O'Hara here; aren't you, Tim?"

"I am," said O'Hara grimly.

"I'm going to go round and ask your views, and you must each make your own decision," continued Forester. "What about you, Doctor Willis?"

Willis looked up and his face was strained. "It's difficult, isn't it? You see, I'm not much of a fighter. Then again, it's a question of the odds—can we win? I don't see much reason in putting up a fight if we're certain of losing—and I don't see any chance at all of our winning out." He paused, then said hesitantly, "But I'll go with the majority vote."

Willis, you bastard, you're a fine example of a fence-sitter, thought O'Hara.

"Peabody?" Forester's voice cut like a lash.

"What the hell has this got to do with us?" exploded Peabody. "I'm damned if I'm going to risk my life for any wop politician. I say hand the bastard over and let's get the hell out of here."

"What do you say, Miss Ponsky?"

She gave Peabody a look of scorn, then hesitated. All the talk seemed to be knocked out of her, leaving her curiously deflated. At last she said in a small voice, "I know I'm only a woman and I can't do much in the way of fighting, and I'm scared to death—but I think we ought to fight." She ended in a rush and looked defiantly at Peabody. "And that's my vote."

Good for you, Miss Ponsky, cheered O'Hara silently. That's three to fight. It's now up to Armstrong—he can tip it for fighting or make a deadlock, depending on his vote.

"Doctor Armstrong, what do you have to say?" queried Forester.

Armstrong sucked on his pipe and it made an obscene noise. "I suppose I'm more an authority on this kind of situation than anyone present," he observed. "With the possible exception of Señor Aguillar, who at present is cooking our lunch, I see. Give me a couple of hours and I could quote a hundred parallel examples drawn from history."

Peabody muttered in exasperation. "What the hell!"

"The question at issue is whether to hand Señor Aguillar to the gentlemen on the other side of the river. The important point, as I see it affecting us, is what would they do with him? And I can't really see that there is anything they can do

62

with him other than kill him. Keeping high-standing politicians as prisoners went out of fashion a long time ago. Now, if they kill him they will automatically be forced to kill us. They would not dare take the risk of letting this story loose upon the world. They would be most painfully criticised, perhaps to the point of losing what they have set out to gain. In short, the people of Cordillera would not stand for it. So you see, we are not fighting for the life of Señor Aguillar; we are fighting for our own lives."

He put his pipe back into his mouth and made another rude noise.

"Does that mean that you are in favour of fighting?" asked Forester.

"Of course," said Armstrong in surprise. "Haven't you been listening to what I've been saying?"

Peabody looked at him in horror. "Jesus!" he said. "What have I got myself into?" He buried his head in his hands.

Forester grinned at O'Hara, and said, "Well, Doctor Willis?"

"I fight," said Willis briefly.

O'Hara chuckled. One academic man had convinced another.

Forester said, "Ready to change your mind, Peabody?"

Peabody looked up. "You really think they're going to rub us all out?"

"If they kill Aguillar I don't see what else they can do," said Armstrong reasonably. "And they will kill Aguillar, you know."

"Oh, hell," said Peabody in an anguish of indecision.

"Come on," Forester ordered harshly. "Put up or shut up."

"I guess I'll have to throw in with you," Peabody said morosely.

"That's it, then," said Forester. "A unanimous vote. I'll tell Aguillar and we'll discuss how to fight over some food." Miss Ponsky went to help the Aguillars with their cooking and O'Hara went back to the river to see what Rohde was doing. He looked back and saw that Armstrong was talking to Willis and again drawing on the ground with a stick. Willis looked interested.

Rohde had chosen a better place for observation and at first O'Hara could not find him. At last he saw the sole of a boot protruding from behind a rock and joined Rohde, who

63

seemed pleased. "They have not yet come out of their holes," he said. "It has been an hour. One bullet that missed has held them up for an hour."

"That's great," said O'Hara sardonically. "Ten bullets —ten hours."

"It is better than that," protested Rohde. "They have thirty planks to put in—that would take them fifteen hours without my bullets. With the shooting it will take them twenty-five hours. They will not work at night—so that is two full days."

O'Hara nodded. "It gives us time to decide what to do next," he admitted. But when the bullets were finished and the bridge completed a score of armed and ruthless men would come boiling over the river. It would be a slaughter.

"I will stay here," said Rohde. "Send some food when it is ready." He nodded towards the bridge. "It takes a brave man to walk on that, knowing that someone will shoot at him. I do not think these men are very brave—maybe it will be more than one hour to a bullet."

O'Hara went back and told Forester what was happening and Forester grimaced. "Two days—maybe—two days to come up with something. But with what?"

O'Hara said, "I think a Committee of Ways and Means is indicated."

They all sat in a circle on the sparse grass and Benedetta and Miss Ponsky served the food on the aluminium plates they had found at the camp. Forester said, "This is a war council, so please stick to the point and let's have no idle chit-chat—we've no time to waste. Any sensible suggestions will be welcome."

There was a dead silence, then Miss Ponsky said, "I suppose the main problem is to stop them repairing the bridge. Well, couldn't we do something at this end—cut the ropes or something?"

"That's good in principle," said Forester. "Any objections to it?" He glanced at O'Hara, knowing what he would say.

O'Hara looked at Forester sourly; it seemed as though he was being cast as the cold-water expert and he did not fancy the role. He said deliberately, "The approaches to the bridge from this side are wide open; there's no cover for at least a hundred yards—you saw what happened to Benedetta and me this morning. Anyone who tried to get to the bridge along the road would be cut down before he'd got half-way. It's point blank range, you know—they don't have to be crack shots." He paused. "Now I know it's the only way we *can* get at the bridge, but it seems impossible to me."

"What about a night attack?" asked Willis.

"That sounds good," said Forester.

O'Hara hated to do it, but he spoke up. "I don't want to sound pessimistic, but I don't think those chaps over there are entirely stupid. They've got two trucks and four jeeps, maybe more, and those vehicles have at least two headlights apiece. They'll keep the bridge well lit during the dark hours."

There was silence again.

Armstrong cleared his throat. "Willis and I have been doing a little thinking and maybe we have something that will help. Again I find myself in the position of being something of an expert. You know that my work is the study of medieval history, but it so happens that I'm a specialist, and my speciality is medieval warfare. The position as I see it is that we are in a castle with a moat and a drawbridge. The drawbridge is fortuitously pulled up, but our enemies are trying to rectify that state of affairs. Our job is to stop them."

"With what?" asked O'Hara. "A push of a pike?"

"I wouldn't despise medieval weapons too much, O'Hara," said Armstrong mildly. "I admit that the people of those days weren't as adept in the art of slaughter as we are, but still, they managed to kill each other off at a satisfactory rate. Now, Rohde's pistol is highly inaccurate at the range he is forced to use. What we want is a more efficient missile weapon than Rohde's pistol."

"So we all make like Robin Hood," said Peabody derisively. "With the jolly old longbow, what? For Christ's sake, Professor!"

"Oh, no," said Armstrong. "A longbow is very chancy in the hands of a novice. It takes five years at least to train a good bowman."

"I can use the bow," said Miss Ponsky unexpectedly. Everyone looked at her and she coloured. "I'm president of the South Bridge Ladies' Greenwood Club. Last year I won our own little championship in the Hereford Round."

"That's interesting," said Armstrong.

O'Hara said, "Can you use a longbow lying down, Miss Ponsky?"

"It would be difficult," she said. "Perhaps impossible."

O'Hara jerked his head at the gorge. "You stand up there with a longbow and you'll get filled full of holes."

She bridled. "I think you'd do better helping than pouring cold water on all our ideas, Mr. O'Hara."

"I've got to do it," said O'Hara evenly. "I don't want anyone killed uselessly."

"For God's sake," exclaimed Willis. "How did a longbow come into this? That's out—we can't make one; we haven't the material. Now, will you listen to Armstrong; he has a point to make." His voice was unexpectedly firm.

The flat crack of Rohde's pistol echoed on the afternoon air and there was the answering rattle of shots from the other side of the gorge. Peabody ducked and O'Hara looked at his watch. It had been an hour and twenty minutes—and they had nine bullets left.

Forester said, "That's one good thing—we're safe here. Their rifles won't shoot round corners. Make your point, Doctor Armstrong."

"I was thinking of something more on the lines of a prodd or crossbow," said Armstrong. "Anyone who can use a rifle can use a crossbow and it has an effective range of over a hundred yards." He smiled at O'Hara. "You can shoot it lying down, too."

O'Hara's mind jumped at it. They could cover the bridge and also the road on the other side where it turned north and followed the edge of the gorge and where the enemy trucks were. He said, "Does it have any penetrative power?"

"A bolt will go through mail if it hits squarely," said Armstrong.

"What about a petrol tank?"

"Oh, it would penetrate a petrol tank quite easily."

"Now, take it easy," said Forester. "How in hell can we make a crossbow?"

"You must understand that I'm merely a theoretician where this is concerned," explained Armstrong. "I'm no mechanic or engineer. But I described what I want to Willis and he thinks we can make it."

"Armstrong and I were rooting round up at the camp," said Willis. "One of the huts had been a workshop and there was a lot of junk lying about—you know, the usual bits and pieces that you find in a metal-working shop. I reckon they didn't think it worthwhile carting the stuff away when they abandoned the place. There are some flat springs and odd bits of metal rod; and there's some of that concrete reinforcing steel that we can cut up to make arrows."

"Bolts," Armstrong corrected mildly. "Or quarrels, if

you prefer. I thought first of making a prodd, you know; that's a type of crossbow which fires bullets, but Willis has convinced me that we can manufacture bolts more easily."

"What about tools?" asked O'Hara. "Have you anything that will cut metal?"

"There are some old hacksaw blades," Willis said. "And I saw a couple of worn-out files. And there's a hand-powered grindstone that looks as though it came out of the Ark. I'll make out; I'm good with my hands and I can adapt Armstrong's designs with the material available."

O'Hara looked at Forester, who said slowly, "A weapon accurate to a hundred yards built out of junk seems too good to be true. Are you certain about this, Doctor Armstrong?"

"Oh, yes," said Armstrong cheerfully. "The crossbow has killed thousands of men in its time—I see no reason why it shouldn't kill a few more. And Willis seems to think he can make it." He smiled. "I've drawn the blueprints there." He pointed to a few lines scratched in the dust.

"If we're going to do this, we'd better do it quickly," said O'Hara.

"Right." Forester looked up at the sun. "You've got time to make it up to the camp by nightfall. It's uphill, but you'll be travelling light. You go too, Peabody; Willis can use another pair of hands."

Peabody nodded quickly. He had no taste for staying too near the bridge.

"One moment," said Aguillar, speaking for the first time. "The bridge is made of rope and wood—very combustible materials. Have you considered the use of fire? Señor O'Hara gave me the idea when he spoke of petrol tanks."

"Um," said O'Hara. "But how to get the fire to the bridge?"

"Everyone think of that," said Forester. "Now let's get things moving."

Armstrong, Willis and Peabody left immediately on the long trudge up to the camp. Forester said, "I didn't know what to make of Willis—he's not very forthcoming—but I've got him tagged now. He's the practical type; give him something to do and he'll get it done, come hell or high water. He'll do."

Aguillar smiled. "Armstrong is surprising, too."

"My God!" said Forester. "Crossbows in this day and age!"

O'Hara said, "We've got to think about making camp.

67

There's no water here, and besides, our main force is too close to the enemy. There's a pond about half a mile back—I think that's a good spot."

"Benedetta, you see to that," Aguillar commanded. "Miss Ponsky will help you." He watched the two women go, then turned with a grave face. "There is something we must discuss, together with Miguel. Let us go over there."

Rohde was happy. "They have not put a plank in the bridge yet. They ran again like the rabbits they are."

Aguillar told him what was happening and he said uncertainly, "A crossbow?"

"I think it's crazy, too," said Forester. "But Armstrong reckons it'll work."

"Armstrong is a good man," said Aguillar. "He is thinking of immediate necessities—but I think of the future. Suppose we hold off these men; suppose we destroy the bridge—what then?"

"We're not really any better off," said O'Hara reflectively. "They've got us pinned down anyway."

"Exactly," said Aguillar. "True, we have plenty of food, but that means nothing. Time is very valuable to these men, just as it is to me. They gain everything by keeping me inactive."

"By keeping you here they've removed you from the game," agreed Forester. "How long do you think it will be before they make their *coup d'état*?"

Aguillar shrugged. "One month—maybe two. Certainly not longer. We advanced our own preparations because the communists showed signs of moving. It is a race between us with the destiny of Cordillera as the prize—maybe the destiny of the whole of Latin America is at stake. And the time is short."

"Your map, Señor O'Hara," said Rohde suddenly.

O'Hara took out the chart and spread it on a rock, and Rohde traced the course of the river north and south, shaking his head. "This river—this gorge—is a trap, pinning us against the mountains," he said.

"We've agreed it's no use going for the bridge downstream," said Forester. "It's a hell of a long way and it's sure to be guarded."

"What's to stop *them* crossing that bridge and pushing up on this side of the river to outflank us?" asked O'Hara.

"As long as they think they can repair this bridge they won't do that," Aguillar said. "Communists are not supermen; they are as lazy as other people and they would not relish crossing eighty kilometres of mountain country—that would take at least four days. I think they will be content to stop the bolt hole."

Rohde's fingers swept across the map to the west. "That leaves the mountains."

Forester turned and looked at the mountain wall, at the icy peaks. "I don't like the sound of that. I don't think Señor Aguillar could make it."

"I know," said Rohde. "He must stay here. But someone must cross the mountains for help."

"Let's see if it's practicable," said O'Hara. "I was going to fly through the Puerto de las Águilas. That means that anyone going back would have to go twenty miles north before striking west through the pass. And he'd have to go pretty high to get round this bloody gorge. The pass isn't so bad—it's only about fourteen thousand feet."

"A total of about thirty miles before he got into the Santos Valley," said Forester. "That's on straight line courses. It would probably be fifty over the ground."

"There is another way," said Rohde quietly. He pointed to the mountains. "This range is high, but not very wide. On the other side lies the Santos Valley. If you draw a line on the map from here to Altemiros in the Santos Valley you will find that it is not more than twenty-five kilometres."

O'Hara bent over the map and measured the distance. "You're right; about fifteen miles—but it's all peaks."

"There is a pass about two miles north-west of the mine," said Rohde. "It has no name because no one is so foolish as to use it. It is about five thousand eight hundred metres."

Forester rapidly translated. "Wow! Nineteen thousand feet."

"What about lack of oxygen?" asked O'Hara. "We've had enough trouble with that already. Could a man go over that pass without oxygen?"

"I have done so," said Rohde. "Under more favourable conditions. It is a matter of acclimatisation. Mountaineers know this; they stay for days at one level and then move up the mountain to another camp and stay a few days there also before moving to a higher level. It is to attune their bodies to the changing conditions." He looked up at the mountains. "If I went up to the camp to-morrow and spent a day there then went to the mine and stayed a day there—I think I could cross that pass."

Forester said, "You couldn't go alone."

"I'll go with you," said O'Hara promptly.

"Hold on there," said Forester. "Are you a mountaineer?"

"No," said O'Hara.

"Well, I am. I mean, I've scrambled about in the Rockies —that should count for something." He appealed to Rohde. "Shouldn't it?"

Aguillar said, "You should not go alone, Miguel."

"Very well," said Rohde. "I will take one man—you." He nodded to Forester and smiled grimly. "But I promise you—you will be sorry."

Forester grinned cheerfully and said, "Well, Tim, that leaves you as garrison commander. You'll have your hands full."

"*Si*," said Rohde. "You must hold them off."

A new sound was added to the noise of the river and Rohde immediately wriggled up to his observation post, then beckoned to O'Hara. "They are starting their engines," he said. "I think they are going away."

But the vehicles did not move. "What are they doing?" asked Rohde in perplexity.

"They're charging their batteries," said O'Hara. "They're making sure that they'll have plenty of light to-night."


II


O'Hara and Aguillar went back to help the women make camp, leaving Rohde and Forester to watch the bridge. There was no immediate danger of the enemy forcing the crossing and any unusual move could soon be reported. Forester's attitude had changed as soon as the decision to cross the mountains had been made. He no longer drove hard for action, seemingly being content to leave it to O'Hara. It was as though he had tacitly decided that there could be only one commander and the man was O'Hara.

O'Hara's lips quirked as he mentally reviewed his garrison. An old man and a young girl; two sedentary academic types; a drunk and someone's maiden aunt; and himself—a broken-down pilot. On the other side of the river were at least twenty ruthless men—with God knows how many more to back them up. His muscles tensed at the thought that they were communists; sloppy South American communists, no doubt—but still communists.

Whatever happens, they're not going to get me again, he thought.

Benedetta was very quiet and O'Hara knew why. To be shot at for the first time took the pith out of a person— one came to the abrupt realisation that one was a soft bag of wind and liquids, vulnerable and defenceless against steel-jacketed bullets which could rend and tear. He remembered the first time he had been in action, and felt very sorry for Benedetta; at least he had been prepared, however inadequately, for the bullets—the bullets and the cannon shells.

He looked across at the scattered rocks on the bleak hillside. "I wonder if there's a cave over there?" he suggested. "That would come in handy right now." He glanced at Benedetta. "Let's explore a little."

She looked at her uncle who was helping Miss Ponsky check the cans of food. "All right," she said.

They crossed the road and struck off at right angles, making their way diagonally up the slope. The ground was covered with boulders and small pebbles and the going was difficult, their feet slipping as the stones shifted. O'Hara thought that one could break an ankle quite easily and a faint idea stirred at the back of his mind.

After a while they separated, O'Hara to the left and the girl to the right. For an hour they toiled among the rocks, searching for something that would give shelter against the night wind, however small. O'Hara found nothing, but he heard a faint shout from Benedetta and crossed the hillside to see what she had found.

It was not a cave, merely a fortuitous tumbling of the rocks. A large boulder had rolled from above and wedged itself between two others, forming a roof. It reminded O'Hara of a dolmen he had seen on Dartmoor, although the whole thing was very much bigger. He regarded it appreciatively. At least it would be shelter from snow and rain and it gave a little protection from the wind.

He went inside and found a hollow at the back. "This is good," he said. "This will hold a lot of water—maybe twenty gallons."

He turned and looked at Benedetta. The exercise had brought some colour into her cheeks and she looked better. He produced his cigarettes. "Smoke?"

She shook her head. "I don't."

"Good!" he said with satisfaction. "I was hoping you

71

didn't." He looked into the packet—there were eleven left. "I'm a selfish type, you know; I want these for myself."

He sat down on a rock and lit his cigarette, voluptuously inhaling the smoke. Benedetta sat beside him and said, "I'm glad you decided to help my uncle."

O'Hara grinned. "Some of us weren't too sure. It needed a little tough reasoning to bring them round. But it was finally unanimous."

She said in a low voice, "Do you think there's any chance of our coming out of this?"

O'Hara bit his lip and was silent for a time. Then he said, "There's no point in hiding the truth—I don't think we've got a cat in hell's chance. If they bust across the bridge and we're as defenceless as we are now, we won't have a hope." He waved his hand at the terrain. "There's just one chance—if we split up, every man for himself heading in a different direction, then they'll have to split up, too. This is rough country and one of us might get away to tell what happened to the rest. But that's pretty poor consolation."

"Then why did you decide to fight?" she said in wonder.

O'Hara chuckled. "Armstrong put up some pretty cogent arguments," he said, and told her about it. Then he added, "But I'd have fought anyway. I don't like those boys across the river; I don't like what they do to people. It makes no difference if their skins are yellow, white or brown—they're all of the same stripe."

"Señor Forester was telling me that you fought together in Korea," Benedetta said.

"We might have—we probably did. He was in an American squadron which we flew with sometimes. But I never met him."

"It must have been terrible," she said. "All that fighting."

"It wasn't too bad," said O'Hara. "The fighting part of it." He smiled. "You *do* get used to being shot at, you know. I think that people can get used to anything if it goes on long enough—most things, anyway. That's the only way wars can be fought—because people can adapt and treat the craziest things as normal. Otherwise they couldn't go through with it."

She nodded. "I know. Look at us here. Those men shoot at us and Miguel shoots back—he regards it as the normal thing to do."

"It *is* the normal thing to do," said O'Hara harshly. "The

human being is a fighting animal; it's that quality which has put him where he is—the king of this planet." His lips twisted. " It's also the thing that's maybe holding him back from bigger things." He laughed abruptly. " Christ, this is no time for the philosophy of war—I'd better leave that to Armstrong."

" You said something strange," said Benedetta. " You said that Korea wasn't too bad—the fighting part of it. What *was* bad, if it wasn't the fighting?"

O'Hara looked into the distance. " It was when the fighting stopped—when *I* stopped fighting—when I couldn't fight any more. Then it was bad."

" You were a prisoner? In the hands of the Chinese? Forester said something of that."

O'Hara said slowly, " I've killed men in combat—in hot blood—and I'll probably do it again, and soon, at that. But what those communist bastards can do intellectually and with cold purpose is beyond . . ." He shook his head irritably. " I prefer not to talk about it."

He had a sudden vision of the bland, expressionless features of the Chinese lieutenant, Feng. It was something that had haunted his dreams and woken him screaming ever since Korea. It was the reason he preferred to go to sleep in a sudden, dreamless and mindless coma. He said, " Let's talk about you. You speak good English—where did you learn it?"

She was aware that she had trodden on forbidden and shaky ground. " I'm sorry if I disturbed you, Señor O'Hara," she said contritely.

" That's all right. But less of the Señor O'Hara; my name is Tim."

She smiled quickly. " I was educated in the United States, Tim. My uncle sent me there after Lopez made the revolution." She laughed. " I was taught English by a teacher very like Miss Ponsky."

" Now there's a game old trout," said O'Hara. " Your uncle sent you? What about your parents?"

" My mother died when I was a child. My father—Lopez had him shot."

O'Hara sighed. " We both seem to be scraping on raw nerves, Benedetta. I'm sorry."

She said sadly, " It's the way the world is, Tim."

He agreed sombrely. " Anyone who expects fair play in this world is a damn fool. That's why we're in this jam.

Come on, let's get back; this isn't getting us anywhere." He pinched off his cigarette and carefully put the stub back in the packet.

As Benedetta rose she said, "Do you think that Señor Armstrong's idea of a crossbow will work?"

"I don't," said O'Hara flatly. "I think that Armstrong is a romantic. He's specialised as a theoretician in wars a thousand years gone, and I can't think of anything more futile than that. He's an ivory-tower man—an academician—blood-thirsty in a theoretical way, but the sight of blood will turn his stomach. And I think he's a little bit nuts."

### III

Armstrong's pipe gurgled as he watched Willis rooting about in the rubbish of the workshop. His heart was beating rapidly and he felt breathless, although the altitude did not seem to affect him as much as the previous time he had been at the hutted camp. His mind was turning over the minutiæ of his profession—the science of killing without gunpowder. He thought coldly and clearly about the ranges, trajectories and penetrations that could be obtained from pieces of bent steel and twisted gut, and he sought to adapt the ingenious mechanisms so clearly diagrammed in his mind to the materials and needs of the moment. He looked up at the roof beams of the hut and a new idea dawned on him. But he put it aside—the crossbow came first.

Willis straightened, holding a flat spring. "This came from an auto—will it do for the bow?"

Armstrong tried to flex it and found it very stiff. "It's very strong," he said. "Probably stronger than anything they had in the Middle Ages. This will be a very powerful weapon. Perhaps this is too strong—we must be able to bend it."

"Let's go over that problem again," Willis said.

Armstrong drew on the back of an envelope. "For the light sporting bows they had a goat's-foot lever, but that is not strong enough for the weapon we are considering. For the heavier military bows they had two methods of bending —the cranequin, a ratchet arranged like this, which was de-mounted for firing, and the other was a windlass built into the bow which worked a series of pulleys."

Willis looked at the rough sketches and nodded. "The

74

windlass is our best bet," he said. "That ratchet thing would be difficult to make. And if necessary we can weaken the spring by grinding it down." He looked around. "Where's Peabody?"

"I don't know," said Armstrong. "Let's get on with this."

"You'd better find him," Willis said. "We'll put him on to making arrows—that should be an easy job."

"Bolts or quarrels," said Armstrong patiently.

"Whatever they're called, let's get on with it," Willis said. They found Peabody taking it easy in one of the huts, heating a can of beans. Reluctantly he went along to the workshop and they got to work. Armstrong marvelled at the dexterity of Willis's fingers as he contrived effective parts from impossible materials and worse tools. They found the old grindstone to be their most efficient cutting tool, although it tended to waste material. Armstrong sweated in turning the crank and could not keep it up for long, so they took it in turns, he and Willis silently, Peabody with much cursing.

They ripped out electric wiring from a hut and tore down conduit tubing. They cut up reinforcing steel into lengths and slotted the ends to take flights. It was cold and their hands were numb and the blood oozed from the cuts made when their makeshift tools slipped.

They worked all night and dawn was brightening the sky as Armstrong took the completed weapon in his hands and looked at it dubiously. "It's a bit different from how I imagined it, but I think it will do." He rubbed his eyes wearily. "I'll take it down now—they might need it."

Willis slumped against the side of the hut. "I've got an idea for a better one," he said. "That thing will be a bastard to cock. But I must get some sleep first—and food." His voice trailed to a mumble and he blinked his eyes rapidly.

All that night the bridge had been illuminated by the headlamps of the enemy vehicles and it was obviously hopeless to make a sortie in an attempt to cut the cables. The enemy did not work on the bridge at night, not relishing being in a spotlight when a shot could come out of the darkness.

Forester was contemptuous of them. "The goddam fools," he said. "If we can't hit them in daylight then it's sure we can't at night—but if they'd any sense they'd see that they could spot our shooting at night and they'd send a man on to the bridge to draw our fire—then they'd fill our man full of holes."

But during the daylight hours the enemy *had* worked on the bridge, and had been less frightened of the shots fired at them. No one had been hit and it had become obvious that there was little danger other than that from a freakishly lucky shot. By morning there were but six bullets left for Rohde's pistol and there were nine more planks in the bridge.

By nine o'clock Rohde had expended two more bullets and it was then that Armstrong stumbled down the road carrying a contraption. "Here it is," he said. "Here's your crossbow." He rubbed his eyes which were red-rimmed and tired. "Professionally speaking, I'd call it an arbalest."

"My God, that was quick," said O'Hara.

"We worked all night," Armstrong said tiredly. "We thought you'd need it in a hurry."

"How does it work?" asked O'Hara, eyeing it curiously.

"The metal loop on the business end is a stirrup," said Armstrong. "You put it on the ground and put your foot in it. Then you take this cord and clip the hook on to the bowstring and start winding on this handle. That draws back the bowstring until it engages on this sear. You drop a bolt in this trough and you're ready to shoot. Press the trigger and the sear drops to release the bowstring."

The crossbow was heavy in O'Hara's hands. The bow itself was made from a car spring and the bowstring was a length of electric wire woven into a six-strand cord to give it strength. The cord which drew it back was also electric wire woven of three strands. The seat and trigger were carved from wood, and the trough where the bolt went was made from a piece of electric conduit piping.

It was a triumph of improvisation.

"We had to weaken the spring," said Armstrong. "But it's still got a lot of bounce. Here's a bolt—we made a dozen."

The bolt was merely a length of round steel, three-eighths of an inch in diameter and fifteen inches long. It was very rusty. One end was slotted to hold metal flights cut from a dried-milk can and the other end was sharpened to a point. O'Hara hefted it thoughtfully; it was quite heavy. "If this thing doesn't kill immediately, anyone hit will surely die of blood-poisoning. Does it give the range you expected?"

"A little more," said Armstrong. "These bolts are heavier than the medieval originals because they're steel throughout instead of having a wooden shaft—but the bow is very powerful and that makes up for it. Why don't you try it out?"

O'Hara put his foot in the stirrup and cranked the windlass handle. He found it more difficult than he had anticipated —the bow was very strong. As he slipped a bolt into the trough he said, "What should I shoot at?"

"What about that earth bank over there?"

The bank was about sixty yards away. He raised the crossbow and Armstrong said quickly, "Try it lying down, the way we'll use it in action. The trajectory is very flat so you won't have much trouble with sighting. I thought we'd wait until we got down here before sighting in." He produced a couple of gadgets made of wire. "We'll use a ring-and-pin sight."

O'Hara lay down and fitted the rough wooden butt awkwardly into his shoulder. He peered along the trough and sighted as best he could upon a brown patch of earth on the bank. Then he squeezed the trigger and the crossbow bucked hard against his shoulder as the string was released.

There was a puff of dust from the extreme right of the target at which he had aimed. He got up and rubbed his shoulder. "My God!" he said with astonishment. "She's got a hell of a kick."

Armstrong smiled faintly. "Let's retrieve the bolt."

They walked over to the bank but O'Hara could not see it. "It went in about here," he said. "I saw the dust distinctly —but where is it?"

Armstrong grinned. "I told you this weapon was powerful. There's the bolt."

O'Hara grunted with amazement as he saw what Armstrong meant. The bolt had penetrated more than its own length into the earth and had buried itself completely. As Armstrong dug it out, O'Hara said, "We'd better all practise with this thing and find out who's the best shot." He looked at Armstrong. "You'd better get some sleep; you look pooped."

"I'll wait until I see the bow in action," said Armstrong. "Maybe it'll need some modification. Willis is making another —he has some ideas for improvements—and we put Peabody to making more bolts." He stood upright with the bolt in his hands. "And I've got to fix the sights."

All of them, excepting Aguillar and Rohde, practised with the crossbow, and—perhaps not surprisingly—Miss Ponsky turned out to be the best shot, with Forester coming next and O'Hara third. Shooting the bow was rough on Miss Ponsky's shoulder, but she made a soft shoulder-pad and eight times out of ten she put a bolt into a twelve-inch circle, clucking deprecatingly when she missed.

"She's not got the strength to crank it," said Forester. "But she's damned good with the trigger."

"That settles it," said O'Hara. "She gets first crack at the enemy—if she'll do it." He crossed over to her and said with a smile, "It looks as though you're elected to go into action first. Will you give it a go?"

Her face paled and her nose seemed even sharper. "Oh, my!" she said, flustered. "Do you think I can do it?"

"They've put in another four planks," said O'Hara quietly. "And Rohde's saving his last four bullets until he's reasonably certain of making a hit. This is the only other chance we've got—and you're the best shot."

Visibly she pulled herself together and her chin rose in determination. "All right," she said. "I'll do my best."

"Good! You'd better come and have a look at the bridge to get your range right—and maybe you'd better take a few practice shots at the same range."

He took her up to where Rohde was lying. "Miss Ponsky's going to have a go with the crossbow," he said.

Rohde looked at it with interest. "Does it work?"

"It's got the range and the velocity," O'Hara told him. "It should work all right." He turned his attention to the bridge. Two men had just put in another plank and were retreating. The gap in the bridge was getting very small— soon it would be narrow enough for a determined man to leap. "You'd better take the nearest man the next time they come out," he said. "What would you say the range is?"

Miss Ponsky considered. "A little less than the range I've been practising at," she said. "I don't think I need to practise any more." There was a tremor in her voice.

O'Hara regarded her. "This has got to be done, Miss Ponsky. Remember what they did to Mrs. Coughlin—and what they'll do to us if they get across the bridge."

"I'll be all right," she said in a low voice.

O'Hara nodded in satisfaction. "You take Rohde's place. I'll be a little way along. Take your time—you needn't hurry. Regard it as the target practice you've just been doing."

Forester had already cocked the bow and handed it up to Miss Ponsky. She put a bolt in the trough and slid forward on her stomach until she got a good view of the bridge. O'Hara waited until she was settled, then moved a little way farther along the edge of the gorge. He looked back and saw Forester talking to Armstrong, who was lying full-length on the ground, his eyes closed.

He found a good observation post and lay waiting. Presently the same two men appeared again, carrying a plank. They crawled the length of the bridge, pushing the plank before them until they reached the gap—even though none of them had been hit, they weren't taking unnecessary chances. Once at the gap they got busy, lashing the plank to the two main ropes.

O'Hara found his heart thumping and the wait seemed intolerably long. The nearest man was wearing a leather jacket similar to his own and O'Hara could see quite clearly the flicker of his eyes as he gazed apprehensively at the opposite bank from time to time. O'Hara clenched his fist. "Now!" he whispered. "For God's sake—now!"

He did not hear the twang as the crossbow fired, but he saw the spurt of dust from the man's jacket as the bolt hit him, and suddenly a shaft of steel sprouted from the man's back just between the shoulder blades. There was a faint cry above the roar of the river and the man jerked his legs convulsively. He thrust his arms forward, almost in an imploring gesture, then he toppled sideways and rolled off the edge of the bridge, to fall in a spinning tangle of arms and legs into the raging river.

The other man paused uncertainly, then ran back across the bridge to the other side of the gorge. The bridge swayed under his pounding feet and as he ran he looked back fearfully. He joined the group at the end of the bridge and O'Hara saw him indicate his own back and another man shaking his head in disbelief.

Gently he withdrew and ran back to the place from which Miss Ponsky had fired the shot. She was lying on the ground, her body racked with sobs, and Forester was bending over her. "It's all right, Miss Ponsky," he was saying. "It had to be done."

"But I've killed a man," she wailed. "I've taken a life."

Forester got her to her feet and led her away, talking softly to her all the time. O'Hara bent and picked up the crossbow. "What a secret weapon!" he said in admiration. "No noise, no flash—just *zing*." He laughed. "They still don't know what happened—not for certain. Armstrong, you're a bloody genius."

But Armstrong was asleep.

79

The enemy made no further attempts to repair the bridge that morning. Instead, they kept up a steady, if slow, light barrage of rifle fire, probing the tumble of rocks at the edge of the gorge in the hope of making hits. O'Hara withdrew everyone to safety, including Rohde. Then he borrowed a small mirror from Benedetta and contrived a makeshift periscope, being careful to keep the glass in the shadow of a rock so that it would not reflect direct sunlight. He fixed it so that an observer could lie on his back in perfect cover, but could still keep an eye on the bridge. Forester took first watch.

O'Hara said, " If they come on the bridge again use the gun—just one shot. We've got them off-balance now and a bit nervous. They don't know if that chap fell off the bridge by accident, whether he was shot and they didn't hear the report, or whether it was something else. *We* know it was something else and so does the other man who was on the bridge, but I don't think they believe him. There was a hell of an argument going on the last I saw of it. At any rate, I think they'll be leery of coming out now, and a shot ought to put them off."

Forester checked the pistol and looked glumly at the four remaining bullets. " I feel a hell of a soldier—firing off twenty-five per cent of the available ammunition at one bang."

" It's best this way," said O'Hara. " They don't know the state of our ammunition, the crossbow is our secret weapon, and by God we must make the best use of it. I have ideas about that, but I want to wait for the second crossbow." He paused. " Have you any idea how many of the bastards are across there?"

" I tried a rough count," said Forester. " I made it twenty-three. The leader seems to be a big guy with a Castro beard. He's wearing some kind of uniform—jungle-green pants and a bush-jacket." He rubbed his chin and said thoughtfully, " It's my guess that he's a Cuban specialist."

" I'll look out for him," said O'Hara. " Maybe if we can nail him, the rest will pack up."

" Maybe," said Forester non-committally.

O'Hara trudged back to the camp which had now been transferred to the rock shelter on the hillside. That was a better defensive position and could not be so easily rushed, the attackers having to move over broken ground. But O'Hara had no great faith in it; if the enemy crossed the bridge they could move up the road fast, outflanking the rock shelter to move in behind and surround them. He had cudgelled his brain to find a way of blocking the road but had not come up with anything.

But there it was—a better place than the camp by the pond and the roadside. The trouble was water, but the rock hollow at the rear of the shelter had been filled with twenty-five gallons of water, transported laboriously a canful at a time, much of it spilling on the way. And it was a good place to sleep, too.

Miss Ponsky had recovered from her hysteria but not from her remorse. She was unaccustomedly quiet and withdrawn, speaking to no one. She had helped to transport the water and the food but had done so mechanically, as if she did not care. Aguillar was grave. "It is not right that this should be," he said. "It is not right that a lady like Miss Ponsky should have to do these things."

O'Hara felt exasperated. "Dammit, we didn't start this fight," he said. "The Coughlins are dead, and Benedetta was nearly killed—not to mention me. I'll try not to let it happen again, but she *is* the best shot and we *are* fighting for our lives."

"You are a soldier," said Aguillar. "Almost I seem to hear you say, with Napoleon, that one cannot make an omelette without breaking eggs." His voice was gently sardonic.

O'Hara disregarded that. "We must all practise with the bow—we must learn to use it while we have time."

Aguillar tapped him on the arm. "Señor O'Hara, perhaps if I gave myself to these people they would be satisfied."

O'Hara stared at him. "You know they wouldn't; they can't let us go—knowing what we know."

Aguillar nodded. "I know that; I was wondering if you did." He shrugged half-humorously. "I wanted you to convince me there is nothing to gain by it—and you have. I am sorry to have brought this upon all these innocent people."

O'Hara made an impatient noise and Aguillar continued, "There comes a time when the soldier takes affairs out of the hands of the politician—all ways seem to lead to violence. So I must cease to be a politician and become a soldier. I will learn how to shoot this bow well, señor."

"I wouldn't do too much, Señor Aguillar," said O'Hara.

"You must conserve your strength in case we must move suddenly and quickly. You're not in good physical shape, you know."

Aguillar's voice was sharp. "Señor, I will do what I must."

O'Hara said no more, guessing he had touched on Spanish-American pride. He went to talk to Miss Ponsky.

She was kneeling in front of the pressure stove, apparently intent on watching a can of water boil, but her eyes were unfocused and staring far beyond. He knew what she was looking at—a steel bolt that had sprouted like a monstrous growth in the middle of a man's back.

He said, "Killing another human being is a terrible thing, Miss Ponsky. I know—I've done it, and I was sickened for days afterwards. The first time I shot down an enemy fighter in Korea I followed him down—it was a dangerous thing to do, but I was young and inexperienced then. The Mig went down in flames, and his ejector seat didn't work, so he opened the canopy manually and jumped out against the slipstream.

"It was brave or desperate of that man to do that. But he had the Chinese sort of courage—or maybe the Russian courage, for all I know. You see, I didn't know the nationality or even the colour of the man I had killed. He fell to earth, a spinning black speck. His parachute didn't open. I knew he was a dead man."

O'Hara moistened his lips. "I felt bad about that, Miss Ponsky; it sickened me. But then I thought that the same man had been trying to kill me—he nearly succeeded, too. He had pumped my plane full of holes before I got him and I crash-landed on the air-strip. I was lucky to get away with it—I spent three weeks in hospital. I finally worked it out that it was a case of him or me, and I was the lucky one. I don't know if he would have had regrets if he had killed me—I think probably not. Those people aren't trained to have much respect for life."

He regarded her closely. "These people across the river are the same that I fought in Korea, no matter that their skins are a different colour. We have no fight with them if they will let us go in peace—but they won't do that, Miss Ponsky. So it's back to basics; kill or be killed and the devil take the loser. You did all right, Miss Ponsky; what you did may have saved all our lives and maybe the lives of a lot of people in this country. Who knows?"

As he lapsed into silence she turned to him and said in a husky, broken voice, "I'm a silly old woman, Mr. O'Hara.

For years I've been talking big, like everyone else in America, about fighting the communists; but I didn't have to do it myself, and when it comes to doing it yourself it's a different matter. Oh, we women cheered our American boys when they went to fight—there's no one more bloodthirsty than one who doesn't have to do the fighting. But when you do your own killing, it's a dreadful thing, Mr. O'Hara."

"I know," he said. "The only thing that makes it bearable is that if you don't kill, then you are killed. It reduces to a simple choice in the end."

"I realise that now, Mr. O'Hara," she said. "I'll be all right now."

"My name is Tim," he said. "The English are pretty stuffy about getting on to first-name terms, but not we Irish."

She gave him a tremulous smile. "I'm Jennifer."

"All right, Jenny," said O'Hara. "I'll try not to put you in a spot like that again."

She turned her head away and said in a muffled voice, "I think I'm going to cry." Hastily she scrambled to her feet and ran out of the shelter.

Benedetta said from behind O'Hara, "That was well done, Tim."

He turned and looked at her stonily. "Was it? It was something that had to be done." He got up and stretched his legs. "Let's practise with that crossbow."

v

For the rest of the day they practised, learning to allow for wind and the effect of a change of range. Miss Ponsky tightened still-further her wire-drawn nerves and became instructress, and the general level of performance improved enormously.

O'Hara went down to the gorge and, by triangulation, carefully measured the distance to the enemy vehicles and was satisfied that he had the range measured to a foot. Then he went back and measured the same distance on the ground and told everyone to practise with the bow at that range. It was one hundred and eight yards.

He said to Benedetta, "I'm making you my chief-of-staff —that's a sort of glorified secretary that a general has. Have you got pencil and paper?"

She smiled and nodded, whereupon he reeled off a dozen things that had to be done. "You pass on that stuff to the right people in case I forget—I've got a hell of a lot of things on my mind right now and I might slip up on something important when the action starts."

He set Aguillar to tying bunches of rags around half a dozen bolts, then shot them at the target to see if the rags made any difference to the accuracy of the flight. There was no appreciable difference, so he soaked one of them in paraffin and lit it before firing, but the flame was extinguished before it reached the target.

He swore and experimented further, letting the paraffin burn fiercely before he pulled the trigger. At the expense of a scorched face he finally landed three fiercely burning bolts squarely in the target and observed happily that they continued to burn.

"We'll have to do this in the day-time," he said. "It'll be bloody dangerous in the dark—they'd spot the flame before we shot." He looked up at the sun. "To-morrow," he said. "We've got to drag this thing out as long as we can."

It was late afternoon before the enemy ventured on to the bridge again and they scattered at a shot from Rohde who, after a long sleep, had taken over again from Forester. Rohde fired another shot before sunset and then stopped on instructions from O'Hara. "Keep the last two bullets," he said. "We'll need them."

So the enemy put in three more planks and stepped up their illumination that night, although they dared not move on the bridge.

## Chapter IV

Forester awoke at dawn. He felt refreshed after having had a night's unbroken sleep. O'Hara had insisted that he and Rohde should not stand night watches but should get as much sleep as they could. This was the day that he and Rohde were to go up to the hutted camp to get acclimatised and the next day to go on up to the mine.

He looked up at the white mountains and felt a sudden chill in his bones. He had lied to O'Hara when he said he had mountaineered in the Rockies—the highest he had climbed

84

was to the top of the Empire State Building in an elevator. The high peaks were blindingly bright as the sun touched them and he wrinkled his eyes to see the pass that Rohde had pointed out. Rohde had said he would be sorry and Forester judged he was right; Rohde was a tough cookie and not given to exaggeration.

After cleaning up he went down to the bridge. Armstrong was on watch, lying on his back beneath the mirror. He was busy sketching on a scrap of paper with a pencil stub, glancing up at the mirror every few minutes. He waved as he saw Forester crawling up and said, " All quiet. They've just switched off the lights."

Forester looked at the piece of paper. Armstrong had drawn what looked like a chemist's balance. " What's that?" he asked. " The scales of justice?"

Armstrong looked startled and then pleased. " Why, sir, you have identified it correctly," he said.

Forester did not press it further. He thought Armstrong was a nut—clever, but still a nut. That crossbow of his had turned out to be some weapon—but it took a nut to think it up. He smiled at Armstrong and crawled away to where he could get a good look at the bridge.

His mouth tightened when he saw how narrow the gap was. Maybe he wouldn't have to climb the pass after all; maybe he'd have to fight and die right where he was. He judged that by the afternoon the gap would be narrow enough for a man to jump and that O'Hara had better prepare himself for a shock. But O'Hara had seemed untroubled and talked of a plan, and Forester hoped to God that he knew what he was doing.

When he got back to the rock shelter he found that Willis had come down from the hutted camp. He had hauled a *travois* the whole way and it was now being unpacked. He had brought more food, some blankets and another crossbow which he was demonstrating to O'Hara.

" This will be faster loading," he said. " I found some small gears, so I built them into the windlass—they make the cranking a lot easier. How did the other bow work?"

" Bloody good," said O'Hara. " It killed a man."

Willis paled a little and the unshaven bristles stood out against his white skin. Forester smiled grimly. The backroom boys always felt squeamish when they heard the results of their tinkering.

O'Hara turned to Forester. " As soon as they start work

85

on the bridge we'll give them a surprise," he said. "It's time we put a bloody crimp in their style. We'll have breakfast and then go down to the bridge—you'd better stick around and see the fun; you can leave immediately afterwards."

He swung around. "Jenny, don't bother about helping with the breakfast. You're our star turn. Take a crossbow and have a few practice shots at the same range as yesterday." As she paled, he smiled and said gently, "We'll be going down to the bridge and you'll be firing at a stationary, inanimate target."

Forester said to Willis, "Where's Peabody?"

"Back at the camp—making more arrows."

"Have any trouble with him?"

Willis grinned briefly. "He's a lazy swine but a couple of kicks up the butt soon cured that," he said, unexpectedly coarsely. "Where's Armstrong?"

"On watch down by the bridge."

Willis rubbed his chin with a rasping noise. "That man's got ideas," he said. "He's a whole Manhattan Project by himself. I want to talk to him."

He headed down the hill and Forester turned to Rohde, who had been talking to Aguillar and Benedetta in Spanish. "What do we take with us?"

"Nothing from here," Rohde said. "We can get what we want at the camp; but we must take little from there—we travel light."

O'Hara looked up from the can of stew he was opening. "You'd better take warm clothing—you can have my leather jacket," he offered.

"Thanks," Forester said.

O'Hara grinned. "And you'd better take your boss's vicuna coat—he may need it. I hear it gets cold in New York."

Forester smiled and took the can of hot stew. "I doubt if he'll appreciate it," he said dryly.

They had just finished breakfast when Willis came running back. "They've started work on the bridge," he shouted. "Armstrong wants to know if he should shoot."

"Hell no," said O'Hara. "We've only got two bullets." He swung on Rohde. "Go down there, get the gun from Armstrong and find yourself a good spot for shooting—but don't shoot until I tell you."

Rohde plunged down the hill and O'Hara turned to the others. "Everyone gather round," he ordered. "Where's Jenny?"

"I'm here," called Miss Ponsky from inside the shelter. "Come to the front, Jenny; you'll play a big part in all this." O'Hara squatted down and drew two parallel lines in the dust with a sharp stone. "That's the gorge and this is the bridge. Here is the road; it crosses the bridge, turns sharply on the other side and runs on the edge of the gorge, parallel to the river."

He placed a small stone on his rough diagram. "Just by the bridge there's a jeep, and behind it another jeep. Both are turned so that their lights illuminate the bridge. Behind the second jeep there's a big truck half full of timber." O'Hara placed a larger stone. "Behind the truck there's another jeep. There are some other vehicles farther down, but we're not concerned with those now."

He shifted his position. "Now for our side of the gorge. Miguel will be here, upstream of the bridge. He'll take one shot at the men on the bridge. He won't hit anyone—he hasn't yet, anyway—but that doesn't matter. It'll scare them and divert their attention, which is what I want.

"Jenny will be *here*, downstream of the bridge and immediately opposite the truck. The range is one hundred and eight yards, and we know the crossbow will do it because Jenny was shooting consistently well at that range all yesterday afternoon. As soon as she hears the shot she lets fly at the petrol tank of the truck."

He looked up at Forester. "You'll be right behind Jenny. As soon as she has fired she'll hand you the bow and tell you if she's hit the tank. If she hasn't, you crank the bow, reload it and hand it back to her for another shot. If she *has* hit it, then you crank it, run up to where Benedetta will be waiting and give it to her cocked but unloaded."

He placed another small stone. "I'll be there with Benedetta right behind me. She'll have the other crossbow ready cocked and with a fire-bolt in it." He looked up at her. "When I give you the signal you'll light the paraffin rags on the bolt and hand the crossbow to me, and I'll take a crack at the truck. We might need a bit of rapid fire at this point, so crank up the bows. You stick to seeing that the bolts are properly ignited before the bows are handed to me, just like we did yesterday in practice."

He stood up and stretched. "Is that clear to everyone?"

Willis said, "What do I do?"

"Anyone not directly concerned with this operation will keep his head down and stay out of the way." O'Hara paused.

"But stand by in case anything goes wrong with the bows."

"I've got some spare bowstrings," said Willis. "I'll have a look at that first bow to see if it's okay."

"Do that," said O'Hara. "Any more questions?"

There were no questions. Miss Ponsky held up her chin in a grimly determined manner; Benedetta turned immediately to collect the fire-bolts which were her care; Forester merely said, "Okay with me."

As they were going down the hill, though, he said to O'Hara, "It's a good plan, but your part is goddam risky. They'll see those fire-bolts before you shoot. You stand a good chance of being knocked off."

"You can't fight a war without risk," said O'Hara. "And that's what this is, you know; it's as much a war as any bigger conflict."

"Yeah," said Forester thoughtfully. He glanced at O'Hara sideways. "What about me doing this fire-bolt bit?"

O'Hara laughed. "You're going with Rohde—you picked it, you do it. You said I was garrison commander, so while you're here you'll bloody well obey orders."

Forester laughed too. "It was worth a try," he said.

Close to the gorge they met Armstrong. "What's going on?" he asked plaintively.

"Willis will tell you all about it," said O'Hara. "Where's Rohde?"

Armstrong pointed. "Over there."

O'Hara said to Forester, "See that Jenny has a good seat for the performance," and went to find Rohde.

As always, Rohde had picked a good spot. O'Hara wormed his way next to him and asked, "How much longer do you think they'll be fixing that plank?"

"About five minutes." Rohde lifted the pistol, obviously itching to take a shot.

"Hold it," O'Hara said sharply. "When they come with the next plank give them five minutes and then take a crack. We've got a surprise cooking for them."

Rohde raised his eyebrows but said nothing. O'Hara looked at the massive stone buttresses which carried the cables of the bridge. "It's a pity those abutments aren't made of timber —they'd have burnt nicely. What the hell did they want to build them so big for?"

"The Incas always built well," said Rohde.

"You mean this is Inca work?" said O'Hara, astonished.

Rohde nodded. "It was here before the Spaniards came.

The bridge needs constant renewal, but the buttresses will last for ever."

"Well, I'm damned," said O'Hara. "I wonder why the Incas wanted a bridge here—in the middle of nowhere."

"The Incas did many strange things." Rohde paused. "I seem to remember that the ore deposit of this mine was found by tracing the surface workings of the Incas. They would need the bridge if they worked metals up here."

O'Hara watched the men on the other side of the gorge. He spotted the big man with the beard whom Forester thought was the leader, wearing a quasi-uniform and with a pistol at his waist. He walked about bellowing orders and when he shouted men certainly jumped to it. O'Hara smiled grimly as he saw that they did not bother to take cover at all. No one had been shot at while on the other side—only when on the bridge and that policy was now going to pay off.

He said to Rohde, "You know what to do. I'm going to see to the rest of it." He slid back cautiously until it was safe to stand, then ran to where the rest were waiting, skirting the dangerous open ground at the approach to the bridge.

He said to Benedetta, "I'll be posted there; you'd better get your stuff ready. Have you got matches?"

"I have Señor Forester's cigarette-lighter."

"Good. You'd better keep it burning all the time, once the action starts. I'm just going along to see Jenny, then I'll be back."

Miss Ponsky was waiting with Forester a little farther along. She was bright-eyed and a little excited and O'Hara knew that she'd be all right if she didn't have to kill anyone. Well, that was all right, too; she would prepare the way and he'd do the killing. He said, "Have you had a look?"

She nodded quickly. "The gas tank is that big cylinder fastened under the truck."

"That's right; it's a big target. But try to hit it squarely—a bolt might glance off unless you hit it in the middle."

"I'll hit it," she said confidently.

He said, "They've just about finished putting a plank in. When they start to fasten the next one Rohde is going to give them five minutes and then pop off. That's your signal."

She smiled at him. "Don't worry, Tim, I'll do it."

Forester said, "I'll keep watch. When they bring up the plank Jenny can take over."

"Right," said O'Hara and went back to Benedetta. Armstrong was cocking the crossbow and Benedetta had arranged the fire-bolts in an arc, their points stuck in the earth. She lifted a can. "This is the last of the kerosene; we'll need more for cooking."

O'Hara smiled at this incongruous domestic note, and Willis said, "There's plenty up at the camp; we found two forty-gallon drums."

"Did you, by God?" said O'Hara. "That opens up possibilities." He climbed up among the rocks to the place he had chosen and tried to figure what could be done with a forty-gallon drum of paraffin. But then two men walked on to the bridge carrying a plank and he froze in concentration. One thing at a time, Tim, my boy, he thought.

He turned his head and said to Benedetta who was standing below, "Five minutes."

He heard the click as she tested the cigarette-lighter and turned his attention to the other side of the gorge. The minutes ticked by and he found the palms of his hands sweating. He wiped them on his shirt and cursed suddenly. A man had walked by the truck and was standing negligently in front of it—dead in front of the petrol tank.

"For Christ's sake, move on," muttered O'Hara. He knew that Miss Ponsky must have the man in her sights—but would she have the nerve to pull the trigger? He doubted it.

Hell's teeth, I should have told Rohde what was going on, he thought. Rhode wouldn't know about the crossbow and would fire his shot on time, regardless of the man covering the petrol tank. O'Hara ground his teeth as the man, a short, thick-set Indian type, produced a cigarette and carelessly struck a match on the side of the truck.

Rohde fired his shot and there was a yell from the bridge. The man by the truck stood frozen for a long moment and then started to run. O'Hara ignored him from then on—the man disappeared, that was all he knew—and his attention was riveted on the petrol tank. He heard a dull *thunk* even at that distance, and saw a dark shadow suddenly appear in the side of the tank, and saw the tank itself shiver abruptly.

Miss Ponsky had done it!

O'Hara wiped the sweat from his eyes and wished he had binoculars. Was that petrol dropping on to the road? Was that dark patch in the dust beneath the truck the spreading stain of leaking petrol, or was it just imagination? The trigger-happy bandits on the other side were letting go with all they had in their usual futile barrage, but he ignored the racket and strained his aching eyes.

The Indian came back and looked with an air of puzzlement at the truck. He sniffed the air suspiciously and then bent down to look underneath the vehicle. Then he let out a yell and waved violently.

By God, thought O'Hara exultantly, it *is* petrol!

He turned and snapped his fingers at Benedetta who immediately lit the fire-bolt waiting ready in the crossbow. O'Hara thumped the rock impatiently with his fist while she waited until it got well alight. But he knew this was the right way—if the rags were not burning well the flame would be extinguished in flight.

She thrust the bow at him suddenly and he twisted with it in his hands, the flame scorching his face. Another man had run up and was looking incredulously under the truck. O'Hara peered through the crude wire sight and through the flames of the burning bolt and willed himself to take his time. Gently he squeezed the trigger.

The butt lurched against his shoulder and he quickly twisted over to pass the bow back into Benedetta's waiting hands, but he had time to see the flaming bolt arch well over the truck to bury itself in the earth on the other side of the road.

This new bow was shooting too high.

He grabbed the second bow and tried again, burning his fingers as he incautiously put his hand in the flame. He could feel his eyebrows shrivelling as he aimed and again the butt slammed his shoulder as he pulled the trigger. The shot went too far to the right and the bolt skidded on the road surface, sending up a shower of sparks.

The two men by the truck had looked up in alarm when the first bolt had gone over their heads. At the sight of the second bolt they both shouted and pointed across the gorge.

Let this one be it, prayed O'Hara, as he seized the bow from Benedetta. This is the one that shoots high, he thought, as he deliberately aimed for the lip of the gorge. As he squeezed the trigger a bullet clipped the rock by his head and a granite splinter scored a bloody line across his forehead. But the bolt went true, a flaming line drawn across the gorge which passed between the two men and beneath the truck.

With a soft thud the dripping petrol caught alight and the truck was suddenly enveloped in flames. The Indian staggered out of the inferno, his clothing on fire, and ran screaming down the road, his hands clawing at his eyes. O'Hara did not see the other man; he had turned and was grabbing for the second bow.

But he didn't get off another shot. He had barely lined up the sights on one of the jeeps when the bow slammed into him before he touched the trigger. He was thrown back violently and the bow must have sprung of its own volition, for he saw a fire-bolt arch into the sky. Then his head struck a rock and he was knocked unconscious.

### 11

He came round to find Benedetta bathing his head, looking worried. Beyond, he saw Forester talking animatedly to Willis and beyond them the sky, disfigured by a coil of black, greasy smoke. He put his hand to his head and winced. "What the hell hit me?"

"Hush," said Benedetta. "Don't move."

He grinned weakly and lifted himself up on his elbow. Forester saw that he was moving. "Are you all right, Tim?"

"I don't know," said O'Hara. "I don't think so." His head ached abominably. "What happened?"

Willis lifted the crossbow. "A rifle bullet hit this," he said. "It smashed the stirrup—you were lucky it didn't hit you. You batted your head against a rock and passed out."

O'Hara smiled painfully at Benedetta. "I'm all right," he said and sat up. "Did we do the job?"

Forester laughed delightedly. "Did we do the job? Oh, boy!" He knelt down next to O'Hara. "To begin with, Rohde actually hit his man on the bridge when he shot—plugged him neatly through the shoulder. That caused all the commotion we needed. Jenny Ponsky had a goddam tricky time with that guy in front of the gas tank, but she did her job in the end. She was shaking like a leaf when she gave me the bow."

"What about the truck?" asked O'Hara. "I saw it catch fire—that's about the last thing I did see."

"The truck's gone," said Forester. "It's still burning —and the jeep next to it caught fire when the second gas tank on the other side of the truck blew up. Hell, they were running about like ants across there." He lowered his voice.

92

"Both the men who were by the truck were killed. The Indian ran plumb over the edge of the gorge—I reckon he was blinded—and the other guy was burned to a crisp. Jenny didn't see it and I didn't tell her."

O'Hara nodded; it would be a nasty thing for her to live with.

"That's about it," said Forester. "They've lost all their timber—it burned with the truck. They've lost the truck and a jeep and they've abandoned the jeep by the bridge—they couldn't get it back past the burning truck. All the other vehicles they've withdrawn a hell of a long way down the road where it turns away from the gorge. I'd say it's a good half-mile. They were hopping mad, judging by the way they opened up on us. They set up the damnedest barrage of rifle fire—they must have all the ammunition in the world."

"Anybody hurt?" demanded O'Hara.

"You're our most serious casualty—no one else got a scratch."

"I must bandage your head, Tim," said Benedetta.

"We'll go up to the pond," said O'Hara.

As he got to his feet Aguillar approached. "You did well, Señor O'Hara," he said.

O'Hara swayed and leaned on Forester for support. "Well enough, but they won't fall for that trick again. All we've bought is time." His voice was sober.

"Time is what we need," said Forester. "Earlier this morning I wouldn't have given two cents for our scheme to cross the mountains. But now Rohde and I can leave with an easy conscience." He looked at his watch. "We'd better get on the road."

Miss Ponsky came up. "Are you all right, Mr. O'Hara —Tim?"

"I'm fine," he said. "You did all right, Jenny."

She blushed. "Why—thank you, Tim. But I had a dreadful moment. I really thought I'd have to shoot that man by the truck."

O'Hara looked at Forester and grinned weakly and Forester suppressed a macabre laugh. "You did just what you were supposed to do," said O'Hara, "and you did it very well." He looked around. "Willis, you stay down here—get the gun from Rohde and if anything happens fire the last bullet. But I don't think anything will happen—not yet a while. The rest of us will have a war council up by the pond. I'd like to do that before Ray goes off."

"Okay," said Forester.

They went up to the pond and O'Hara walked over to the water's edge. Before he took a cupped handful of water he caught sight of his own reflection and grimaced distastefully. He was unshaven and very dirty, his face blackened by smoke and dried blood and his eyes red-rimmed and sore from the heat of the fire-bolts. My God, I look like a tramp, he thought.

He dashed cold water at his face and shivered violently, then turned to find Benedetta behind him, a strip of cloth in her hands. "Your head," she said. "The skin was broken."

He put a hand to the back of his head and felt the stickiness of drying blood. "Hell, I must have hit hard," he said.

"You're lucky you weren't killed. Let me see to it."

Her fingers were cool on his temples as she washed the wound and bandaged his head. He rubbed his hand raspingly over his cheek; Armstrong is always clean-shaven, he thought; I must find out how he does it.

Benedetta tied a neat little knot and said, "You must take it easy to-day, Tim. I think you are concussed a little."

He nodded, then winced as a sharp pain stabbed through his head. "I think you're right. But as for taking it easy—that isn't up to me; that's up to the boys on the other side of the river. Let's get back to the others."

Forester rose up as they approached. "Miguel thinks we should get going," he said.

"In a moment," said O'Hara. "There are a few things I want to find out." He turned to Rohde. "You'll be spending a day at the camp and a day at the mine. That's two days used up. Is this lost time necessary?"

"It is necessary and barely enough," said Rohde. "It should be longer."

"You're the expert on mountains," said O'Hara. "I'll take your word for it. How long to get across?"

"Two days," said Rohde positively. "If we have to take longer we will not do it at all."

"That's four days," said O'Hara. "Add another day to convince someone that we're in trouble and another for that someone to do something about it. We've got to hold out for six days at least—maybe longer."

Forester looked grave. "Can you do it?"

"We've got to do it," said O'Hara. "I think we've gained one day. They've got to find some timber from somewhere, and that means going back at least fifty miles to a town. They might have to get another truck as well—and it all takes time. I don't think we'll be troubled until to-morrow—maybe not until the next day. But I'm thinking about your troubles— how are you going to handle things on the other side of the mountain?"

Miss Ponsky said, " I've been wondering about that, too. You can't go to the government of this man Lopez. He would help Señor Aguillar, would he?"

Forester smiled mirthlessly. " He wouldn't lift a finger. Are there any of your people in Altemiros, Señor Aguillar?"

" I will give you an address," said Aguillar. " And Miguel will know. But you may not have to go as far as Altemiros."

Forester looked interested and Aguillar said to Rohde, " The airfield."

" Ah," said Rohde. " But we must be careful."

" What's this about an airfield?" Forester asked.

" There is a high-level airfield in the mountains this side of Altemiros," said Aguillar. " It is a military installation which the fighter squadrons use in rotation. Cordillera has four squadrons of fighter aircraft—the eighth, the tenth, the fourteenth and the twenty-first squadrons. We—like the communists—have been infiltrating the armed forces. The fourteenth squadron is ours; the eighth is communist; and the other two still belong to Lopez."

" So the odds are three to one that any squadron at the airfield will be a rotten egg," commented Forester.

" That is right," said Aguillar. " But the airfield is directly on your way to Altemiros. You must tread carefully and act discreetly, and perhaps you can save much time. The commandant of the fourteenth squadron, Colonel Rodriguez, is an old friend of mine—he is safe."

" If he's there," said Forester. " But it's worth the chance. We'll make for this airfield as soon as we've crossed the mountains."

" That's settled," said O'Hara with finality. " Doctor Armstrong, have you any more tricks up your medieval sleeve?"

Armstrong removed his pipe from his mouth. " I think I have. I had an idea and I've been talking to Willis about it and he thinks he can make it work." He nodded towards the gorge. " Those people are going to be more prepared when they come back with their timber. They're not going to stand up and be shot at like tin ducks in a shooting gallery—they're going to have their defences against our crossbows. So what we need now is a trench mortar."

"For Christ's sake," exploded O'Hara. "Where the devil are we going to get a trench mortar?"

"Willis is going to make it," Armstrong said equably. "With the help of Señor Rohde, Mr. Forester and myself—and Mr. Peabody, of course, although he isn't much help, really."

"So I'm going to make a trench mortar," said Forester helplessly. He looked baffled. "What do we use for explosives? Something cleverly cooked up out of match-heads?"

"Oh, you misunderstand me," said Armstrong. "I mean the medieval equivalent of a trench mortar. We need a machine that will throw a missile in a high trajectory to lob *behind* the defences which our enemies will undoubtedly have when they make their next move. There are no really new principles in modern warfare, you know; merely new methods of applying the old principles. Medieval man knew all the principles."

He looked glumly at his empty pipe. "They had a variety of weapons. The onager is no use for our purpose, of course. I did think of the mangonel and the ballista, but I discarded those too, and finally settled on the trebuchet. Powered by gravity, you know, and very effective."

If the crossbows had not been such a great success O'Hara would have jeered at Armstrong, but now he held his peace, contenting himself with looking across at Forester ironically. Forester still looked baffled and shrugged his shoulders. "What sort of missile would the thing throw?" he asked.

"I was thinking of rocks," said Armstrong. "I explained the principle of the trebuchet to Willis and he has worked it all out. It's merely the application of simple mechanics, you know, and Willis has got all that at his fingertips. We'll probably make a better trebuchet than they could in the Middle Ages—we can apply the scientific principles with more understanding. Willis thinks we can throw a twenty-pound rock over a couple of hundred yards with no trouble at all."

"Wow!" said O'Hara. He visualised a twenty-pound boulder arching in a high trajectory—it would come out of the sky almost vertically at that range. "We can do the bridge a bit of no good with a thing like that."

"How long will it take to make?" asked Forester.

"Not long," said Armstrong. "Not more than twelve hours, Willis thinks. It's a very simple machine, really."

O'Hara felt in his pocket and found his cigarette packet. He took one of his last cigarettes and gave it to Armstrong. "Put that in your pipe and smoke it. You deserve it."

Armstrong smiled delightedly and began to shred the cigarette. "Thanks," he said. "I can think much better when I smoke."

O'Hara grinned. "I'll give you all my cigarettes if you can come up with the medieval version of the atom bomb."

"That was gunpowder," said Armstrong seriously. "I think that's beyond us at the moment."

"There's just one thing wrong with your idea," O'Hara commented. "We can't have too many people up at the camp. We must have somebody down at the bridge in case the enemy does anything unexpected. We've got to keep a fighting force down here."

"I'll stay," said Armstrong, puffing at his pipe contentedly. "I'm not very good with my hands—my fingers are all thumbs. Willis knows what to do; he doesn't need me."

"That's it, then," said O'Hara to Forester. "You and Miguel go up to the camp, help Willis and Peabody build this contraption, then push on to the mine to-morrow. I'll go down and relieve Willis at the bridge."

III

Forester found the going hard as they climbed up to the camp. His breath wheezed in his throat and he developed slight chest pains. Rohde was not so much affected and Willis apparently not at all. During the fifteen-minute rest at the half-way point he commented on it. "That is acclimatisation," Rohde explained. "Señor Willis has spent much time at the camp—to come down means nothing to him. For us going up it is different."

"That's right," said Willis. "Going down to the bridge was like going down to sea-level, although the bridge must be about twelve thousand feet up."

"How high is the camp?" asked Forester.

"I'd say about fourteen and a half thousand feet," said Willis. "I'd put the mine at a couple of thousand feet higher."

Forester looked up at the peaks. "And the pass is nineteen thousand. Too close to heaven for my liking, Miguel."

Rohde's lips twisted. "Not heaven—it is a cold hell."

When they arrived at the camp Forester was feeling bad and said so. "You will be better to-morrow," said Rohde.

"But to-morrow we're going higher," said Forester morosely.

"One day at each level is not enough to acclimatise," Rohde admitted. "But it is all the time we can afford."

Willis looked around the camp. "Where the hell is Peabody? I'll go and root him out."

He wandered off and Rohde said, "I think we should search this camp thoroughly. There may be many things that would be of use to O'Hara."

"There's the kerosene," said Forester. "Maybe Armstrong's gadget can throw fire bombs. That would be one way of getting at the bridge to burn it."

They began to search the huts. Most of them were empty and disused, but three of them had been fitted out for habitation and there was much equipment. In one of the huts they found Willis shaking a recumbent Peabody, who was stretched out on a bunk.

"Five arrows," said Willis bitterly. "That's all this bastard has done—made five arrows before he drank himself stupid."

"Where's he getting the booze?" asked Forester.

"There's a case of the stuff in one of the other huts."

"Lock it up if you can," said Forester. "If you can't, pour it away—I ought to have warned you about this, but I forgot. We can't do much about him now—he's too far gone."

Rohde who had been exploring the hut grunted suddenly as he took a small leather bag from a shelf. "This is good."

Forester looked with interest at the pale green leaves which Rohde shook out into the palm of his hand. "What's that?"

"Coca leaves," said Rohde. "They will help us when we cross the mountain."

"Coca?" said Forester blankly.

"The curse of the Andes," said Rohde. "This is where cocaine comes from. It has been the ruin of the *indios*—this and *aguardiente*. Señor Aguillar intends to restrict the growing of coca when he comes into power." He smiled slowly. "It would be asking too much to stop it altogether."

"How is it going to help us?" asked Forester.

"Look around for another bag like this one containing

a white powder," said Rohde. As they rummaged among the shelves, he continued, " In the great days of the Incas the use of coca was restricted to the nobles. Then the royal messengers were permitted to use it because it increased their running power and stamina. Now all the *indios* chew coca—it is cheaper than food."

" It isn't a substitute for food, is it?"

" It anæsthetises the stomach lining," said Rohde. " A starving man will do anything to avoid the pangs of hunger. It is also a narcotic, bringing calmness and tranquillity—at a price."

" Is this what you're looking for?" asked Forester. He opened a small bag he had found and tipped out some of the powder. " What is it?"

" Lime," said Rohde. " Cocaine is an alkaloid and needs a base for it to precipitate. While we are waiting for Señor Willis to tell us what to do, I will prepare this for us."

He poured the coca leaves into a saucer and began to grind them, using the back of a spoon as a pestle. The leaves were brittle and dry and broke up easily. When he had ground them to a powder he added lime and continued to grind until the two substances were thoroughly mixed. Then he put the mixture into an empty tin and added water, stirring until he had a light green paste. He took another tin and punched holes in the bottom, and, using it as a strainer, he forced the paste through.

He said, " In any of the villages round here you can see the old women doing this. Will you get me some small, smooth stones?"

Forester went out and got the stones and Rohde used them to roll and squeeze the paste like a pastrycook. Finally the paste was rolled out for the last time and Rohde cut it into rectangles with his pocket-knife. " These must dry in the sun," he said. " Then we put them back in the bags."

Forester looked dubiously at the small green squares. " Is this stuff habit-forming?"

" Indeed it is," said Rohde. " But do not worry; this amount will do us no harm. And it will give us the endurance to climb the mountains."

Willis came back. " We can swing it," he said. " We've got the material to make this—what did Armstrong call it?"

" A trebuchet," Forester said.

" Well, we can do it," said Willis. He stopped and looked down at the table. " What's that stuff?"

99

Forester grinned. "A substitute for prime steak; Miguel just cooked it up." He shook his head. "Medieval artillery and pep pills—what a hell of a mixture."

"Talking about steak reminds me that I'm hungry," said Willis. "We'll eat before we get started."

They opened some cans of stew and prepared a meal. As Forester took the first mouthful, he said, "Now, tell me—what the hell is a trebuchet?"

Willis smiled and produced a stub of pencil. "Just an application of the lever," he said. "Imagine a thing like an out-of-balance see-saw—like this." Rapidly he sketched on the soft pine top of the table. "The pivot is here and one arm is, say, four times as long as the other. On the short arm you sling a weight, of, say, five hundred pounds, and on the other end you have your missile—a twenty-pound rock."

He began to jot down calculations. "Those medieval fellows worked empirically—they didn't have the concepts of energy that we have. We can do the whole thing precisely from scratch. Assuming your five-hundred-pound weight drops ten feet. The acceleration of gravity is such that, taking into account frictional losses at the pivot, it will take half a second to fall. That's five thousand foot-pounds in a half-second, six hundred thousand foot-pounds to the minute, eighteen horse-power of energy applied instantaneously to a twenty-pound rock on the end of the long arm."

"That should make it move," said Forester.

"I can tell you the speed," said Willis. "Assuming the ratio between the two arms is four to one, then the . . . the . . ." He stopped, tapped on the table for a moment, then grinned. "Let's call it the muzzle velocity, although this thing hasn't a muzzle. The muzzle velocity will be eighty feet per second."

"Is there any way of altering the range?"

"Sure," said Willis. "Heavy stones won't go as far as light stones. You want to decrease the range, you use a heavier rock. I must tell O'Hara that—he'd better get busy collecting and grading ammunition."

He began to sketch on the table in more detail. "For the pivot we have the back axle of a wrecked truck that's back of the huts. The arms we make from the roof beams of a hut. There'll have to be a cup of some kind to hold the missile—we'll use a hub cap bolted on to the end of the long arm. The whole thing will need a mounting but we'll figure that out when we come to it."

Forester looked at the sketch critically. "It's going to be damned big and heavy. How are we going to get it down the mountain?"

Willis grinned. "I've figured that out too. The whole thing will pull apart and we'll use the axle to carry the rest of it. We'll wheel the damn thing down the mountain and assemble it again at the bridge."

"You've done well," said Forester.

"It was Armstrong who thought it up," said Willis. "For a scholar, he has the most murderous tendencies. He knows more ways of killing people—say, have you ever heard of Greek fire?"

"In a vague sort of way."

"Armstrong says it was as good as napalm, and that the ancients used to have flame-throwers mounted on the prows of their warships. We've done a bit of thinking along those lines and got nowhere." He looked broodingly at his sketch. "He says this thing is nothing to the siege weapons they had. They used to throw dead horses over city walls to start a plague. How heavy is a horse?"

"Maybe horses weren't as big in those days," said Forester.

"Any horse that could carry a man in full armour was no midget," Willis pointed out. He spooned the last of the gravy from his plate. "We'd better get started—I don't want to work all night again."

Rohde nodded briefly and Forester looked over at Peabody, snoring on the bunk. "I think we'll start with a bucket of the coldest water we can get," he said.

I V

O'Hara looked across the gorge.

Tendrils of smoke still curled from the burnt-out vehicles and he caught the stench of burning rubber. He looked speculatively at the intact jeep at the bridgehead and debated whether to do something about it, but discarded the idea almost as soon as it came to him. It would be useless to destroy a single vehicle—the enemy had plenty more—and he must husband his resources for more vital targets. It was not his intention to wage a war of attrition; the enemy could beat him hands down at that game.

He had been along the edge of the gorge downstream to where the road turned away, half a mile from the bridge, and had picked out spots from which crossbowmen could keep up a harassing fire. Glumly, he thought that Armstrong was right—the enemy would not be content to be docile targets; they would certainly take steps to protect themselves against further attack. The only reason for the present success was the unexpectedness of it all, as though a rabbit had taken a weasel by the throat.

The enemy was still vigilant by the bridge. Once, when O'Hara had incautiously exposed himself, he drew a concentrated fire that was unpleasantly accurate and it was only his quick reflexes and the fact that he was in sight for so short a time that saved him from a bullet in the head. We can take no chances, he thought; no chances at all.

Now he looked at the bridge with the twelve-foot gap yawning in the middle and thought of ways of getting at it. Fire still seemed the best bet and Willis had said that there were two drums of paraffin up at the camp. He measured with his eye the hundred-yard approach to the bridge; there was a slight incline and he thought that, given a good push, a drum would roll as far as the bridge. It was worth trying.

Presently Armstrong came down to relieve him. "Grub's up," he said.

O'Hara regarded Armstrong's smooth cheeks. "I didn't bring my shaving-kit," he said. "Apparently you did."

"I've got one of those Swiss wind-up dry shavers," said Armstrong. "You can borrow it if you like. It's up at the shelter in my coat pocket."

O'Hara thanked him and pointed out the enemy observation posts he had spotted. "I don't think they'll make an attempt on the bridge to-day," he said, "so I'm going up to the camp this afternoon. I want those drums of paraffin. But if anything happens while I'm gone and the bastards get across, then you scatter. Aguillar, Benedetta and Jenny rendezvous at the mine—not the camp—and they go up the mountain the hard way, steering clear of the road. You get up to the camp by the road as fast as you can—you'd better move fast because they'll be right on your tail."

Armstrong nodded. "I have the idea. We stall them off at the camp, giving the others time to get to the mine."

"That's right," said O'Hara. "But you're the boss in my absence and you'll have to use your own judgment."

He left Armstrong and went back to the shelter, where he found the professor's coat and rummaged in the pockets. Benedetta smiled at him and said, "Lunch is ready."

"I'll be back in a few minutes," he said, and went down the hill towards the pond, carrying the dry shaver.

Aguillar pulled his overcoat tighter about him and looked at O'Hara's retreating figure with curious eyes. "That one is strange," he said. "He is a fighter but he is too cold—too objective. There is no hot blood in him, and that is not good for a young man."

Benedetta bent her head and concentrated on the stew. "Perhaps he has suffered," she said.

Aguillar smiled slightly as he regarded Benedetta's averted face. "You say he was a prisoner in Korea?" he asked.

She nodded.

"Then he must have suffered," agreed Aguillar. "Perhaps not in the body, but certainly in the spirit. Have you asked him about it?"

"He will not talk about it."

Aguillar wagged his head. "That is also very bad. It is not good for a man to be so self-contained—to have his violence pent-up. It is like screwing down the safety-valve on a boiler—one can expect an explosion." He grimaced. "I hope I am not near when that young man explodes."

Benedetta's head jerked up. "You talk nonsense, Uncle. His anger is directed against those others across the river. He would do us no harm."

Aguillar looked at her sadly. "You think so, child? His anger is directed against himself as the power of a bomb is directed against its casing—but when the casing shatters everyone around is hurt. O'Hara is a dangerous man."

Benedetta's lips tightened and she was going to reply when Miss Ponsky approached, lugging a crossbow. She seemed unaccountably flurried and the red stain of a blush was ebbing from her cheeks. Her protection was volubility. "I've got both bows sighted in," she said rapidly. "They're both shooting the same now, and very accurately. They're very strong too—I was hitting a target at one hundred and twenty yards. I left the other with Doctor Armstrong; I thought he might need it."

"Have you seen Señor O'Hara?" asked Benedetta.

Miss Ponsky turned pink again. "I saw him at the pond," she said in a subdued voice. "What are we having for lunch?" she continued brightly.

Benedetta laughed. "As always—stew."

Miss Ponsky shuddered delicately. Benedetta said, "It is

all that Señor Willis brought from the camp—cans of stew. Perhaps it is his favourite food."

"He ought to have thought of the rest of us," complained Miss Ponsky.

Aguillar stirred. "What do you think of Señor Forester, madam?"

"I think he is a very brave man," she said simply. "He and Señor Rohde."

"I think so too," said Aguillar. "But also I think there is something strange about him. He is too much the man of action to be a simple businessman."

"Oh, I don't know," Miss Ponsky demurred. "A good businessman must be a man of action, at least in the States."

"Somehow I don't think Forester's idea is the pursuit of the dollar," Aguillar said reflectively. "He is not like Peabody."

Miss Ponsky flared. "I could *spit* when I think of that man. He makes me ashamed to be an American."

"Do not be ashamed," Aguillar said gently. "He is not a coward because he is an American; there are cowards among all people."

O'Hara came back. He looked better now that he had shaved the stubble from his cheeks. It had not been easy; the clockwork rotary shaver had protested when asked to attack the thicket of his beard, but he had persisted and was now smooth-cheeked and clean. The water in the pond had been too cold for bathing, but he had stripped and taken a sponge-bath and felt the better for it. Out of the corner of his eye he had seen Miss Ponsky toiling up the hill towards the shelter and hoped she had not seen him—he did not want to offend the susceptibilities of maiden ladies.

"What have we got?" he asked.

"More stew," said Aguillar wryly.

O'Hara groaned and Benedetta laughed. He accepted the aluminium plate and said, "Maybe I can bring something else when I go up to the camp this afternoon. But I won't have room for much—I'm more interested in the paraffin."

Miss Ponsky asked, "What is it like by the river?"

"Quiet," said O'Hara. "They can't do much to-day so they're contenting themselves with keeping the bridge covered. I think it's safe enough for me to go up to the camp."

"I'll come with you," said Benedetta quickly.

O'Hara paused, his fork in mid-air. "I don't know if . . ."

"We need food," she said. "And if you cannot carry it, somebody must."

O'Hara glanced at Aguillar, who nodded tranquilly. "It will be all right," he said.

O'Hara shrugged. "It will be a help," he admitted.

Benedetta sketched a curtsy at him, but there was a flash of something in her eyes that warned O'Hara he must tread gently. "Thank you," she said, a shade too sweetly. "I'll try not to get in the way."

He grinned at her. "I'll tell you when you are."

v

Like Forester, O'Hara found the going hard on the way up to the camp. When he and Benedetta took a rest half-way, he sucked in the thin, cold air greedily, and gasped, "My God, this is getting tough."

Benedetta's eyes went to the high peaks. "What about Miguel and Señor Forester? They will have it worse."

O'Hara nodded, then said, "I think your uncle ought to come up to the camp to-morrow. It is better that he should do it when he can do it in his own time, instead of being chased. And it will acclimatise him in case we have to retreat to the mine."

"I think that is good," she said. "I will go with him to help, and I can bring more food when I return."

"He might be able to help Willis with his bits and pieces," said O'Hara. "After all, he can't do much down at the bridge anyway, and Willis wouldn't mind another pair of hands."

Benedetta pulled her coat about her. "Was it as cold as this in Korea?"

"Sometimes," O'Hara said. He thought of the stone-walled cell in which he had been imprisoned. Water ran down the walls and froze into ice at night—and then the weather got worse and the walls were iced day and night. It was then that Lieutenant Feng had taken away all his clothing. "Sometimes," he repeated bleakly.

"I suppose you had warmer clothing than we have," said Benedetta. "I am worried about Forester and Miguel. It will be very cold up in the pass."

O'Hara felt suddenly ashamed of himself and his self-pity. He looked away quickly from Benedetta and stared at the snows above. "We must see if we can improvise a tent for them. They'll spend at least one night in the open up there." He stood up. "We'd better get on."

The camp was busy with the noise of hammering and the trebuchet was taking shape in the central clearing between the huts. O'Hara stood unnoticed for a moment and looked at it. It reminded him very much of something he had once seen in an avant-garde art magazine; a modern sculptor had assembled a lot of junk into a crazy structure and had given it some high-falutin' name, and the trebuchet had the same appearance of wild improbability.

Forester paused and leaned on the length of steel he was using as a crude hammer. As he wiped the sweat from his eyes he caught sight of the newcomers and hailed them. "What the hell are you doing here? Is anything wrong?"

"All's quiet," said O'Hara reassuringly. "I've come for one of the drums of paraffin—and some grub." He walked round the trebuchet. "Will this contraption work?"

"Willis is confident," said Forester. "That's good enough for me."

"You won't be here," O'Hara said stonily. "But I suppose I'll have to trust the boffins. By the way—it's going to be bloody cold up there—have you made any preparations?"

"Not yet. We've been too busy on this thing."

"That's not good enough," said O'Hara sternly. "We're depending on you to bring the good old U.S. cavalry to the rescue. You've *got* to get across that pass—if you don't, then this piece of silly artillery will be wasted. Is there anything out of which you can improvise a tent?"

"I suppose you're right," said Forester. "I'll have a look around."

"Do that. Where's the paraffin?"

"Paraffin? Oh, you mean the kerosene. It's in that hut there. Willis locked it up; he put all the booze in there—we had to keep Peabody sober somehow."

"Um," said O'Hara. "How's he doing?"

"He's not much good. He's out of condition and his disposition doesn't help. We've got to drive him."

"Doesn't the bloody fool realise that if the bridge is forced he'll get his throat cut?"

Forester sighed. "It doesn't seem to make any difference —logic isn't his strong-point. He goofs off at the slightest opportunity."

O'Hara saw Benedetta going into one of the huts. "I'd better get that paraffin. We must have it at the bridge before it gets dark."

He got the key of the hut from Willis and opened the door. Just inside was a crate, half-filled with bottles. There was a stir of longing in his guts as he looked at them, but he suppressed it firmly and switched his attention to the two drums of paraffin. He tested the weight of one of them, and thought, this is going to be a bastard to get down the mountain.

He heaved the drum on to its side and rolled it out of the hut. Across the clearing he saw Forester helping Benedetta to make a *travois*, and crossed over to them. "Is there any rope up here?"

"Rope we've got," replied Forester. "But Rohde was worried about that—he said we'll need it in the mountains, rotten though it is; and Willis needs it for the trebuchet, too. But there's plenty of electric wire that Willis ripped out to make crossbow-strings with."

"I'll need some to help me get that drum down the mountain—I suppose the electric wire will have to do."

Peabody wandered over. His face had a flabby, unhealthy look about it and he exuded the scent of fear. "Say, what is this?" he demanded. "Willis tells me that you and the spic are making a getaway over the mountains."

Forester's eyes were cold. "If you want to put it that way —yes."

"Well, I wanna come," said Peabody. "I'm not staying here to be shot by a bunch of commies."

"Are you crazy?" said Forester.

"What's so crazy about it? Willis says it's only fifteen miles to this place Altemiros."

Forester looked at O'Hara speechlessly. O'Hara said quietly, "Do you think it's going to be like a stroll in Central Park, Peabody?"

"Hell, I'd rather take my chance in the mountains than with the commies," said Peabody. "I think you're crazy if you think you can hold them off. What have you got? You've got an old man, a silly bitch of a school-marm, two nutty scientists and a girl. And you're fighting with bows and arrows, for God's sake." He tapped Forester on the chest. "If you're making a getaway, I'm coming along."

Forester slapped his hand away. "Now get this, Peabody; you'll do as you're damn well told."

"Who the hell are you to give orders?" said Peabody with venom. "To begin with I take no orders from a limey—and I don't see why you should be so high and mighty, either. I'll do as I damn well please."

O'Hara caught Forester's eye. "Let's see Rohde," he said hastily. He had seen Forester balling his fist and wanted to prevent trouble, for an idea was crystallising in his mind.

Rohde was positively against it. "This man is in no condition to cross the mountains," he said. "He will hold us back, and if he holds us back none of us will get across. We cannot spend more than one night in the open."

"What do you think?" Forester asked O'Hara.

"I don't like the man," said O'Hara. "He's weak and he'll break under pressure. If he breaks it might be the end of the lot of us. I can't trust him."

"That's fair enough," Forester agreed. "He's a weak sister, all right. I'm going to overrule you, Miguel; he comes with us. We can't afford to leave him with O'Hara."

Rohde opened his mouth to protest but stopped when he saw the expression on Forester's face. Forester grinned wolfishly and there was a hard edge to his voice when he said, "If he holds us up, we'll drop the bastard into the nearest crevasse. Peabody will have to put up or shut up."

He called Peabody over. "All right, you come with us. But let's get this straight right from the start. You take orders."

Peabody nodded. "All right," he mumbled. "I'll take orders from you."

Forester was merciless. "You'll take orders from anyone who damn well gives them from now on. Miguel is the expert round here and when he gives an order—you jump fast."

Peabody's eyes flickered, but he gave in. He had no option if he wanted to go with them. He shot a look of dislike at Rohde and said, "Okay, but when I get back Stateside the State Department is going to get an earful from me. What kind of place is this where good Americans can be pushed around by spics and commies?"

O'Hara looked at Rohde quickly. His face was as placid as though he had not heard. O'Hara admired his self-control—but he pitied Peabody when he got into the mountains.

Half an hour later he and Benedetta left. She was pulling the *travois* and he was clumsily steering the drum of paraffin.

There were two loops of wire round the drum in a sling so that he could have a measure of control. They had wasted little time in saying good-bye to Rohde and Forester, and still less on Peabody. Willis had said, "We'll need you up here to-morrow; the trebuchet will be ready then."

"I'll be here," promised O'Hara. "If I haven't any other engagements."

It was difficult going down the mountain, even though they were on the road. Benedetta hauled on the *travois* and had to stop frequently to rest, and more often to help O'Hara with the drum. It weighed nearly four hundred pounds and seemed to have a malevolent mind of its own. His idea of being able to steer it by pulling on the wires did not work well. The drum would take charge and go careering at an angle to wedge itself in the ditch at the side of the road. Then it would be a matter of sweat and strain to get it out, whereupon it would charge into the opposite ditch.

By the time they got down to the bottom O'Hara felt as though he had been wrestling with a malign and evil adversary. His muscles ached and it seemed as though someone had pounded him with a hammer all over his body. Worse, in order to get the drum down the mountain at all he had been obliged to lighten the load by jettisoning a quarter of the contents and had helplessly watched ten gallons of invaluable paraffin drain away into the thirsty dust.

When they reached the valley Benedetta abandoned the *travois* and went for help. O'Hara had looked at the sky and said, "I want this drum at the bridge before nightfall."

Night swoops early on the eastern slopes of the Andes. The mountain wall catches the setting sun, casting long shadows across the hot jungles of the interior. At five in the afternoon the sun was just touching the topmost peaks and O'Hara knew that in an hour it would be dark.

Armstrong came up to help and O'Hara immediately asked, "Who's on watch?"

"Jenny. She's all right. Besides, there's nothing doing at all."

With two men to control the erratic drum it went more easily and they manœuvred it to the bridgehead within half an hour. Miss Ponsky came running up. "They switched on their lights just now and I think I heard an auto engine from way back along there." She pointed downstream.

"I would have liked to try and put out the headlamps on

109

this jeep," she said. "But I didn't want to waste an arrow —a quarrel—and in any case there's something in front of the glass."

"They have stone guards in front of the lights," said Armstrong. "Heavy mesh wire."

"Go easy on the bolts, anyway," said O'Hara. "Peabody was supposed to be making some but he's been loafing on the job." He carefully crept up and surveyed the bridgehead. The jeep's headlights illuminated the whole bridge and its approaches and he knew that at least a dozen sharp pairs of eyes were watching. It would be suicidal to go out there.

He dropped back and looked at the drum in the fading light. It was much dented by its careering trip down the mountain road but he thought it would roll a little farther. He said, "This is the plan. We're going to burn the bridge. We're going to play the same trick that we played this morning but we'll apply it on this side of the bridge."

He put his foot on top of the drum and rocked it gently. "If Armstrong gives this one good heave it should roll right down to the bridge—if we're lucky. Jenny will be standing up there with her crossbow and when it gets into the right position she'll puncture it. I'll be in position too, with Benedetta to hand me the other crossbow with a fire-bolt. If the drum is placed right then we'll burn through the ropes on this side and the whole bloody bridge will drop into the water."

"That sounds all right," said Armstrong.

"Get the bows, Jenny," said O'Hara and took Armstrong to one side, out of hearing of the others. "It's a bit more tricky than that," he said. "In order to get the drum in the right place you'll have to come into the open." He held his head on one side; the noise of the vehicle had stopped. "So I want to do it before they get any more lights on the job."

Armstrong smiled gently. "I think your little bit is more dangerous than mine. Shooting those fire-bolts in the dark will make you a perfect target—it won't be as easy as this morning, and then you nearly got shot."

"Maybe," said O'Hara. "But this has got to be done. This is how we do it. When that other jeep—or whatever it is—comes up, maybe the chaps on the other side won't be so vigilant. My guess is that they'll tend to watch the vehicle manœuvre into position; I don't think they're a very disciplined crowd. Now, while that's happening is the time to do your stuff. I'll give you the signal."

"All right, my boy," said Armstrong. "You can rely on me."

O'Hara helped him to push the drum into the position easiest for him, and then Miss Ponsky and Benedetta came up with the crossbows. He said to Benedetta, "When I give Armstrong the signal to push off the drum, you light the first fire-bolt. This has got to be done quickly if it's going to be done at all."

"All right, Tim," she said.

Miss Ponsky went to her post without a word.

He heard the engine again, this time louder. He saw nothing on the road downstream and guessed that the vehicle was coming slowly and without lights. He thought they'd be scared of being fired on during that half-mile journey. By God, he thought, if I had a dozen men with a dozen bows I'd make life difficult for them. He smiled sourly. Might as well wish for a machine-gun section—it was just as unlikely a possibility.

Suddenly the vehicle switched its lights on. It was quite near the bridge and O'Hara got ready to give Armstrong the signal. He held his hand until the vehicle—a jeep—drew level with the burnt-out truck, then he said in a whispered shout, "Now!"

He heard the rattle as the drum rolled over the rocks and out of the corner of his eye saw the flame as Benedetta ignited the fire-bolt. The drum came into sight on his left, bumping down the slight incline which led towards the bridge. It hit a larger stone which threw it off course. Christ, he whispered, we've bungled it.

Then he saw Armstrong run into the open, chasing after the drum. A few faint shouts came from across the river and there was a shot. "You damned fool," yelled O'Hara. "Get back." But Armstrong kept running forward until he had caught up with the drum and, straightening it on course again, he gave it another boost.

There was a *rafale* of rifle-fire and spurts of dust flew about Armstrong's feet as he ran back at full speed, then a metallic *thunk* as a bullet hit the drum and, as it turned, O'Hara saw a silver spurt of liquid rise in the air. The enemy were divided in their intentions—they did not know which was more dangerous, Armstrong or the drum. And so Armstrong got safely into cover.

Miss Ponsky raised the bow. "Forget it, Jenny," roared O'Hara. "They've done it for us."

Again and again the drum was hit as it rolled towards the bridge and the paraffin spurted out of more holes, rising in gleaming jets into the air until the drum looked like some strange kind of liquid catherine wheel. But the repeated impact of bullets was slowing it down and there must have been a slight and unnoticed rise in the ground before the bridge because the drum rolled to a halt just short of the abutments.

O'Hara swore and turned to grasp the crossbow which Benedetta was holding. Firing in the dark with a fire-bolt was difficult; the flame obscured his vision and he had to will himself consciously to take aim slowly. There was another babble of shouts from over the river and a bullet ricocheted from a rock nearby and screamed over his head.

He pressed the trigger gently and the scorching heat was abruptly released from his face as the bolt shot away into the opposing glare of headlamps. He ducked as another bullet clipped the rock by the side of his head and thrust the bow at Benedetta for reloading.

It was not necessary. There was a dull explosion and a violent flare of light as the paraffin around the drum caught fire. O'Hara, breathing heavily, moved to another place where he could see what was happening. It would have been very foolish to pop his head up in the same place from which he had fired his bolt.

It was with dejection that he saw a raging fire arising from a great pool of paraffin just short of the bridge. The drum had stopped too soon and although the fire was spectacular it would do the bridge no damage at all. He watched for a long time, hoping the drum would explode and scatter burning paraffin on the bridge, but nothing happened and slowly the fire went out.

He dropped back to join the others. "Well, we messed that one up," he said bitterly.

"I should have pushed it harder," Armstrong said.

O'Hara flared up in anger. "You damned fool, if you hadn't run out and given it another shove it wouldn't have gone as far as it did. Don't do an idiotic thing like that again—you nearly got killed!"

Armstrong said quietly, "We're all of us on the verge of getting killed. Someone has to risk something besides you."

"I should have surveyed the ground more carefully," said O'Hara self-accusingly.

Benedetta put a hand on his arm. "Don't worry, Tim; you did the best you could."

"Sure you did," said Miss Ponsky militantly. "And we've shown them we're still here and fighting. I bet they're scared to come across now for fear of being burned alive."

"Come," said Benedetta. "Come and eat." There was a flash of humour in her voice. "I didn't bring the *travois* all the way down, so it will be stew again."

Wearily O'Hara turned his back on the bridge. It was the third night since the plane crash—and six more to go!

## Chapter V

Forester attacked his baked beans with gusto. The dawn light was breaking, dimming the bright glare of the Coleman lamp and smoothing out the harsh shadows on his face. He said, "One day at the mine—two days crossing the pass— another two days getting help. We must cut that down somehow. When we get to the other side we'll have to act quickly."

Peabody looked at the table morosely, ignoring Forester. He was wondering if he had made the right decision, done the right thing by Joe Peabody. The way these guys talked, crossing the mountains wasn't going to be so easy. Aw, to hell with it—he could do anything any other guy could do— especially any spic.

Rohde said, "I thought I heard rifle-fire last night—just at sunset." His face was haunted by the knowledge of his helplessness.

"They should be all right. I don't see how the commies could have repaired the bridge and got across so quickly," said Forester reasonably. "That O'Hara's a smart cookie. He must have been doing something with that drum of kerosene he took down the hill yesterday. He's probably cooked the bridge to a turn."

Rohde's face cracked into a faint smile. "I hope so."

Forester finished his beans. "Okay, let's get the show on the road." He turned round in his chair and looked at the huddle of blankets on the bunk. "What about Willis?"

"Let him sleep," said Rohde. "He worked harder and longer than any of us."

Forester got up and examined the packs they had made up the previous night. Their equipment was pitifully inadequate for the job they had to do. He remembered the books he had read about mountaineering expeditions—the special rations they had, the lightweight nylon ropes and tents, the windproof clothing and the specialised gear—climbing-boots, ice-axes, pitons. He smiled grimly—yes, and porters to help hump it.

There was none of that here. Their packs were roughly cobbled together from blankets; they had an ice-axe which Willis had made—a roughly shaped metal blade mounted on the end of an old broom handle; their ropes were rotten and none too plentiful, scavenged from the rubbish heap of the camp and with too many knots and splices for safety; their climbing-boots were clumsy miners' boots made of thick, unpliant leather, heavy and graceless. Willis had discovered the boots and Rohde had practically gone into raptures over them.

He lifted his pack and wished it was heavier—heavier with the equipment they needed. They had worked far into the night improvising, with Willis and Rohde being the most inventive. Rohde had torn blankets into long strips to make puttees, and Willis had practically torn down one of the huts single-handed in his search for extra long nails to use as pitons. Rohde shook his head wryly when he saw them. "The metal is too soft, but they will have to do."

Forester heaved the pack on to his back and fastened the crude electric wiring fastenings. Perhaps it's as well we're staying a day at the mine, he thought; maybe we can do better than this. There are suitcases up there with proper straps; there is the plane—surely we can find something in there we can use. He zipped up the front of the leather jacket and was grateful to O'Hara for the loan of it. He suspected it would be windy higher up, and the jacket was windproof.

As he stepped out of the hut he heard Peabody cursing at the weight of his pack. He took no notice but strode on through the camp, past the trebuchet which crouched like a prehistoric monster, and so to the road which led up the mountain. In two strides Rohde caught up and came abreast of him. He indicated Peabody trailing behind. "This one will make trouble," he said.

Forester's face was suddenly bleak. "I meant what I said, Miguel. If he makes trouble, we get rid of him."

It took them a long time to get up to the mine. The air became very thin and Forester could feel that his heartbeat had accelerated and his heart thumped in his chest like a swinging stone. He breathed faster and was cautioned by Rohde against forced breathing. My God, he thought; what is it going to be like in the pass?

They reached the air-strip and the mine at midday. Forester felt dizzy and a little nauseated and was glad to reach the first of the deserted huts and to collapse on the floor. Peabody had been left behind long ago; they had ignored his pleas for them to stop and he had straggled farther and farther behind on the trail until he had disappeared from sight. "He'll catch up," Forester said. "He's more scared of the commies than he is of me." He grinned with savage satisfaction. "But I'll change that before we're through."

Rohde was in nearly as bad shape as Forester, although he was more used to the mountains. He sat on the floor of the hut, gasping for breath, too weary to shrug off his pack. They both relaxed for over half an hour before Rohde made any constructive move. At last he fumbled with numb fingers at the fastenings of his pack, and said, "We must have warmth; get out the kerosene."

As Forester undid his pack Rohde took the small axe which had been brought from the Dakota and left the hut. Presently Forester heard him chopping at something in one of the other huts and guessed he had gone for the makings of a fire. He got out the bottle of kerosene and put it aside, ready for when Rohde came back.

An hour later they had a small fire going in the middle of the hut. Rohde had used the minimum of kerosene to start it and small chips of wood built up in a pyramid. Forester chuckled. "You must have been a boy scout."

"I was," said Rohde seriously. "That is a fine organisation." He stretched. "Now we must eat."

"I don't feel hungry," objected Forester.

"I know—neither do I. Nevertheless, we must eat." Rohde looked out of the window towards the pass. "We must fuel ourselves for to-morrow."

They warmed a can of beans and Forester choked down his share. He had not the slightest desire for food, nor for anything except quietness. His limbs felt flaccid and heavy and he felt incapable of the slightest exertion. His mind was affected, too, and he found it difficult to think clearly and to stick to a single line of thought. He just sat there in a corner of the hut, listlessly munching his lukewarm beans and hating every mouthful.

He said, " Christ, I feel terrible."

" It is the *soroche*," said Rohde with a shrug. " We must expect to feel like this." He shook his head regretfully. " We are not allowing enough time for acclimatisation."

" It wasn't as bad as this when we came out of the plane," said Forester.

" We had oxygen," Rohde pointed out. " And we went down the mountain quickly. You understand that this is dangerous?"

" Dangerous? I know I feel goddam sick."

" There was an American expedition here a few years ago, climbing mountains to the north of here. They went quickly to a level of five thousand metres—about as high as we are now. One of the Americans lost consciousness because of the *soroche*, and although they had a doctor, he died while being taken down the mountain. Yes, it is dangerous, Señor Forester."

Forester grinned weakly. " In a moment of danger we ought to be on a first-name basis, Miguel. My name is Ray."

After a while they heard Peabody moving outside. Rohde heaved himself to his feet and went to the door. " We are here, señor."

Peabody stumbled into the hut and collapsed on the floor. " You lousy bastards," he gasped. " Why didn't you wait?"

Forester grinned at him. " We'll be moving really fast when we leave here," he said. " Coming up from the camp was like a Sunday morning stroll compared to what's coming next. We'll not wait for you then, Peabody."

" You son of a bitch. I'll get even with you," Peabody threatened.

Forester laughed. " I'll ram those words down your throat —but not now. There'll be time enough later."

Rohde put out a can of beans. " You must eat, and we must work. Come, Ray."

" I don't wanna eat," moaned Peabody.

" Suit yourself," said Forester. " I don't care if you starve to death." He got up and went out of the hut, following Rohde. " This loss of appetite—is that *soroche*, too?"

Rohde nodded. " We will eat little from now on—we

116

must live on the reserves of our bodies. A fit man can do it —but that man . . .? I don't know if he can do it."

They walked slowly down the air-strip towards the crashed Dakota. To Forester it seemed incredible that O'Hara had found it too short on which to land because to him it now appeared to be several miles long. He plodded on, mechanically putting one foot in front of the other, while the cold air rasped in his throat and his chest heaved with the drudging effort he was making.

They left the air-strip and skirted the cliff over which the plane had plunged. There had been a fresh fall of snow which mantled the broken wings and softened the jagged outlines of the holes torn in the fuselage. Forester looked down over the cliff, and said, " I don't think this can be seen from the air—the snow makes perfect camouflage. If there is an air search I don't think they'll find us."

Walking with difficulty over the broken ground, they climbed to the wreck and got inside through the hole O'Hara had chopped when he and Rohde had retrieved the oxygen cylinder. It was dim and bleak inside the Dakota and Forester shivered, not from the cold which was becoming intense, but from the odd idea that this was the corpse of a once living and vibrant thing. He shook the idea from him, and said, " There were some straps on the luggage rack—complete with buckles. We could use those, and O'Hara says there are gloves in the cockpit."

" That is good," agreed Rohde. " I will look towards the front for what I can find."

Forester went aft and his breath hissed when he saw the body of old Coughlin, a shattered smear of frozen flesh and broken bones on the rear seat. He averted his eyes and turned to the luggage-rack and began to unbuckle the straps. His fingers were numb with the cold and his movements clumsy, but at last he managed to get them free—four broad canvas straps which could be used on the packs. That gave him an idea and he turned his attention to the seat belts, but they were anchored firmly and it was hopeless to try to remove them without tools.

Rohde came aft carrying the first-aid box which he had taken from the bulkhead. He placed it on a seat and opened it, carefully moving his fingers among the jumbled contents. He grunted. " Morphine."

" Damn," said Forester. " We could have used that on Mrs. Coughlin."

Rohde held up the shattered end of an ampoule. "It would have been no use; they are all broken."

He put some bandages away in his pocket, then said, "This will be useful—aspirin." The bottle was cracked, but it still held together and contained a hundred tablets. They both took two tablets and Rohde put the bottle in his pocket. There was nothing more in the first-aid box that was usable.

Forester went into the cockpit. The body of Grivas was there, tumbled into an obscene attitude, and still with the look of deep surprise frozen into the open eyes which were gazing at the shattered instrument panel. Forester moved forward, thinking that there must be something in the wreck of an aircraft that could be salvaged, when he kicked something hard that slid down the inclined floor of the cockpit.

He looked down and saw an automatic pistol.

My God, he thought; we'd forgotten that. It was Grivas's gun, left behind in the scramble to get out of the Dakota. It would have been of use down by the bridge, he thought, picking it up. But it was too late for that now. The metal was cold in his hand and he stood for a moment, undecided, then he slipped it into his pocket, thinking of Peabody and of what lay on the other side of the pass.

Equipment for well-dressed mountaineers, he thought sardonically; one automatic pistol.

They found nothing more that was of use in the Dakota, so they retraced their steps along the air-strip and back to the hut. Forester took the straps and a small suitcase belonging to Miss Ponsky which had been left behind. From these unlikely ingredients he contrived a serviceable pack which sat on his shoulders more comfortably than the one he had.

Rohde went to look at the mine and Peabody sat slackly in a corner of the hut watching Forester work with lacklustre eyes. He had not eaten his beans, nor had he attempted to keep the fire going. Forester, when he came into the hut, had looked at him with contempt but said nothing. He took the axe and chipped a few shavings from the baulk of wood that Rohde had brought in, and rebuilt the fire.

Rohde came in, stamping the snow from his boots. "I have selected a tunnel for O'Hara," he said. "If the enemy force the bridge then O'Hara must come up here; I think the camp is indefensible."

Forester nodded. "I didn't think much of it myself," he said, remembering how they had "assaulted" the empty camp on the way down the mountain.

"Most of the tunnels drive straight into the mountain," said Rohde. "But there is one which has a sharp bend about fifty metres from the entrance. It will give protection against rifle fire."

"Let's have a look at it," said Forester.

Rohde led the way to the cliff face behind the huts and pointed out the tunnels. There were six of them driven into the base of the cliff. "That is the one," he said.

Forester investigated. It was a little over ten feet high and not much wider, just a hole blasted into the hard rock of the mountainside. He walked inside, finding it deepening from gloom to darkness the farther he went. He put his hands before him and found the side wall. As Rohde had said, it bent to the left sharply and, looking back, he saw that the welcome blue sky at the entrance was out of sight.

He went no farther, but turned around and walked back until he saw the bulk of Rohde outlined against the entrance. He was surprised at the relief he felt on coming out into the daylight, and said, "Not much of a home from home—it gives me the creeps."

"Perhaps that is because men have died there."

"Died?"

"Too many men,". said Rohde. "The government closed the mine—that was when Señor Aguillar was President."

"I'm surprised that Lopez didn't try to coin some money out of it," commented Forester.

Rohde shrugged. "It would have cost a lot of money to put back into operation. It was uneconomical when it ran—just an experiment in high-altitude mining. I think it would have closed anyway."

Forester looked around. "When O'Hara comes up here he'll be in a hell of a hurry. What about building him a wall at the entrance here? We can leave a note in the hut telling him which tunnel to take."

"That is well thought," said Rohde. "There are many rocks about."

"Three will do better than two," said Forester. "I'll roust out Peabody." He went back to the hut and found Peabody still in the same corner gazing blankly at the wall. "Come on, buster," Forester commanded. "Rise and shine; we've got a job of work on hand."

Peabody's eyelid twitched. "Leave me alone," he said thickly.

Forester stooped, grasped Peabody by the lapels and hauled

119

him to his feet. "Now, listen, you crummy bastard; I told you that you'd have to take orders and that you'd have to jump to it. I've got a lower boiling-point than Rohde, so you'd better watch it."

Peabody began to beat at him ineffectually and Forester shoved and slammed him against the wall. "I'm sick," gasped Peabody. "I can't breathe."

"You can walk and you can carry rocks," said Forester callously. "Whether you breathe or not while you do it is immaterial. Personally, I'll be goddam glad when you *do* stop breathing. Now, are you going to leave this hut on your own two feet or do I kick you out?"

Muttering obscenities Peabody staggered to the door. Forester followed him to the tunnel and told him to start gathering rocks and then he pitched to with a will. It was hard physical labour and he had to stop and rest frequently, but he made sure that Peabody kept at it, driving him unmercifully.

They carried the rocks to the tunnel entrance, where Rohde built a rough wall. When they had to stop because of encroaching darkness, they had built little more than a breastwork. Forester sagged to the ground and looked at it through swimming eyes. "It's not much, but it will have to do." He beat his arms against his body. "God, but it's cold."

"We will go back to the hut," said Rohde. "There is nothing more we can do here."

So they went back to the hut, relit the fire and prepared a meal of canned stew. Again, Peabody would not eat, but Rohde and Forester forced themselves, choking over the succulent meat and the rich gravy. Then they turned in for the night.

II

Oddly enough, Forester was not very tired when he got up at dawn and his breathing was much easier. He thought— if we could spend another day here it would be much better. I could look forward to the pass with confidence. Then he rejected the thought—there was no more time.

In the dim light he saw Rohde wrapping strips of blanket puttee-fashion around his legs and silently he began to do the same. Neither of them felt like talking. Once that was done he went across to the huddle in the corner and stirred Peabody gently with his foot.

"Lemme alone," mumbled Peabody indistinctly.

Forester sighed and dropped the tip of his boot into Peabody's ribs. That did the trick. Peabody sat up cursing and Forester turned away without saying anything.

"It seems all right," said Rohde from the doorway. He was staring up at the mountains.

Forester caught a note of doubt in his voice and went to join him. It was a clear crystal dawn and the peaks, caught by the rising sun, stood out brilliantly against the dark sky behind. Forester said, "Anything wrong?"

"It is very clear," said Rohde. Again there was a shadow of doubt in his voice. "Perhaps too clear."

"Which way do we go?" asked Forester.

Rohde pointed. "Beyond that mountain is the pass. We go round the base of the peak and then over the pass and down the other side. It is this side which will be difficult—the other side is nothing."

The mountain Rohde had indicated seemed so close in the clear morning air that Forester felt that he could put out his hand and touch it. He sighed with relief. "It doesn't look too bad."

Rohde snorted. "It will be worse than you ever dreamed," he said and turned away. "We must eat again."

Peabody refused food again and Forester, after a significant glance from Rohde, said, "You'll eat even if I have to cram the stuff down your gullet. I've stood enough nonsense from you, Peabody; you're not going to louse this up by passing out through lack of food. But I warn you, if you do—if you hold us up for as little as one minute—we'll leave you."

Peabody looked at him with venom but took the warmed-up can and began to eat with difficulty. Forester said, "How are your boots?"

"Okay, I guess," said Peabody ungraciously.

"Don't guess," said Forester sharply. "I don't care if they pinch your toes off and cut your feet to pieces—I don't care if they raise blisters as big as golf balls—I don't care as far as you're concerned. But I am concerned about you holding us up. If those boots don't fit properly, say so now."

"They're all right," said Peabody. "They fit all right."

Rohde said, "We must go. Get your packs on."

Forester picked up the suitcase and fastened the straps

121

about his body. He padded the side of the case with the blanket material of his old pack so that it fitted snugly against his back, and he felt very pleased with his ingenuity.

Rohde took the primitive ice-axe and stuck the short axe from the Dakota into his belt. He eased the pack on his back so that it rested comfortably and looked pointedly at Peabody, who scrambled over to the corner where his pack lay. As he did so, something dropped with a clatter to the floor.

It was O'Hara's flask.

Forester stooped and picked it up, then fixed Peabody with a cold stare. "So you're a goddam thief, too."

"I'm not," yelled Peabody. "O'Hara gave it to me."

"O'Hara wouldn't give you the time of day," snarled Forester. He shook the flask and found it empty. "You little shit," he shouted, and hurled the flask at Peabody. Peabody ducked, but was too late and the flask hit him over the right eye.

Rohde thumped the butt of the ice-axe on the floor. "Enough," he commanded. "This man cannot come with us—we cannot trust him."

Peabody looked at him in horror, his hand dabbing at his forehead. "But you gotta take me," he whispered. "You gotta. You can't leave me to those bastards down the mountain."

Rohde's lips tightened implacably and Peabody whimpered. Forester took a deep breath and said, "If we leave him here he'll only go back to O'Hara; and he's sure to ball things up down there."

"I don't like it," said Rohde. "He is likely to kill us on the mountain."

Forester felt the weight of the gun in his pocket and came to a decision. "You're coming with us, Peabody," he said harshly. "But one more fast move and you're a dead duck." He turned to Rohde. "He won't hold us up—not for one minute, I promise you." He looked Rohde in the eye and Rohde nodded with understanding.

"Get your pack on, Peabody," said Forester. "And get out of that door on the double."

Peabody lurched away from the wall and seemed to cringe as he picked up his pack. He scuttled across the hut, running wide of Forester, and bolted through the door. Forester pulled a scrap of paper and a pencil from his pocket. "I'll leave a note for Tim, telling him of the right tunnel. Then we'll go."

It was comparatively easy at first, at least to Forester's later recollection. Although they had left the road and were striking across the mountainside, they made good time. Rohde was in the lead with Peabody following and Forester at the rear, ready to flail Peabody if he lagged. But to begin with there was no need for that; Peabody walked as though he had the devil at his heels.

At first the snow was shallow, dry and powdery, but then it began to get deeper, with a hard crust on top. It was then that Rohde stopped. "We must use the ropes."

They got out their pitiful lengths of rotten rope and Rohde carefully tested every knot. Then they tied themselves together, still in the same order, and carried on. Forester looked up at the steep white slope which seemed to stretch unendingly to the sky and thought that Rohde had been right—this wasn't going to be easy.

They plodded on, Rohde as trailbreaker and the other two thankful that he had broken a path for them in the thickening snow. The slope they were crossing was steep and swept dizzyingly below them and Forester found himself wondering what would happen if one of them fell. It was likely that he would drag down the other two and they would all slide, a tangled string of men and ropes, down the thousands of feet to the sharp rocks below.

Then he shook himself irritably. It wouldn't be like that at all. That was the reason for the ropes, so that a man's fall could be arrested.

From ahead he heard a rumble like thunder and Rohde paused. "What is it?" shouted Forester.

"Avalanche," replied Rohde. He said no more and resumed his even pace.

My God, thought Forester; I hadn't thought of avalanches. This could be goddam dangerous. Then he laughed to himself. He was in no more danger than O'Hara and the others down by the bridge—possibly less. His mind played about with the relativity of things and presently he was not thinking at all, just putting one foot in front of the other with mindless precision, an automaton toiling across the vast white expanse of snow like an ant crawling across a bed sheet.

He was jolted into consciousness by stumbling over Peabody, who lay sprawled in the snow, panting stertorously, his mouth opening and closing like a goldfish. "Get up, Peabody," he mumbled. "I told you what would happen if you held us up. Get up, damn you."

"Rohde's . . . Rohde's stopped," panted Peabody.

Forester looked up and squinted against a vast dazzle. Specks danced in front of his eyes and coalesced into a vague shape moving towards him. "I am sorry," said Rohde, unexpectedly closely. "I am a fool. I forgot this."

Forester rubbed his eyes. I'm going blind, he thought in an access of terror; I'm losing my sight.

"Relax," said Rohde. "Close your eyes; rest them."

Forester sank into the snow and closed his eyes. It felt as though there were hundreds of grains of sand beneath the lids and he felt the cold touch of tears on his cheeks. "What is it?" he asked.

"Ice glare," said Rohde. "Don't worry; it will be all right. Just keep your eyes closed for a few minutes."

He kept his eyes closed and gradually felt his muscles lose tension and he was grateful for this pause. He felt tired—more tired than he had ever felt in his life—and he wondered how far they had come. "How far have we come?" he asked.

"Not far," said Rohde.

"What time is it?"

There was a pause, then Rohde said, "Nine o'clock."

Forester was shocked. "Is that all?" He felt as though he had been walking all day.

"I'm going to rub something on your eyes," said Rohde, and Forester felt cold fingers massaging his eyelids with a substance at once soft and gritty.

"What is it, Miguel?"

"Wood ash. It is black—it will cut the glare, I think. I have heard it is an old Eskimo practice; I hope it will work."

After a while Forester ventured to open his eyes. To his relief he could see, not as well as he could normally, but he was not as blind as during that first shocking moment when he thought he had lost his sight. He looked over to where Rohde was ministering to Peabody and thought—yes, that's another thing mountaineers have—dark glasses. He blinked painfully.

Rohde turned and Forester burst out laughing at the sight of him. He had a broad, black streak across his eyes and looked like a Red Indian painted to go on the warpath.

Rohde smiled. "You too look funny, Ray," he said. Then more soberly, "Wrap a blanket round your head like a hood, so that it cuts out some of the glare from the side." Forester unfastened his pack and regretfully tore out the blanket from the side of the case. His pack would not be so comfortable from now on. The blanket provided enough material to make hoods for the three of them, and then Rohde said, "We must go on."

Forester looked back. He could still see the huts and estimated that they had not gained more than five hundred feet of altitude although they had come a considerable distance. Then the rope tugged at his waist and he stepped out, following the stumbling figure of Peabody.

It was midday when they rounded the shoulder of the mountain and were able to see their way to the pass. Forester sank to his knees and sobbed with exhaustion and Peabody dropped in his tracks as though knocked on the head. Only Rohde remained on his feet, staring up towards the pass, squinting with sore eyes. "It is as I remembered it," he said. "We will rest here."

Ignoring Peabody, he squatted beside Forester. "Are you all right?"

"I'm a bit bushed," said Forester, "but a rest will make a lot of difference."

Rohde took off his pack and unfastened it. "We will eat now."

"My God, I couldn't," said Forester.

"You will be able to stomach this," said Rohde, and produced a can of fruit. "It is sweet for energy."

There was a cold wind sweeping across the mountainside and Forester pulled the jacket round him as he watched Rohde dig into the snow. "What are you doing?"

"Making a wind break." He took a Primus stove and put it into the hole he had dug where it was sheltered from the wind. He lit it, then handed an empty bean can to Forester. "Fill that with snow and melt it; we must drink something hot. I will see to Peabody."

At the low atmospheric pressure the snow took a long time to melt and the resulting water was merely tepid. Rohde dropped a bouillon cube into it, and said, "You first."

Forester gagged as he drank it, and then filled the can with snow again. Peabody had revived and took the next canful, then Forester melted more snow for Rohde. "I haven't looked up the pass," he said. "What's it like?"

Rohde looked up from the can of fruit he was opening. "Bad," he said. "But I expected that." He paused. "There is a glacier with many crevasses."

Forester took the proffered can silently and began to eat. He found the fruit acceptable to his taste and his stomach—it was the first food he had enjoyed since the plane crash and it put new life into him. He looked back; the mine was out of sight, but far away he could see the river gorge, many thousands of feet below. He could not see the bridge.

He got to his feet and trudged forward to where he could see the pass. Immediately below was the glacier, a jumble of ice blocks and a maze of crevasses. It ended perhaps three thousand feet lower and he could see the blue waters of a mountain lake. As he looked he heard a whip-crack as of a stroke of lightning and the mutter of distant thunder and saw a plume of white leap up from the blue of the lake.

Rohde spoke from behind him. "That is a *laguna*," he said. "The glaciers are slowly retreating here and there is always a lake between the glacier and the moraine. But that is of no interest to us; we must go there." He pointed across the glacier and swept his arm upwards.

Across the valley of the pass white smoke appeared suddenly on the mountainside and a good ten seconds afterwards came a low rumble. "There is always movement in the mountains," said Rohde. "The ice works on the rock and there are many avalanches."

Forester looked up. "How much higher do we have to climb?"

"About five hundred metres—but first we must go down a little to cross the glacier."

"I don't suppose we could go round it," said Forester.

Rohde pointed downwards towards the lake. "We would lose a thousand metres of altitude and that would mean another night on the mountain. Two nights up here would kill us."

Forester regarded the glacier with distaste; he did not like what he saw and for the first time a cold knot of fear formed in his belly. So far there had been nothing but exhausting work, the labour of pushing through thick snow in bad and unaccustomed conditions. But here he was confronted with danger itself—the danger of the toppling ice block warmed to the point of insecurity by the sun, the trap of the snow-covered crevasse. Even as he watched he saw a movement on the glacier, a sudden alteration of the scene, and he heard a dull rumble.

Rohde said, "We will go now."

They went back to get their packs. Peabody was sitting in the snow, gazing apathetically at his hands folded in his lap. Forester said, "Come on, man; get your pack on," but Peabody did not stir. Forester sighed regretfully and kicked him in the side, not too violently. Peabody seemed to react only to physical stimuli, to threats of violence.

Obediently he got up and put on his pack and Rohde refastened the rope about him, careful to see that all was secure. Then they went on in the same order. First the more experienced Rohde, then Peabody, and finally Forester.

The climb down to the glacier—a matter of about two hundred feet—was a nightmare to Forester, although it did not seem to trouble Rohde and Peabody was lost in the daze of his own devising and was oblivious of the danger. Here the rock was bare of snow, blown clean by the strong wind which swept down the pass. But it was rotten and covered with a slick layer of ice, so that any movement at all was dangerous. Forester cursed as his feet slithered on the ice; we should have spikes, he thought; this is madness.

It took an hour to descend to the glacier, the last forty feet by what Rohde called an *abseil*. There was a vertical ice-covered cliff and Rohde showed them what to do. He hammered four of their makeshift pitons into the rotten rock and looped the rope through them. They went down in reverse order, Forester first, with Rohde belaying the rope. He showed Forester how to loop the rope round his body so that he was almost sitting in it, and how to check his descent if he went too fast.

"Try to keep facing the cliff," he said. "Then you can use your feet to keep clear—and try not to get into a spin."

Forester was heartily glad when he reached the bottom—this was not his idea of fun. He made up his mind that he would spend his next vacation as far from mountains as he could, preferably in the middle of Kansas.

Then Peabody came down, mechanically following Rohde's instructions. He had no trace of fear about him—his face was as blank as his mind and all fear had been drained out of him long before, together with everything else. He was an automaton who did precisely what he was told.

Rohde came last with no one to guard the rope above him. He dropped heavily the last ten feet as the pitons gave way one after the other in rapid succession and the rope dropped in coils about his prostrate body. Forester helped him to his feet. "Are you okay?"

Rohde swayed. "I'm all right," he gasped. "The pitons —find the pitons."

Forester searched about in the snow and found three of the pitons; he could not find the fourth. Rohde smiled grimly. "It is as well I fell," he said. "Otherwise we would have had to leave the pitons up there, and I think we will need them later. But we must keep clear of rock; the *verglas*—the ice on the rock—is too much for us without crampons."

Forester agreed with him from the bottom of his heart, although he did not say so aloud. He recoiled the rope and made one end fast about his waist while Rohde attended to Peabody. Then he looked at the glacier.

It was as fantastic as a lunar landscape—and as dead and removed from humanity. The pressures from below had squeezed up great masses of ice which the wind and the sun had carved into grotesque shapes, all now mantled with thick snow. There were great cliffs with dangerous overhanging columns which threatened to topple, and there were crevasses, some open to the sky and some, as Forester knew, treacherously covered with snow. Through this wilderness, this maze of ice, they had to find their way.

Forester said, "How far to the other side?"

Rohde reflected. "Three-quarters of one of your North American miles." He took the ice-axe firmly in his hand. "Let us move—time is going fast."

He led the way, testing every foot with the butt of the ice-axe. Forester noticed that he had shortened the intervals between the members of the party and had doubled the ropes, and he did not like the implication. The three of them were now quite close together and Rohde kept urging Peabody to move faster as he felt the drag on the rope when Peabody lagged. Forester stooped and picked up some snow; it was powdery and did not make a good snowball, but every time Peabody dragged on Rohde's rope he pelted him with snow.

The way was tortuous and more than once Rohde led them into a dead end, the way blocked by vertical ice walls or wide crevasses, and they would have to retrace their steps and hunt for a better way. Once, when they were seemingly entrapped in a maze of ice passages, Forester totally lost his sense of direction and wondered hopelessly if they would be condemned to wander for ever in this cold hell.

His feet were numb and he had no feeling in his toes. He
128

mentioned this to Rohde, who stopped immediately. " Sit down," he said. " Take off your boots."

Forester stripped the puttees from his legs and tried to untie his boot-laces with stiff fingers. It took him nearly fifteen minutes to complete this simple task. The laces were stiffened with ice, his fingers were cold, and his mind did not seem able to control the actions of his body. At last he got his boots off and stripped off the two pairs of socks he wore.

Rohde closely examined his toes and said, " You have the beginning of frost-bite. Rub your left foot—I'll rub the right."

Forester rubbed away violently. His big toe was bone-white at the tip and had a complete lack of sensation. Rohde was merciless in his rubbing; he ignored Forester's yelp of anguish as the circulation returned to his foot and continued to massage with vigorous movements.

Forester's feet seemed to be on fire as the blood forced its way into the frozen flesh and he moaned with the pain. Rohde said sternly, " You must not let this happen. You must work your toes all the time—imagine you are playing a piano with your feet—your toes. Let me see your fingers."

Forester held out his hands and Rohde inspected them. " All right," he said. " But you must watch for this. Your toes, your fingers and the tips of your ears and the nose. Keep rubbing them." He turned to where Peabody was sitting slackly. " And what about him?"

With difficulty Forester thrust his feet into his frozen boots, retied the laces and wrapped the puttees round his legs. Then he helped Rohde to take off Peabody's boots. Handling him was like handling a dummy—he neither hindered nor helped, letting his limbs be moved flaccidly.

His toes were badly frostbitten and they began to massage his feet. After working on him for ten minutes he suddenly moaned and Forester looked up to see a glimmer of intelligence steal into the dead eyes. " Hell!" Peabody protested. " You're hurting me."

They took no notice of him and continued to work away. Suddenly Peabody screamed and began to thrash about, and Forester grabbed his arms. " Be sensible, man," he shouted. He looked up at Peabody. " Keep moving your toes. Move them all the time in your boots."

Peabody was moaning with pain but it seemed to have the effect of bringing him out of his private dream. He was able to put on his own socks and boots and wrap the puttees round his legs, and all the time he swore in a dull monotone, uttering a string of obscenities directed against the mountains, against Rohde and Forester for being uncaring brutes, and against the fates in general for having got him into this mess.

Forester looked across at Rohde and grinned faintly, and Rohde picked up the ice-axe and said, " We must move—we must get out of here."

Somewhere in the middle of the glacier Rohde, after casting fruitlessly in several directions, led them to a crevasse and said, " Here we must cross—there is no other way."

There was a snow bridge across the crevasse, a frail span connecting the two sides. Forester went to the edge and looked down into the dim green depths. He could not see the bottom.

Rohde said, " The snow will bear our weight if we go over lying flat so that the weight is spread." He tapped Forester on the shoulder. " You go first."

Peabody said suddenly, " I'm not going across there. You think I'm crazy?"

Forester had intended to say the same but the fact that a man like Peabody had said it put some spirit into him. He said harshly—and the harshness was directed at himself for his moment of weakness—" Do as you're damn well told."

Rohde re-roped them so that the line would be long enough to stretch across the crevasse, which was about fifteen feet wide, and Forester approached cautiously. " Not on hands and knees," said Rohde. " Lie flat and wriggle across with your arms and legs spread out."

With trepidation Forester lay down by the edge of the crevasse and wriggled forward on to the bridge. It was only six feet wide and, as he went forward on his belly in the way he had been taught during his army training, he saw the snow crumble from the edge of the bridge to fall with a soft sigh into the abyss.

He was very thankful for the rope which trailed behind him, even though he knew it was probably not strong enough to withstand a sudden jerk, and it was with deep thankfulness that he gained the other side to lie gasping in the snow, beads of sweat trickling into his eyes.

After a long moment he stood up and turned. " Are you all right?" asked Rohde.

" I'm fine," he said, and wiped the sweat from his forehead before it froze.

"To hell with this," shouted Peabody. "You're not going to get me on that thing."

"You'll be roped from both sides," said Forester. "You can't possibly fall—isn't that right, Miguel?"

"That is so," said Rohde.

Peabody had a hunted look about him. Forester said, "Oh, to hell with him. Come across, Miguel, and leave the stupid bastard."

Peabody's voice cracked. "You can't leave me *here*," he screamed.

"Can't we?" asked Forester callously. "I told you what would happen if you held us up."

"Oh, Jesus!" said Peabody tearfully, and approached the snow bridge slowly.

"Get down," said Rohde abruptly.

"On your belly," called Forester.

Peabody lay down and began to inch his way across. He was shaking violently and twice he stopped as he heard snow swish into the crevasse from the crumbling edge of the bridge. As he approached Forester he began to wriggle along faster and Forester became intent on keeping the rope taut, as did Rohde, paying out as Peabody moved away from him.

Suddenly Peabody lost his nerve and got up on to his hands and knees and scrambled towards the end of the bridge. "Get down, you goddam fool," Forester yelled.

Suddenly he was enveloped in a cloud of snow dust and Peabody cannoned into him, knocking him flat. There was a roar as the bridge collapsed into the crevasse in a series of diminishing echoes, and when Forester got to his feet he looked across through the swirling fog of powdery snow and saw Rohde standing helplessly on the other side.

He turned and grabbed Peabody, who was clutching at the snow in an ecstasy of delight at being on firm ground. Hauling him to his feet, Forester hit him with his open palm in a vicious double slap across the face. "You selfish bastard," he shouted. "Can't you ever do anything right?"

Peabody's head lolled on his shoulders and there was a vacant look in his eyes. When Forester let him go he dropped to the ground, muttering incomprehensibly, and grovelled at Forester's feet. Forester kicked him for good measure and turned to Rohde. "What the hell do we do now?"

Rohde seemed unperturbed. He hefted the ice-axe like a spar and said, "Stand aside." Then he threw it and it stuck into the snow in front of Forester. "I think I can swing across," he said. "Hammer the axe into the snow as deep as you can."

Forester felt the rope at his waist. "This stuff isn't too strong, you know. It won't bear much weight."

Rohde measured the gap with his eye. "I think there is enough to make a triple strand," he said. "That should take my weight."

"It's your neck," said Forester, and began to beat the ice-axe into the snow. But he knew that *all* their lives were at stake. He did not have the experience to make the rest of the trip alone—his chances were still less if he was hampered by Peabody. He doubted if he could find his way out of the glacier safely.

He hammered the axe into the snow and ice for three-quarters of its length and tugged at it to make sure it was firm. Then he turned to Peabody, who was sobbing and drooling into the snow and stripped the rope from him. He tossed the ends across to Rohde who tied them round his waist and sat on the edge of the crevasse, looking into the depths between his knees and appearing as unconcerned as though he was sitting in an arm-chair.

Forester fastened the triple rope to the ice-axe and belayed a loop around his body, kicking grooves in the snow for his heels. "I've taken as much of the strain as I can," he called.

Rohde tugged on the taut rope experimentally, and seemed satisfied. He paused. "Put something between the rope and the edge to stop any chafing." So Forester stripped off his hood and wadded it into a pad, jamming it between the rope and the icy edge of the crevasse.

Rohde tugged again and measured his probable point of impact fifteen feet down on the farther wall of the crevasse.

Then he launched himself into space.

Forester saw him disappear and felt the sudden strain on the rope, then heard the clash of Rohde's boots on the ice wall beneath. Thankfully he saw that there was no sudden easing of the tension on the rope and knew that Rohde had made it. All that remained now was for him to climb up.

It seemed an age before Rohde's head appeared above the edge and Forester went forward to haul him up. This is one hell of a man, he thought; this is one hell of a good joe. Rohde sat down not far from the edge and wiped the sweat from his face. "That was not a good thing to do," he said.

Forester cocked his head at Peabody. "What do we do about him? He'll kill us all yet." He took the gun from his pocket and Rohde's eyes widened. "I think this is the end of the trail for Peabody."

Peabody lay in the snow muttering to himself and Forester spoke as though he were not there, and it is doubtful if Peabody heard what was being said about him.

Rohde looked Forester in the eye. "Can you shoot a defenceless man—even him?"

"You're damned right I can," snapped Forester. "We don't have only our own lives to think of—there are the others down at the bridge depending on us; this crazy fool will let us all down."

He lifted the pistol and aimed at the back of Peabody's head. He was just taking up the slack on the trigger when his wrist was caught by Rohde. "No, Ray; you are not a murderer."

Forester tensed the muscles of his arm and fought Rohde's grip for a moment, then relaxed, and said, "Okay, Miguel; but you'll see I'm right. He's selfish and he'll never do anything right—but I guess we're stuck with him."


IV


Altogether it took them three hours to cross the glacier and by then Forester was exhausted, but Rohde would allow no rest. "We must get as high as we can while there is still light," he said. "To-night will weaken us very much—it is not good to spend a night in the open without a tent or the right kind of clothing."

Forester managed a grin. Everything to Rohde was either *good* or *not good*; black and white with no shades of grey. He kicked Peabody to his feet and said tiredly, "Okay; lead on, MacDuff."

Rohde looked up at the pass. "We lost height in crossing the glacier; we still have to ascend between five and six hundred metres to get to the top."

Sixteen hundred to two thousand feet, Forester translated silently. He followed Rohde's gaze. To their left was the glacier, oozing imperceptibly down the mountain and scraping

133

itself by a rock wall. Above, the clean sweep of snow was broken by a line of cliffs half way up to the top of the pass. "Do we have to climb *that*?" he demanded.

Rohde scrutinised the terrain carefully, then shook his head. "I think we can go by the cliffs there—on the extreme right. That will bring us on top of the cliffs. We will bivouac there to-night."

He put his hand in his pocket and produced the small leather bag of coca quids he had compounded back in the camp. "Hold out your hand," he said. "You will need these now."

He shook a dozen of the green squares into Forester's palm and Forester put one into his mouth and chewed it. It had an acrid and pungent taste which pleasantly warmed the inside of his mouth. "Not too many," warned Rohde. "Or your mouth will become inflamed."

It was useless giving them to Peabody. He had relapsed into his state of automatism and followed Rohde like a dog on a lead, obedient to the tugs on the rope. As Rohde set out on the long climb up to the cliffs he followed, mechanically going through the proper climbing movements as though guided by something outside himself. Forester, watching him from behind, hoped there would be no crisis; as long as things went well Peabody would be all right, but in an emergency he would certainly break, as O'Hara had prophesied.

He did not remember much of that long and toilsome climb. Perhaps the coca contributed to that, for he found himself in much the same state as he imagined Peabody to be in. Rhythmically chewing the quid, he climbed automatically, following the trail broken by the indefatigable Rohde.

At first the snow was thick and crusted, and then, as they approached the extreme right of the line of cliffs, the slope steepened and the snow cover became thinner and they found that under it was a sheet of ice. Climbing in these conditions without crampons was difficult, and, as Rohde confessed a little time afterwards, would have been considered impossible by anyone who knew the mountains.

It took them two hours to get above the rock cliffs and to meet a great disappointment. Above the cliffs and set a few feet back was a continuous ice wall over twenty feet high, surmounted by an overhanging snow cornice. The wall stretched across the width of the pass in an unbroken line.

Forester, gasping for breath in the thin air, looked at it in dismay. We've had it, he thought; how can we get over this? But Rohde, gazing across the pass, did not lose hope. He pointed. "I think the ice wall is lower there in the middle. Come, but stay away from the edge of the cliff."

They started out along the ledge between the ice wall and the edge of the cliff. At first the ledge was narrow, only a matter of feet, but as they went on it became broader and Rohde advanced more confidently and faster. But he seemed worried. "We cannot stay here," he said. "It is very dangerous. We must get above this wall before nightfall."

"What's the hurry?" asked Forester. "If we stay here, the wall will shelter us from the wind—it's from the west and I think it's rising."

"It is," replied Rohde. He pointed upwards. "That is what I worry about—the cornice. We cannot stay below it —it might break away—and the wind in the west will build it to breaking-point. It is going to snow—look down."

Forester looked into the dizzying depths below the cliffs and saw a gathering greyness of mist. He shivered and retreated to safety, then followed the shambling figure of Peabody.

It was not five minutes later when he felt his feet suddenly slide on the ice. Frantically he tried to recover his balance but to no effect, and he found himself on his back, swooping towards the edge of the cliff. He tried to brake himself with his hands and momentarily saw the smear of blood on the ice as, with a despairing cry, he went over the edge.

Rohde, hearing the cry and feeling the tug of Peabody on the rope, automatically dug the ice-axe firmly into the ice and took the strain. When he turned his head he saw only Peabody scrabbling at the edge of the cliff, desperately trying to prevent himself from being pulled off. He was screaming incoherently, and of Forester there was no sign.

Forester found the world wheeling crazily before his eyes, first a vast expanse of sky and a sudden vista of valleys and mountains half obscured by wreaths of mist, then the grey rock close by as he spun and dangled on the end of the rope, suspended over a sheer drop of three hundred feet on the steep snow slopes beneath. His chest hurt and he found that the rope had worked itself under his armpits and was constricting his ribs. From above he heard the terrified yammerings of Peabody.

With a heave Rohde cracked the muscles of his back and hoped the rotten rope would not break. He yelled to Peabody, "Pull on the rope—get him up." Instead he saw the flash of

135

steel and saw that Peabody had a clasp-knife and was sawing at the rope where it went over the edge of the cliff.

Rohde did not hesitate. His hand went to his side and found the small axe they had taken from the Dakota. He drew it from his belt, reversing it quickly so that he held it by the handle. He lifted it, poised, for a second, judging his aim, and then hurled it at Peabody's head.

It struck Peabody squarely on the nape of the neck, splitting his skull. The terrified yelping stopped and from below Forester was aware of the startling silence and looked up. A knife dropped over the edge of the cliff and the blade cut a gash in his cheek before it went spinning into the abyss below, and a steady drip of blood rained on him from above.

## Chapter VI

O'Hara had lost his flask.

He thought that perhaps he had left it in the pocket of the leather jacket he had given Forester, but then he remembered going through the pockets first. He looked about the shelter, trying not to draw attention to himself, but still could not find it and decided that it must be up at the camp.

The loss worried him unreasonably. To have a full flask at his side had comforted him; he knew that whenever he wanted a drink then it was there ready to hand, and because it was there he had been able, in some odd way, to resist the temptation. But now he felt an aching longing in the centre of his being for a drink, for the blessed relief of alcohol and the oblivion it would bring.

It made him very short-tempered.

The night had been quiet. Since the abortive attempt to burn the bridge the previous evening, nothing had happened. Now, in the dawn light, he was wondering whether it would be safe to bring down the trebuchet. His resources in manpower were slender and to bring the trebuchet from the camp would leave the bridge virtually defenceless. True, the enemy was quiet, but that was no guarantee of future inactivity. He had no means of telling how long it would take them to obtain more timber and to transport it.

It was the common dilemma of the military man—trying to guess what the enemy was doing on the other side of the hill and balancing guesses against resources.

He heard the clatter of a stone and turned his head to find Benedetta coming towards him. He waved her back and slid down from his observation post. "Jenny has made coffee," she said. "I will keep watch. Has anything happened?"

He shook his head. "Everything's quiet. They're still there, of course; if you stick your neck out you'll get your head blown off—so be careful." He paused; he badly needed to discuss his problems with someone else, not to shrug off responsibility but to clarify the situation in his own mind. He missed Forester.

He told Benedetta what he was thinking and she said immediately, "But, of course, I will come up to the camp."

"I might have known," he said unreasonably. "You won't be separated from your precious uncle."

"It is not like that," she said sharply. "All you men are needed to bring down this machine, but what good can Jenny *and* I do down here? If we are attacked we can only run; and it does not take two to watch. Four can bring the machine from the camp quicker than three—even though one of them *is* a woman. If the enemy attacks in force Jenny will warn us."

He said slowly, "We'll have to take the risk, of course; we've got no choice. And the sooner we move the better."

"Send Jenny down quickly," said Benedetta. "I'll wait for you at the pond."

O'Hara went up to the shelter and was glad of the mug of steaming coffee that was thrust into his hands. In between gulps he rapidly detailed his plan and ended by saying, "It puts a great deal on your shoulders, Jenny. I'm sorry about that."

"I'll be all right," she said quietly.

"You can have two shots—no more," he said. "We'll leave both bows cocked for you. If they start to work on the bridge, fire two bolts and then get up to the camp as fast as you can. With luck, the shots will slow them down enough for us to get back in time to fight them off. And for God's sake don't fire them both from the same place. They're getting smart over there and they have all our favourite posts spotted."

He surveyed the small group. "Any questions?"

Aguillar stirred. "So I am to return to the camp. I feel I am a drag on you; so far I have done nothing—nothing."

137

"God in heaven!" exclaimed O'Hara. "You're our king-pin—you're the reason for all this. If we let them get you we'll have fought for nothing."

Aguillar smiled slowly. "You know as well as I do that I do not matter any more. True, it is me they want, but they cannot let you live as well. Did not Doctor Armstrong point out that very fact?"

Armstrong removed his pipe from his mouth. "That might be so, but you're in no condition to fight," he said bluntly. "And while you're down here you are taking O'Hara's mind off his job. You'd be better out of the way up at the camp where you can do something constructive, like making new bolts."

Aguillar bent his head. "I stand corrected and rightly so. I am sorry, Señor O'Hara, for making more trouble than I need."

"That's all right," said O'Hara awkwardly. He felt sorry for Aguillar; the man had courage, but courage was not enough—or perhaps it was not the right kind of courage. Intellectual bravery was all very well in its place.

It was nearer three hours than two before they arrived at the camp, the slowness being caused by Aguillar's physical weakness, and O'Hara was fretting about what could have happened at the bridge. At least he had heard no rifle fire, but the wind was blowing away from the mountains and he doubted if he would have heard it anyway. This added to his tension.

Willis met them. "Did Forester and Rohde get away all right—and our good friend Peabody?" asked O'Hara.

"They left before I awoke," said Willis. He looked up at the mountains. "They should be at the mine by now."

Armstrong circled the trebuchet, making pleasurable noises. "I say, you've done a good job here, Willis."

Willis coloured a little. "I did the best I could in the time we had—and with what we had."

"I can't see how it can possibly work," said O'Hara.

Willis smiled. "Well, it's stripped down for transport. It's more or less upside-down now; we can wheel it down the road on the axle."

Armstrong said, "I was thinking of the Russo-Finnish war; a bit out of my field, I know, but the Finns were in very much the same case as we are—dreadfully under-equipped and using their ingenuity to the utmost. I seem to remember they invented the Molotov Cocktail."

O'Hara's mind leapt immediately to the remaining drum of paraffin and to the empty bottles he had seen lying round the camp. "My God, you've done it again," he said. "Gather together all the bottles you can find."

He strode across to the hut where the paraffin was stored, and Willis called after him, "It's open—I was in there this morning."

He pushed open the door and paused as he saw the crate of liquor. Slowly he bent down and pulled out a bottle. He cradled it in his hand, then held it up to the light; the clear liquid could have been water, but he knew the deception. This was the water of Lethe which brought blessed forgetfulness, which untied the knots in his soul. His tongue crept out to lick his lips.

He heard someone approaching the hut and quickly put the bottle on a shelf, pushing it behind a box and out of sight. When Benedetta came in he was bending over the paraffin drum, unscrewing the cap.

She was laden with empty bottles. "Willis said you wanted these. What are they for?"

"We're making bombs of a sort. We'll need some strips of cloth to make wicks and stoppers; see if you can find something."

He began to fill the bottles and presently Benedetta came back with the cloth and he showed her how to stuff the necks of the bottles, leaving an easily ignitable wick. "Where are the others?" he asked.

"Willis had an idea," she said. "Armstrong and my uncle are helping him."

He filled another bottle. "Do you mind leaving your uncle up here alone?"

"What else can we do?" she asked. She bent her head. "He has always been alone. He never married, you know. And then he has known a different kind of loneliness—the loneliness of power."

"And have *you* been lonely—since . . ."

"Since my family were killed?" She looked up and there was something in her dark eyes that he could not fathom. "Yes, I have. I joined my uncle and we were two lonely people together in foreign countries." Her lip curved. "I think you are also a lonely man, Tim."

"I get along," he said shortly, and wiped his hands on a piece of rag.

She stood up. "What will you do when we leave here?"

139

"Don't you mean, *if* we leave here?" He stood too and looked down at her upraised face. " I think I'll move on; there's nothing for me in Cordillera now. Filson will never forgive me for bending one of his aeroplanes."

" Is there nothing you want to stay for?"

Her lips were parted and on impulse he bent his head and kissed her. She clung to him and after a long moment he sighed. A sudden wonder had burst upon him and he said in surprise, " Yes, I think there is something to stay for."

They stood together quietly for a few minutes, not speaking. It is in the nature of lovers to make plans, but what could they plan for? So there was nothing to say.

At last Benedetta said, " We must go, Tim. There is work to do."

He released her. " I'll see what the others are doing. You'd better throw the booze out of the liquor crate and put the paraffin bottles in it; we can strap it on to the trebuchet."

He walked out of the hut and up to the other end of the camp to see what was happening. Half way there he stopped in deep thought and cursed quietly. He had at last recognised the strange look in Benedetta's eyes. It had been compassion.

He took a deep breath, then straightened his shoulders and walked forward again, viciously kicking at a stone. He heard voices to his left and tramped over to the hillside, where he saw Willis, Armstrong and Aguillar grouped round an old cable drum.

" What's all this?" he asked abruptly.

" Insurance," said Armstrong cheerfully. " In case the enemy gets across the bridge."

Willis gave another bang with the rock he was holding and O'Hara saw he had hammered a wedge to hold the drum in position. " You know what this is," he said. " It's one of those wooden drums used to transport heavy cable—looks like a big cotton reel, doesn't it?"

It did indeed look like a cotton reel, eight feet in diameter. " Well?" said O'Hara.

" The wood is rotten, of course—it must have been standing in the open for years," said Willis. " But it's heavy and it will roll. Take a few steps down the hill and tell me what you see."

O'Hara walked down the hill and came to a steep drop, and found he was overlooking a cutting, blasted when the road was being made. Willis said from behind him, " The drum is out of sight of the road. We wait until a jeep or a truck is coming up, then we pull away the chocks and with a bit of luck we cause a smash and block the road."

O'Hara looked back at Aguillar, whose grey face told of the exertions he had made. He felt anger welling up inside him and jerked his head curtly to Willis and Armstrong. He walked out of earshot of Aguillar, then said evenly, suppressing his anger, " I think it would be a good idea if we didn't go off half-cocked on independent tracks."

Willis looked surprised and his face flushed. " But——"

O'Hara cut him short. " It's a bloody good idea, but you might have had some consultation about it. I could have helped to get the drum down into position and the old man could have filled paraffin bottles. You know he's got a heart condition, and if he drops dead on us those swine on the other side of the river have won." He tapped Willis on the chest. " And I don't intend to let that happen if I have to kill you, me and every other member of this party to get Aguillar away to safety."

Willis looked shocked. " Speak for yourself, O'Hara," he said angrily. " I'm fighting for my own life."

" Not while I'm in command, you're not. You'll bloody well obey orders and you'll consult me on everything you do."

Willis flared up. " And who put *you* in command?"

" I did," said O'Hara briefly. He stared at Willis. " Want to make an issue of it?"

" I might," said Willis tightly.

O'Hara stared him down. " You won't," he said with finality.

Willis's eyes flickered away. Armstrong said quietly, " It would be a good idea if we didn't fight among ourselves." He turned to Willis. " O'Hara is right, though; we shouldn't have let Aguillar push the drum."

" Okay, okay," said Willis impatiently. " But I don't go for this death-or-glory stuff."

" Look," said O'Hara. " You know what I think? I think I'm a dead man as I stand here right now. I don't think we've a hope in hell of stopping those communist bastards crossing the bridge; we might slow them down but we can't stop them. And once they get across they'll hunt us down and slaughter us like pigs—that's why I think I'm a dead man. It's not that I particularly like Aguillar, but the com-

141

munists want him and I'm out to stop them—that's why I'm so tender of him."

Willis had gone pale. "But what about Forester and Rohde?"

"I think they're dead too," said O'Hara coldly. "Have you any idea what it's like up there? Look, Willis; I flew men and equipment for two Yankee mountaineering expeditions and one German. And with all their modern gadgets they failed in their objectives three-quarters of the time." He waved his arm at the mountains. "Hell, half these mountains don't even have names, they're so inaccessible."

Armstrong said, "You paint a black picture, O'Hara."

"Is it a true picture?"

"I fear it is," said Armstrong ruefully.

O'Hara shook his head irritably. "This isn't doing any good. Let's get that contraption down to the bridge."


## II

It was not as difficult as O'Hara anticipated getting the trebuchet down the mountain road. Willis had done a good job in mounting it for ease of transportation and it took only three hours to get back, the main difficulty being to manœuvre the clumsy machine round the hairpin bends. At every bend he half expected to see Miss Ponsky running up to tell them that the communists had made their attack, but all was quiet and he did not even hear the crack of a rifle. Things were too quiet, he thought; maybe they were running out of ammunition—there was none of the desultory firing that had gone on the previous day.

They pushed the trebuchet off the road to the place indicated by Willis, and O'Hara said expressionlessly, "Benedetta, relieve Jenny; tell her to come up and see me."

She looked at him curiously, but he had turned away to help Willis and Armstrong dismantle the trebuchet preparatory to erecting it as a weapon. They were going to mount it on a small knoll in order to get the height, so that the heavy weight on the shorter arm could have a good fall.

Miss Ponsky came up to him and told him that everything had been quiet. He thought for a moment and then said, "Did you hear any trucks?"

"Not since they took away the jeep this morning."

He rubbed his chin. "Maybe we hit them harder than we thought. You're sure they're still there?"

"Oh, yes," she said brightly. "I had that thought myself some hours ago so I waggled something in full view." She blushed. "I put my hat on a stick—I've seen it done on old movies on TV."

He smiled. "Did they hit it?"

"No—but they came close."

"You're doing all right, Jenny."

"You must be hungry—I'll make a meal." Her lips twitched. "I think this is fun, you know." She turned and hurried up the road, leaving him standing dumbfounded. Fun!

Assembling the trebuchet took two hours and when it was completed Armstrong, begrimed but happy, said with satisfaction, "There, now; I never expected to see one of these in action." He turned to O'Hara. "Forester came upon me sketching a trebuchet for Willis; he asked if I were drawing the scales of justice and I said that I was. He must have thought me mad, but it was perceptive of him."

He closed his eyes and recited as though quoting a dictionary entry. "From the medieval Latin *trebuchetum*; old French, *trébuchet*; a pair of scales, an assay balance." He opened his eyes and pointed. "You see the resemblance?"

O'Hara did see. The trebuchet looked like a warped balance, very much out of proportion, with one arm much longer than the other. He said, "Does this thing have much of a kick—much recoil?"

"Nothing detectable; the impact is absorbed by the ground."

O'Hara looked at the crazy system of ropes and pulleys. "The question is now—will the beast work?"

There was an edge of irritability to Willis's voice. "Of course it will work. Let's chuck this thing." He pointed to a round boulder about the size of a man's head.

"All right," said O'Hara. "Let's give it a bang. What do we do?"

"First we haul like hell on this rope," said Willis.

The rope was connected, through a three-part pulley arrangement, to the end of the long arm. As O'Hara and Willis pulled, the arm came down and the shorter arm with the weight rose into the air. The weight was a big, rusty iron bucket which Willis had found and filled with stones. As the long arm came to the ground, Armstrong stepped forward and threw over a lever and a wooden block dropped over the

143

arm, holding it down. Willis picked up the boulder and placed it in the hub-cap which served as a cup.

"We're ready," he said. "I've already aligned the thing in the general direction of the bridge; we need someone down there to call the fall of the shot."

"I'll go," said O'Hara. He walked across to where Benedetta was keeping watch and slid down beside her, being careful to keep his head down. "They're going to let fly," he said.

She turned her head to look at the trebuchet. "Do you think this will work?"

"I don't know." He grimaced. "All I know is that it's a hell of a way to fight a war."

"We're ready," shouted Armstrong.

O'Hara waved and Armstrong pulled the firing lever sharply. The weight dropped and the long arm bearing the missile flipped up into the air. There was an almighty crash as the iron bucket hit the ground, but O'Hara's attention was on the rock as it arched over his head. It was in the air a long time and went very high; then it reached the top of its trajectory and started to fall to earth, gaining speed appreciably as it plummeted. It fell far on the other side of the bridge, beyond the road and the burned vehicles, into the mountainside. A plume of dust fountained from the side of the hill to mark its fall.

"Jesus!" whispered O'Hara. "The thing has range." He slipped from his place and ran back. "Thirty yards over —fifteen to the right. How heavy was that rock?"

"About thirty pounds," said Willis offhandedly. "We need a bigger one." He heaved on the trebuchet. "We'll swing her a bit to the left."

O'Hara could hear a babble of voices from across the river and there was a brief rattle of rifle fire. Or should I call it musketry? he thought, just to keep it in period. He laughed and smote Armstrong on the back. "You've done it again," he roared. "We'll pound that bridge to matchwood."

But it was not to prove as easy as he thought. It took an hour to fire the next six shots—and not one of them hit the bridge. They had two near misses and one that grazed the catenary rope on the left, making the bridge shiver from end to end. But there were no direct hits.

Curiously, too, there was no marked reaction from the enemy. A lot of running about and random shooting followed each attempt, but there was no coherent action. What could they do after all, O'Hara thought; nothing could stop the rocks once they were in flight.

"Why can't we get the range right—what the hell's the matter with this thing?" he demanded at last.

Armstrong said mildly, "I knew a trebuchet wasn't a precision weapon, in a general way, of course; but this brings it home. It does tend to scatter a bit, doesn't it?"

Willis looked worried. "There's a bit of a whip in the arm," he said. "It isn't stiff enough. Then again, we haven't a standard shot; there are variations in weight and that causes the overs and unders. It's the whip that's responsible for the variations from side to side."

"Can you do anything about the whip in the arm?"

Willis shook his head. "A steel girder would help," he said ironically.

"There must be some way of getting a standard weight of shot."

So the ingenious Willis made a rough balance which, he said, would match one rock against another to the nearest half-pound. And they started again. Four shots later, they made the best one of the afternoon.

The trebuchet crashed again and a cloud of dust rose from where the bucket smashed into the ground. The long arm came over, just like a fast bowler at cricket, thought O'Hara, and the rock soared into the sky, higher and higher. Over O'Hara's head it reached it highest point and began to fall, seeming to go true to its target. "This is it," said O'Hara urgently. "This is going to be a smash hit."

The rock dropped faster and faster under the tug of gravity and O'Hara held his breath. It dropped right between the catenary ropes of the bridge and, to O'Hara's disgust, fell plumb through the gap in the middle, sending a plume of white spray leaping from the boiling river to splash on the underside of the planking.

"God Almighty!" he howled. "A perfect shot—and in the wrong bloody place."

But he had a sudden hope that what he had said to Willis up at the camp would prove to be wrong; that he was *not* a dead man—that the enemy would *not* get over the bridge—that they all had a fighting chance. As hope surged in him a knot of tension tightened in his stomach. When he had no hope his nerves had been taut enough, but the offer of continued life made life itself seem more precious and not to be lost or thrown away—and so the tension was redoubled.

A man who considers himself dead has no fear of dying, but with hope came a trace of fear.

He went back to the trebuchet. "You're a bloody fine artillery man," he said to Willis in mock-bitter tones.

Willis bristled. "What do you mean?"

"I mean what I say—you're a bloody fine artillery man. That last shot was perfect—but the bridge wasn't there at that point. The rock went through the gap."

Willis grinned self-consciously and seemed pleased. "It looks as though we've got the range."

"Let's get at it," said O'Hara.

For the rest of the afternoon the trebuchet thumped and crashed at irregular intervals. They worked like slaves hauling on the ropes and bringing rocks to the balance. O'Hara put Miss Ponsky in charge of the balance and as the afternoon wore on they became expert at judging the weight—it was no fun to carry a forty-pound rock a matter of a couple of hundred yards, only to have it rejected by Miss Ponsky.

O'Hara kept an eye on his watch and recorded the number of shots, finding that the rate of fire had speeded up to above twelve an hour. In two and a half hours they fired twenty-six rocks and scored about seven hits; about one in four. O'Hara had seen only two of them land but what he saw convinced him that the bridge could not take that kind of pounding for long. It was a pity that the hits were scattered on the bridge —a concentration would have been better—but they had opened a new gap of two planks and several more were badly bent. It was not enough to worry a man crossing the bridge—not yet—but no one would take a chance with a vehicle.

He was delighted—as much by the fact that the enemy was helpless as by anything else. There was nothing they could do to stop the bridge being slowly pounded into fragments, short of bringing up a mortar to bombard the trebuchet. At first there had been the usual futile rifle-fire, but that soon ceased. Now there was merely a chorus of jeers from the opposite bank when a shot missed and a groan when a hit was scored.

It was half an hour from nightfall when Willis came to him and said, "We can't keep this up. The beast is taking a hell of a battering—she's shaking herself to pieces. Another two or three shots and she'll collapse."

O'Hara swore and looked at the grey man—Willis was covered in dust from head to foot. He said slowly, "I had

146

hoped to carry on through the night—I wanted to ruin the bridge beyond repair."

"We can't," said Willis flatly. "She's loosened up a lot and there's a split in the arm—it'll break off if we don't bind it up with something. If that happens the trebuchet is the pile of junk it started out as."

O'Hara felt impotent fury welling up inside him. He turned away without speaking and walked several paces before he said over his shoulder, "Can you fix it?"

"I can try," said Willis. "I think I can."

"Don't try—don't think. Fix it," said O'Hara harshly, as he walked away. He did not look back.

III

Night.

A sheath of thin mist filmed the moon, but O'Hara could still see as he picked his way among the rocks. He found a comfortable place in which to sit, his back resting against a vertical slab. In front of him was a rock shelf on which he carefully placed the bottle he carried. It reflected the misted moon deep in its white depths as though enclosing a nacreous pearl.

He looked at it for a long time.

He was tired; the strain of the last few days had told heavily on him and his sleep had been a matter of a few hours snatched here and there. But Miss Ponsky and Benedetta were now taking night watches and that eased the burden. Over by the bridge Willis and Armstrong were tinkering with the trebuchet, and O'Hara thought he should go and help them but he did not. To hell with it, he thought; let me have an hour to myself.

The enemy—the peculiarly faceless enemy—had once more brought up another jeep and the bridge was again well illuminated. They weren't taking any chances of losing the bridge by a sudden fire-burning sortie. For two days they had not made a single offensive move apart from their futile barrages of rifle-fire. They're cooking something up, he thought; and when it comes, it's going to surprise us.

He looked at the bottle thoughtfully.

Forester and Rohde would be leaving the mine for the pass at dawn and he wondered if they would make it. He had been quite honest with Willis up at the camp—he honestly did

147

not think they had a hope. It would be cold up there and they had no tent and, by the look of the sky, there was going to be a change in the weather. If they did not cross the pass —maybe even if they did—the enemy had won; the God of Battles was on their side because they had the bigger battalions.

With a deep sigh he picked up the bottle and unscrewed the cap, giving way to the lurking devils within him.


## IV


Miss Ponsky said, "You know, I'm enjoying this—really I am."

Benedetta looked up, startled. "Enjoying it!"

. "Yes, I am," said Miss Ponsky comfortably, "I never thought I'd have such an adventure."

Benedetta said carefully, "You know we might all be killed?"

"Oh, yes, child; I know that. But I know now why men go to war. It's the same reason that makes them gamble, but in war they play for the highest stake of all—their own lives. It adds a certain edge to living."

She pulled her coat closer about her and smiled. "I've been a school teacher for thirty years," she said. "And you know how folk think of spinster schoolmarms—they're supposed to be prissy and sexless and unromantic, but I was never like that. If anything I was too romantic, surely too much so for my own good. I saw life in terms of old legends and historical novels, and of course life isn't like that at all. There was a man, you know, once . . ."

Benedetta was silent, not wishing to break the thread of this curious revelation.

Miss Ponsky visibly pulled herself together. "Anyway, there I was—a very romantic young girl growing into middle age and rising a little in her profession. I became a head-mistress—a sort of dragon to a lot of children. I suppose my romanticism showed a little by what I did in my spare time; I was quite a good fencer when I was younger, and of course, later there was the archery. But I wished I could have been a man and gone away and had adventures—men are so much *freer,* you know. I had almost given up hope when this happened."

She chuckled happily. "And now here I am, rising fifty-five and engaged in a desperate adventure. Of course I know I might be killed but it's all worth it, every bit of it; it makes up for such a lot."

Benedetta looked at her sadly. What was happening threatened to destroy her uncle's hopes for their country and Miss Ponsky saw it in the light of dream-like romanticism, something from Robert Louis Stevenson to relieve the sterility of her life. She had jibbed at killing a man, but now she was blooded and would never look upon human life in the same light again. And when—or if—she went back home again, dear safe old South Bridge, Connecticut, would always seem a little unreal to her—reality would be a bleak mountainside with death coming over a bridge and a sense of quickened life as her blood coursed faster through parched veins.

Miss Ponsky said briskly, "But I mustn't run on like this. I must go down to the bridge; I promised Mr. O'Hara I would. He's such a handsome young man, isn't he? But he looks so sad sometimes."

Benedetta said in a low voice, "I think he is unhappy."

Miss Ponsky nodded wisely. "There has been a great grief in his life," she said, and Benedetta knew that she was casting O'Hara as a dark Byronic hero in the legend she was living. But he's not like that, she cried to herself; he's a man of flesh and blood, and a stupid man too, who will not allow others to help him, to share his troubles. She thought of what had happened up at the camp, of O'Hara's kisses and the way she had been stirred by them—and then of his inexplicable coldness towards her soon afterwards. If he would not share himself, she thought, perhaps such a man was not for her—but she found herself wishing she was wrong.

Miss Ponsky went out of the shelter. "It's becoming a little misty," she said. "We must watch all the more carefully."

Benedetta said, "I'll come down in two hours."

"Good," said Miss Ponsky gaily, and clattered her way down to the bridge.

Benedetta sat for a while repairing a rent in her coat with threads drawn out of the hem and using the needle which she always carried stuck in the lining of her handbag. The small domestic task finished, she thought, Tim's shirt is torn —perhaps I can mend that.

He had been glumly morose during the evening meal and had gone away immediately afterwards to the right along the mountainside, away from the bridge. She had recognised

149

that he had something on his mind and had not interrupted, but had marked the way he had gone. Now she got up and stepped out of the shelter.

She came upon him suddenly from behind after being guided by the clink of glass against stone. He was sitting gazing at the moon, the bottle in his hand, and was quietly humming a tune she did not know. The bottle was half-empty.

He turned as she stepped forward out of the shadows and held out the bottle. "Have a drink; it's good for what ails you." His voice was slurred and furry.

"No, thank you, Tim." She stepped down and sat beside him. "You have a tear in your shirt—I'll mend it if you come back to the shelter."

"Ah, the little woman. Domesticity in a cave." He laughed humourlessly.

She indicated the bottle. "Do you think this is good—at this time?"

"It's good at this or any other time—but especially at this time." He waved the bottle. "Eat, drink and be merry—for to-morrow we certainly die." He thrust it at her. "Come on, have a snort."

She took the proffered bottle and quickly smashed it against a rock. He made a movement as though to save it, and said, "What the hell did you do that for?" in an aggrieved voice.

"Your name is not Peabody," she said cuttingly.

"What do you know about it? Peabody and I are old pals—bottle-babies, both of us." He stooped and groped. "Maybe it's not all gone—there might be some to be saved." He jerked suddenly. "Damn, I've cut my bloody finger," he said and laughed hysterically. "Look, I've got a bloody finger."

She saw the blood dripping from his hand, black in the moonlight. "You're irresponsible," she said. "Give me your hand." She lifted her skirt and ripped at her slip, tearing off a strip of cloth for a bandage.

O'Hara laughed uproariously. "The classic situation," he said. "The heroine bandages the wounded hero and does all the usual things that Hollywood invented. I suppose I should turn away like the gent I'm supposed to be, but you've got nice legs and I like looking at them."

She was silent as she bandaged his finger. He looked down at her dark head and said, "Irresponsible? I suppose I am.

150

So what? What is there to be responsible for? The world can go to hell in a hand-basket for all I care." He crooned. " Naked came I into the world and naked I shall go out of it —and what lies between is just a lot of crap."

" That's a sad philosophy of life," she said, not raising her head.

He put his hand under her chin to lift her head and stared at her. " Life? What do you know about life? Here you are—fighting the good fight in this crummy country—and for what? So that a lot of stupid Indians can have something that, if they had any guts at all, they'd get for themselves. But there's a big world outside which is always interfering— and you'll kowtow to Russia or America in the long run; you can't escape that fate. If you think that you'll be masters in your own country, you're even more stupid than I thought you were."

She met his eyes steadily. In a quiet and tranquil voice she said, " We can try."

" You'll never do it," he answered, and dropped his hand. " This is a world of dog eat dog and this country is one of the scraps that the big dogs fight over. It's a world of eat or be eaten—kill or be killed."

" I don't believe that," she said.

He gave a short laugh. " Don't you? Then what the hell are we doing here? Why don't we pack up our things and just go home? Let's pretend there's no one on the other side of the river who wants to kill us on sight."

She had no answer to that. He put his arm round her and she felt his hand on her knee, moving up her thigh under her skirt. She struggled loose and hit him with her open palm as hard as she could. He looked at her and there was a shocked expression in his eyes as he rubbed his cheek.

She cried, " You are one of the weak ones, Tim O'Hara, you are one of those who are killed and eaten. You have no courage and you always seek refuge—in the bottom of a bottle, in the arms of a woman, what does it matter? You're a pitiful, twisted man."

" Christ, what do you know about me?" he said, stung by the contempt in her voice but knowing that he liked her contempt better than her compassion.

" Not much. And I don't particularly like what I know. But I do know that you're worse than Peabody—he's a weak man who can't help it; you're a strong man who refuses to be strong. You spend all your time staring at your own navel

151

in the belief that it's the centre of the universe, and you have no human compassion at all."

"Compassion?" he shouted. "I have no need of *your* compassion—I've no time for people who are sorry for me. I don't need it."

"Everyone needs it," she retorted. "We're all afraid—that's the human predicament, to be afraid, and any man who says he isn't is a liar." In a quieter voice she went on, "You weren't always like this, Tim—what caused it?"

He dropped his head into his hands. He could feel something breaking within him; there was a shattering and a crumbling of his defences, the walls he had hidden behind for so long. He had just realised the truth of what Benedetta said; that his fear was not an abnormality but the normal situation of mankind and that it was not weakness to admit it.

He said in a muffled voice, "Good Christ, Benedetta, I'm frightened—I'm scared of falling into their hands again."

"The communists?"

He nodded.

"What did they do to you?"

So he told her and in the telling her face went white. He told her of the weeks of lying naked in his own filth in that icy cell; of the enforced sleeplessness, the interminable interrogations; of the blinding lamps and the electric shocks; of Lieutenant Feng. "They wanted me to confess to spreading plague germs," he said. He raised his head and she saw the streaks of tears in the moonlight. "But I didn't; it wasn't true, so I didn't." He gulped. "But I nearly did."

In her innermost being she felt a scalding contempt for herself—she had called *this* man weak. She cradled his head to her breast and felt the deep shudders which racked him. "It's all right now, Tim," she said. "It's all right."

He felt a draining of himself, a purging of the soul in the catharsis of telling to another human being that which had been locked within him for so long. And in a strange way, he felt strengthened and uplifted as he got rid of all the psychic pus that had festered in his spirit. Benedetta took the brunt of this verbal torrent calmly, comforting him with disconnected, almost incoherent endearments. She felt at once older and younger than he, which confused her and made her uncertain of what to do.

At last the violence of his speech ebbed and gradually he fell silent, leaning back against the rock as though physically exhausted. She held both his hands and said, "I'm sorry, Tim—for what I said."

He managed a smile. "You were right—I *have* been a thorough bastard, haven't I?"

"With reason."

"I must apologise to the others," he said. "I've been riding everybody too hard."

She said carefully, "We aren't chess pieces, Tim, to be moved as though we had no feelings. And that's what you have been doing, you know; moving my uncle, Willis and Armstrong—Jenny, too—as though they were just there to solve the problem. You see, it isn't only your problem—it belongs to all of us. Willis has worked harder than any of us; there was no need to behave towards him as you did when the trebuchet broke down."

O'Hara sighed. "I know," he said. "But it seemed the last straw. I was feeling bloody-minded about everything just then. But I'll apologise to him."

"A better thing would be to help him."

He nodded. "I'll go now." He looked at her and wondered if he had alienated her for ever. It seemed to him that no woman could love him who knew about him what this woman knew. But then Benedetta smiled brilliantly at him, and he knew with relief that everything was going to be all right.

"Come," she said. "I'll walk with you as far as the shelter." She felt an almost physical swelling pain her bosom, a surge of wild, unreasonable happiness, and she knew that she had been wrong when she had felt that Tim was not for her. This was the man with whom she would share her life —for as long as her life lasted.

He left her at the shelter and she kissed him before he went on. As she saw the dark shadow going away down the mountain she suddenly remembered and called, "What about the tear in your shirt?"

His answer came back almost gaily. "To-morrow," he shouted, and went on to the glimmer of light where Willis was working against time.

v

The morning dawned mistily but the rising sun soon burned away the haze. They held a dawn conference by the trebuchet to decide what was to be done next. "What do you think?" O'Hara asked Willis. "How much longer will it take?"

Armstrong clenched his teeth round the stem of his pipe and observed O'Hara with interest. Something of note had happened to this young man; something good. He looked over to where Benedetta was keeping watch on the bridge— her radiance this morning had been unbelievable, a shining effulgence that cast an almost visible glow about her. Armstrong smiled—it was almost indecent how happy these two were.

Willis said, "It'll be better now we can see what we're doing. I give us another couple of hours." His face was drawn and tired.

"We'll get to it," said O'Hara. He was going to continue but he paused suddenly, his head on one side. After a few seconds Armstrong also caught what O'Hara was listening to —the banshee whine of a jet plane approaching fast.

It was on them suddenly, coming low up-river. There was a howl and a wink of shadow as the aircraft swept over them to pull up into a steep climb and a sharp turn. Willis yelled, "They've found us—they've found us." He began to jump up and down in a frenzy of excitement, waving his arms.

"It's a Sabre," O'Hara shouted. "And it's coming back."

They watched the plane reach the top of its turning climb and come back at them in a shallow dive. Miss Ponsky screamed at the top of her voice, her arms going like a sema-phore, but O'Hara said suddenly, "I don't like this—everyone scatter—take cover."

He had seen aircraft behave like that in Korea, and he had done it himself; it had all the hallmarks of the beginning of a strafing attack.

They scattered like chickens at the sudden onset of a hawk and again the Sabre roared over, but there was no chatter of guns—just the diminishing whine of the engine as it went away down river. Twice more it came over them and the tough grass standing in clumps trembled stiff stems in the wake of its passage. And then it was gone in a long, almost vertical climb heading west over the mountains.

They came out of cover and stood in a group looking towards the peaks. Willis was the first to speak. "Damn you," he shouted at O'Hara. "Why did you make us hide? That plane must have been searching for us."

"Was it?" asked O'Hara. "Benedetta, does Cordillera have Sabres in the Air Force?"

"That was an Air Force fighter," she said. "I don't know which squadron."

"I missed the markings," said O'Hara. "Did anyone get them?"

No one had.

"I'd like to know which squadron that was," mused O'Hara. "It could make a difference."

"I tell you it was part of the search," insisted Willis.

"Nothing doing," said O'Hara. "The pilot of that plane knew exactly where to come—he wasn't searching. Someone had given him a pinpoint map position. There was nothing uncertain about his passes over us. We didn't tell him; Forester didn't tell him—they're only just leaving the mine now—so who did?"

Armstrong used his pipe as a pointer. "They did," he said, and pointed across the river. "We must assume that it means nothing good."

O'Hara was galvanised into activity. "Let's get this bloody beast working again. I want that bridge ruined as soon as possible. Jenny, take a bow and go down-river to where you can get a good view of the road where it bends away. If anyone comes through, take a crack at them and then get back here as fast as you can. Benedetta, you watch the bridge—the rest of us will get cracking here."

Willis had been too optimistic, because two hours went by and the trebuchet was still in pieces and far from being in working order. He wiped a grimy hand across his face. "It's not so bad now—another hour will see it right."

But they did not get another hour. Benedetta called out, "I can hear trucks." Following immediately upon her words came the rattle of rifle shots from down-river and another sound that chilled O'Hara—the unmistakable rat-a-tat of a machine-gun. He ran over to Benedetta and said breathlessly, "Can you see anything?"

"No," she answered; then, "Wait—yes, three trucks—big ones."

"Come down," said O'Hara. "I want to see this."

She climbed down from among the rocks and he took her place. Coming up the road at a fast clip and trailing a cloud of dust was a big American truck and behind it another, and another. The first one was full of men, at least twenty of

155

them, all armed with rifles. There was something odd about it that O'Hara could not at first place, then he saw the deep skirting of steel plate below the truck body which covered the petrol tank. The enemy was taking precautions.

The truck pulled to a halt by the bridge and the men piled out, being careful to keep the truck between themselves and the river. The second truck stopped behind; this was empty of men apart from two in the cab, and O'Hara could not see what the covered body contained. The third truck also contained men, though not as many, and O'Hara felt cold as he saw the light machine-gun being unloaded and taken hurriedly to cover.

He turned and said to Benedetta, " Give me that bow, and get the others over here." But when he turned back there was no target for him; the road and mountainside opposite seemed deserted of life, and the three trucks held no profit for him.

Armstrong and Willis came up and he told them what was happening. Willis said, " The machine-gun sounds bad, I know, but what can they do with it that they can't do with the rifles they've got? It doesn't make us much worse off."

" They can use it like a hose-pipe," said O'Hara. " They can squirt a stream of bullets and systematically hose down the side of the gorge. It's going to be bloody dangerous using the crossbow from now on."

" You say the second truck was empty," observed Armstrong thoughtfully.

" I didn't say that; I said it had no men. There must be something in there but the top of the body is swathed in canvas and I couldn't see." He smiled sourly. " They've probably got a demountable mountain howitzer or a mortar in there— and if they have anything like that we've had our chips."

Armstrong absently knocked his pipe against a rock, forgetting it was empty. " The thing to do now is have a parley," he said unexpectedly. " There never was a siege I studied where there wasn't a parley somewhere along the line."

" For God's sake, talk sense," said O'Hara. " You can only parley when you've got something to offer. These boys are on top and they know it; why should they parley? Come to that—why should *we*? We know they'll offer us the earth, and we know damned well they'll not keep their promises— so what's the use?"

" We have something to offer," said Armstrong calmly.

156

"We have Aguillar—they want him, so we'll offer him." He held up his hands to silence the others' protests. "We know what they'll offer us—our lives, and we know what their promises are worth, but that doesn't matter. Oh, we don't give them Aguillar, but with a bit of luck we can stretch the parley out into a few hours, and who knows what a few hours may mean later on?"

O'Hara thought about it. "What do you think, Willis?"

Willis shrugged. "We don't stand to lose anything," he said, "and we stand to gain time. Everything we've done so far has been to gain time."

"We could get the trebuchet into working order again," mused O'Hara. "That alone would be worth it. All right, let's try it out."

"Just a minute," said Armstrong. "Is anything happening across there yet?"

O'Hara looked across the gorge; everything was still and quiet. "Nothing."

"I think we'd better wait until they start to do something," counselled Armstrong. "It's my guess that the new arrivals and the old guard are in conference; they may take a while and there's no point in breaking it up. *Any* time we gain is to our advantage, so let's wait awhile."

Benedetta, who was standing by quietly, now spoke. "Jenny hasn't come back yet."

O'Hara whirled. "Hasn't she?"

Willis said, "Perhaps she'll have been hit; that machine-gun . . ." His voice tailed away.

"I'll go and see," said Benedetta.

"No," said O'Hara sharply. "I'll go—she may need to be carried and you can't do that. You'd better stay here on watch and the others can get on with repairing the trebuchet."

He plunged away and ran across the level ground, skirting the bridgehead where there was no cover and began to clamber among the rocks on the other side, making his way down-river. He had a fair idea of the place Miss Ponsky would have taken and he made straight for it. As he went he swore and cursed under his breath; if she had been killed he would never forgive himself.

It took him over twenty minutes to make the journey—good time considering the ground was rough—but when he arrived at the most likely spot she was not there. But there were three bolts stuck point first in the ground and a small pool of sticky blood staining the rock.

He bent down and saw another blood-spot and then another. He followed this bloody spoor and back-tracked a hundred yards before he heard a weak groan and saw Miss Ponsky lying in the shadow of a boulder, her hand clutching her left shoulder. He dropped to his knee beside her and lifted her head. "Where were you hit, Jenny? In the shoulder?"

Her eyes flickered open and she nodded weakly.

"Anywhere else?"

She shook her head and whispered, "Oh, Tim, I'm sorry. I lost the bow."

"Never mind that," he said, and ripped the blouse from her shoulder, careful not to jerk her. He sighed in relief; the wound was not too bad, being through the flesh part of the shoulder and not having broken the bone so far as he could judge. But she had lost a lot of blood and that had weakened her, as had the physical shock.

She said in a stronger voice, "But I shouldn't have lost it —I should have held on tight. It fell into the river, Tim; I'm so sorry."

"Damn the bow," he said. "You're more important." He plugged the wound on both sides with pieces torn from his shirt, and made a rough bandage. "Can you walk?"

She tried to walk and could not, so he said cheerfully, "Then I'll have to carry you—fireman's lift. Up you come." He slung her over his shoulder and slowly made his way back to the bridge. By the time he got to the shelter and delivered her to Benedetta she was unconscious again.

"All the more need for a parley," he said grimly to Armstrong. "We must get Jenny on her feet again and capable of making a run for it. Has anything happened across there?"

"Nothing. But we've nearly finished the trebuchet."

It was not much later that two men began to strip the canvas from the second truck and O'Hara said, "Now we give it a go." He filled his lungs and shouted in Spanish, "Señors—Señors! I wish to speak to your leader. Let him step forward—we will not shoot."

The two men stopped dead and looked at each other. Then they stared across the gorge, undecided. O'Hara said, in a sardonic aside to Armstrong, "Not that we've got much to shoot with."

The men appeared to make up their minds. One of them ran off and presently the big man with the beard appeared from among the rocks, climbed down and walked to the abutments of the bridge. He shouted, " Is that Señor Aguillar?"

" No," shouted O'Hara, changing into English. " It is O'Hara."

" Ah, the pilot." The big man responded in English, rather startling O'Hara with his obvious knowledge of their identities. " What do you want, Señor O'Hara?"

Benedetta had returned to join them and now said quickly, " This man is not a Cordilleran; his accent is Cuban."

O'Hara winked at her. " Señor Cuban, why do you shoot at us?"

The big man laughed jovially. " Have you not asked Señor Aguillar? Or does he still call himself Montes?"

" Aguillar is nothing to do with me," called O'Hara. " His fight is not mine—and I'm tired of being shot at."

The Cuban threw back his head and laughed again, slapping his thigh. " So?"

" I want to get out of here."

" And Aguillar?"

" You can have him. That's what you're here for, isn't it?"

The Cuban paused as though thinking deeply, and O'Hara said to Benedetta, " When I pinch you, scream your head off." She looked at him in astonishment, then nodded.

" Bring Aguillar to the bridge and you can go free, Señor O'Hara."

" What about the girl?" asked O'Hara.

" The girl we want too, of course."

O'Hara pinched Benedetta in the arm and she uttered a blood-curdling scream, artistically chopping it off as though a hand had been clapped to her mouth. O'Hara grinned at her and waited a few moments before he raised his voice. " Sorry, Señor Cuban; we had some trouble." He let caution appear in his tone. " I'm not the only one here—there are others."

" You will all go free," said the big man with an air of largesse. " I myself will escort you to San Croce. Bring Aguillar to the bridge now; let us have him and you can all go."

" That is impossible," O'Hara protested. " Aguillar is at the upper camp. He went there when he saw what was happening here at the bridge. It will take time to bring him down."

The Cuban lifted his head suspiciously. " Aguillar ran away?" he asked incredulously.

O'Hara swore silently; he had not thought that Aguillar

would be held in such respect by his enemies. He quickly improvised. "He was sent away by Rohde, his friend. But Rohde has been killed by your machine-gun."

"Ah, the man who shot at us on the road just now." The Cuban looked down at his tapping foot, apparently undecided. Then he lifted his head. "Wait, Señor O'Hara."

"How long?"

"A few minutes, that is all." He walked up the road and disappeared among the rocks.

Armstrong said, "He's gone to consult with his second-in-command."

"Do you think he'll fall for it?"

"He might," said Willis. "It's an attractive proposition. You baited it well—he thinks that Rohde has been keeping us in line and that now he's dead we're about to collapse. It was very well done."

The Cuban was away for ten minutes, then he came back to the bridge accompanied by another man, a slight, swarthy Indian type. "Very well," he called. "As the *norteamericanos* say, you have made a deal. How long to bring Aguillar?"

"It's a long way," shouted O'Hara. "It will take some time—say, five hours."

The two men conferred and then the Cuban shouted, "All right, five hours."

"And we have an armistice?" shouted O'Hara. "No shooting from either side?"

"No shooting," promised the Cuban.

O'Hara sighed. "That's it. We must get the trebuchet finished. We've got five hours' grace. How's Jenny, Benedetta?"

"She will be all right. I gave her some hot soup and wrapped her in a blanket. She must be kept warm."

"Five hours isn't a long time," said Armstrong. "I know we were lucky to get it, but it still isn't long. Maybe we can string it out a little longer."

"We can try," said O'Hara. "But not for much longer. They'll get bloody suspicious when the five hours have gone and we haven't produced Aguillar."

Armstrong shrugged. "What can they do that they haven't been trying to do for the last three days?"

The day wore on.

The trebuchet was repaired and O'Hara made plans for the rage that was to come. He said, "We have one crossbow and a pistol with one bullet—that limits us if it comes to in-fighting. Benedetta, you take Jenny up to the camp as soon as she can walk. She won't be able to move fast, so you'd better get a head start in case things blow up here. I still don't know what they've got in the second truck, but it certainly isn't intended to do us any good."

So Benedetta and Miss Ponsky went off, taking a load of Molotov cocktails with them. Armstrong and O'Hara watched the bridge, while Willis tinkered with the trebuchet, doing unnecessary jobs. On the other side of the river men had popped out from among the rocks, and the hillside seemed alive with them as they unconcernedly smoked and chatted. It reminded O'Hara of the stories he had heard of the first Christmas of the First World War.

He counted the men carefully and compared notes with Armstrong. "I make it thirty-three," he said.

"I get thirty-five," said Armstrong. "But I don't suppose the difference matters." He looked at the bowl of his pipe. "I wish I had some tobacco," he said irritably.

"Sorry, I'm out of cigarettes."

"You're a modern soldier," said Armstrong. "What would you do in their position? I mean, how would you handle the next stage of the operation?"

O'Hara considered. "We've done the bridge a bit of no good with the trebuchet, but not enough. Once they've got that main gap repaired they can start rushing men across, but not vehicles. I'd make a rush and form a bridgehead at this end, spreading out along this side of the gorge where we are now. Once they've got us away from here it won't be much trouble to repair the rest of the bridge to the point where they can bring a couple of jeeps over. Then I'd use the jeeps as tanks, ram them up to the mine as fast as possible—they'd be there before we could arrive on foot. Once they hold both ends of the road where can we retreat to? There's not a lot we can do about it—that's the hell of it."

"Um," said Armstrong glumly. "That's the appreciation

I made." He rolled over on his back. "Look, it's clouding over."

O'Hara turned and looked up at the mountains. A dirty grey cloud was forming and had already blotted out the higher peaks and now swirled in misty coils just above the mine. "That looks like snow," he said. "If there was ever a chance of a real air-search looking for and finding us, it's completely shot now. And it must have caught Ray flat-footed." He shivered. "I wouldn't like to be in their boots."

They watched the cloud for some time and suddenly Armstrong said, "It may be all right for us, though; I believe it's coming low. We could do with a good, thick mist."

When the truce had but one hour to go the first grey tendrils of mist began to curl about the bridge and O'Hara sat up as he heard a motor engine. A new arrival pulled up behind the trucks, a big Mercédès saloon car out of which got a man in trim civilian clothes. O'Hara stared across the gorge as the man walked to the bridge and noted the short square build and the broad features. He nudged Armstrong. "The commissar has arrived," he said.

"A Russian?"

"I'd bet you a pound to a pinch of snuff," said O'Hara.

The Russian—if such he was—conferred with the Cuban and an argument seemed to develop, the Cuban waving his arms violently and the Russian stolidly stone-walling with his hands thrust deep into his coat pockets. He won the argument for the Cuban suddenly turned away and issued a string of rapid orders and the hillside on the other side of the gorge became a sudden ants' nest of activity.

The idling men disappeared behind the rocks again and it was as though the mountain had swallowed them. With frantic speed four men finished stripping the canvas from the second truck and the Cuban shouted to the Russian and waved his arms. The Russian, after one long look over the gorge, nonchalantly turned his back and strolled towards his car.

"By God, they're going to break the truce," said O'Hara tightly. He grabbed the loaded crossbow as the machine-gun suddenly ripped out and stitched the air with bullets. "Get back to the trebuchet." He aimed the bow carefully at the Russian's back, squeezed the trigger and was mortified to miss. He ducked to reload and heard the crash of the trebuchet behind him as Willis pulled the firing lever.

When he raised his head again he found that the trebuchet shot had missed and he paled as he saw what had been pulled out of the truck. It was a prefabricated length of bridging carried by six men who had already set foot on the bridge itself. Following them was a squad of men running at full speed. There was nothing that a single crossbow bolt would do to stop them and there was no time to reload the trebuchet —they would be across the bridge in a matter of seconds.

He yelled at Willis and Armstrong. "Retreat! Get back up the road—to the camp!" and ran towards the bridgehead, bow at the ready.

The first man was already across, scuttling from side to side, a sub-machine-gun at the ready. O'Hara crouched behind a rock and took aim, waiting until the man came closer. The mist was thickening rapidly and it was difficult to judge distances, so he waited until he thought the man was twenty yards away before he pulled the trigger.

The bolt took the man full in the chest, driving home right to the fletching. He shouted in a bubbling voice and threw his hands up as he collapsed, and the tightening death grip on the gun pulled the trigger. O'Hara saw the rest of the squad coming up behind him and the last thing he saw before he turned and ran was the prone figure on the ground quivering as the sub-machine-gun fired its magazine at random.

## Chapter VII

Rohde hacked vigorously at the ice wall with the small axe. He had retrieved it—a grisly job—and now it was coming in very useful, returning to its designed function as an instrument for survival. Forester was lying, a huddled heap of old clothing, next to the ice wall, well away from the edge of the cliff. Rohde had stripped the outer clothing from Peabody's corpse and used it to wrap up Forester as warmly as possible before he pushed the body into the oblivion of the gathering mists below.

They needed warmth because it was going to be a bad night. The ledge was now enveloped in mist and it had started to snow in brief flurries. A shelter was imperative. Rohde stopped for a moment to bend over Forester who was still conscious, and adjusted the hood which had fallen away from his face. Then he resumed his chopping at the ice wall.

Forester had never felt so cold in his life. His hands and

feet were numb and his teeth chattered uncontrollably. He was so cold that he welcomed the waves of pain which rose from his chest; they seemed to warm him and they prevented him from slipping into unconsciousness. He knew he must not let that happen because Rohde had warned him about it, slapping his face to drive the point home.

It had been a damned near thing, he thought. Another couple of slashes from Peabody's knife and the rope would have parted to send him plunging to his death on the snow slopes far below. Rohde had been quick enough to kill Peabody when the need for it arose, even though he had been squeamish earlier. Or perhaps it wasn't that; perhaps he believed in expending just the necessary energy and effort that the job required. Forester, watching Rohde's easy strokes and the flakes of ice falling one by one, suddenly chuckled—a time-and-motion-study killer; that was one for the books. His weak chuckle died away as another wave of pain hit him; he clenched his teeth and waited for it to leave.

When Rohde had killed Peabody he had waited rigidly for a long time, holding the rope taut for fear that Peabody's body would slide over the edge, taking Forester with it. Then he began to dig the ice-axe deeper into the snow, hoping to use it to belay the rope; but he encountered ice beneath the thin layer of snow and, using only one hand, he could not force the axe down.

He changed his tactics. He pulled up the axe and, frightened of being pulled forward on the slippery ice, first chipped two deep steps into which he could put his feet. That gave him the leverage to haul himself upright by the rope and he felt Peabody's body shift under the strain. He stopped because he did not know how far Peabody had succeeded in damaging the rope and he was afraid it might part and let Forester go.

He took the axe and began to chip at the ice, making a large circular groove about two feet in diameter. He found it a difficult task because the head of the axe, improvised by Willis, was set at an awkward angle on the shaft and it was not easy to use. After nearly an hour of chipping he deepened the groove enough to take the rope, and carefully unfastening it from round his waist he belayed it round the ice mushroom he had created.

That left him free to walk to the edge of the cliff. He did not go forward immediately but stood for a while, stamping his feet and flexing his muscles to get the blood going again.

He had been lying in a very cramped position. When he looked over the edge he saw that Forester was unconscious, dangling limply on the end of the rope, his head lolling.

The rope was badly frayed where Peabody had attacked it, so Rohde took a short length from round his waist and carefully knotted it above and below the potential break. That done, he began to haul up the sagging and heavy body of Forester. It was hopeless to think of going farther that day. Forester was in no condition to move; the fall had tightened the rope cruelly about his chest and Rohde, probing carefully, thought that some ribs were cracked, if not broken. So he rolled Forester up in warm clothing and relaxed on the ledge between the rock cliff and the ice wall, wondering what to do next.

It was a bad place to spend a night—even a good night—and this was going to be a bad one. He was afraid that if the wind rose to the battering strength that it did during a blizzard, then the overhanging cornice on the ice wall would topple—and if it did they would be buried without benefit of grave-diggers. Again, they must have shelter from the wind and the snow, so he took the small axe, wiped the blood and the viscous grey matter from the blade, and began to chip a shallow cave in the ice wall.

I I

The wind rose just after nightfall and Rohde was still working. As the first fierce gusts came he stopped and looked around wearily; he had been working for nearly three hours, chipping away at the hard ice with a blunt and inadequate instrument more suited to chopping household firewood. The small cleft he had made in the ice would barely hold the two of them but it would have to do.

He dragged Forester into the ice cave and propped him up against the rear wall, then he went out and brought in the three packs, arranging them at the front of the cave to form a low and totally inadequate wall which, however, served as some sort of bulwark against the drifting snow. He fumbled in his pocket and turned to Forester. "Here," he said urgently. "Chew these."

Forester mumbled and Rohde slapped him. "You must not sleep—not yet," he said. "You must chew coca." He forced open Forester's mouth and thrust a coca quid into it.

165

It took him over half an hour to open a pack and assemble the Primus stove. His fingers were cold and he was suffering from the effects of high altitude—the loss of energy and the mental haziness which dragged the time of each task to many times its normal length. Finally, he got the stove working. It provided little heat and less light, but it was a definite improvement.

He improvised a windshield from some pitons and pieces of blanket. Fortunately the wind came from behind, from the top of the pass and over the ice wall, so that they were in a relatively sheltered position. But vicious side gusts occasionally swept into the cave, bringing a flurry of snowflakes and making the Primus flare and roar. Rohde was glum when he thought of the direction of the wind. It was good as far as their present shelter went, but the snow cornice on top of the wall would begin to build up and as it grew heavier it would be more likely to break off. And, in the morning when they set off again, they would be climbing in the teeth of a gale. He prayed the wind would change direction before then.

Presently he had melted enough snow to make a warm drink, but Forester found the taste of the bouillon nauseating and could not drink it, so he heated some more water and they drank that; at least it put some warmth into their bellies.

Then he got to work on Forester, examining his hands and feet and pummelling him violently over many protests. After this Forester was wide awake and in full possession of his senses and did the same for Rohde, rubbing hands and feet to bring back the circulation. "Do you think we'll make it, Miguel?" he asked.

"Yes," said Rohde shortly; but he was having his first doubts. Forester was not in good condition for the final assault on the pass and the descent of the other side. It was not a good thing for a man with cracked ribs. He said, "You must keep moving—your fingers and toes, move them all the time. You must rub your face, your nose and ears. You must not sleep."

"We'd better talk," suggested Forester. "Keep each other awake." He raised his head and listened to the howls of the wind. "It'll be more like shouting, though, if this racket keeps up. What shall we talk about?"

Rohde grunted and pulled the hood about his ears. "O'Hara told me you were an airman."

"Right," said Forester. "I flew towards the end of the

war—in Italy mostly. I was flying Lightnings. Then when Korea came I was dragged in again—I was in the Air Force Reserve, you see. I did a conversion on to jets and then I flew Sabres all during the Korean war, or at least until I was pulled out to go back Stateside as an instructor. I think I must have flown some missions with O'Hara in Korea."

"So he said. And after Korea?"

Forester shrugged. "I was still bitten with the airplane bug; the company I work for specialises in airplane maintenance." He grinned. "When all this happened I was on my way to Santillana to complete a deal with your Air Force for maintenance equipment. You still have Sabres, you know; I sometimes get to flying them if the squadron commandant is a good guy." He paused. "If Aguillar pulls off his *coup d'état* the deal may go sour—I don't know why the hell I'm taking all this trouble."

Rohde smiled, and said, "If Señor Aguillar comes into power your business will be all right—he will remember. And you will not have to pay the bribes you have already figured into your costing." His voice was a little bitter.

"Hell," said Forester. "You know what it's like in this part of the world—especially under Lopez. Make no mistake, I'm for Aguillar; we businessmen like an honest government—it makes things easier all round." He beat his hands together. "Why are you for Aguillar?"

"Cordillera is my country," said Rohde simply, as though that explained everything, and Forester thought that meeting an honest patriot in Cordillera was a little odd, like finding a hippopotamus in the Arctic.

They were silent for a while, then Forester said, "What time is it?"

Rohde fumbled at his wrist-watch. "A little after nine."

Forester shivered. "Another nine hours before sunrise." The cold was biting deep into his bones and the wind gusts which flailed into their narrow shelter struck right through his clothing, even through O'Hara's leather jacket. He wondered if they would be alive in the morning; he had heard and read too many tales of men dying of exposure, even back home and closer to civilisation, to have any illusions about the precariousness of their position.

Rohde stirred and began to empty two of the packs. Carefully he arranged the contents where they would not roll out of the cave, then gave an empty pack to Forester. "Put your feet in this," he said. "It will be some protection against the cold."

Forester took the pack and flexed the blanket material, breaking off the encrusted ice. He put his feet into it and pulled the draw-string about the calves of his legs. "Didn't you say you'd been up here before?" he asked.

"Under better conditions," answered Rohde. "It was when I was a student many years ago. There was a mountaineering expedition to climb this peak—the one to our right here."

"Did they make it?"

Rohde shook his head. "They tried three times—they were brave, those Frenchmen. Then one of them was killed and they gave up."

"Why did you join them?" asked Forester curiously.

Rohde shrugged. "I needed the money—students always need money—and they paid well for porters. And, as a medical student, I was interested in the *soroche*. Oh, the equipment those men had! Fleece-lined under-boots and thick leather over-boots with crampons for the ice; quilted jackets filled with down; strong tents of nylon and long lengths of nylon rope—and good steel pitons that did not bend when you hammered them into the rock." He was like a starving man voluptuously remembering a banquet he had once attended.

"And you came over the pass?"

"From the other side—it was easier that way. I looked down over this side from the top and was glad we did not have to climb it. We had a camp—camp three—on top of the pass; and we came up slowly, staying some days at each camp to avoid the *soroche*."

"I don't know why men climb mountains," said Forester, and there was a note of annoyance in his voice. "God knows I'm not doing it because I want to; it beats me that men do it for pleasure."

"Those Frenchmen were geologists," said Rohde. "They were not climbing for the sake of climbing. They took many rock samples from the mountains around here. I saw a map they had made—published in Paris—and I read they had found many rich minerals."

"What's the use?" queried Forester. "No one can work up here."

"Not now," agreed Rohde. "But later—who knows?" His voice was serenely confident.

168

They talked together for a long time, each endeavouring to urge along the lagging clock. After a time Rohde began to sing—folk-songs of Cordillera and later the half-forgotten German songs that his father had taught him. Forester contributed some American songs, avoiding the modern pop tunes and sticking to the songs of his youth. He was half-way through " I've Been Working on the Railroad " when there was a thunderous crash from the left which momentarily drowned even the howls of the gale.

" What's that?" he asked, startled.

" The snow cornice is falling," said Rohde. " It has built up because of the wind; now it is too heavy and not strong enough to bear its own weight." He raised his eyes to the roof of the ice cave. " Let us pray that it does not fall in this place; we would be buried."

" What time is it?"

" Midnight. How do you feel?"

Forester had his arms crossed over his chest. " Goddam cold."

" And your ribs—how are they?"

" Can't feel a thing."

Rohde was concerned. " That is bad. Move, my friend; move yourself. You must not allow yourself to freeze." He began to slap and pummel Forester until he howled for mercy and could feel the pain in his chest again.

Just after two in the morning the snow cornice over the cave collapsed. Both Rohde and Forester had become dangerously moribund, relapsing into a half-world of cold and numbness. Rohde heard the preliminary creaking and stirred feebly, then sagged back weakly. There was a noise as of a bomb exploding as the cornice broke and a cloud of dry, powdery snow was driven into the shelter, choking and cold.

Rohde struggled against it, waving his arms in swimming motions as the tide of snow covered his legs and crept up to his chest. He yelled to Forester, " Keep a space clear for yourself."

Forester moaned in protest and waved his hands ineffectually, and luckily the snow stopped its advance, leaving them buried to their shoulders. After a long, dying rumble which seemed to come from an immense distance they became aware that it was unnaturally quiet; the noise of the blizzard which had battered at their ears for so long that they had ceased to be aware of it had gone, and the silence was loud and ear-splitting.

169

"What's happened?" mumbled Forester. Something was holding his arms imprisoned and he could not get them free. In a panic he began to struggle wildly until Rohde shouted, "Keep still." His voice was very loud in the confined space.

For a while they lay still, then Rohde began to move cautiously, feeling for his ice-axe. The snow in which he was embedded was fluffy and uncompacted, and he found he could move his arms upwards. When he freed them he began to push the snow away from his face and to plaster and compress it against the wall of the cave. He told Forester to do the same and it was not long before they had scooped out enough space in which to move. Rohde groped in his pocket for matches and tried to strike one, but they were all wet, the soggy ends crumbling against the box.

Forester said painfully, "I've got a lighter," and Rohde heard a click and saw a bright point of blinding light. He averted his eyes from the flame and looked about him. The flame burned quite still without flickering and he knew that they were buried. In front, where the opening to the cave had been, was an unbroken wall of compacted snow.

He said, "We must make a hole or suffocate," and groped in the snow for the small axe. It took him a long time to find it and his fingers encountered several other items of their inadequate equipment before he succeeded. These he put carefully to one side—everything would be important from now on.

He took the axe and, sitting up with his legs weighed down with snow, he began to hew at the wall before him. Although it was compacted it was not as hard to cut as the ice from which he had chopped the cave and he made good progress. But he did not know how much snow he had to go through before he broke through to the other side. Perhaps the fall extended right across the ledge between the ice wall and the cliff edge and he would come out upon a dizzying drop.

He put the thought out of his mind and diligently worked with the axe, cutting a hole only of such size as he needed to work in. Forester took the snow as it was scooped out of the hole and packed it to one side, observing after a while, "We're not going to have much room if this goes on much longer."

Rohde kept silent, cutting away in the dark, for he had blown out the small flame. He worked by sense of touch and at last he had penetrated as far as he could with the small axe, thrusting his arm right up to the shoulder into the hole

170

he had made. He had still not come to the other side of the snow fall, and said abruptly, " The ice-axe."

Forester handed it to him and Rohde thrust it into the hole, driving vigorously. There was no room to cut with this long axe, so he pushed, forcing it through by sheer muscle power. To his relief, something suddenly gave and there was a welcome draught of cold air. It was only then he realised how fœtid the atmosphere had become. He collapsed, half on top of Forester, panting with his exertions and taking deep breaths of air.

Forester pushed him and he rolled away. After a while he said, " The fall is about two metres thick—we should have no trouble in getting through."

" We'd better get at it, then," said Forester.

Rohde considered the proposition and decided against it. " This might be the best thing for us. It is warmer in here now, the snow is shielding us from the wind. All we have to do is to keep that hole clear. And there will not be another fall."

" Okay," said Forester. " You're the boss."

Warmth was a relative term. Cutting the hole had made Rohde sweat freely and now he could feel the sweat freezing to ice on his body under his clothing. Awkardly he began to strip and had Forester rub his body all over. Forester gave a low chuckle as he massaged, and said, " A low-temperature Turkish bath—I'll have to introduce it to New York. We'll make a mint of money."

Rohde dressed again, and asked, " How are you feeling?"

" Goddam cold," said Forester. " But otherwise okay."

" That shock did us good," said Rohde. " We were sinking fast—we must not let that happen again. We have another three hours to go before dawn—let us talk and sing."

So they sang lustily, the sound reverberating from the hard and narrow confines of the ice cave, making them sound, as Forester put it, " like a pair of goddam bathroom Carusos."


III


Half an hour before dawn Rohde began to cut their way out and he emerged into a grey world of blustery wind and driving snow. Forester was shocked at the conditions outside the cave. Although it was daylight, visibility was restricted to less than ten yards and the wind seemed to pierce right through him. He put his lips to Rohde's ear and shouted, "Draughty, isn't it?"

Rohde turned, his lips curled back in a fierce grin. "How is your chest?"

Forester's chest hurt abominably, but his smile was amiable. "Okay. I'll follow where you go." He knew they could not survive another night on the mountain—they had to get over the pass this day or they would die.

Rohde pointed upward with the ice-axe. "The cornice is forming again, but it is not too bad; we can go up here. Get the packs together." He stepped to the ice wall and began to cut steps skilfully, while Forester repacked their equipment. There was not much—some had been lost, buried under the snow fall, and some Rohde had discarded as being unnecessary deadweight to carry on this last desperate dash. They were stripped down to essentials.

Rohde cut steps in the fifteen-foot ice wall as high as he could reach while standing on reasonably firm ground, then climbed up and roped himself to pitons and stood in the steps he had already cut, chopping vigorously. He cut the steps very deep, having Forester in mind, and it took him nearly an hour before he was satisfied that Forester could climb the wall safely.

The packs were hauled up on a rope and then Forester began the climb, roped to Rohde. It was the most difficult task he had faced in his life. Normally he could have almost run up the broad and deep steps that Rohde had cut but now the bare ice burned his hands, even through the gloves, his chest ached and stabbing pains pierced him as he lifted his arms above his head, and he felt weak and tired as though the very breath of life had been drained from him. But he made it and collapsed at Rohde's feet.

Here the wind was a howling devil driving down the pass and bearing with it great clouds of powdery snow and ice particles which stung the face and hands. The din was indescribable, a freezing pandemonium from an icy hell, deafening in its loudness. Rohde bent over Forester, shielding him from the worst of the blast, and made him sit up. "You can't stay here," he shouted. "We must keep moving. There is no more hard climbing—just the slope to the top and down the other side."

Forester flinched as the ice particles drove like splinters into his face and he looked up into Rohde's hard and indomitable eyes. "Okay, buster," he croaked harshly. "Where you go, so can I."

Rohde thrust some coca quids into his hand. "You will need these." He checked the rope round Forester's waist and then picked up both packs, tentatively feeling their weight. He ripped them open and consolidated the contents into one pack, which he slung on his back despite Forester's protests. The empty pack was snatched by the wind and disappeared into the grey reaches of the blizzard behind them.

Forester stumbled to his feet and followed in the tracks that Rohde broke. He hunched his shoulders and held his head down, staring at his feet in order to keep the painful wind from his face. He wrapped the blanket hood about the lower part of his face but could do nothing to protect his eyes, which became red and sore. Once he looked up and the wind caught him right in the mouth, knocking the breath out of him as effectively as if he had been punched in the solar plexus. Quickly he bent his head again and trudged on.

The slope was not very steep, much less so than below the cliffs, but it meant that to gain altitude they had that much farther to go. He tried to work it out; they had to gain a thousand feet of height and the slope was, say, thirty degrees —but then his bemused mind bogged down in the intricacies of trigonometry and he gave up the calculation.

Rohde plodded on, breaking the deep snow and always testing the ground ahead with the ice-axe, while the wind shrieked and plucked at him with icy fingers. He could not see more than ten yards ahead but he trusted to the slope of the mountainside as being sufficient guide to the top of the pass. He had never climbed this side of the pass but had looked down from the top, and he hoped his memory of it was true and that what he had told Forester was correct —that there would be no serious climbing—just this steady plod.

Had he been alone he could have moved much faster, but he deliberately reduced his pace to help Forester. Besides, it helped conserve his own energy, which was not inexhaustible, although he was in better condition than Forester. But then, he had not fallen over a cliff. Like Forester, he went forward bent almost double, the wind tearing at his clothing and the snow coating his hood with a thickening film of ice.

After an hour they came to a slight dip where the slope eased and found that the ground became almost level. Here the snow had drifted and was very deep, getting deeper the

173

farther they went on. Rohde raised his head and stared upwards, shielding his eyes with his hand and looking through the slits made by his fingers. There was nothing to be seen beyond the grey whirling world in which they were enclosed. He waited until Forester came abreast of him and shouted, " Wait here; I will go ahead a little way."

Forester nodded wearily and sank to the snow, turning his back to the gale and hunching himself into a fœtus-like attitude. Rohde unfastened the rope around his waist and dropped it by Forester's side, then went on. He had gone a few paces when he turned to look back and saw the dim huddle of Forester and, between them, the broken crust of the snow. He was satisfied that he could find his way back by following his own trail, so he pressed on into the blizzard.

Forester put another coca quid into his mouth and chewed it slowly. His gloved hand was clumsy and he pulled off the glove to pick up the quid from the palm of his hand. He was cold, numb to the bone, and his mouth was the only part of him that was pleasantly warm, a synthetic warmth induced by the coca. He had lost all sense of time; his watch had stopped long ago and he had no way of knowing how long they had been trudging up the mountain since scaling the ice wall. The cold seemed to have frozen his mind as well as his body, and he had the distinct impression that they had been going for several hours—or perhaps it was only several minutes; he did not know. All he knew was that he did not care much. He felt he was condemned to walk and climb for ever in this cold and bleak mountain world.

He lay apathetically in the snow for a long time and then, as the coca took effect, he roused himself and turned to look in the direction Rohde had gone. The wind flailed his face and he jerked and held up his hand, noticing absently that his knuckles had turned a scaly lizard-blue and that his fingers were cut in a myriad places by the wind-driven ice.

There was no sign of Rohde and Forester turned away, feeling a little surge of panic in his belly. What if Rohde could not find him again? But his mind was too torpid, too drugged by the cold and the coca, to drive his body into any kind of constructive action, and he slumped down to the snow again, where Rohde found him when he came back.

He was aroused by Rohde shaking him violently by the shoulder. " Move, man. You must not sit there and freeze. Rub your face and put on your glove."

Mechanically he brought up his hand and dabbed ineffectually at his face. He could feel no contact at all, both hand and face were anæsthetised by the cold. Rhode struck his face twice with vigorous open hand slaps and Forester was annoyed. "All right," he croaked. "No need to hit me." He slapped his hands together until the circulation came back and then began to massage his face.

Rohde shouted, "I went about two hundred metres—the snow was waist-deep and getting deeper. We cannot go that way; we must go round."

Forester felt a moment of despair. Would this never end? He staggered to his feet and waited while Rohde tied the rope, then followed him in a direction at right-angles to the course they had previously pursued. The wind was now striking at them from the side and, walking as they were across the slope, the buffeting gusts threatened to knock them off their feet and they had to lean into the wind to maintain a precarious balance.

The route chosen by Rohde skirted the deep drifts, but he did not like the way they tended to lose altitude. Every so often he would move up again towards the pass, and every time was forced down again by deepening snow. At last he found a way upwards where the slope steepened and the snow cover was thinner, and once more they gained altitude in the teeth of the gale.

Forester followed in a half-conscious stupor, mechanically putting one foot in front of the other in an endless lurching progression. From time to time as he cautiously raised his eyes he saw the dim snow-shrouded figure of Rohde ahead, and after a time his mind was wiped clean of all other considerations but that of keeping Rohde in sight and the rope slack. Occasionally he stumbled and fell forward and the rope would tighten and Rohde would wait patiently until he recovered his feet, and then they would go on again, and upwards—always upwards.

Suddenly Rohde halted and Forester shuffled to his side. There was a hint of desperation in Rohde's voice as he pointed forward with the ice-axe. "Rock," he said slowly. "We have come upon rock again." He struck the ice-glazed outcrop with the axe and the ice shattered. He struck again at the bare rock and it crumbled, flakes falling away to dirty the white purity of the snow. "The rock is rotten," said Rohde. "It is most dangerous. And there is the *verglas*."

Forester forced his lagging brain into action. "How far up do you think it extends?"

"Who knows?" said Rhode. He turned and squatted with his back to the wind and Forester followed his example. "We cannot climb this. It was bad enough on the other side of the glacier yesterday when we were fresh and there was no wind. To attempt this now would be madness." He beat his hands together.

"Maybe it's just an isolated outcrop," suggested Forester. "We can't see very far, you know."

Rohde grasped the ice-axe. "Wait here. I will find out."

Once again he left Forester and scrambled upwards. Forester heard the steady chipping of the axe above the noise of the wind and pieces of ice and flakes of rock fell down out of the grey obscurity. He paid out rope as Rohde tugged and the hood about his head flapped loose and the wind stung his cheeks smartly.

He had just lifted his hand to wrap the hood about his face when Rohde fell. Forester heard the faint shout and saw the shapeless figure hurtling towards him from above out of the screaming turmoil. He grabbed the rope, turned and dug his heels into the snow ready to take the shock. Rohde tumbled past him in an uncontrollable fall and slid down the slope until he was brought up sharply on the end of the rope by a jerk which almost pulled Forester off his feet.

Forester hung on until he was sure that Rohde would go no farther down the slope. He saw him stir and then roll over to sit up and rub his leg. He shouted, "Miguel, are you okay?" then began to descend.

Rohde turned his face upwards and Forester saw that each hair of his beard stubble was coated with rime. "My leg," he said. "I've hurt my leg."

Forester bent over him and straightened the leg, probing with his fingers. The trouser-leg was torn and, as Forester put his hand inside, he felt the sticky wetness of blood. After a while he said, "It's not broken, but you've scraped it badly."

"It is impossible up there," said Rohde, his face twisted in pain. "No man could climb that—even in good weather."

"How far does the rock go?"

"As far as I could see, but that was not far." He paused. "We must go back and try the other side."

Forester was appalled. "But the glacier is on the other side; we can't cross the glacier in this weather."

"Perhaps there is a good way up this side of the glacier," said Rohde. He turned his head and looked up towards the rocks from which he had fallen. "One thing is certain—that way is impossible."

"We want something to bind this trouser-leg together," said Forester. "I don't know much about it, but I don't think it would be a good thing if this torn flesh became frostbitten."

"The pack," said Rohde. "Help me with the pack."

Forester helped him take off the pack and he emptied the contents into the snow and tore up the blanket material into strips which he bound tightly round Rohde's leg. He said wryly, "Our equipment gets less and less. I can put some of this stuff into my pocket, but not much."

"Take the Primus," said Rohde. "And some kerosene. If we have to go as far as the glacier perhaps we can find a place beneath an ice fall that is sheltered from the wind, where we can make a hot drink."

Forester put the bottle of kerosene and a handful of bouillon cubes into his pocket and slung the pressure stove over his shoulder suspended by a length of electric wire. As he did so, Rhode sat up suddenly and winced as he put unexpected pressure on his leg. He groped in the snow with scrabbling fingers. "The ice-axe," he said frantically. "The ice-axe—where is it?"

"I didn't see it," said Forester.

They both looked into the whirling grey darkness down the slope and Rohde felt an empty sensation in the pit of his stomach. The ice-axe had been invaluable; without it they could not have come as far as they had, and without it he doubted if they could get to the top of the pass. He looked down and saw that his hands were shaking uncontrollably and he knew he was coming to the end of his strength—physical and mental.

But Forester felt a renewed access of spirit. He said, "Well, what of it? This goddam mountain has done its best to kill us and it hasn't succeeded yet—and my guess is that it won't. If we've come this far we can go the rest of the way. It's only another five hundred feet to the top—five hundred lousy feet—do you hear that, Miguel?"

Rohde smiled wearily. "But we have to go down again."

"So what? It's just another way of getting up speed. I'll lead off this time. I can follow our tracks back to where we turned off."

And it was in this spirit of unreasonable and unreasoning

177

optimism that Forester led the way down with Rohde limping behind. He found it fairly easy to follow their tracks and followed them faithfully, even when they wavered where Rohde had diverged. He had not the same faith in his own wilderness path-finding that he had in Rohde's, and he knew that if he got off track in this blizzard he would never find it again. As it was, when they reached where they had turned off to the right and struck across the slope, the track was so faint as to be almost indistinguishable, the wind having nearly obliterated it with drifting snow.

He stopped and let Rohde catch up. " How's the leg?"

Rohde's grin was a snarl. " The pain has stopped. It is numb with the cold—and very stiff."

" I'll break trail then," said Forester. " You'd better take it easy for a while." He smiled and felt the stiffness of his cheeks. " You can use the rope like a rein to guide me—one tug to go left, two tugs to go right."

Rohde nodded without speaking, and they pressed on again. Forester found the going harder in the unbroken snow, especially as he did not have the ice-axe to test the way ahead. It's not so bad here, he thought; there are no crevasses—but it'll be goddam tricky if we have to cross the glacier. In spite of the hard going, he was better mentally than he had been; the task of leadership kept him alert and forced his creaking brain to work.

It seemed to him that the wind was not as strong and he hoped it was dropping. From time to time he swerved to the right under instruction from Rohde, but each time came to deep drifts and had to return to the general line of march. They came to the jumbled ice columns of the glacier without finding a good route up to the pass.

Forester dropped to his knees in the snow and felt tears of frustration squeeze out on to his cheeks. " What now?" he asked—not that he expected a good answer.

Rohde fell beside him, half-sitting, half-lying, his stiff leg jutting out before him. " We go into the glacier a little way to find shelter. The wind will not be as bad in there." He looked at his watch then held it to his ear. " It is two o'clock—four hours to nightfall; we cannot spare the time but we must drink something hot, even if it is only hot water."

" Two o'clock," said Forester bitterly. " I feel as though I've been wandering round this mountain for a hundred years, and made personal acquaintance with every goddam snowflake."

They pushed on into the tangled ice maze of the glacier and Forester was deathly afraid of hidden crevasses. Twice he plunged to his armpits in deep snow and was hauled out with difficulty by Rohde. At last they found what they were looking for—a small cranny in the ice sheltered from the wind—and they sank into the snow with relief, glad to be out of the cutting blast.

Rohde assembled the Primus and lit it and then melted some snow. As before, they found the rich meaty taste of the bouillon nauseating and had to content themselves with hot water. Forester felt the heat radiating from his belly and was curiously content. He said, "How far to the top from here?"

"Seven hundred feet, maybe," said Rohde.

"Yes, we slipped about two hundred feet by coming back." Forester yawned. "Christ, it's good to be out of the wind; I feel a good hundred per cent warmer—which brings me up to freezing-point." He pulled the jacket closer about him and regarded Rohde through half-closed eyes. Rohde was looking vacantly at the flaring Primus, his eyes glazed with fatigue.

Thus they lay in their ice shelter while the wind howled about them and flurries of driven snow eddied in small whirlpools in that haven of quiet.

I V

Rohde dreamed.

He dreamed, curiously enough, that he was asleep—asleep in a vast feather bed into which he sank with voluptuous enjoyment. The bed enfolded him in soft comfort, seeming to support his tired body and to let him sink at the same time. Both he and the bed were falling slowly into a great chasm, drifting down and down and down, and suddenly he knew to his horror that this was the comfort of death and that when he reached the bottom of the pit he would die.

Frantically he struggled to get up, but the bed would not let him go and held him back in cloying folds and he heard a quiet maniacal tittering of high-pitched voices laughing at him. He discovered that his hand held a long, sharp knife and he stabbed at the bed with repeated plunges of his arm, ripping the fabric and releasing a fountain of feathers which whirled in the air before his eyes.

He started and screamed and opened his eyes. The scream came out as a dismal croak and he saw that the feathers were snowflakes dancing in the wind and beyond was the wilderness of the glacier. He was benumbed with the cold and he knew that if he slept he would not wake again.

There was something strange about the scene that he could not place and he forced himself to analyse what it was, and suddenly he knew—the wind had dropped. He got up stiffly and with difficulty and looked at the sky; the mist was clearing rapidly and through the dissipating wreaths he saw a faint patch of blue sky.

He turned to Forester who was lying prostrate, his head on one side and his cheek touching the ice, and wondered if he was dead. He leaned over him and shook him and Forester's head flopped down on to his chest. "Wake up," said Rohde, the words coming rustily to his throat. "Wake up—come on, wake up."

He took Forester by the shoulder and shook him and Forester's head lolled about, almost as though his neck was broken. Rohde seized his wrist and felt for the pulse; there was a faint fluttering beneath the cold skin and he knew that Forester was still alive—but only just.

The Primus stove was empty—he had fallen asleep with it still burning—but there was a drain of kerosene left in the bottle. He poured it into the Primus and heated some water with which he bathed Forester's head, hoping that the warmth would penetrate somehow and unfreeze his brain. After a while Forester stirred weakly and mumbled something incoherently.

Rohde slapped his face. "Wake up; you cannot give in now." He dragged Forester to his feet and he promptly collapsed. Again Rohde hauled him up and supported him. "You must walk," he said. "You must not sleep." He felt in his pocket and found one last coca quid which he forced into Forester's mouth. "Chew," he shouted. "Chew and walk."

Gradually Forester came round—never fully conscious but able to use his legs in an automatic manner, and Rohde walked him to-and-fro in an effort to get the blood circulating again. He talked all the time, not because he thought Forester could understand him, but to break the deathly silence that held the mountain now that the wind had gone. "Two hours to nightfall," he said. "It will be dark in two hours. We must get to the top before then—long before then. Here, stand still while I fasten the rope."

Forester obediently stood still, swaying slightly on his feet, and Rohde fastened the rope around his waist. "Can you follow me? Can you?"

Forester nodded slowly, his eyes half open.

"Good," said Rohde. "Then come on."

He led the way out of the glacier and on to the mountain slopes. The mist had now gone and he could see right to the top of the pass, and it seemed but a step away—a long step. Below, there was an unbroken sea of white cloud, illumined by the late afternoon sun into a blinding glare. It seemed solid and firm enough to walk on.

He looked at the snow slopes ahead and immediately saw what they had missed in the darkness of the blizzard—a definite ridge running right to the top of the pass. The snow cover would be thin there and would make for easy travel. He twitched on the rope and plunged forward, then glanced back at Forester to see how he was doing.

Forester was in the middle of a cold nightmare. He had been so warm, so cosily and beautiful warm, until Rohde had so rudely brought him back to the mountains. What the devil was the matter with the guy? Why couldn't he let a man sleep when he wanted to instead of pulling him up a mountain? But Rohde was a good joe, so he'd do what he said—but why was he doing it? Why was he on this mountain?

He tried to think but the reason eluded him. He dimly remembered a fall over a cliff and that this guy Rohde had saved his life. Hell, that was enough, wasn't it? If a guy saves your life he was entitled to push you around a little afterwards. He didn't know what he wanted, but he was with him all the way.

And so Forester shambled on, not knowing where or why, but content to follow where Rohde led. He kept falling because his legs were rubbery and he could not make them do precisely what he wanted, and every time he fell Rohde would return the length of the rope and help him to his feet. Once he started to slide and Rohde almost lost his balance and they both nearly tumbled down the slope, but Rohde managed to dig his heels into the snow and so stopped them.

Although Rohde's stiff leg impeded him, Forester impeded him more. But even so they made good time and the top of the pass came nearer and nearer. There was only two hundred feet of altitude to make when Forester collapsed for the last time. Rohde went back along the rope but Forester could not stand. Cold and exhaustion had done their work in sapping the life energy from a strong man, and he lay in the snow unable to move.

A glimmer of intelligence returned to him and he peered at Rohde through red-rimmed eyes. He swallowed painfully and whispered, " Leave me, Miguel; I can't make it. You've *got* to get over the pass."

Rohde stared down at him in silence.

Forester croaked, " Goddam it—get the hell out of here." Although his voice was almost inaudible it was as loud as he could shout and the violence of the effort was too much for him and he relapsed into unconsciousness.

Still in silence Rohde bent down and gathered Forester into his arms. It was very difficult to lift him on to his shoulder in a fireman's lift—there was the steepness of the slope, his stiff leg and his general weakness—but he managed it and, staggering a little under the weight, he put one foot in front of the other.

And then the other.

And so on up the mountain. The thin air wheezed in his throat and the muscles of his thighs cracked under the strain. His stiff leg did not hurt but it was a hindrance because he had to swing it awkwardly sideways in an arc in order to take a step. But it was beautifully firm when he took the weight on it. Forrester's arms swung limply, tapping against the backs of his legs with every movement and this irritated him for a while until he no longer felt the tapping. Until he no longer felt anything at all.

His body was dead and it was only a bright hot spark of will burning in his mind that kept him going. He looked dispassionately at this flame of will, urging it to burn brighter when it flickered and screening out all else that would quench it. He did not see the snow or the sky or the crags and peaks which flanked him. He saw nothing at all, just a haze of darkness shot with tiny sparks of light flaring inside his eyeballs.

One foot forward easily—that was his good foot. The next foot brought round in a stiff semi-circle to grope for a footing. This was harder because the foot was dead and he could not feel the ground. Slowly, very slowly, take the weight. Right—that was good. Now the other foot—easy again.

He began to count, got up to eleven and lost count. He started again and this time got up to eight. After that he did not bother to count but just went forward, content to know that one foot was moving in front of the other.

Pace . . . halt . . . swing . . . grope . . . halt . . . pace . . . halt . . . swing . . . grope . . . halt . . . pace . . . halt . . . swing . . . grope . . . halt . . . swing . . . something glared against his closed eyes and he opened them to stare full into the sun.

He stopped and then closed his eyes painfully, but not before he had seen the silver streak on the horizon and knew it was the sea. He opened his eyes again and looked down on the green valley and the white scattering of houses that was Altemiros lying snugly between the mountain and the lesser foothills beyond.

His tongue came out to lick ice-cracked lips stiffly. " Forester," he whispered. " Forester, we are on top."

But Forester was past caring, hanging limply unconscious across Rohde's broad shoulder.


*Chapter VIII*


Aguillar looked dispassionately at a small cut on his hand—one of many—from which the blood was oozing. I will never be a mechanic, he thought; I can guide people, but not machines. He laid down the broken piece of hacksaw-blade and wiped away the blood, then sucked the wound. When the blood ceased to flow he picked up the blade and got to work on the slot he was cutting in the length of steel reinforcing rod.

He had made ten bolts for the crossbows, or at least he had slotted them and put in the metal flights. To sharpen them was beyond his powers; he could not turn the old grindstone and sharpen a bolt at the same time, but he was confident that, given another pair of hands, the ten bolts would be usable within the hour.

He had also made an inventory of the contents of the camp, checked the food supplies and the water, and in general had behaved like any army quartermaster. He had a bitter-sweet feeling about being sent to the camp. He recognised that he was no use in a fight; he was old and weak and had heart trouble

183

—but there was more to it than that. He knew that he was a man of ideas and not a man of action, and the fact irked him, making him feel inadequate.

His sphere of action lay in the making of decisions and in administration; in order to get into a position to make valid decisions and to have something to administer he had schemed and plotted and manipulated the minds of men, but he had never fought physically. He did not believe in fighting, but hitherto he had thought about it in the abstract and in terms of large-scale conflicts. This sudden plunge into the realities of death by battle had led him out of his depth.

So here he was, the eternal politician, with others, as always, doing the fighting and dying and suffering—even his own niece. As he thought of Benedetta the blade slipped and he cut his hand again. He muttered a brief imprecation and sucked the blood, then looked at the slot he had cut and decided it was deep enough. There would be no more bolts; the teeth of the hacksaw-blade were worn smooth and would hardly cut cheese, let alone steel.

He fitted the flight into the slot, wedging it as Willis had shown him, and then put the unsharpened bolt with the others. It was strange, he thought, that night was falling so suddenly, and went out of the hut to be surprised by the deepening mist. He looked up towards the mountains, now hidden from sight, and felt deep sorrow as he thought of Rohde. And of Forester, yes—he must not forget Forester and the other *norteamericano*, Peabody.

Faintly from the river he heard the sound of small-arms fire and his ears pricked. Was that a machine-gun? He had heard that sound when Lopez and the army had ruthlessly tightened their grip on Cordillera five years earlier, and he did not think he was mistaken. He listened again but it was only some freak of the mountain winds that had brought the sound to his ears and he heard nothing more. He hoped that it was not a machine-gun—the dice were already loaded enough.

He sighed and went back into the hut and selected a can of soup from the shelf for his belated midday meal. He had just finished eating the hot soup half an hour later when he heard his niece calling him. He went out of the hut, tightening his coat against the cold air, and found that the mist was very much thicker. He shouted to Benedetta to let her know where he was and soon a dim figure loomed through the fog, a strange figure, misshapen and humped, and for a moment he felt fear.

Then he saw that it was Benedetta supporting someone and he ran forward to help her. She was breathing painfully and gasped, " It's Jenny, she's hurt."

" Hurt? How?"

" She was shot," said Benedetta briefly.

He was outraged. " This American lady—shot! This is criminal."

" Help me take her inside," said Benedetta. They got Miss Ponsky into the hut and laid her in a bunk. She was conscious and smiled weakly as Benedetta tucked in a blanket, then closed her eyes in relief. Benedetta looked at her uncle. " She killed a man and helped to kill others—why shouldn't she be shot at? I wish I were like her."

Aguillar looked at her with pain in his eyes. He said slowly, " I find all this difficult to believe. I feel as though I am in a dream. Why should these people shoot a woman?"

" They didn't know she was a woman," said Benedetta impatiently. " And I don't suppose they cared. She was shooting at them when it happened, anyway. I wish I could kill some of them." She looked up at Aguillar. " Oh, I know you always preach the peaceful way, but how can you be peaceful when someone is coming at you with a gun? Do you bare your breast and say, ' Kill me and take all I have '?"

Aguillar did not answer. He looked down at Miss Ponsky and said, " Is she badly hurt?"

" Not dangerously," said Benedetta. " But she has lost a lot of blood." She paused. " As we were coming up the road I heard a machine-gun."

He nodded. " I thought I heard it—but I was not sure." He held her eyes. " Do you think they are across the bridge?"

" They might be," said Benedetta steadily. " We must prepare. Have you made bolts? Tim has the crossbow and he will need them."

" Tim? Ah—O'Hara." He raised his eyebrows slightly, then said, " The bolts need sharpening."

" I will help you."

She turned the crank on the grindstone while Aguillar sharpened the steel rods to a point. As he worked he said, " O'Hara is a strange man—a complicated man. I do not think I fully understand him." He smiled slightly. " That is an admission from me."

" I understand him—now," she said. Despite the cold, a film of sweat formed on her forehead as she turned the heavy crank.

"So? You have talked with him?"

While the showers of sparks flew and the acrid stink of burning metal filled the air she told Aguillar about O'Hara and his face grew pinched as he heard the story. "That is the enemy," she said at length. "The same who are on the other side of the river."

Aguillar said in a low voice, "There is so much evil in the world—so much evil in the hearts of men."

They said nothing more until all the bolts were sharpened and then Benedetta said, "I am going out on the road. Will you watch Jenny?"

He nodded silently and she walked along the street between the two rows of huts. The mist was getting even thicker so that she could not see very far ahead, and tiny droplets of moisture condensed on the fabric of her coat. If it gets colder it will snow, she thought.

It was very quiet on the road, and very lonely. She did not hear a sound except for the occasional splash of a drop of water falling from a rock. It was as though being in the middle of a cloud was like being wrapped in cotton-wool; this was very dirty cotton-wool, but she had done enough flying to know that from above the cloud bank would be clean and shining.

After some time she walked off the road and crossed the rocky hillside until the gigantic cable drum loomed through the mist. She paused by the enormous reel, then went forward to the road cutting and looked down. The road surface was barely visible in the pervading greyness and she stood there uncertainly, wondering what to do. Surely there was something she could be doing.

Fire, she thought suddenly, we can fight them with fire. The drum was already poised to crash into a vehicle coming up the road, and fire would add to the confusion. She hurried back to the camp and collected the bottles of paraffin she had brought back from the bridge, stopping briefly to see how Miss Ponsky was.

Aguillar looked up as she came in. "There is soup," he said. "It will be good in this cold, my dear."

Benedetta spread her hands gratefully to the warmth of the paraffin heater and was aware that she was colder than she had thought. "I would like some soup," she said. She looked over to Miss Ponsky. "How are you, Jenny?"

Miss Ponsky, now sitting up, said briskly, "Much better,

thank you. Wasn't it silly of me to get shot? I shouldn't have leaned out so far—and then I missed. And I lost the bow."

"I would not worry," said Benedetta with a quick smile. "Does your shoulder hurt?"

"Not much," said Miss Ponsky. "It will be all right if I keep my arm in a sling. Señor Aguillar helped me to make one."

Benedetta finished her soup quickly and mentioned the bottles, which she had left outside. "I must take them up to the road," she said.

"Let me help you," said Aguillar.

"It is too cold out there, *tío*," she said. "Stay with Jenny."

She took the bottles down to the cable drum and then sat on the edge of the cutting, listening. A wind was rising and the mist swirled in wreaths and coils, thinning and thickening in the vagaries of the breeze. Sometimes she could see as far as the bend in the road, and at other times she could not see the road at all although it was only a few feet below her. And everything was quiet.

She was about to leave, sure that nothing was going to happen, when she heard the faint clatter of a rock from far down the mountain. She felt a moment of apprehension and scrambled to her feet. The others would not be coming unless they were in retreat, and in that case it could just as well be an enemy as a friend. She turned and picked up one of the bottles and felt for matches in her pocket.

It was a long time before she heard anything else and then it was the thud of running feet on the road. The mist had thinned momentarily and she saw a dim figure come round the bend and up the road at a stumbling run. As the figure came closer she saw that it was Willis.

"What is happening?" she called.

He looked up, startled to hear a voice from above his head and in a slight panic until he recognised it. He stopped, his chest heaving, and went into a fit of coughing. "They've come across," he gasped. "They broke across." He coughed again, rackingly. "The others are just behind me," he said. "I heard them running—unless . . ."

"You'd better come up here," she said.

He looked up at Benedetta, vaguely outlined at the top of the fifteen-foot cutting. "I'll come round by the road," he said, and began to move away at a fast walk.

By the time he joined her she had already heard someone else coming up the road, and, remembering Willis's *unless*, she lay down by the edge and grasped the bottle. It was Armstrong, coming up at a fast clip. "Up here," she called. "To the drum."

He cast a brief glance upwards but wasted no time in greeting, nor did he slacken his pace. She watched him go until he was lost in the mist and waited for him to join them.

They were both exhausted, having made the five-mile journey uphill in a little over an hour and a half. She let them rest a while and get their breath before she asked them, "What happened?"

"I don't know," said Willis. "We were on the trebuchet; we'd let fly when O'Hara told us to—it was ready loaded—and then he yelled for us to clear out, so we took it on the run. There was a devil of a lot of noise going on—a lot of shooting, I mean."

She looked at Armstrong. He said, "That's about it. I think O'Hara got one of them—I heard a man scream in a choked sort of way. But they came across the bridge; I saw them as I looked back—and I saw O'Hara run into the rocks. He should be along any minute now."

She sighed with relief.

Willis said, "And he'll have the whole pack of them on his heels. What the hell are we going to do?" There was a hysterical note in his voice.

Armstrong was calmer. "I don't think so. O'Hara and I talked about this and we came to the conclusion that they'll play it safe and repair the bridge while they can, and then run jeeps up to the mine before we can get there." He looked up at the cable drum. "This is all we've got to stop them."

Benedetta held up the bottle. "And some of these."

"Oh, good," said Armstrong approvingly. "Those should help." He thought a little. "There's not much your uncle can do—or Miss Ponsky. I suggest that they get started for the mine right now—and if they hear anyone or anything coming up the road behind them to duck into the rocks until they're sure it's safe. Thank God for this mist."

Benedetta did not stir and he said, "Will you go and tell them?"

She said, "I'm staying here. I want to fight."

"I'll go," said Willis. He got up and faded into the mist.

188

Armstrong caught the desperate edge in Benedetta's voice and patted her hand in a kindly, fatherly manner. "We all have to do the best we can," he said. "Willis is frightened, just as I am, and you are, I'm sure." His voice was grimly humorous. "O'Hara was talking to me about the situation back at the bridge and I gathered he didn't think much of Willis. He said he wasn't a leader—in fact, his exact words were, 'He couldn't lead a troop of boy scouts across a street.' I think he was being a bit hard on poor Willis—but, come to that, I gathered that he didn't think much of me either, from the tone of his voice." He laughed.

"I'm sure he didn't mean it," said Benedetta. "He has been under a strain."

"Oh, he was right," said Armstrong. "I'm no man of action. I'm a man of ideas, just like Willis."

"And my uncle," said Benedetta. She sat up suddenly. "Where *is* Tim? He should have been here by now." She clutched Armstrong's arm. "*Where is he?*"

II

O'Hara was lying in a crack in the rocks watching a pair of stout boots that stamped not more than two feet from his head, and trying not to cough. Events had been confused just after the rush across the bridge, he had not been able to get to the road—he would have been cut down before going ten yards in the open—so he had taken to the rocks, scuttling like a rabbit for cover.

It was then that he had slipped on a mist-wetted stone and turned his ankle, to come crashing to the ground. He had lain there with all the wind knocked out of him, expecting to feel the thud of bullets that would mean his death, but nothing like that happened. He heard a lot of shouting and knew his analysis of the enemy intentions had proved correct; they were spreading out along the edge of the gorge and covering the approaches to the bridge.

The mist helped, of course. He still had the crossbow and was within hearing distance of the noisy crowd which surrounded the man he had shot through the chest. He judged that they did not relish the task of winkling out a man with a silent killing weapon from the hillside, especially when death could come from the mist. There was a nervous snapping

189

edge to the voices out there and he smiled grimly; knives they knew and guns they understood, but this was something different, something they regarded with awe.

He felt his ankle. It was swollen and painful and he wondered if it would bear his weight, but this was neither the time nor the place to stand. He took his small pocket-knife and slit his trousers, cutting a long strip. He did not take off his shoe because he knew he would not be able to get it on again, so he tied the strip of cloth tightly around the swelling and under the instep of his shoe, supporting his ankle.

He was so intent on this that he did not see the man approach. The first indication was the slither of a kicked pebble and he froze rigid. From the corner of his eye he saw the man standing sideways to him, looking back towards the bridge. O'Hara kept very still, except for his arm which groped for a handy-sized rock. The man scratched his ribs in a reflective sort of way, moved on and was lost in the mist.

O'Hara let loose his pent-up breath in a silent sigh and prepared to move. He had the crossbow and three bolts which had a confounded tendency to clink together unless he was careful. He slid forward on his belly, worming his way among the rocks, trying to go upwards, away from the bridge. Again he was warned of imminent peril by the rattle of a rock and he rolled into a crack between two boulders and then he saw the boots appear before his face and struggled with a tickle in his throat, fighting to suppress the cough.

The man stamped his feet noisily and beat his hands together, breathing heavily. Suddenly he turned with a clatter of boots and O'Hara heard the metallic snap as a safety-catch went off. " *Quien?* "

" Santos."

O'Hara recognised the voice of the Cuban. So his name was Santos—he'd remember that and look him up if he ever got out of this mess.

The man put the rifle back on safety and Santos said in Spanish, " See anything?"

" Nothing."

Santos grunted in his throat. " Keep moving; go up the hill—they won't hang about here."

The other man said, " The Russian said we must stay down here."

" To hell with him," growled Santos. " If he had not interfered we would have old Aguillar in our hands right now. Move up the hill—and get the others going too."

The other did not reply but obediently moved off, and O'Hara heard him climbing higher. Santos stayed only a moment and then clattered away noisily in his steel-shod boots, and again O'Hara let out his breath softly.

He waited a while and thought of what to do next. If Santos was moving the men away up the hill, then his obvious course was to go down. But the enemy seemed to be divided into two factions and the Russian might still have kept some men below. Still, he would have to take that chance.

He slid out of the crack and began to crawl back the way he had come, inching his way along on his belly and being careful of his injured ankle. He was pleased to see that the mist was thickening and through it he heard shouts from the bridge and the knocking of steel on wood. They were getting on with their repairs and traffic in the vicinity of the bridge would be heavy, so it was a good place to stay away from. He wanted to find a lone man far away from his fellows and preferably armed to the teeth. A crossbow was all very well, but he could do with something that had a faster rate of fire.

He altered course and headed for the trebuchet, stopping every few yards to listen and to peer through the mist. As he approached he heard laughter and a few derogatory comments shouted in Spanish. There was a crowd round the trebuchet and apparently they found it a humorous piece of machinery. He stopped and cocked the crossbow awkwardly, using the noise of the crowd as cover for any clinkings he might make. Then he crawled closer and took cover behind a boulder.

Presently he heard the bull-roar of Santos. "Up the hill, you lot. In the name of Jesus, what are you doing wasting time here? Juan, you stay here; the rest of you get moving."

O'Hara flattened behind the boulder as the men moved off to the accompaniment of many grumbles. None of them came close to him, but he waited a few minutes before he began to crawl in a wide circle round the trebuchet, looking for the man left on guard. The bridge was illuminated by headlights and their glow lit the mist with a ghostly radiance, and at last he crept up on the guard who was just in the right position—silhouetted against the light.

Juan, the guard, was very young—not more than twenty—and O'Hara hesitated. Then he steeled himself because there was more at stake here than the life of a misguided youth. He lifted the crossbow and aimed carefully, then hesitated again, his finger on the trigger. His hesitation this time was for a different reason; Juan was playing soldiers, strutting about with his sub-machine-gun at the ready, and, O'Hara suspected, with the safety-catch off. He remembered the man he had shot by the bridge and how a full magazine had emptied in a dead hand, so he waited, not wanting any noise when he pulled the trigger.

At last Juan got tired of standing sentry and became more interested in the trebuchet. He leaned over to look at the mechanism which held down the long arm, found his gun in his way and let it fall to be held by the shoulder-sling. He never knew what hit him as the heavy bolt struck him between the shoulders at a range of ten yards. It knocked him forward against the long arm, the bolt protruding through his chest and skewering him to the baulk of timber. He was quite dead when O'Hara reached him.

Ten minutes later O'Hara was again ensconced among the rocks, examining his booty. He had the sub-machine-gun, three full magazines of ammunition, a loaded pistol and a heavy broad-bladed knife. He grinned in satisfaction—now he was becoming dangerous, he had got himself some sharp teeth.


III


Benedetta, Armstrong and Willis waited in the cold mist by the cable drum. Willis fidgeted, examining the wedge-shaped chock that prevented the drum from rolling on to the road and estimated the amount of force needed to free it when the time came. But Benedetta and Armstrong were quite still, listening intently for any sound that might come up the hill.

Armstrong was thinking that they would have to be careful; any person coming up might be O'Hara and they would have to make absolutely sure before jumping him, something that would be difficult in this mist. Benedetta's mind was emptied of everything except a deep sorrow. Why else was O'Hara not at the camp unless he were dead, or worse, captured? She knew his feelings about being captured again and she knew he would resist that, come what may. That made the likelihood of his being dead even more certain, and something within her died at the thought.

Aguillar had been difficult about retreating to the mine. He had wanted to stay and fight, old and unfit as he was, but

Benedetta had overruled him. His eyes had widened in surprise as he heard the incisive tone of command in her voice. "There are only three of us fit to fight," she said. "We can't spare one to help Jenny up to the mine. Someone must help her and you are the one. Besides, it is even higher up there than here, remember—you will have to go slowly so you must get away right now."

Aguillar glanced at the other two men. Willis was morosely kicking at the ground and Armstrong smiled slightly, and Aguillar saw that they were content to let Benedetta take the lead and give the orders in the absence of O'Hara. She has turned into a young Amazon, he thought; a raging young lioness. He went up to the mine road with Miss Ponsky without further argument.

Willis stopped fiddling with the chock. "Where are they?" he demanded in a high voice. "Why don't they come and get it over with?"

Benedetta glanced at Armstrong who said, "Quiet! Not so loud."

"All right," said Willis, whispering. "But what's keeping them from attacking us?"

"We have already discussed that," said Benedetta. She turned to Armstrong. "Do you think we can defend the camp?"

He shook his head. "It's indefensible. We haven't a hope. If we can block the road, our next step is to retreat to the mine."

"Then the camp must be burned," said Benedetta decisively. "We must not leave it to give comfort and shelter to them." She looked at Willis. "Go back and splash kerosene in the huts—all of them. And when you hear noise and shooting from here, set everything on fire."

"And then what?" he asked.

"Then you make your way up to the mine as best you can." She smiled slightly. "I would not come up this way again—go straight up and find the road at a higher level. We will be coming up too—as fast as we can."

Willis withdrew and she said to Armstrong, "That one is frightened. He tries to hide it, but it shows. I cannot trust him here."

"I'm frightened too. Aren't you?" asked Armstrong curiously.

"I was," she said. "I was afraid when the airplane crashed and for a long time afterwards. My bones were jelly—

193

my legs were weak at the thought of fighting and dying. Then I had a talk with Tim and he taught me not to be that way." She paused. "That was when he told me how frightened he was."

"What a damned silly situation this is," said Armstrong in wonder. "Here we are waiting to kill men whom we don't know and who don't know us. But that's always the way in a war, of course." He grinned. "But it is damned silly all the same; a middle-aged professor and a young woman lurking on a mountain with murderous intent. I think——"

She put her hand on his arm. "Hush!"

He listened. "What is it?"

"I thought I heard something."

They lay quietly, their ears straining and hearing nothing but the sough of the wind on the mist-shrouded mountain. Then Benedetta's hand tightened on his arm as she heard, far away, the characteristic sound of a gear change. "Tim was right," she whispered. "They're coming up in a truck or a jeep. We must get ready."

"I'll release the drum," Armstrong said. "You stay on the edge here, and give a shout when you want it to go." He scrambled to his feet and ran back to the drum.

Benedetta ran along the edge of the cutting where she had placed the Molotov cocktails. She lit the wicks of three of them and each flamed with a halo in the mist. The rags, slightly damp with exposure, took a long time to catch alight well. She did not think their light could be seen from the road below; nevertheless, she put them well back from the edge.

The vehicle was labouring heavily, the engine coughing in the thin air. Twice it stopped and she heard the revving of the self-starter. This was no supercharged engine designed for high-altitude operation and the vehicle could not be making more than six or seven miles an hour up the steep slopes of the road. But it was moving much faster than a man could climb under the same conditions.

Benedetta lay on the edge of the cutting and looked down the road towards the bend. The mist was too thick to see that far and she hoped the vehicle had lights strong enough to give her an indication of its position. The growling of the engine increased and then faded as the vehicle twisted and turned round the hairpin bends, and she thought she heard a double note as of two engines. One or two, she thought; it does not matter.

Armstrong crouched by the cable drum, grasping the short

length of electric wire which was fastened to the chock. He peered towards the cutting but saw nothing but a blank wall of grey mist. His face was strained as he waited.

Down the road Benedetta saw a faint glow at the corner of the road and knew that the first vehicle was coming up on the other side of the bend. She glanced back to see if the paraffin wicks were still burning, then turned back and saw two misty eyes of headlamps as the first vehicle made the turn. She had already decided when to shout to Armstrong —a rock was her mark and when the headlights drew level with it, that was the time.

She drew her breath as the engine coughed and died away and the jeep—for through the mist she could now see what it was—drew to a halt. There was a whine from the starter and the jeep began to move again. Behind it two more headlights came into view as a second vehicle pulled round the bend.

Then the headlights of the jeep were level with the rock, and she jumped up, shouting, "Now! Now! Now!"

There was a startled shout from below as she turned and grabbed the paraffin bottles, easy to see as they flamed close at hand. There was a rumble as the drum plunged forward and she looked up to see it charging down the slope like a juggernaut to crash over the side of the cutting.

She heard the smash and rending of metal and a man screamed. Then she ran back to the edge and hurled a bottle into the confusion below.

The heavy drum had dropped fifteen feet on to the front of the jeep, crushing the forepart entirely and killing the driver. The bottle broke beside the dazed passenger in the wrecked front seat and the paraffin ignited in a great flare and he screamed again, beating at the flames that enveloped him and trying to release his trapped legs. The two men in the back tumbled out and ran off down the road towards the truck coming up behind.

Armstrong ran up to Benedetta just as she threw the second bottle. He had two more in his hand which he lit from the flaming wick of the remaining one and ran along the edge of the cutting towards the truck, which had drawn to a halt. There was a babble of shouts from below and a couple of wild shots which came nowhere near him as he stood on the rim and looked into the truck full of men.

Deliberately he threw one bottle hard at the top of the cab. It smashed and flaming paraffin spread and dripped down past the open window and there came an alarmed cry from the driver. The other bottle he tossed into the body of the truck and in the flickering light he saw the mad scramble to get clear. No one had the time or inclination to shoot at him.

He ran back to Benedetta who was attempting to light another bottle, her hand shaking and her breath coming in harsh gasps. Exertion and the reaction of shock were taking equal toll of her fortitude. "Enough," he panted. "Let's get out of here." As he spoke, there was an explosion and a great flaring light from the jeep and he grinned tightly. "That wasn't paraffin—that was petrol. Come on."

As they ran they saw a glow from the direction of the camp —and then another and another. Willis was doing his job of arson.


IV


O'Hara's ankle was very painful. Before making his move up the hill he had rebound it, trying to give it some support, but it still could not bear his full weight. It made clambering among the rocks difficult and he made more noise than he liked.

He was following in the line of beaters that Santos had organised and luckily they were making more noise than he as they stumbled and fell about in the mist, and he thought they weren't making too good a job of it. He had his own troubles; the crossbow and the sub-machine-gun together were hard to handle and he thought of discarding the bow, but then thought better of it. It was a good, silent weapon and he still had two bolts.

He had a shock when he heard the roar of Santos ordering his men to return to the road and he shrank behind a boulder in case any of the men came his way. None did, and he smiled as he thought of the note of exasperation in Santos's voice. Apparently the Russian was getting his own way after all, and he was certain of it when he heard the engines start up from the direction of the bridge.

That was what they should have done in the first place— this searching of the mountain in the mist was futile. The Russian was definitely a better tactician than Santos; he had not fallen for their trick of promising to give up Aguillar, and now he was preparing to ram his force home to the mine.

196

O'Hara grimaced as he wondered what would happen at the camp.

Now that the mountainside ahead of him was clear of the enemy he made better time, and deliberately stayed as close as he could to the road. Soon he heard the groan of engines again and knew that the communist mechanised division was on its way. He saw the headlights as a jeep and a truck went past and he paused, listening for what was coming next. Apparently that was all, so he boldly stepped out on to the road and started to hobble along on the smooth surface.

He thought it was safe enough; he could hear if another truck came up behind and there was plenty of time to take cover. Still, as he walked he kept close to the edge of the road, the sub-machine-gun at the ready and his eyes carefully scanning the greyness ahead.

It took him a very long time to get anywhere near the camp and long before that he heard a few scattered shots and what sounded like an explosion, and he thought he could detect a glow up the mountain but was not sure whether his eyes were playing tricks. He redoubled his caution, which was fortunate, because presently he heard the thud of boots ahead of him and he slipped in among the rocks on the roadside, sweating with exertion.

A man clattered past at a dead run, and O'Hara heard the wheezing of his breath. He stayed hidden until there was nothing more to be heard, then came on to the road again and resumed his hobbling climb. Half an hour later he heard the sound of an engine from behind him and took cover again and watched a jeep go by at a crawl. He thought he could see the Russian but was not sure, and the jeep had gone by before he thought to raise the gun.

He cursed himself at the missed opportunity. He knew there was no point in killing the rank-and-file indiscriminately —there were too many of them—but if he could knock out the king-pins, then the whole enemy attack would collapse. The Russian and the Cuban would be his targets in future, and all else would be subordinated to the task of getting them in his sights.

He knew that something must have happened up ahead and tried to quicken his pace. The Russian had been sent for and that meant the enemy had run into trouble. He wondered if Benedetta was safe and felt a quick anger at these ruthless men who were harrying them like animals.

As he climbed higher he found that his eyes had not

deceived him—there was a definite glow of fire from up ahead, reflected and subdued by the surrounding mist. He stopped and considered. The fire seemed to be localised in two patches; one small patch which seemed to be on the road and another, which was so large that he could not believe it. Then he smiled—of course, that was the camp; the whole bloody place was going up in flames.

He had better give both localities a wide berth, he thought; so he left the road again, intending to cast a wide circle and come upon the road again above the camp. But curiosity drew him back to where the smaller fire was and where he suspected the Russian had gone.

The mist was too thick to see exactly what had happened but from the shouts he gathered that the road was blocked. Hell, he thought; that's the cutting where Willis was going to dump the cable drum. It looks as though it's worked. But he could not explain the fire which was now guttering out, so he tried to get closer.

His ankle gave way suddenly and he fell heavily, the crossbow falling from his grasp with a terrifying loud noise as it hit a rock, and he came down hard on his elbow and gasped with pain. He lay there, just by the side of the road and close by the Russian's jeep, his lips drawn back from his teeth in agony as he tried to suppress the groan which he felt was coming, and waited for the surprised shout of discovery.

But the enemy were making too much noise themselves as they tried to clear the road and O'Hara heard the jeep start up and drive a little way forward. Slowly the pain ebbed away and cautiously he tried to get up, but to his horror he found that his arm seemed to be trapped in a crevice between the rocks. Carefully he pulled and heard the clink as the sub-machine-gun he was holding came up against stone, and he stopped. Then he pushed his arm down and felt nothing.

At any other time he would have found it funny. He was like a monkey that had put its hand in the narrow neck of a bottle to grasp an apple and could not withdraw it without releasing the apple. He could not withdraw his arm without letting go of the gun, and he dared not let it go in case it made a noise. He wriggled cautiously, then stopped as he heard voices from close by.

"I say my way was best." It was the Cuban.

The other voice was flat and hard, speaking in badly-accented Spanish. "What did it get you? Two sprained ankles and a broken leg. You were losing men faster than

198

Aguillar could possibly kill them for you. It was futile to think of searching the mountain in this weather. You've bungled this right from the start."

"Was your way any better?" demanded Santos in an aggrieved voice. "Look at what has happened here—a jeep and a truck destroyed, two men killed and the road blocked. I still say that men on foot are better."

The other man—the Russian—said coldly, "It happened because you are stupid—you came up here as though you were driving through Havana. Aguillar is making you look like a fool, and I think he is right. Look, Santos, here is a pack of defenceless airline passengers and they have held you up four days; they have killed six of your men and you have a lot more wounded and out of action because of your own stupidity. Right from the start you should have made certain of the bridge—you should have been at the mine when Grivas landed the plane—but you bungled even there. Well, I am taking over from now, and when I come to write my report you are not going to look very good in Havana—not to mention Moscow."

O'Hara heard him walk away and sweated as he tried to free his arm. Here he had the two of them together and he could not do a damn' thing about it. With one burst he could have killed them both and chanced getting away afterwards, but he was trapped. He heard Santos shuffle his feet indecisively and then walk quickly after the Russian, mumbling as he went.

O'Hara lay there while they hooked up the Russian's jeep to the burned-out truck and withdrew it, to push it off the road and send it plunging down the mountain. Then they dragged out the jeep and did the same with it, and finally got to work on the cable drum. It took them two hours and, to O'Hara, sweating it out not more than six yards from where they were working, it seemed like two days.

V

Willis struggled to get back his breath as he looked down at the burning camp, thankful for the long hours he had put in at that high altitude previously. He had left Benedetta and Armstrong, glad to get away from the certainty of a hand-to-hand fight, defenceless against the ruthless armed men who were coming to butcher them. He could see no prospect

199

of any success; they had fought for days against tremendous odds and the outlook seemed blacker than ever. He did not relish the fact of his imminent death.

With difficulty he had rolled out the drum of paraffin and went from hut to hut, soaking the interior woodwork as thoroughly as possible. While in the last hut he thought he heard an engine and stepped outside to listen, catching the sound of the grinding of gears.

He struck a match, then paused. Benedetta had told him to wait for the shooting or noise and that had not come yet. But it might take some time for the huts to catch alight properly and, from the expression he had seen on Benedetta's face, the shooting was bound to come.

He tossed the match near a pool of paraffin and it caught fire in a flare of creeping flame which ran quickly up the woodwork. Hastily he lit the bundle of paraffin-soaked rags he held and ran along the line of huts, tossing them inside. As he reached the end of the first line he heard a distant crash from the road and a couple of shots. Better make this quick, he thought; now's the time to get out of here.

By the time he left the first line of huts was well aflame, great gouts of fire leaping from the windows. He scrambled up among the rocks above the camp and headed for the road, and when he reached it looked back to see the volcano of the burning camp erupting below. He felt satisfaction at that—he always liked to see a job well done. The mist was too thick to see more than the violent red and yellow glow, but he could make out enough to know that all the huts were well alight and there were no significant gaps. They won't sleep in there to-night, he thought, and turned to run up the road.

He went on for a long time, stopping occasionally to catch his labouring breath and to listen. He heard nothing once he was out of earshot of the camp. At first he had heard a faint shouting, but now everything was silent on the mountainside apart from the eerie keening of the wind. He did not know whether Armstrong and Benedetta were ahead of him or behind, but he listened carefully for any sound coming from the road below. Hearing nothing, he turned and pushed on again, feeling the first faint intimation of lack of oxygen as he went higher.

He was nearing the mine when he caught up with the others, Armstrong turning on his heels with alarm as he heard Willis's footsteps. Aguillar and Miss Ponsky were there also, having made very slow progress up the road. Armstrong said, falsely cheerful, " Bloody spectacular, wasn't it?"

Willis stopped, his chest heaving. " They'll be cold to-night —maybe they'll call off the final attack until to-morrow."

Armstrong shook his head in the gathering darkness. " I doubt it. Their blood is up—they're close to the kill." He looked at Willis, who was panting like a dog. " You'd better take it easy and help Jenny here—she's pretty bad. Benedetta and I can push up to the mine and see what we can do up there."

Willis stared back. " Do you think they're far behind?"

" Does it matter?" asked Benedetta. " We fight here or we fight at the mine." She absently kissed Aguillar and said something to him in Spanish, then gestured to Armstrong and they went off fairly quickly.

It did not take them long to get to the mine, and as Armstrong surveyed the three huts he said bleakly, " These are as indefensible as the camp. However, let's see what we can do."

He entered one of the huts and looked about in the gloom despairingly. He touched the wooden wall and thought, bullets will go through these like paper—we'd be better off scattered on the hillside facing death by exposure. He was roused by a cry from Benedetta, so he went outside.

She was holding a piece of paper in her hand and peering at it in the light of a burning wooden torch. She said excitedly, " From Forester—they prepared one of the mine tunnels for us."

Armstrong jerked up his head. " Where?" He took the piece of paper and examined the sketch on it, then looked about. " Over there," he said, pointing.

He found the tunnel and the low wall of rocks which Forester and Rohde had built. " Not much, but it's home," he said, looking into the blackness. " You'd better go back and bring the others, and I'll see what it's like inside."

By the time they all assembled in the tunnel mouth he had explored it pretty thoroughly with the aid of a smoky torch. " A dead end," he said. " This is where we make our last stand." He pulled a pistol from his belt. " I've still got Rohde's gun—with one bullet; can anyone shoot better than me?" He offered the gun to Willis. " What about you, General Custer?"

Willis looked at the pistol. " I've never fired a gun in my life."

Armstrong sighed. "Neither have I, but it looks as though this is my chance." He thrust the pistol back in his belt and said to Benedetta, "What's that you've got?"

"Miguel left us some food," she said. "Enough for a cold meal."

"Well, we won't die hungry," said Armstrong sardonically.

Willis made a sudden movement. "For God's sake, don't talk that way."

"I'm sorry," said Armstrong. "How are Miss Ponsky and Señor Aguillar?"

"As well as might be expected," said Benedetta bitterly. "For a man with a heart condition and an elderly lady with a hole in her shoulder, trying to breathe air that is not there." She looked up at Armstrong. "You think there is any chance for Tim?"

He averted his head. "No," he said shortly, and went to the mouth of the tunnel, where he lay down behind the low breastwork of rocks and put the gun beside him. If I wait I might kill someone, he thought; but I must wait until they're very close.

It was beginning to snow.


VI

It was very quiet by the cutting, although O'Hara could hear voices from farther up the road by the burning camp. There was not much of a glow through the mist now, and he judged that the huts must just about have burned down to their foundations. Slowly he relaxed his hand and let the sub-machine-gun fall. It clattered to the rocks and he pulled up his arm and massaged it.

He felt very damp and cold and wished he had been able to strip the llama-skin coat from the sentry by the trebuchet —young Juan would not have needed it. But it would have taken too long, apart from being a gruesome job, and he had not wanted to waste the time. Now he wished he had taken the chance.

He stayed there, sitting quietly for some time, wondering if anyone had noticed the noise of metal on stone. Then he set himself to retrieve the gun. It took him ten minutes to fish it from the crevice with the aid of the crossbow, and then he set off up the mountain again, steering clear of the road. At least the enforced halt had rested him.

Three more trucks had come up. They had not gone straight up to the mine—not yet; the enemy had indulged in a futile attempt to quench the fires of the flaming camp and that had taken some time. Knowing that the trucks were parked above the camp, he circled so as to come out upon them. His ankle was bad, the flesh soft and puffy, and he knew he could not walk very much farther—certainly not up to the mine. It was in his mind to get himself a truck the same way he got himself a gun—by killing for it.

A crowd of men were climbing into the trucks when he got back to the road and he felt depressed but brightened a little when he saw that only two trucks were being used. The jeep was drawn up alongside and O'Hara heard the Russian giving orders in his pedantic Spanish and fretted because he was not within range. Then the jeep set off up the road and the trucks rolled after it with a crashing of gears, leaving the third parked.

He could not see whether a guard had been left so he began to prowl forward very cautiously. He did not think that there was a guard—the enemy would not think of taking such a precaution, as everyone was supposed to have been driven up to the mine. So he was very shocked when he literally fell over a sentry, who had left his post by the truck and was relieving himself among the rocks by the roadside.

The man grunted in surprise as O'Hara cannoned into him. "*Cuidado!*" he said, and then looked up. O'Hara dropped both his weapons as the man opened his mouth and clamped the palm of his hand over the other's jaw before he could shout. They strained against each other silently, O'Hara forcing back the man's head, his fingers clawing for the vulnerable eyes. His other arm was wrapped around the man's chest, clutching him tight.

His opponent flailed frantically with both arms and O'Hara knew that he was in no condition for a real knock-down-drag-out fight with this man. He remembered the knife in his belt and decided to take a chance, depending on swiftness of action to kill the man before he made a noise. He released him suddenly, pushing him away, and his hand went swiftly to his waist. The man staggered and opened his mouth again and O'Hara stepped forward and drove the knife in a straight stab into his chest just below the breastbone, giving it an upward turn as it went in.

The man coughed in a surprised hiccuping fashion and leaned forward, toppling straight into O'Hara's arms. As

O'Hara lowered him to the ground he gave a deep sigh and died. Breathing heavily, O'Hara plucked out the knife and a gush of hot blood spurted over his hand. He stood for a moment, listening, and then picked up the sub-machine-gun from where he had dropped it. He felt a sudden shock as his finger brushed the safety-catch—it was in the off position; the sudden jar could well have fired a warning shot.

But that was past and he was beyond caring. He knew he was living from minute to minute and past possibilities and actions meant nothing to him. All that mattered was to get up to the mine as quickly as possible—to nail the Cuban and the Russian—and to find Benedetta.

He looked into the cab of the truck and opened the door. It was a big truck and from where he sat when he pulled himself into the cab he could see the dying embers of the camp. He did not see any movement there, apart from a few low flames and a curl of black smoke which was lost immediately in the mist. He turned back, looked ahead and pressed the starter.

The engine fired and he put it into gear and drove up the road, feeling a little light-headed. In a very short space of time he had killed three men, the first he had ever killed face to face, and he was preparing to go on killing for as long as was necessary. His mind had returned to the tautness he remembered from Korea before he had been shot down; all his senses were razor-sharp and his mind emptied of everything but the task ahead.

After a while he switched off the lights. It was risky, but he had to take the chance. There was the possibility that in the mist he could lose the road on one of the bends and go down the mountain out of control; but far worse was the risk that the enemy in the trucks ahead would see him and lay an ambush.

The truck ground on and on and the wheel bucked against his hand as the jolts were transmitted from the road surface. He went as fast as he thought safe, which was really not fast at all, but at last, rounding a particularly hair-raising corner, he saw a red tail-light disappearing round the next bend. At once he slowed down, content to follow at a discreet distance. There was nothing he could do on the road—his time would come at the mine.

He put out his hand to the sub-machine-gun resting on the seat next to him and drew it closer. It felt very comforting.

He reached a bend he remembered, the final corner before

the level ground at the mine. He drew into the side of the road and put on the brake, but left the engine running. Taking the gun, he dropped to the ground, wincing as he felt the weight on his bad ankle, and hobbled up the road. From ahead he could hear the roar of engines stopping one by one, and when he found a place from where he could see, he discovered the other trucks parked by the huts and in the glare of headlights he saw the movement of men.

The jeep revved up and started to move, the beams of its lights stabbing through the mist and searching along the base of the cliff where the mine tunnels had been driven. First one black cavern was illuminated and then another, and then there was a raised shout of triumph, a howl of fierce joy, as the beams swept past the third tunnel and returned almost immediately to show a low rock wall at the entrance and the white face of a man who quickly dodged back out of sight.

O'Hara wasted no time in wondering who it was. He hobbled back to his truck and put it in gear. Now was the time to enter that bleak arena.

## Chapter IX

Forester felt warm and at ease, and to him the two were synonymous. Strange that the snow is so warm and soft, he thought; and opened his eyes to see a glare of white before him. He sighed and closed his eyes again, feeling a sense of disappointment. It *was* snow, after all. He supposed he should make an effort to move and get out of this deliciously warm snow or he would die, but he decided it was not worth the effort. He just let the warmth lap him in comfort and for a second before he relapsed into unconsciousness he wondered vaguely where Rohde had got to.

The next time he opened his eyes the glare of white was still there but now he had recovered enough to see it for what it was—the brilliance of sunlight falling on the crisply laundered white counterpane that covered him. He blinked and looked again, but the glare hurt his eyes, so he closed them. He knew he should do something but what it was he could not remember, and he passed out again while struggling to keep awake long enough to remember what it was.

Vaguely, in his sleep, he was aware of the passage of time

and he knew he must fight against this, that he must stop the clock, hold the moving fingers, because he had something to do that was of prime urgency. He stirred and moaned, and a nurse in a trim white uniform gently sponged the sweat from his brow.

But she did not wake him.

At last he woke fully and stared at the ceiling. That was also white, plainly white-washed with thick wooden beams. He turned his head and found himself looking into kindly eyes. He licked dry lips and whispered, "What happened?"

"*No comprendo,*" said the nurse. "No talk—I bring doctor."

She got up and his eyes moved as she went out of the room. He desperately wanted her to come back, to tell him where he was and what had happened and where to find Rohde. As he thought of Rohde it all came back to him—the night on the mountain and the frustrating attempts to find a way over the pass. Most of it he remembered, although the end bits were hazy—and he also remembered why that impossible thing had been attempted.

He tried to sit up but his muscles had no strength in them and he just lay there, breathing hard. He felt as though his body weighed a thousand pounds and as though he had been beaten all over with a rubber hose. Every muscle was loose and flabby, even the muscles of his neck, as he found when he tried to raise his head. And he felt very, very tired.

It was a long time before anyone came into the room, and then it was the nurse bearing a bowl of hot soup. She would not let him talk and he was too weak to insist, and every time he opened his mouth she ladled a spoonful of soup into it. The broth gave him new strength and he felt better, and when he had finished the bowl he said, "Where is the other man—*el otro hombre?*"

"Your friend will be all right," she said in Spanish, and whisked out of the room before he could ask anything else.

Again it was a long time before anyone came to see him. He had no watch, but by the position of the sun he judged it was about midday. But which day? How long had he been there? He put up his hand to scratch an intolerable itching in his chest and discovered why he felt so heavy and uncomfortable; he seemed to be wrapped in a couple of miles of adhesive tape.

A man entered the room and closed the door. He said in an American accent, "Well, Mr. Forester, I hear you're better." He was dressed in hospital white and could have been a doctor. He was elderly but still powerfully built, with a shock of white hair and the crowsfeet of frequent laughter around his eyes.

Forester relaxed. "Thank God—an American," he said. His voice was much stronger.

"I'm McGruder—Doctor McGruder."

"How did you know my name?" asked Forester.

"The papers in your pocket," said McGruder. "You carry an American passport."

"Look," said Forester urgently. "You've got to let me out of here. I've got things to do. I've got to——"

"You're not leaving here for a long time," said McGruder abruptly. "And you couldn't stand if you tried."

Forester sagged back in the bed. "Where is this place?"

"San Antonio Mission," said McGruder. "I'm the Big White Chief here. Presbyterian, you know."

"Anywhere near Altemiros?"

"Sure. Altemiros village is just down the road—almost two miles away."

"I want a message sent," said Forester rapidly. "Two messages—one to Ramón Sueguerra in Altemiros and one to Santillana to the——"

McGruder held up his hand. "Whoa up, there; you'll have a relapse if you're not careful. Take it easy."

"For God's sake," said Forester bitterly. "This is urgent."

"For God's sake nothing is urgent," said McGruder equably. "He has all the time there is. What I'm interested in right now is why one man should come over an impossible pass in a blizzard carrying another man."

"Did Rohde carry me? How is he?"

"As well as can be expected," said McGruder. "I'd be interested to know why he carried you."

"Because I was dying," said Forester. He looked at McGruder speculatively, sizing him up. He did not want to make a blunder—the communists had some very unexpected friends in the strangest places—but he did not think he could go wrong with a Presbyterian doctor, and McGruder *looked* all right. "All right," he said at last. "I suppose I'll have to tell you. You look okay to me."

McGruder raised his eyebrows but said nothing, and Forester told him what was happening on the other side of the mountains, beginning with the air crash but leaving out such irrelevancies as the killing of Peabody, which, he thought,

207

might harm his case. As he spoke McGruder's eyebrows crawled up his scalp until they were almost lost in his hair.

When Forester finished he said, "Now that's as improbable a story as I've ever heard. You see, Mr. Forester, I don't entirely trust you. I had a phone call from the Air Force base—there's one quite close—and they were looking for you. Moreover, you were carrying this." He put his hand in his pocket and pulled out a pistol. "I don't like people who carry guns—it's against my religion."

Forester watched as McGruder skilfully worked the action and the cartridges flipped out. He said, "For a man who doesn't like guns you know a bit too much about their workings."

"I was a Marine at Iwo Jima," said McGruder. "Now why would the Cordilleran military be interested in you?"

"Because they've gone communist."

"Tchah!" said McGruder disgustedly. "You talk like an old maid who sees burglars under every bed. Colonel Rodriguez is as communist as I am."

Forester felt a sudden hope. Rodriguez was the commandant of Fourteenth Squadron and the friend of Aguillar. "Did you speak to Rodriguez?" he asked.

"No," said McGruder. "It was some junior officer." He paused. "Look, Forester, the military want you and I'd like you to tell me why."

"Is Fourteenth Squadron still at the airfield?" countered Forester.

"I don't know. Rodriguez did say something about moving —but I haven't seen him for nearly a month."

So it was a toss-up, thought Forester disgustedly. The military were friend or foe and he had no immediate means of finding out—and it looked as though McGruder was quite prepared to hand him over. He said speculatively, "I suppose you try to keep your nose clean. I suppose you work in with the local authorities and you don't interfere in local politics."

"Indeed I don't," said McGruder. "I don't want this mission closed. We have enough trouble as it is."

"You *think* you have trouble with Lopez, but that's nothing to the trouble you'll have when the commies move in," snapped Forester. "Tell me, is it against your religion to stand by and wait while your fellow human beings—some of them fellow countrymen, not that that matters—are slaughtered not fifteen miles from where you are standing?"

McGruder whitened about the nostrils and the lines deepened about his mouth. "I almost think you are telling the truth," he said slowly.

"You're damn right I am."

Ignoring the profanity McGruder said, "You mentioned a name—Sueguerra. I know Señor Sueguerra very well. I play chess with him whenever I get into the village. He is a good man, so that is a point for you. What was the other message—to Santillana?"

"The same message to a different man," said Forester patiently. "Bob Addison of the United States Embassy. Tell them both what I've told you—and tell Addison to get the lead out of his breeches fast."

McGruder wrinkled his brow. "Addison? I believe I know all the Embassy staff, but I don't recall an Addison."

"You wouldn't," said Forester. "He's an officer of the Central Intelligence Agency of the United States. We don't advertise."

McGruder's eyebrows crawled up again. "We?"

Forester grinned weakly. "I'm a C.I.A. officer, too. But you'll have to take it on trust—I don't carry the information tattooed on my chest."


II


Forester was shocked to hear that Rohde was likely to lose his leg. "Frostbite in a very bad open wound is not conducive to the best of health," said McGruder dryly. "I'm very sorry about this; I'll try to save the leg, of course—it's a pity that this should happen to so brave a man."

McGruder now appeared to have accepted Forester's story, although he had taken a lot of convincing and had doubts about the wisdom of the State Department. "They're stupid," he said. "We don't want open American interference down here—that's certain to stir up anti-Americanism. It's giving the communists a perfect opening."

"For God's sake, I'm not interfering actively," protested Forester. "We knew that Aguillar was going to make his move and my job was to keep a friendly eye on him, to see that he got through safely." He looked at the ceiling and said bitterly, "I seem to have balled it up, don't I?"

"I don't see that you could have done anything different,"

209

observed McGruder. He got up from the bedside. " I'll check up on which squadron is at the airfield, and I'll go to see Sueguerra myself."

" Don't forget the Embassy."

" I'll put a phone call through right away."

But that proved to be difficult because the line was not open. McGruder sat at his desk and fumed at the unresponsive telephone. This was something that happened about once a week and always at a critical moment. At last he put down the hand-set and turned to take off his white coat, but hesitated as he heard the squeal of brakes from the courtyard. He looked through his office window and saw a military staff car pull up followed by a truck and a military ambulance. A squad of uniformed and armed men debussed from the truck under the barked orders of an N.C.O., and an officer climbed casually out of the staff car.

McGruder hastily put on the white coat again and when the officer strode into the room he was busy writing at his desk. He looked up and said, " Good day—er—Major. To what do I owe this honour?"

The officer clicked his heels punctiliously. " Major Garcia, at your service."

The doctor leaned back in his chair and put both his hands flat on the desk. " I'm McGruder. What can I do for you, Major?"

Garcia flicked his glove against the side of his well-cut breeches. " We—the Cordilleran Air Force, that is—thought we might be of service," he said easily. " We understand that you have two badly injured men here—the men who came down from the mountain. We offer the use of our medical staff and the base hospital at the airfield." He waved. " The ambulance is waiting outside."

McGruder swivelled his eyes to the window and saw the soldiers taking up position outside. They looked stripped for action. He flicked his gaze back to Garcia. " And the escort!"

Garcia smiled. " *No es nada*," he said casually. " I was conducting a small exercise when I got my orders, and it was as easy to bring the men along as to dismiss them and let them idle."

McGruder did not believe a word of it. He said pleasantly, " Well, Major, I don't think we need trouble the military. I haven't been in your hospital at the airfield, but this place

210

of mine is well enough equipped to take care of these men. I don't think they need to be moved."

Garcia lost his smile. "But we insist," he said icily.

McGruder's mobile eyebrows shot up. "Insist, Major Garcia? I don't think you're in a position to insist."

Garcia looked meaningly at the squad of soldiers in the courtyard. "No?" he asked silkily.

"No," said McGruder flatly. "As a doctor, I say that these men are too sick to be moved. If you don't believe me, then trot out your own doctor from that ambulance and let *him* have a look at them. I am sure he will tell you the same."

For the first time Garcia seemed to lose his self-possession. "Doctor?" he said uncertainly. "Er . . . we have brought no doctor."

"No doctor?" said McGruder in surprise. He wiggled his eyebrows at Garcia. "I am sure you have misinterpreted your orders, Major Garcia. I don't think your commanding officer would approve of these men leaving here unless under qualified supervision; and I certainly don't have the time to go with you to the airfield—I am a busy man."

Garcia hesitated and then said sullenly, "Your telephone—may I use it?"

"Help yourself," said McGruder. "But it isn't working—as usual."

Garcia smiled thinly and spoke into the mouthpiece. He got an answer too, which really surprised McGruder and told him of the seriousness of the position. This was not an ordinary breakdown of the telephone system—it was planned; and he guessed that the exchange was under military control.

When next Garcia spoke he came to attention and McGruder smiled humourlessly; that would be his commanding officer and it certainly wouldn't be Rodriguez—he didn't go in for that kind of spit-and-polish. Garcia explained McGruder's attitude concisely and then listened to the spate of words which followed. There was a grim smile on his face as he put down the telephone. "I regret to tell you, Doctor McGruder, that I must take those men."

He stepped to the window and called his sergeant as McGruder came to his feet in anger. "And I say the men are too ill to be moved. One of those men is an American, Major Garcia. Are you trying to cause an international incident?"

"I am obeying orders," said Garcia stiffly. His sergeant came to the window and he gave a rapid stream of instructions, then turned to McGruder. "I have to inform you that these men stand accused of plotting against the safety of the State. I am under instructions to arrest them."

"You're nuts," said McGruder. "You take these men and you'll be up to your neck in diplomats." He moved over to the door.

Garcia stood in front of him. "I must ask you to move away from the door, Doctor McGruder, or I will be forced to arrest you, too." He spoke over McGruder's shoulder to a corporal standing outside. "Escort the doctor into the courtyard."

"Well, if you're going to feel like that about it, there's nothing I can do," said McGruder, "But that commanding officer of yours—what's his name . . .?"

"Colonel Coello."

"Colonel Coello is going to find himself in a sticky position." He stood aside and let Garcia precede him into the corridor.

Garcia waited for him, slapping the side of his leg impatiently. "Where are the men?"

McGruder led the way down the corridor at a rapid pace. Outside Forester's room he paused and deliberately raised his voice. "You realise I am letting these men go under protest. The military have no jurisdiction here and I intend to protest to the Cordilleran government through the United States Embassy. And I further protest upon medical grounds—neither of these men is fit to be moved."

"Where are the men?" repeated Garcia.

"I have just operated on one of them—he is recovering from an anæsthetic. The other is also very ill and I insist on giving him a sedative before he is moved."

Garcia hesitated and McGruder pressed him. "Come, Major; military ambulances have never been noted for smooth running—you would not begrudge a man a pain-killer." He tapped Garcia on the chest. "This is going to make headlines in every paper across the United States. Do you want to make matters worse by appearing anti-humanitarian?"

"Very well," said Garcia unwillingly.

"I'll get the morphine from the surgery," said McGruder, and went back, leaving Garcia standing in the corridor.

Forester heard the raised voices as he was polishing the plate of the best meal he had ever enjoyed in his life. He realised that something was amiss and that McGruder was making him appear sicker than he was. He was willing to play along with that, so he hastily pushed the tray under the bed and when the door opened he was lying flat on his back with his eyes closed. As McGruder touched him he groaned.

McGruder said, "Mr. Forester, Major Garcia thinks you will be better looked after in another hospital, so you are being moved." As Forester opened his eyes McGruder frowned at him heavily. "I do not agree with this move, which is being done under *force majeure*, and I am going to consult the appropriate authorities. I am going to give you a sedative so that the journey will not harm you, although it is not far —merely to the airfield."

He rolled up the sleeve of Forester's pyjamas and dabbed at his arm with cotton-wool, then produced a hypodermic syringe which he filled from an ampoule. He spoke casually. "The tape round your chest will support your ribs but I wouldn't move around much—not unless you have to." There was a subtle emphasis on the last few words and he winked at Forester.

As he pushed home the needle in Forester's arm he leaned over and whispered, "It's a stimulant."

"What was that?" said Garcia sharply.

"What was what?" asked McGruder, turning and skewering Garcia with an icy glare. "I'll trouble you not to interfere with a doctor in his duties. Mr. Forester is a very sick man, and on behalf of the United States government I am holding you and Colonel Coello responsible for what happens to him. Now, where are your stretcher-bearers?"

Garcia snapped to the sergeant at the door, "*Una camilla.*" The sergeant bawled down the corridor and presently a stretcher was brought in. McGruder fussed about while Forester was transferred from the bed, and when he was settled said, "There, you can take him."

He stepped back and knocked a kidney basin to the floor with a clatter. The noise was startling in that quiet room, and everyone's attention was diverted McGruder hastily thrust something hard under Forester's pillow.

Then Forester was borne down the corridor and into the open courtyard and he winced as the sun struck his eyes. Once in the ambulance he had to wait a long time before anything else happened and he closed his eyes, feigning sleep, because the soldier on guard kept peering at him. Slowly he brought his hand up under the coverlet towards the pillow and eventually touched the butt of a gun.

Good old McGruder, he thought; the Marines to the rescue. He hooked his finger in the trigger guard and gradually

213

brought the gun down to his side, where he thrust it into the waistband of his pyjamas at the small of his back where it could not be seen when he was transferred to another bed. He smiled to himself; at other times lying on a hard piece of metal might be thought extremely uncomfortable, but he found the touch of the gun very comforting.

And what McGruder had said was comforting, too. The tape would hold him together and the stimulant would give him strength to move. Not that he thought he needed it; his strength had returned rapidly once he had eaten, but no doubt the doctor knew best.

Rohde was pushed into the ambulance and Forester looked across at the stretcher. He was unconscious and there was a hump under the coverlet where his legs were. His face was pale and covered with small beads of sweat and he breathed stertorously.

Two soldiers climbed into the ambulance and the doors were slammed, and after a few minutes it moved off. Forester kept his eyes closed at first—he wanted the soldiers to believe that the hypothetical sedative was taking effect. But after a while he decided that these rank and file would probably not know anything about a sedative being given to him, so he risked opening his eyes and turned his head to look out of the window.

He could not see much because of the restricted angle of view, but presently the ambulance stopped and he saw a wrought-iron gate and through the bars a large board. It depicted an eagle flying over a snow-capped mountain, and round this emblem in a scroll and written in ornate letters were the words: ESQUADRON OCTAVO.

He closed his eyes in pain. They had drawn the wrong straw; this was the communist squadron.

III

McGruder watched the ambulance leave the courtyard followed by the staff car. Then he went into his office, stripped off his white coat and put on his jacket. He took his car keys from a drawer and went round to the hospital garage, where he got a shock. Lounging outside the big doors was a soldier in a sloppy uniform—but there was nothing sloppy about the rifle he was holding, nor about the gleaming bayonet.

He walked over and barked authoritatively, " Let me pass."

The soldier looked at him through half-closed eyes and shook his head, then spat on the ground. McGruder got mad and tried to push his way past but found the tip of the bayonet pricking his throat. The soldier said, "You see the sergeant —if he says you can take a car, then you take a car."

McGruder backed away, rubbing his throat. He turned on his heel and went to look for the sergeant, but got nowhere with him. The sergeant was a sympathetic man when away from his officers and his broad Indian face was sorrowful. "I'm sorry, Doctor," he said. "I just obey orders—and my orders are that no one leaves the mission until I get contrary orders."

"And when will that be?" demanded McGruder.

The sergeant shrugged. "Who knows?" he said with the fatalism of one to whom officers were a race apart and their doings incomprehensible.

McGruder snorted and withdrew to his office, where he picked up the telephone. Apparently it was still dead, but when he snapped, "Get me Colonel Coello at the military airfield," it suddenly came to life and he was put through— not to Coello, but to some underling.

It took him over fifteen minutes before he got through to Coello and by then he was breathing hard with ill-suppressed rage. He said aggressively, "McGruder here. What's all this about closing down San Antonio Mission?"

Coello was suave. "But the mission is not closed, Doctor; anyone can enter."

"But I can't leave," said McGruder. "I have work to do."

"Then do it," said Coello. "Your work is in the mission, Doctor; stick to your job—like the cobbler. Do not interfere in things which do not concern you."

"I don't know what the hell you mean," snarled McGruder with a profanity he had not used since his Marine days. "I have to pick up a consignment of drugs at the railroad depot in Altemiros. I need them and the Cordilleran Air Force is stopping me getting them—that's how I see it. You're not going to look very good when this comes out, Colonel."

"But you should have said this earlier," said Coello soothingly. "I will send one of the airfield vehicles to pick them up for you. As you know, the Cordilleran Air Force is always ready to help your mission. I hear you run a very good hospital, Doctor McGruder. We are short of good hospitals in this country."

McGruder heard the cynical amusement in the voice. He

said irascibly, "All right," and banged the phone down. Mopping his brow he thought that it was indeed fortunate there *was* a consignment of drugs waiting in Altemiros. He paused, wondering what to do next, then he drew a sheet of blank paper from a drawer and began writing.

Half an hour later he had the gist of Forester's story on paper. He folded the sheets, sealed them in an envelope and put the envelope into his pocket. All the while he was conscious of the soldier posted just outside the window who was keeping discreet surveillance of him. He went out into the corridor to find another soldier lounging outside the office door whom he ignored, carrying on down towards the wards and the operating theatre. The soldier stared after him with incurious eyes and drifted down the corridor after him.

McGruder looked for Sánchez, his second-in-command, and found him in one of the wards. Sánchez looked at his face and raised his eyebrows. "What is happening, Doctor?"

"The local military have gone berserk," said McGruder unhappily. "And I seem to be mixed up in it—they won't let me leave the mission."

"They won't let *anyone* leave the mission," said Sánchez. "I tried."

"I must get to Altemiros," said McGruder. "Will you help me? I know I'm usually non-political, but this is different. There's murder going on across the mountains."

"Eight Squadron came to the airfield two days ago—I have heard strange stories about Eight Squadron," said Sánchez reflectively. "You may be non-political, Doctor McGruder, but I am not. Of course I will help you."

McGruder turned and saw the soldier gazing blankly at him from the entrance of the ward. "Let's go into your office," he said.

They went to the office and McGruder switched on an X-ray viewer and pointed out the salient features of an X-ray plate to Sánchez. He left the door open and the soldier leaned on the opposite wall of the corridor, solemnly picking his teeth. "This is what I want you to do," said McGruder in a low voice.

Fifteen minutes later he went to find the sergeant and spoke to him forthrightly. "What are your orders concerning the mission?" he demanded.

The sergeant said, "Not to let anyone leave—and to watch you, Doctor McGruder." He paused. "I'm sorry."

"I seem to have noticed that I've been watched," said

216

McGruder with heavy irony. "Now, I'm going to do an operation. Old Pedro must have his kidneys seen to or he will die. I can't have any of your men in the operating theatre, spitting all over the floor; we have enough trouble attaining asepsis as it is."

"We all know you *norteamericanos* are very clean," acknowledged the sergeant. He frowned. "This room—how many doors?"

"One door—no windows," said McGruder. "You can come and look at it if you like; but don't spit on the floor."

He took the sergeant into the operating theatre and satisfied him that there was only one entrance. "Very well," said the sergeant. "I will put two men outside the door—that will be all right."

McGruder went into the sluice room and prepared for the operation, putting on his gown and cap and fastening the mask loosely about his neck. Old Pedro was brought up on a stretcher and McGruder stood outside the door while he was pushed into the theatre. The sergeant said, "How long will this take?"

McGruder considered. "About two hours—maybe longer. It is a serious operation, Sergeant."

He went into the theatre and closed the door. Five minutes later the empty stretcher was pushed out and the sergeant looked through the open door and saw the doctor, masked and bending over the operating table, a scalpel in his hand. The door closed, the sergeant nodded to the sentries and wandered towards the courtyard to find a sunny spot. He quite ignored the empty stretcher being pushed by two chattering nurses down the corridor.

In the safety of the bottom ward McGruder dropped from under the stretcher where he had been clinging and flexed the muscles of his arms. Getting too old for these acrobatics, he thought, and nodded to the nurses who had pushed in the stretcher. They giggled and went out, and he changed his clothes quickly.

He knew of a place where the tide of prickly pear which covered the hillside overflowed into the mission grounds. For weeks he had intended to cut down the growth and tidy it up, but now he was glad that he had let it be. No sentry in his right mind would deliberately patrol in the middle of a grove of sharp-spined cactus, no matter what his orders, and McGruder thought he had a chance of getting through.

He was right. Twenty minutes later he was on the other

side of a low rise, the mission out of sight behind him and the houses of Altemiros spread in front. His clothes were torn and so was his flesh—the cactus had not been kind.

He began to run.

Forester was still on his stretcher. He had expected to be taken into a hospital ward and transferred to a bed, but instead the stretcher was taken into an office and laid across two chairs. Then he was left alone, but he could hear the shuffling feet of a sentry outside the door and knew he was well guarded.

It was a large office overlooking the airfield, and he guessed it belonged to the commanding officer. There were many maps on the walls and some aerial photographs, mainly of mountain country. He looked at the décor without interest; he had been in many offices like this when he was in the American Air Force and it was all very familiar, from the group photographs of the squadron to the clock let into the boss of an old wooden propeller.

What interested him was the scene outside. One complete wall of the office was a window and through it he could see the apron outside the control tower and, farther away, a group of hangars. He clicked his tongue as he recognised the aircraft standing on the apron—they were Sabres.

Good old Uncle Sam, he thought in disgust; always willing to give handouts, even military handouts, to potential enemies. He looked at the fighter planes with intense curiosity. They were early model Sabres, now obsolete in the major air forces, but quite adequate for the defence of a country like Cordillera which had no conceivable military enemies of any strength. As far as he could see, they were the identical model he had flown in Korea. I could fly one of those, he thought, if I could just get into the cockpit.

There were four of them standing in a neat line and he saw they were being serviced. Suddenly he sat up—no, not serviced—those were rockets going under the wings. And those men standing on the wings were not mechanics, they were armourers loading cannon shells. He did not have to be close enough to see the shells; he had seen this operation performed many times in Korea and he knew automatically that these planes were being readied for instant action.

Christ! he thought bitterly; it's like using a steam hammer to crack a nut. O'Hara and the others won't have a chance against this lot. But then he became aware of something else —this must mean that O'Hara was still holding out; that the communists across the bridge were still baffled. He felt exhilarated and depressed at the same time as he watched the planes being readied.

He lay back again and felt the gun pressing into the small of his back. This was the time to prepare for action, he realised, so he pulled out the gun, keeping a wary eye on the door, and examined it. It was the pistol he had brought over the mountain—Grivas's pistol. Cold and exposure to the elements had not done it any good—the oil had dried out and the action was stiff—but he thought it would work. He snapped the action several times, catching the rounds as they flipped from the breech, then he reloaded the magazine and worked the action again, putting a round in the breech ready for instant shooting.

He stowed the pistol by his side under the coverlet and laid his hand on the butt. Now he was ready—as ready as he could be.

He waited a long time and began to get edgy. He felt little tics all over his body as small muscles jumped and twitched, and he had never been so wide-awake in his life. That's McGruder's stimulant he thought; I wonder what it was and if it'll mix with all the coca I've taken.

He kept an eye on the Sabres outside. The ground crews had completed their work long before someone opened the door of the office, and Forester looked up to see a man with a long, saturnine face looking down at him. The man smiled. "*Colonel Coello, a sus ordines.*" He clicked his heels.

Forester blinked his eyes, endeavouring to simulate sleepiness. "Colonel who?" he mumbled.

The colonel sat behind the desk. "Coello," he said pleasantly. "I am the commandant of this fighter squadron."

"It's the damnedest thing," said Forester with a baffled look. "One minute I was in hospital, and the next minute I'm in this office. Familiar surroundings, too; I woke up and became interested in those Sabres."

"You have flown?" asked Coello politely.

"I sure have," said Forester. "I was in Korea—I flew Sabres there."

"Then we can talk together as comrades," said Coello heartily. "You remember Doctor McGruder?"

"Not much," said Forester. "I woke up and he pumped me full of stuff to put me to sleep again—then I found myself here. Say, shouldn't I be in hospital or something?"

"Then you did not talk to McGruder about anything—anything at all?"

"I didn't have the chance," said Forester. He did not want to implicate McGruder in this. "Say, Colonel, am I glad to see you. All hell is breaking loose on the other side of the mountains. There's a bunch of bandits trying to murder some stranded airline passengers. We were on our way here to tell you."

"On your way *here*?"

"That's right; there was a South American guy told us to come here—now, what was his name?" Forester wrinkled his brow.

"Aguillar—perhaps?"

"Never heard that name before," said Forester. "No, this guy was called Montes."

"And Montes told you to come *here*?" said Coello incredulously. "He must have thought that fool Rodriguez was here. You were two days too late, Mr. Forester." He began to laugh.

Forester felt a cold chill run through him but pressed on with his act of innocence. "What's so funny?" he asked plaintively. "Why the hell are you sitting there laughing instead of doing something about it?"

Coello wiped the tears of laughter from his eyes. "Do not worry, Señor Forester; we know all about it already. We are making preparations for . . . er . . . a rescue attempt."

I'll bet you are, thought Forester bitterly, looking at the Sabres drawn up on the apron. He said, "What the hell! Then I nearly killed myself on the mountain for nothing. What a damned fool I am."

Coello opened a folder on his desk. "Your name is Raymond Forester; you are South American Sales Manager for the Fairfield Machine Tool Corporation, and you were on your way to Santillana." He smiled as he looked down at the folder. "We have checked, of course; there is a Raymond Forester who works for this company, and he *is* sales manager in South America. The C.I.A. can be efficient in small matters, Mr. Forester."

"Huh!" said Forester. "C.I.A.? What the devil are you talking about?"

Coello waved his hand airily. "Espionage! Sabotage! Corruption of public officials! Undermining the will of the people! Name anything bad and you name the C.I.A.—and also yourself, Mr. Forester."

"You're nuts," said Forester disgustedly.

"You are a meddling American," said Coello sharply. "You are a plutocratic, capitalistic lackey. One could forgive you if you were but a tool; but you do your filthy work in full awareness of its evil. You came to Cordillera to foment an imperialistic revolution, putting up that scoundrel Aguillar as a figurehead for your machinations."

"Who?" said Forester. "You're still nuts."

"Give up, Forester; stop this pretence. We know all about the Fairfield Machine Tool Corporation. It is a cover that capitalistic Wall Street has erected to hide your imperialistic American secret service. We know all about you and we know all about Addison in Santillana. He has been removed from the game—and so have you, Forester."

Forester smiled crookedly. "The voice is Spanish-American, but the words come from Moscow—or is it Peking this time?" He nodded towards the armed aircraft. "Who is really doing the meddling round here?"

Coello smiled. "I am a servant of the present government of General Lopez. I am sure he would be happy to know that Aguillar will soon be dead."

"But I bet you won't tell him," said Forester. "Not if I know how you boys operate. You'll use the threat of Aguillar to drive Lopez out as soon as it suits you." He tried to scratch his itching chest but was unsuccessful. "You jumped me and Rohde pretty fast—how did you know we were at McGruder's hospital?"

"I am sure you are trying to sound more stupid than you really are," said Coello. "My dear Forester, we are in radio communication with our forces on the other side of the mountains." He sounded suddenly bitter. "Inefficient though they are, they have at least kept their radio working. You were seen by the bridge. And when men come over that pass, do you think the news can be kept quiet? The whole of Altemiros knows of the mad American who has done the impossible."

But they don't know why I did it, thought Forester savagely; and they'll never find out if this bastard has his way.

221

Coello held up a photograph. "We suspected that the C.I.A. might have someone with Aguillar. It was only a suspicion then, but now we know it to be a fact. This photograph was taken in Washington six months ago."

He skimmed it over and Forester looked at it. It was a glossy picture of himself and his immediate superior talking together on the steps of a building. He flicked the photograph with his fingernail. "Processed in Moscow?"

Coello smiled and asked silkily, "Can you give me any sound reasons why you should not be shot?"

"Not many," said Forester off-handedly. "But enough." He propped himself up on one elbow and tried to make it sound good. "You're killing Americans on the other side of those mountains, Coello. The American government is going to demand an explanation—an investigation."

"So? There is an air crash—there have been many such crashes even in North America. Especially can they occur on such ill-run air lines as Andes Airlift, which, incidentally, is owned by one of your own countrymen. An obsolete aircraft with a drunken pilot—what more natural? There will be no bodies to send back to the United States, I assure you. Regrettable, isn't it?"

"You don't know the facts of life," said Forester. "My government is going to be very interested. Now, don't get me wrong; they're not interested in air crashes as such. But *I* was in that airplane and they're going to be goddam suspicious. There'll be an official investigation—Uncle Sam will goose the I.A.T.A. into making one—and there'll be a concurrent under-cover investigation. This country will be full of operatives within a week—you can't stop them all and you can't hide all the evidence. The truth is going to come out and the U.S. government will be delighted to blow the lid off. Nothing would please them more."

He coughed, sweating a little—now it had to sound really good. "Now, there's a way round all that." He sat up on the stretcher. "Have you a cigarette?"

Coello's eyes narrowed as he picked up a cigarette-box from the desk and walked round to the stretcher. He offered the open box and said, "Am I to understand that you're trying to bargain for your life?"

"You're dead right," said Forester. He put a whine in his voice. "I've no hankering to wear a wooden overcoat, and I know how you boys operate on captured prisoners."

Thoughtfully Coello flicked his lighter and lit Forester's cigarette. "Well?"

Forester said, "Look, Colonel; supposing I was the only survivor of that crash—thrown clear by some miraculous chance. Then I could say that the crash was okay; that it was on the up-and-up. Why wouldn't they believe me? I'm one of their bright boys."

Coello nodded. "You are bright." He smiled. "What guarantee have we that you will do this for us?"

"Guarantee? You know damn well I can't give you one. But I tell you this, buddy-boy; you're not the boss round here —not by a long shot. And I'm stuffed full of information about the C.I.A.—operation areas, names, faces, addresses, covers—you ask for it, I've got it. And if your boss ever finds out that you've turned down a chance like this you're going to be in trouble. What have you got to lose? All you have to do is to put it to your boss and let him say 'yes' or 'no.' If anything goes wrong he'll have to take the rap from higher up, but you'll be in the clear."

Coello tapped his teeth with a fingernail. "I think you're playing for time, Forester." He thought deeply. "If you can give me a sensible answer to the next question I might believe you. You say you are afraid of dying. If you are so afraid, why did you risk your life in coming over the pass?"

Forester thought of Peabody and laughed outright. "Use your brains. I was being shot at over there by that goddam bridge. Have you ever tried to talk reasonably with someone who shoots at you if you bat an eyelid? But you're not shooting at me, Colonel; I can talk to you. Anyway, I reckoned it was a sight safer on the mountain than down by the bridge— and I've proved it, haven't I? I'm here and I'm still alive."

"Yes," said Coello pensively. "You are still alive." He went to his desk. "You might as well begin by proving your goodwill immediately. We sent a reconnaissance plane over to see what was happening and the pilot took these photographs. What do you make of them?"

He tossed a sheaf of glossy photographs on to the foot of the stretcher. Forester leaned over and gasped. "Have a heart, Colonel; I'm all bust up inside—I can't reach."

Coello leaned over with a ruler and flicked them within his reach, and Forester fanned them out. They were good; a little blurred because of the speed of the aircraft, but still sharp enough to make out details. He saw the bridge and a scattering of upturned faces, white blobs against a grey background. And he saw the trebuchet. So they'd got it down from the camp all right. "Interesting," he said.

Coello leaned over. "What is that?" he asked. "Our experts have been able to make nothing of it." His finger was pointing at the trebuchet.

Forester smiled. "I'm not surprised," he said. "There's a nut-case over there; a guy called Armstrong. He conned the others into building that gadget; it's called a trebuchet and it's for throwing stones. He said the last time it was used was when Cortes besieged Mexico City and then it didn't work properly. It's nothing to worry about."

"No?" said Coello. "They nearly broke down the bridge with it."

Forester gave a silent cheer, but said nothing. He was itching to pull out his gun and let Coello have it right where it hurt most, but he would gain nothing by that—just a bullet in the brain from the guard and no chance of doing anything more damaging.

Coello gathered the photographs together and tapped them on his hand. "Very well," he said. "We will not shoot you—yet. You have possibly gained yourself another hour of life—perhaps much longer. I will consult my superior and let him decide what to do with you."

He went to the door, then turned. "I would not do anything foolish; you realise you are well guarded."

"What the hell can I do?" growled Forester. "I'm bust up inside and all strapped up; I'm as weak as a kitten and full of dope. I'm safe enough."

When Coello closed the door behind him Forester broke out into a sweat. During the last half-hour Coello had nearly been relieved of the responsibility of him, for he had almost had a heart attack on three separate occasions. He hoped he had established the points he had tried to make; that he could be bought—something which might gain precious time; that he was too ill to move—Coello might get a shock on that one; and that Coello himself had nothing to lose by waiting a little—nothing but his life, Forester hoped.

He touched the butt of the gun and gazed out of the window. There was action about the Sabres on the apron; a truck had pulled up and a group of men in flying kit were getting out—three of them. They stood about talking for some time and then went to their aircraft and got settled in the cockpits with the assistance of the ground crews. Forester heard the whine of the engines as the starter truck rolled from one plane to another and, one by one, the planes slowly taxied forward until they went out of his sight.

He looked at the remaining Sabre. He knew nothing about the Cordilleran Air Force insignia, but the three stripes on the tail looked important. Perhaps the good colonel was going to lead this strike himself; it would be just his mark, thought Forester with animosity.

v

Ramón Sueguerra was the last person he would have expected to be involved in a desperate enterprise involving the overthrow of governments, thought McGruder, as he made his devious way through the back streets of Altemiros towards Sueguerra's office. What had a plump and comfortable merchant to do with revolution? Yet perhaps the Lopez régime was hurting him more than most—his profits were eaten up by bribes; his markets were increasingly more restricted; and the fibre of his business slackened as the general economic level of the country sagged under the misrule of Lopez. Not all revolutions were made by the starving proletariat.

He came upon the building which housed the multitudinous activities of Sueguerra from the rear and entered by the back door. The front door was, of course, impossible; directly across the street was the post and telegraph office, and McGruder suspected that the building would be occupied by men of Eighth Squadron. He went into Sueguerra's office as he had always done—with a cheery wave to his secretary—and found Sueguerra looking out of the window which faced the street.

He was surprised to see McGruder. "What brings you here?" he asked. "It's too early for chess, my friend." A truck roared in the street outside and his eyes flickered back to the window and McGruder saw that he was uneasy and worried.

"I won't waste your time," said McGruder, pulling the envelope from his pocket. "Read this—it will be quicker than my explanations."

As Sueguerra read he sank into his chair and his face whitened. "But this is incredible," he said. "Are you sure of this?"

"They took Forester and Rohde from the mission," said McGruder. "It was done by force."

"The man Forester I do not know—but Miguel Rohde should have been here two days ago," said Sueguerra. "He is supposed to take charge in the mountains when . . ."

"When the revolution begins?"

Sueguerra looked up. "All right—call it revolution if you will. How else can we get rid of Lopez?" He cocked his head to the street. "This explains what is happening over there; I was wondering about that."

He picked up a white telephone. "Send in Juan."

"What are you going to do?" asked McGruder.

Sueguerra stabbed his finger at the black telephone. "That is useless, my friend, as long as the post office is occupied. And this local telephone exchange controls all the communications in our mountain area. I will send Juan, my son, over the mountains, but he has a long way to go and it will take time—you know what our roads are like."

"It will take him four hours or more," agreed McGruder.

"Still, I will send him. But we will take more direct action." Sueguerra walked over to the window and looked across the street at the post office. "We must take the post office."

McGruder's head jerked up. "You will fight Eighth Squadron?"

Sueguerra swung round. "We must—there is more than telephones involved here." He walked over to his desk and sat down. "Doctor McGruder, we always knew that when the revolution came and if Eighth Squadron was stationed here, then Eighth Squadron would have to be removed from the game. But how to do it—that was the problem."

He smiled slightly. "The solution proved to be ridiculously easy. Colonel Rodriguez has mined all important installations on the airfield. The mines can be exploded electrically—and the wires lead from the airfield to Altemiros; they were installed under the guise of telephone cables. It just needs one touch on a plunger and Eighth Squadron is out of action."

Then he thumped the desk and said savagely, "An extra lead was supposed to be installed in my office this morning —as it is, the only way we can do it is to take the post office by force, because that is where the electrical connection is."

McGruder shook his head. "I'm no electrical engineer, but surely you can tap the wire *outside* the post office."

"It was done by Fourteenth Squadron engineers in a

hurry," said Sueguerra. "And they were pulled out when Eighth Squadron so unexpectedly moved in. There are hundreds of wires in the civil and military networks and no one knows which is the right one. But I know the right connection *inside* the post office—Rodriguez showed it to me."

They heard the high scream of a jet as it flew over Altemiros from the airfield, and Sueguerra said, "We must act quickly —Eighth Squadron must not be allowed to fly."

He burst into activity and McGruder paled when he saw the extent of his preparations. Men assembled in his warehouses as though by magic and innocent tea-chests and bales of hides disgorged an incredible number of arms—both rifles and automatic weapons. The lines deepened in McGruder's face and he said to Sueguerra, "I will not fight, you know."

Sueguerra clapped him on the back. "We do not need you —what is one extra man? And in any case we do not want a *norteamericano* involved. This is a home-grown revolution. But there may be some patching-up for you to do when this is over."

But there was little fighting at the post office. The attack was so unexpected and in such overwhelming strength that the Eighth Squadron detachment put up almost no resistance at all, and the only casualty was a corporal who got a bullet in his leg because an inexperienced and enthusiastic amateur rifleman had left off his safety-catch.

Sueguerra strode into the post office. "Jaime! Jaime! Where is that fool of an electrician? Jaime!"

"I'm here," said Jaime, and came forward carrying a large box under his arm. Sueguerra took him into the main switch-room and McGruder followed.

"It's the third bank of switches—fifteenth from the right and nineteenth from the bottom," said Sueguerra, consulting a scrap of paper.

Jaime counted carefully. "That's it," he said. "Those two screw connections there." He produced a screwdriver. "I'll be about two minutes."

As he worked a plane screamed over the town and then another and another. "I hope we're not too late," whispered Sueguerra.

McGruder put his hand on his arm. "What about Forester and Rohde?" he said in alarm. "They are at the airfield."

"We do not destroy hospitals," said Sueguerra. "Only the important installations are mined—the fuel and ammunition dumps, the hangars, the runways, the control tower. We only want to immobilise them—they are Cordillerans, you know."

Jaime said, "Ready," and Sueguerra lifted the plunger.

"It must be done," he said, and abruptly pushed down hard.

VI

It seemed that Coello *was* leading the strike because the next time he entered the office he was in full flying kit, parachute pack and all. He looked sour. "You have gained yourself more time, Forester. The decision on you will have to wait. I have other, more urgent, matters to attend to. However, I have something to show you—an educative demonstration." He snapped his fingers and two soldiers entered and picked up the stretcher.

"What sort of a demonstration?" asked Forester as he was carried out.

"A demonstration of the dangers of lacking patriotism," answered Coello, smiling. "Something you may be accused of by *your* government one day, Mr. Forester."

Forester lay limply on the stretcher as it was carried out of the building and wondered what the hell was going on. The bearers veered across the apron in front of the control tower, past the single Sabre fighter, and Coello called to a mechanic, "*Diez momentos*." The man saluted, and Forester thought, Ten minutes? Whatever it is, it won't take long.

He turned his head as he heard the whine of an aircraft taking off and saw a Sabre clearing the ground, its wheels retracting. Then there was another, and then the third. They disappeared over the horizon and he wondered where they were going—certainly in the wrong direction if they intended to strafe O'Hara.

The small party approached one of the hangars. The big sliding doors were closed and Coello opened the wicker door and went inside, the stretcher-bearers following. There were no aircraft in the hangar and their footfalls echoed hollowly in dull clangour from the metal walls. Coello went into a side room, waddling awkwardly in his flying gear, and motioned for the stretcher to be brought in. He saw the stretcher placed across two chairs, then told the soldiers to wait outside.

Forester looked up at him. "What the hell is this?" he demanded.

228

"You will see," said Coello calmly, and switched on the light. He went to the window and drew a cord and the curtains came across. "Now then," he said, and crossed the room to draw another cord and curtains parted on an internal window looking into the hangar. "The demonstration will begin almost immediately," he said, and cocked his head on one side as though listening for something.

Forester heard it too, and looked up. It was the banshee howl of a diving jet plane, growing louder and louder until it threatened to shatter the eardrums. With a shriek the plane passed over the hangar and Forester reckoned with professional interest that it could not have cleared the hangar roof by many feet.

"We begin," said Coello, and indicated the hangar.

Almost as though the diving plane had been a signal, a file of soldiers marched into the hangar and stood in a line, an officer barking at them until they trimmed the rank. Each man carried a rifle at the slope and Forester began to have a prickly foreknowledge of what was to come.

He looked at Coello coldly and began to speak but the howling racket of another diving plane drowned his words. When the plane had gone he turned and saw with rage in his heart that Rohde was being dragged in.

He could not walk and two soldiers were half dragging, half carrying him, his feet trailing on the concrete floor. Coello tapped on the window with a pencil and the soldiers brought Rohde forward. His face was dreadfully battered, both eyes were turning black and he had bruised cheeks. But his eyes were open and he regarded Forester with a lacklustre expression and opened his mouth and said a few words which Forester could not hear. He had some teeth missing.

"You've beaten him up, you bastard," exploded Forester.

Coello laughed. "The man is a Cordilleran national, a traitor to his country, a conspirator against his lawful government. What do you do with traitors in the United States, Forester?"

"You hypocritical son-of-a-bitch," said Forester with heat. "What else are *you* doing but subverting the government?"

Coello grinned. "That is different; *I* have not been caught. Besides, I regard myself as being on the right side—the stronger side is always right, is it not? We will crush all these puling, whining liberals like Miguel Rohde and Aguillar." He bared his teeth. "In fact, we will crush Rohde now—and Aguillar in not more than forty-five minutes."

He waved to the officer in the hangar and the soldiers began to drag Rohde away. Forester began to curse Coello, but his words were destroyed in the quivering air as another plane dived on the hangar. He looked after the pitiful figure of Rohde and waited until it was quiet, then he said, " Why are you doing this?"

" Perhaps to teach you a lesson," said Coello lightly. " Let this be a warning—if you cross us, this can happen to you."

" But you're not too certain of your squadron, are you?" said Forester. " You're going to shoot Rohde and your military vanity makes you relish a firing-squad, but you can't afford a public execution—the men of the squadron might not stand for it. I'm right, aren't I?"

Coello gestured irritably. " Leave these mental probings to your bourgeois psychoanalysts."

" And you've laid on a lot of noise to drown the shots," persisted Forester as he heard another plane begin its dive.

Coello said something which was lost in the roar and Forester looked at him in horror. He did not know what to do. He could shoot Coello, but that would not help Rohde; there were more than a dozen armed men outside, and some were watching through the window. Coello laughed silently and pointed. When Forester could hear what he was saying, he shuddered. " The poor fool cannot stand, he will be shot sitting down."

" God damn you," groaned out Forester. " God damn your lousy soul to hell."

A soldier had brought up an ordinary kitchen chair which he placed against the wall, and Rohde was dragged to it and seated, his stiff leg sticking out grotesquely in front of him. A noose of rope was tossed over his head and he was bound to the chair. The soldiers left him and the officer barked out a command. The firing-squad lifted their rifles as one man and aimed, and the officer lifted his arm in the air.

Forester looked on helplessly but with horrified fascination, unable to drag his eyes away. He talked loudly, directing a stream of vicious obscenities at Coello in English and Spanish, each one viler than the last.

Another Sabre started its dive, the hand of the officer twitched and, as the noise grew to its height, he dropped his arm sharply and there was a rippling flash along the line of men. Rohde jerked convulsively in the chair as the bullets slammed into him and his body toppled on one side, taking the chair with it. The officer drew his pistol and walked over to examine the body.

Coello pulled the drawstring and the curtains closed, shutting off the hideous sight. Forester snarled, "*Hijo de puta!*"

"It will do you no good calling me names," said Coello. "Although as a man of honour I resent them and will take the appropriate steps." He smiled. "Now I will tell you the reason for this demonstration. From your rather crude observations I gather you are in sympathy with the unfortunate Rohde—the late Rohde, I should say. I was instructed to give you this test by my superior and I regret to inform you that you have failed. I think you have proved that you were not entirely sincere in the offer you made earlier, so I am afraid that you must go the same way as Rohde." His hand went to the pistol at his belt. "And after you—Aguillar. He will come to his reckoning not long from now." He began to draw the pistol. "Really, Forester, you should have known better than to——"

His words were lost in the uproar of another diving Sabre and it was then that Forester shot him, very coldly and precisely, twice in the stomach. He did not pull out the gun, but fired through the coverlet.

Coello shouted in pain and surprise and put his hands to his belly, but nothing could be heard over the tremendous racket above. Forester shot him again, this time to kill, right through the heart, and Coello rocked back as the bullet hit him and fell against the desk, dragging the blotter and the inkwell to the floor with him. He stared up with blank eyes at the ceiling, seeming to listen to the departing aircraft.

Forester slid from the stretcher and went to the door, gun in hand. Softly he turned the key, locking himself in, then he cautiously parted the curtain and looked into the hangar. The file of men—the firing-squad—were marching out, followed by the officer, and two soldiers were throwing a piece of canvas over the body of Rohde.

Forester waited until they had gone, then went to the door again and heard a shuffling of feet outside. His personal guard was still there, waiting to take him back to Coello's office or wherever Coello should direct. Something would have to be done about that.

He began to strip Coello's body, bending awkwardly in the mummy-like wrappings of tape which constricted him. His ribs hurt, but not very much, and his body seemed to glory in the prospect of action. The twitchiness had gone now that he was moving about and he blessed McGruder for that enlivening injection.

He and Coello were much of a size and the flying overalls and boots fitted well enough. He strapped on the parachute and then lifted Coello on to the stretcher, covering him with the sheet carefully so that the face could not be seen. Then he put on the heavy plastic flying helmet with the dangling oxygen mask, and picked up the pistol.

When he opened the door he appeared to be having some trouble with the fastenings of the mask, for he was fumbling with the straps, his hand and the mask obscuring his face. He gestured casually with the pistol he held in his other hand and said to the sentries, "*Vaya usted por alli*," pointing to the other end of the hangar. His voice was very indistinct.

He was prepared to shoot it out if either of the soldiers showed any sign of suspicion and his finger was nervous on the trigger. The eyes of one of the men flicked momentarily to the room behind Forester, and he must have seen the shrouded body on the stretcher. Forester was counting on military obedience and the natural fear these men had for their officers. They had already witnessed one execution and if that mad dog, Coello, had held another, more private, killing, what was it to them?

The soldier clicked to attention. "*Si, mio Colonel*," he said, and they both marched stiffly down to the end of the hangar. Forester watched them go out by the bottom door, then locked the office, thrust the pistol into the thigh pocket of the overalls and strode out of the hangar, fastening the oxygen mask as he went.

He heard the whistle of jet planes overhead and looked up to see the three Sabres circling in tight formation. As he watched they broke off into a straight course, climbing eastward over the mountains. They're not waiting for Coello, he thought; and broke into a clumsy run.

The ground crew waiting by the Sabre saw him coming and were galvanised into action. As he approached he pointed to the departing aircraft and shouted, "*Rapidemente! Dése prisa!*" He ran up to the Sabre with averted face and scrambled up to the cockpit, being surprised when one of the ground crew gave him a boost from behind.

He settled himself before the controls and looked at them; they were familiar but at the same time strange through long absence. The starter truck was already plugged in, its crew looking up at him with expectant faces. Damn, he thought; I don't know the command routine in Spanish. He closed his eyes and his hands went to the proper switches and then he waved.

Apparently that was good enough; the engine burst into noisy song and the ground crew ran to uncouple the starter cable. Another man tapped him on the helmet and closed the canopy and Forester waved again, indicating that the wheels should be unchocked. Then he was rolling, and he turned to taxi up the runway, coupling up the oxygen as he went.

At the end of the runway he switched on the radio, hoping that it was already netted in to the control tower; not that he wanted to obey any damned instructions they gave, but he wanted to know what was going on. A voice crackled in the headphones. " Colonel Coello?"

" *Si*," he mumbled.

" You are cleared for take-off."

Forester grinned, and rammed the Sabre straight down the runway. His wheels were just off the ground when all hell broke loose. The runway seemed to erupt before him for its entire length and the Sabre staggered in the air. He went into a steep, climbing turn and looked down at the airfield in astonishment. The ground was alive with the deep red flashes of violent explosions and, even as he watched, he saw the control tower shiver and disintegrate into a pile of rubble and a pillar of smoke coiled up to reach him.

He fought with the controls as a particularly violent eruption shivered the air, making the plane swerve drunkenly. " Who's started the goddam war?" he demanded of no one in particular. There was just a nervous crackle in the earphones to answer him—the control tower had cut out.

He gave up the futile questioning. Whatever it was certainly did him no harm and Eighth Squadron looked as though it was hamstrung for a long time. With one last look at the amazing spectacle on the ground, he set the Sabre in a long climb to the westward and clicked switches on the radio, searching for the other three Sabres. Two channels were apparently not in use, but he got them on the third, carrying on an idle conversation and in total ignorance of the destruction of their base, having already travelled too far to have seen the débâcle.

A sloppy, undisciplined lot, he thought; but' useful. He looked down as he eavesdropped and saw the pass drifting below him, the place where he had nearly died, and decided that flying beat walking. Then he scanned the sky ahead, looking for the rest of the flight. From their talk he gathered that they were orbiting a pre-selected point while waiting for Coello and he wondered if they were already briefed on the operation or whether Coello had intended to brief them in flight. That might make a difference to his tactics.

At last he saw them orbiting the mountain by the side of the pass, but very high. He pulled gently on the control column and went to meet them. These were going to be three very surprised communists.


## Chapter X


Armstrong heard trucks grinding up the mountain road. "They're coming," he said, and looked out over the breast-work of rock, his fingers curling round the butt of the gun.

The mist seemed to be thinning and he could see as far as the huts quite clearly and to where the road debouched on to the level ground; but there was still enough mist to halo the headlights even before the trucks came into view.

Benedetta ran up the tunnel and lay beside him. He said, "You'd better get back; there's nothing you can do here." He lifted the pistol. "One bullet. That's all the fighting we can do."

"They don't know that," she retorted.

"How is your uncle?" he asked.

"Better, but the altitude is not good for him." She hesitated. "I am not happy about Jenny; she is in a fever."

He said nothing; what was a fever or altitude sickness when the chances were that they would all be dead within the hour? Benedetta said, "We delayed them about three hours at the camp."

She was not really speaking sense, just making inconse-quential noises to drown her own thoughts—and all her thoughts were of O'Hara. Armstrong looked at her sideways. "I'm sorry to be pessimistic," he said. "But I think this is the last act. We've done very well considering what we had to fight with, but it couldn't go on for ever. Napoleon was right—God is on the side of the big battalions."

Her voice was savage. "We can still take some of them

with us." She grasped his arm. "Look, they're coming."

The first vehicle was breasting the top of the rise. It was quite small and Armstrong judged it was a jeep. It came forward, its headlights probing the mist, and behind it came a big truck, and then another. He heard shouted commands and the trucks rolled as far as the huts and stopped, and he saw men climbing out and heard the clatter of boots on rock.

The jeep curved in a great arc, its lights cutting a swathe like a scythe, and Armstrong suddenly realised that it was searching the base of the cliffs where the tunnels were. Before he knew it he was fully illuminated, and as he dodged back into cover, he heard the animal roar of triumph from the enemy as he was seen.

"Damn!" he said. "I was stupid."

"It does not matter," Benedetta said. "They would have found us soon." She lay down and cautiously pulled a rock from the pile. "I think I can see through here," she whispered. "There is no need to put your head up."

Armstrong heard steps from behind as Willis came up. "Keep down," he said quietly. "Flat on your stomach."

Willis wriggled alongside him. "What's going on?"

"They've spotted us," said Armstrong. "They're deploying out there; getting ready to attack." He laughed humourlessly. "If they knew what we had to defend ourselves with, they'd just walk in."

"There's another truck coming," said Benedetta bitterly. "I suppose it's bringing more men; they need an army to crush us."

"Let me see," said Armstrong. Benedetta rolled away from the spy-hole and Armstrong looked through. "It's got no lights—that's odd; and it's moving fast. Now it's changing direction and going towards the huts. It doesn't seem to be slowing down."

They could hear the roar of the engine, and Armstrong yelled, "It's going faster—it's going to smash into them." His voice cracked on a scream. "Do you think it could be O'Hara?"

O'Hara held tight to the jolting wheel and rammed the accelerator to the floorboards. He had been making for the jeep but then he had seen something much more important; in the light of the truck headlights a group of men were assembling a light machine-gun. He swung the wheel and the truck swerved, two wheels coming off the ground and then bouncing back with a spine-jolting crash. The truck swayed alarmingly, but he held it on its new course and switched on his lights and saw the white faces of men turn towards him and their hands go up to shield their eyes from the glare.

Then they were running aside but two of them were too late and he heard the squashy thumps as the front of the truck hit them. But he was not concerned with men—he wanted the gun—and the truck lifted a little as he drove the off-side wheels over the machine-gun, grinding it into the rock. Then he had gone past and there was a belated and thin scattering of shots from behind.

He looked for the jeep, hauled the wheel round again, and the careering truck swung and went forward like a projectile. The driver of the jeep saw him coming and tried to run for it; the jeep shot forward, but O'Hara swerved again and the jeep was fully illuminated as he made for a head-on crash. He saw the Russian point a pistol and there was a flash and the truck windscreen starred in front of his face. He ducked involuntarily.

The driver of the jeep swung his wheel desperately, but turned the wrong way and came up against the base of the cliff. The jeep spun again, but the mistake had given O'Hara his chance and he charged forward to ram the jeep broadside on. He saw the Russian throw up his arms and disappear from sight as the light vehicle was hurled on its side with a tearing and rending sound, and then O'Hara had slammed into reverse and was backing away.

He looked back towards the trucks and saw a mob of men running towards him, so he picked up the sub-machine-gun from the floor of the cab and steadied it on the edge of the window. He squeezed the trigger three times, altering his aim slightly between bursts, and the mob broke up into fragments, individual men rolling on the open ground and desperately seeking cover.

As O'Hara engaged in bottom gear, a bullet tore through the body of the truck, and then another, but he took no notice. The front of the truck slammed into the overturned jeep again, catching it on the underside of the chassis. Remorselessly O'Hara pushed forward using the truck as a bulldozer and mashed the jeep against the cliff face with a dull crunching noise. When he had finished no human sounds came from the crushed vehicle.

But that act of anger and revenge was nearly the end of

him. By the time he had reversed the truck and swung clear again he was under heavy fire. He rolled forward and tried to zigzag, but the truck was slow in picking up speed and a barrage of fire came from the semi-circle of men surrounding him. The windscreen shattered into opacity and he could not see where he was heading.

Benedetta, Armstrong and Willis were on their feet yelling, but no bullets came their way—they were not as dangerous as O'Hara. They watched the truck weaving drunkenly and saw sparks fly as steel-jacketed bullets ricocheted from the metal armour Santos had installed. Willis shouted, "He's in trouble," and before they could stop him he had vaulted the rock wall and was running for the truck.

O'Hara was steering with one hand and using the butt of the sub-machine-gun as a hammer in an attempt to smash the useless windscreen before him. Willis leaped on the running-board and just as his fingers grasped the edge of the door O'Hara was hit. A rifle bullet flew the width of the cab and smashed his shoulder, slamming him into the door and nearly upsetting Willis's balance. He gave a great cry and slumped down in his seat.

Willis grabbed the wheel with one hand, turned it awkwardly. He shouted, "Keep your foot on the accelerator," and O'Hara heard him through a dark mist of pain and pushed down with his foot. Willis turned the truck towards the cliff and tried to head for the tunnel. He saw the rear view mirror disintegrate and he knew that the bullet that had hit it had passed between his body and the truck. That did not seem to matter—all that mattered was to get the truck into cover.

Armstrong saw the truck turn and head towards him. "Run," he shouted to Benedetta, and took to his heels, dragging her by the hand and making down the tunnel.

Willis saw the mouth of the tunnel yawn darkly before him and pressed closer to the body of the truck. As the nose of the truck hit the low wall, rocks exploded into the interior, splintering against the tunnel sides.

Then Willis was hit. The bullet took him in the small of the back and he let go of the wheel and the edge of the door. In the next instant, as the truck roared into the tunnel to crash at the bend, Willis was wiped off the running-board by the rock face and was flung in a crumpled heap to the ground just by the entrance.

He stirred slightly as a bullet clipped the rock just above his

237

head and his hands groped forward helplessly, the fingers scrabbling at the cold rock. Then two bullets hit him almost simultaneously and he jerked once and was still.


## 11


It seemed enormously quiet as Armstrong and Benedetta dragged O'Hara from the cab of the truck. The shooting had stopped and there was no sound at all apart from the creakings of the cooling engine and the clatter as Armstrong kicked something loose on the floor of the cab. They were working in darkness because a well-directed shot straight down the tunnel would be dangerous.

At last they got O'Hara into safety round the corner and Benedetta lit the wick of the last paraffin bottle. O'Hara was unconscious and badly injured; his right arm hung limp and his shoulder was a ghastly mess of torn flesh and splintered bone. His face was badly cut too, because he had been thrown forward when the truck had crashed at the bend of the tunnel and Benedetta looked at him with tears in her eyes and wondered where to start.

Aguillar tottered forward, the breath wheezing in his chest, and said with difficulty, " In the name of God, what has happened?"

" You cannot help, *tio*," she said. " Lie down again."

Aguillar looked down at O'Hara with shocked eyes—it was brought home to him that war is a bloody business. Then he said, " Where is Señor Willis?"

" I think he's dead," said Armstrong quietly. " He didn't come back."

Aguillar sank down silently next to O'Hara, his face grey. " Let me help," he said.

" I'll go back on watch," said Armstrong. " Though what use that will be I don't know. It'll be dark soon. I suppose that's what they're waiting for."

He went away into the darkness towards the truck, and Benedetta examined O'Hara's shattered shoulder. She looked up at Aguillar helplessly. " What can I do? This needs a doctor—a hospital; we cannot do anything here."

" We must do what we can," said Aguillar. " Before he recovers consciousness. Bring the light closer."

He began to pick out fragments of bone from the bloody flesh and by the time he had finished and Benedetta had bandaged the wound and put the arm in a sling O'Hara was wide awake, suppressing his groans. He looked up at Benedetta and whispered, "Where's Willis?"

She shook her head slowly and O'Hara turned his face away. He felt a growing rage within him at the unfairness of things; just when he had found life again he must leave it—and what a way to leave; cooped up in a cold, dank tunnel at the mercy of human wolves. From nearby he could hear a woman babbling incoherently. "Who is that?"

"Jenny," said Benedetta. "She is delirious."

They made O'Hara as comfortable as possible and then Benedetta stood up. "I must help Armstrong." Aguillar looked up and saw that her face was taut with anger and fatigue, the skin drawn tightly over her cheekbones and dark smudges below her eyes. He sighed softly and nipped the guttering wick into darkness.

Armstrong was crouched by the truck. "I was waiting for someone," he said.

"Who were you expecting?" she said sarcastically. "We two are the only able-bodied left." Then she said in a low voice. "I'm sorry."

"That's all right," said Armstrong. "How's Tim?"

Her voice was bitter. "He'll live—if he's allowed to."

Armstrong said nothing for a long time, allowing the anger and frustration to seep from her, then he said, "Everything's quiet; they haven't made a move and I don't understand it. I'd like to go up there and have a look when it gets really dark outside."

"Don't be an idiot," said Benedetta in alarm. "What can a defenceless man do?"

"Oh, I wouldn't start anything," said Armstrong. "And I wouldn't be exactly defenceless. Tim had one of those little machine-guns with him, and I think there are some full magazines. I haven't been able to find out how it works in the dark; I think I'll go back and examine it in the light of our lamp. The crossbow is here, too; and a couple of bolts—I'll leave those here with you."

She took his arm. "Don't leave yet."

He caught the loneliness and desolation in her voice and subsided. Presently he said, "Who would have thought that Willis would do a thing like that? It was the act of a really brave man and I never thought he was that."

"Who knows what lies inside a man?" said Benedetta softly, and Armstrong knew she was thinking of O'Hara.

He stayed with her a while and talked the tension out of her, then went back and lit the lamp. O'Hara looked across at him with pain-filled eyes. "Has the truck had it?"

"I don't know," said Armstrong. "I haven't looked yet."

"I thought we might make a getaway in it," said O'Hara.

"I'll have a look at it. I don't think it took much damage from the knocks it had—those chaps had it pretty well armoured against our crossbow bolts. But I don't think the bullets did it any good; the armour wouldn't be proof against those."

Aguillar came closer. "Perhaps we might try in the darkness—to get away, I mean."

"Where to?" asked Armstrong practically. "They'll have the bridge covered—and I wouldn't like to take a truck across that at night—it would be suicidal. And they'll have plenty of light up here, too; they'll keep the entrance to the tunnel well covered." He rubbed the top of his head. "I don't know why they don't just come in and take us right now."

"I think I killed the top man," said O'Hara. "I hope I did. And I don't think Santos has the stomach to push in here—he's scared of what he might meet."

"Who is Santos?" asked Aguillar.

"The Cuban." O'Hara smiled weakly. "I got pretty close to him down below."

"You did a lot of damage when you came up in the truck," observed Armstrong. "I don't wonder they're scared. Maybe they'll give up."

"Not now," said O'Hara with conviction. "They're too close to success to give up now. Anyway, all they have to do now is to camp outside and starve us out."

They were silent for a long time thinking about that, then Armstrong said, "I'd rather go down in glory." He pulled forward the sub-machine-gun. "Do you know how this thing works?"

O'Hara showed him how to work the simple mechanism, and when he had gone back to his post Aguillar said, "I am sorry about your shoulder, señor."

O'Hara bared his teeth in a brief grin. "Not as sorry as I am—it hurts like the devil. But it doesn't matter, you know; I'm not likely to feel pain for long."

Aguillar's asthmatical wheezing stopped momentarily as he caught his breath. "Then you think this is the end?"

"I do."

"A pity, señor. I could have made much use of you in the

240

new Cordillera. A man in my position needs good men—they are as hard to find as the teeth of a hen."

"What use would a broken-down pilot be to you? Men like me come ten a penny."

"I do not think so," said Aguillar seriously. "You have shown much initiative in this engagement and that is a commodity which is scarce. As you know, the military forces of Cordillera are rotten with politics and I need men to lift them out of the political arena—especially the fighter squadrons. If you wish to stay in Cordillera, I think I can promise you a position in the Air Force."

For a moment O'Hara forgot that the hours—and perhaps minutes—of his life were measured. He said simply, "I'd like that."

"I'm glad," said Aguillar. "Your first task would be to straighten out Eighth Squadron. But you must not think that because you are marrying into the President's family that the way will be made easy for you." He chuckled as he felt O'Hara start. "I know my niece very well, Tim. Never has she felt about a man as she feels about you. I hope you will be very happy together."

"We will be," said O'Hara, then fell silent as reality flooded upon him once more—the realisation that all this talk of marriage and future plans was futile. After a while, he said wistfully, "These are pipe dreams, Señor Aguillar; reality is much more frightening. But I do wish . . ."

"We are still alive," said Aguillar. "And while the blood runs in a man nothing is impossible for him."

He said nothing more and O'Hara heard only the rasping of his breath in the darkness.

III

When Armstrong joined Benedetta he looked towards the entrance of the tunnel and saw that night had fallen and there was a bright glare of headlamps flooding the opening. He strained his eyes and said, "The mist seems to be thickening, don't you think?"

"I think so," said Benedetta listlessly.

"Now's the time to scout around," he said.

"Don't," Benedetta implored him. "They'll see you."

"I don't think they can; the mist is throwing the light back at them. They'd see me if I went outside, but I don't

241

intend to do that. I don't think they can see a damned thing in the tunnel."

"All right, then. But be careful."

He smiled as he crawled forward. In their circumstances the word "careful" seemed ridiculous. It was like telling a man who had jumped from an aeroplane without a parachute to be careful. All the same, he was most careful to make no noise as he inched his way towards the entrance, hampered by the shattered remnants of the rock wall.

He stopped some ten yards short of the opening, knowing that to go farther would be too risky, and peered into the misty brightness. At first he could see nothing, but by shielding his eyes from the worst of the glare he managed to pick out some details. Two trucks were parked at an angle to the cliff, one on each side of the tunnel, and when the light from the left truck flickered he knew someone had walked in front of it.

He stayed there for some time and twice he made deliberate movements, but it was as he thought—he could not be seen. After a while he began to crawl about gathering rocks, which he built up into a low wall, barely eighteen inches high. It was not much but it would give solid protection against rifle fire to anyone lying behind it. This took him a long time and there was no action from outside; occasionally he heard a man coughing, and sometimes the sound of voices, but apart from that there was nothing.

Eventually he picked up the sub-machine-gun and went back to the truck. Benedetta whispered from the darkness, "What are they doing?"

"Damned if I know," he said, and looked back. "It's too quiet out there. Keep a good watch; I'm going to have a look at the truck."

He squeezed her hand and then groped his way to the cab of the truck and climbed inside. Everything seemed to be all right, as far as he could judge, barring the windscreen which could not be seen through. He sat in the driving-seat and thought about what would happen if they had to make a break for it.

To begin with, he would be driving—there was no one else who could handle the truck—and he would have to reverse out of the tunnel. There would be one man in the passenger seat beside him and the others in the back.

He examined the rest of the truck, more by feel than sight. Two of the tyres had been badly scored by bullets but miraculously the inner tubes had not been penetrated. The petrol tanks, too, were intact, protected by the deep skirts of mild steel, added to guard against crossbow bolts.

He had fears about the radiator, but a groping journey under the truck revealed no fatal drip of water and he was reassured about that. His only worries were that the final crash might have damaged the steering or the engine, but those could not be tested until the time came to go. He did not want to start the engine now—let sleeping dogs lie, he thought.

He rejoined Benedetta. "That's that," he said with satisfaction. "She seems to be in good fettle. I'll take over here. You'd better see how the others are."

She turned immediately, and he knew she was eager to get back to O'Hara.

"Wait a minute," he said. "You'd better know the drill if we have to make a sudden move." He lifted the gun. "Can you use this?"

"I don't know."

Armstrong chuckled. "I don't know if I can, either—it's too modern for me. But O'Hara reckons it's easy enough; you just pull the trigger and let her go. He says it takes a bit of holding down and you must be careful to slip off the safety-catch. Now, I'll be driving, with your uncle sitting next to me on the floor of the cab. Tim and Jenny will be in the back, flat on the floor. And there'll be you in the back, too —with this gun. It'll be a bit dangerous—you'll have to show yourself if you shoot."

Her voice was stony. "I'll shoot."

"Good girl," he said, and patted her on the shoulder. "Give Tim my love when you give him yours." He heard her go, then moved up the tunnel to the wall he had built and lay behind it, the sub-machine-gun ready to hand. He put his hand in his pocket and felt for his pipe, then uttered a muffled "Damn!" It was broken, the two pieces separate in his hand. He put the stem in his mouth and chewed on the mouthpiece, never taking his eyes from the entrance.

IV

The day dawned mistily, a dazzling whiteness at the mouth of the tunnel, and Armstrong shifted his position for the hundredth time, trying to find a place to ease his aching bones. He glanced across at O'Hara on the other side of the tunnel and thought, it's worse for him than for me.

243

When O'Hara had heard of the rebuilt wall he had insisted on moving there. "I haven't a hope of sleep," he said. "Not with this shoulder. And I've got a fully loaded pistol. I might as well stand—or lie—sentry out there as just lie here. I should be of some use, even if only to allow everyone else to get some sleep."

But in spite of that Armstrong had not slept. He ached too much to sleep, even though he felt more exhausted than ever before in his life, but he smiled cheerily at O'Hara in the growing light and lifted his head above the low barricade.

There was nothing to be seen except the white swirling mist, an impenetrable curtain. He said softly, "Tim, why didn't they jump us in the night?"

"They know we have this gun," said O'Hara. "I wouldn't like to come running into this tunnel knowing that—especially at night."

"Um," said Armstrong in an unconvinced tone. "But why haven't they tried to soften us up with rifle fire? They must know that any fire directed into this tunnel will ricochet from the walls—they don't have to be too accurate."

O'Hara was silent, and Armstrong continued reflectively: "I wonder if there *is* anyone out there?"

"Don't be a damn' fool," said O'Hara. "That's something we can't take a chance on—not yet. Besides, there was someone to turn the lights off not very long ago."

"True," said Armstrong, and turned as he heard a movement in the tunnel, and Benedetta crawled up holding a bundle in her arms.

"The last of the food," she said. "There's not much— and we have no water at all."

Armstrong's mouth turned down. "That's bad."

As he and O'Hara shared the food they heard a stirring outside and the murmur of voices. "Changing the guard," said O'Hara. "I heard it before about four hours ago when you were asleep. They're still there, all right."

"Me! Asleep!" said Armstrong in an aggrieved voice. "I didn't sleep a wink all night."

O'Hara smiled. "You got three or four winks out of the forty." He became serious. "If we really need water we can drain some from the truck radiator, but I wouldn't do that unless absolutely necessary."

Benedetta regarded O'Hara with worry in her eyes. He had a hectic flush and looked too animated for a man who had nearly been shot to death. Miss Ponsky had had the same reaction, and now she was off her head with delirium, unable to eat and crying for water. She said, " I think we ought to have water now; Jenny needs it."

" In that case we'll tap the radiator," said Armstrong. " I hope the anti-freeze compound isn't poisonous; I think it's just alcohol, so it should be all right."

He crawled back with Benedetta and squeezed underneath the truck to unscrew the drain-cock. He tapped out half a can of rusty-looking water and passed it to her. " That will have to do," he said. " We can't take too much—we might need the truck."

The day wore on and nothing happened. Gradually the mist cleared under the strengthening sun and then they could see out of the tunnel, and Armstrong's hopes were shattered as he saw a group of men standing by the huts. Even from their restricted view they could see that the enemy was in full strength.

" But can they see us?" mused O'Hara. " I don't think they can. This cavern must look as dark as the Black Hole of Calcutta from outside."

" What the devil are they doing?" asked Armstrong, his eyes level with the top of a rock.

O'Hara watched for a long time, then he said in wonder, " They're piling rocks on the ground—apart from that they're doing nothing."

They watched for a long time and all the enemy did was to pile stones in a long line stretching away from the tunnel. After a while they appeared to tire of that and congregated into small groups, chatting and smoking. They seemed to have the appearance of men waiting for something, but why they were waiting or what the rocks were for neither O'Hara nor Armstrong could imagine.

It was midday when Armstrong, his nerves cracking under the strain, said, " For God's sake, let's do something—something constructive."

O'Hara's voice was flat and tired. " What?"

" If we're going to make a break in the truck we might have to do it quickly. I suggest we put Jenny in the back of the truck right away, and get the old man settled in the front seat. Come to think of it, he'll be a damn sight more comfortable on a soft seat."

O'Hara nodded. " All right. Leave that sub-machine-gun with me. I might need it."

Armstrong went back to the truck, walking upright. To

hell with crawling on my belly like a snake, he thought; let me walk like a man for once. The enemy either did not see or saw and did not care. No shots were fired.

He saw Miss Ponsky safely into the back of the truck and then he escorted Aguillar to the cab. Aguillar was in a bad way, much worse than he had been. His speech was incoherent and his breathing was bad; he was in a daze and did not appear to know where he was. Benedetta was pale and worried and stayed to look after him.

When Armstrong dropped behind the rock wall, he said, " If we don't get out of here soon that bloody crowd will have won."

O'Hara jerked his head in surprise. " Why?"

" Aguillar—he looks on the verge of a heart attack; if he doesn't get down to where he can breathe more easily he'll peg out."

O'Hara looked outside and gestured with his good arm. " There are nearly two dozen men within sight; they'd shoot hell out of us if we tried to break out now. Look at what happened to me yesterday when they were hampered by mist —there's no mist now and we wouldn't stand a chance. We'll have to wait."

So they waited—and so did the enemy. And the day went on, the sun sloping back overhead into mid-afternoon. It was three o'clock when O'Hara stirred and then relaxed and shook his head. " I thought . . . but no."

He settled himself down, but a moment later his head jerked up again. " It *is*—can't you hear it?"

" Hear what?" asked Armstrong.

" A plane—or planes," said O'Hara excitedly.

Armstrong listened and caught the shrill whine of a jet plane passing overhead, the noise muffled and distorted. " By God, you're right," he said. He looked at O'Hara in sudden consternation. " Ours or theirs?"

But O'Hara had already seen their doom. He leaned up and looked, horrified, to the mouth of the tunnel. Framed in the opening against the sky was a diving plane coming head on and, as he watched, he saw something drop from each wing, and a spurt of vapour.

" Rockets!" he screamed. " For Christ's sake, get down!"

Forester had climbed to meet the three Sabres and as he approached they saw him and fell into a loose formation and awaited him. He came in from behind and increased speed, getting the leader in his sights. He flicked off the safety switches and his thumb caressed the firing-button. This boy would never know what hit him.

All the time there was a continual jabber in his ear-phones as the leader called Coello. At last, assuming that Coello's radio was at fault, he said, " Since you are silent, *mio Colonel,* I will lead the attack." It was then that Forester knew that these men had been briefed on the ground—and he pressed the firing-button.

Once again he felt the familiar jolt in the air, almost a halt, and saw the tracer shells streaking and corkscrewing towards their target. The leading Sabre was a-dance with coruscations of light as the shells burst, and suddenly it blew up in a gout of black smoke with a red heart at the centre.

Forester weaved to avoid wreckage and then went into a sharp turn and climbed rapidly, listening to the horrified exclamations from the other pilots. They babbled for a few moments then one of them said, " Silence. I will take him."

Forester searched the skies and thought—he's quick off the mark. He felt chilled; these boys would be young and have fast reflexes and they would be trained to a hair. He had not flown for nearly ten years, beyond the few annual hours necessary to keep up his rating, and he wondered grimly how long he would last.

He found his enemies. One was swooping in a graceful dive towards the ground and the other was climbing in a wide circle to get behind him. As he watched, the pilot fired his rockets aimlessly. " Oh, no, you don't, you bastard," said Forester. " You don't catch me like that." He knew his opponent had jettisoned his rockets in order to reduce weight and drag and to gain speed. For a moment he was tempted to do the same and to fight it out up there in the clean sky, but he knew he could not take the chance. Besides he had a better use for his rockets.

Instead, he pushed the control column forward and went into a screaming dive. This was dangerous—his opponent would be faster in the dive and it had been drilled into Forester never, *never* to lose height while in combat. He kept his eyes on the mirror and soon the Sabre came into view behind, catching up fast. He waited until the very last moment, until he was sure he was about to be fired on, then pushed the stick forward again and went into a suicidal vertical dive.

His opponent overshot him, taken unaware by the craziness of this manœuvre performed so near the ground. Forester ignored him, confident that he had lost him for the time being; he was more concerned with preventing his plane from splattering itself all over the mountainside. He felt juddering begin as the Sabre approached the sound barrier; the whole fabric of the plane groaned as he dragged it out of the dive and he hoped the wings would not come off.

By the time he was flying level the ground was a scant two hundred feet below, snow and rock merging together in a grey blur. He lifted the Sabre up a few hundred feet and circled widely away from the mountains, looking for the gorge and the bridge. He spotted the gorge immediately—it was too unmistakable to be missed, and a minute later he saw the bridge. He turned over it, scanning the ground, but saw no one, and then it was gone behind and he lifted up to the slope of the mountain, flying over the winding road he had laboriously tramped so often.

Abruptly he changed course, wanting to approach the mine parallel to the mountainside, and as he did so he looked up and saw a Sabre a thousand feet higher, launching two rockets. That's the second one, he thought. I was too late.

He turned again and screamed over the mine, the air-strip unwinding close below. Ahead were the huts and some trucks and a great arrow made of piled rocks pointing to the cliff face. And at the head of the arrow a boiling cloud of smoke and dust where the rockets had driven home into the cliff. "Jesus!" he said involuntarily, "I hope they survived that."

Then he had flashed over and went into a turn to come back. Come back he did with an enemy hammering on his heels. The Sabre he had eluded high in the sky had found him again and its guns were already crackling. But the range was too great and he knew that the other pilot, tricked before, was now waiting for him to play some other trick. This sign of inexperience gave him hope, but the other Sabre was faster and he must drop his rockets.

He had seen a good, unsuspecting target, yet to hit it he would have to come in on a smooth dive and stood a good chance of being hit by his pursuer. His lips curled back over his teeth and he held his course, sighting on the trucks and the huts and the group of men standing in their shelter. With one hand he flicked the rocket-arming switches and then fired, almost in the same instant.

The salvo of rockets streaked from under his wings, spearing down towards the trucks and the men who were looking up and waving. At the last moment, when they saw death coming from the sky, they broke and ran—but it was too late. Eight rockets exploded among them and as Forester roared overhead he saw a three-ton truck heave bodily into the air to fall on its side. He laughed out loud; a rocket that would stop a tank dead in its tracks would certainly shatter a truck.

The Sabre felt more handy immediately the rockets were gone and he felt the increase in speed. He put the nose down and screamed along the airstrip at zero feet, not looking back to see the damage he had done and striving to elude his pursuer by flying as low as he dared. At the end of the runway he dipped even lower over the wreckage of the Dakota and skidded in a frantic sideslip round the mountainside.

He looked in the mirror and saw his opponent take the corner more widely and much higher. Forester grinned; the bastard hadn't dared to come down on the deck and so he couldn't bring his guns to bear and he'd lost distance by his wide turn. Now to do him.

He fled up the mountainside parallel with the slope and barely twenty feet from the ground. It was risky, for there were jutting outcrops of rock which stretched out black fangs to tear out the belly of the Sabre if he made the slightest miscalculation. During the brief half-minute it took to reach clear sky, sweat formed on his forehead.

Then he was free of the mountain, and his enemy stooped to make his kill, but Forester was expecting it and went into a soaring vertical climb with a quick roll on top of the loop and was heading away in the opposite direction. He glanced back and grinned in satisfaction; he had tested the enemy and found him wanting—that young man would not take risks and Forester knew he could take him, so he went in for the kill.

It was brief and brutal. He turned to meet the oncoming plane and made as though to ram deliberately. At the closing speed of nearly fifteen hundred miles an hour the other pilot flinched as Forester knew he would, and swerved aside. By the time he had recovered Forester was on his tail and the end was mercifully quick—a sharp burst from the cannons at minimum range and the inevitable explosion in mid-air Again Forester swerved to avoid wreckage. As he climbed to get his bearings, he reflected that battle experience still counted for a lot and the assessment of personality for still more.

V I

Armstrong was deaf; the echoes of that vast explosion still rumbled in the innermost recesses of the tunnel but he did not hear them. Nor could he see much because of the coils of dust which thickened the air. His hands were vainly clutching the hard rock of the tunnel floor as he pressed himself to the ground and his mind felt shattered.

It was O'Hara who recovered first. Finding himself still alive and able to move, he raised his head to look at the tunnel entrance. Light showed dimly through the dust. He missed, he thought vacantly; the rockets missed—but not by much. Then he shook his head to clear it and stumbled across to Armstrong who was still grovelling on the ground. He shook him by the shoulder. "Back to the truck," he shouted. "We've got to get out. He won't miss the second time round."

Armstrong lifted his head and gazed at O'Hara dumbly, and O'Hara pointed back to the truck and made a dumb show of driving. He got to his feet shakily and followed O'Hara, still feeling his head ringing from the violence of the explosion.

O'Hara yelled, "Benedetta—into the truck." He saw her in and handed her the sub-machine-gun, then climbed in himself with her aid and lay down next to Miss Ponsky. Outside he heard the scream of a jet going by and a series of explosions in the distance. He hoped that Armstrong was in a condition to drive.

Armstrong climbed into the cab and felt the presence of Aguillar in the next seat. "On the floor," he said, pushing him down, and then his attention was wholly absorbed by the task before him. He pressed the starter-button and the starter whined and groaned. He stabbed it again and again until, just as he was giving up hope, the engine fired with a coughing roar.

Putting the gears into reverse, he leaned out of the cab and gazed back towards the entrance and let out the clutch. The truck bumped backwards clumsily and scraped the side wall. He hauled on the wheel and tried to steer a straight course for the entrance—as far as he could tell the steering had not been damaged and it did not take long to do the fifty yards. Then he stopped just short of the mouth of the tunnel in preparation for the dash into the open.

Benedetta gripped the unfamiliar weapon in her hands and held it ready, crouching down in the back of the truck. O'Hara was sitting up, a pistol in his good hand; he knew that if he lay down he would have difficulty in getting up again—he could only use one arm for leverage. Miss Ponsky was mercifully unaware of what was going on; she babbled a little in her stupor and then fell silent as the truck backed jerkily into the open and turned.

O'Hara heard Armstrong battering at the useless wind-screen and prepared himself for a fusillade of rifle fire. Nothing came and he looked round and what he saw made him blink incredulously. It was a sight he had seen before but he had not expected to see it here. The huts and the trucks were shattered and wrecked and bodies lay about them. From a wounded man there came a mournful keening and there were only two men left on their feet, staggering about blindly and in a daze. He looked the awful scene over with a professional eye and knew that an aircraft had fired a ripple of eight rockets at this target, blasting it thoroughly.

He yelled, "Armstrong—get the hell out of here while we can," then sagged back and grinned at Benedetta. "One of those fighter boys made a mistake and hammered the wrong target; he's going to get a strip torn off him when he gets back to base."

Armstrong smashed enough of the windscreen away so that he could see ahead, then put the truck into gear and went forward, turning to go past the huts and down the road. He looked in fascinated horror at the wreckage until it was past and then applied himself to the task of driving an unfamiliar and awkward vehicle down a rough mountain road with its multitude of hairpin bends. As he went, he heard a jet plane whine overhead very low and he tensed, waiting for the slam of more explosions, but nothing happened and the plane went out of hearing.

Above, Forester saw the truck move off. One of them still left, he thought; and dived, his thumb ready on the firing-button. At the last moment he saw the streaming hair of a woman standing in the back and hastily removed his thumb as he screamed over the truck. My God, that was Benedetta—they've got themselves a truck.

251

He pulled the Sabre into a climb and looked about. He had not forgotten the third plane and hoped it had been scared off because a strange lassitude was creeping over him and he knew that the effects of McGruder's stimulant were wearing off. He tried to ease the ache in his chest while circling to keep an eye on the truck as it bounced down the mountain road.

O'Hara looked up at the circling Sabre. "I don't know what to make of that chap," he said. "He must know we're here, but he's doing nothing about it."

"He must think we're on his side," said Benedetta. "He must think that of anyone in a truck."

"That sounds logical," O'Hara agreed. "But someone did a good job of working over our friends up on top and it wasn't a mistake an experienced pilot would make." He winced as the truck jolted his shoulder. "We'd better prepare to pile out if he shows signs of coming in to strafe us. Can you arrange signals with Armstrong?"

Benedetta turned and hung over the side, craning her neck to see Armstrong at the wheel. "We might be attacked from the air," she shouted. "How can we stop you?"

Armstrong slowed for a nasty corner. "Thump like hell on top of the cab—I'll stop quick enough. I'm going to stop before we get to the camp, anyway; there might be someone laying for us down there."

Benedetta relayed this to O'Hara and he nodded. "A pity I can't use that thing," he said, indicating the sub-machine-gun. "If you have to shoot, hold it down; it kicks like the devil and you'll find yourself spraying the sky if you aren't careful."

He looked up at her. The wind was streaming her black hair and moulding the tattered dress to her body. She was cradling the sub-machine-gun in her hands and looking up at the plane and he thought in sudden astonishment, My God, a bloody Amazon—she looks like a recruiting poster for partisans. He thought of Aguillar's offer of an Air Force commission and had a sudden and irrational conviction that they would come through this nightmare safely.

Benedetta threw up her hand and cried in a voice of despair, "Another one—another plane."

O'Hara jerked his head and saw another Sabre curving overhead much higher and the first Sabre going to join it. Benedetta said bitterly, "Always they must hunt in packs—even when they know we are defenceless."

But O'Hara, studying the manœuvring of the two aircraft with a war-experienced eye, was not sure about that. "They're going to fight," he said with wonder. "They're jockeying for position. By God, they're going to fight each other." His raised and incredulous voice was sharply punctuated by the distant clatter of automatic cannon.

Forester had almost been caught napping. He had only seen the third enemy Sabre when it was much too close for comfort and he desperately climbed to get the advantage of height. As it was, the enemy fired first and there was a thump and a large, ragged hole magically appeared in his wing as a cannon shell exploded. He side-slipped evasively, then drove his plane into a sharp, climbing turn.

Below, O'Hara yelled excitedly and thumped with his free hand on the side of the cab. "Forester and Rohde—they've got across the mountain—they must have."

The truck jolted to a sudden stop and Armstrong shot out of the cab like a startled jack-rabbit and dived into the side of the road. From the other side Aguillar stepped down painfully into the road and was walking away slowly when he heard the excited shouts from the truck. He turned and then looked upwards to the embattled Sabres.

The fight was drifting westward and presently the two aircraft disappeared from sight over the mountain, leaving only the white inscription of vapour trails in the blue sky. Armstrong came up to the side of the truck. "What the devil's happening?" he asked with annoyance. "I got the fright of my life when you thumped on the cab."

"I'm damned if I know," said O'Hara helplessly. "But some of these planes seem to be on our side; a couple are having a dogfight now." He threw out his arm. "Look, here they come again."

The two Sabres were much lower as they came in sight round the mountain, one in hot pursuit of the other. There was a flickering on the wings of the rear plane as the cannon hammered and suddenly a stream of oily smoke burst from the leading craft. It dropped lower and a black speck shot upwards. "He's bailed out," said O'Hara. "He's had it."

The pursuing Sabre pulled up in a climb, but the crippled plane settled into a steepening dive to crash on the mountainside. A pillar of black, greasy smoke marked the wreck and a parachute, suddenly opened, drifted across the sky like a blown dandelion seed.

Armstrong looked up and watched the departing victor

253

which was easing into a long turn, obviously intent on coming back. "That's all very well," he said worriedly. "But who won—us or them?"

"Everyone out," said O'Hara decisively. "Armstrong, give Benedetta a hand with Jenny."

But they had no time, for suddenly the Sabre was upon them, roaring overhead in a slow roll. O'Hara, who was cradling Miss Ponsky's head with his free arm, blew out his breath expressively. "Our side seems to have won that one," he said. "But I'd like to know who the hell our side is." He watched the Sabre coming back, dipping its wings from side to side. "Of course, it *couldn't* be Forester—that's impossible. A pity. He always wanted to become an ace, to make his fifth kill."

The plane dipped and turned as it came over again and headed down the mountain and presently they heard cannon-fire again. "Everyone in the truck," commanded O'Hara. "He's shooting up the camp—we'll have no trouble there. Armstrong, you get going and don't stop for a damned thing until we're on the other side of the bridge." He laughed delightedly. "We've got air cover now."

They pressed on and passed the camp. There was a fiercely burning truck by the side of the road, but no sign of anyone living. Half an hour later they approached the bridge and Armstrong drew to a slow halt by the abutments, looking about him anxiously. He heard the Sabre going over again and was reassured, so he put the truck into gear and slowly inched his way on to the frail and unsubstantial structure.

Overhead, Forester watched the slow progress of the truck as it crossed the bridge. He thought there was a wind blowing down there because the bridge seemed to sway and shiver, but perhaps it was only his tired eyes playing tricks. He cast an anxious eye on his fuel gauges and decided it was time to put the plane down—and he hoped he could put it down in one piece. He felt desperately tired and his whole body ached.

Making one last pass at the bridge to make sure that all was well, he headed away following the road, and had gone only a few miles when he saw a convoy of vehicles coming up, some of them conspicuously marked with the Red Cross. So that's that, he thought; McGruder got through and someone got on the phone to this side of the mountains and stirred things up. It couldn't possibly be another batch of communists—what would they want with ambulances?

He lifted his eyes and looked ahead for flat ground and a place to land.

Aguillar watched Armstrong's face lighten as the wheels of the truck rolled off the bridge and they were at last on the other side of the river. So many good people, he thought; and so many good ones dead—the Coughlins, Señor Willis—Miss Ponsky so dreadfully wounded and O'Hara also. But O'Hara would be all right; Benedetta would see to that. He smiled as he thought of them, of all the years of their future happiness. And then there were the others, too—Miguel and the two Americans, Forester and Peabody. The State of Cordillera would honour them all—yes, even Peabody, and especially Miguel Rohde.

It would be much later that he heard of what had happened to Peabody—and to Rohde.

O'Hara looked at Miss Ponsky. "Will she be all right?"

"The wound is clean—not as bad as yours, Tim. A hospital will do you both a lot of good." Benedetta fell silent. "What will you do now?"

"I suppose I should go back to San Croce to hand my resignation to Filson—and to punch him on the nose, too—but I don't think I will. He's not worth it, so I won't bother."

"You are returning to England, then?" She seemed despondent.

O'Hara smiled. "A future President of a South American country has offered me an interesting job. I think I might stick around if the pay is good enough."

He gasped as Benedetta rushed into his one-armed embrace. "Ouch! Careful of this shoulder! And for God's sake, drop that damned gun—you might cause an accident."

Armstrong was muttering to himself in a low chant and Aguillar turned his head. "What did you say, señor?"

Armstrong stopped and laughed. "Oh, it's something about a medieval battle; rather a famous one where the odds were against winning. Shakespeare said something about it which I've been trying to remember—he's not my line, really; he's weak on detail but he gets the spirit all right. It goes something like this." He lifted his voice and declaimed:

"'He that shall live this day, and see old age,
Will yearly on the vigil feast his neighbours,
And say, To-morrow is Saint Crispin's.
Then will he strip his sleeve and show his scars,
And say, These wounds I had on Crispin's day.

Old men forget; yet all shall be forgot,
But he'll remember with advantages
What feats he did that day . . .
We few, we happy few.' "

He fell silent and after a few minutes gave a low chuckle.
"I think Jenny Ponsky will be able to teach that very well
when she returns to her school. Do you think *she'll* ' strip her
sleeve and show her scars '?"

The truck lurched down the road towards freedom.


### THE END